PRAISE FOR

TREASURES

OF THE LOCHS

"Hunter White skillfully weaves well-researched historical mysteries into a taut, modern thriller that propels his characters and this novel's readers along a journey to a rewarding and entertaining payoff."

—ERIC L. HARRY,
author of the best-selling novel *Arc Light*

"Hunter White has written an exciting, genre-crossing tale of mystery, murder, and myth. *Treasures of the Lochs* is a page-turner, and I really enjoyed and admired it."

—MARC GROSSBERG,
author of the #1 Amazon best-selling novel
The Best People: A Tale of Trials and Errors

TREASURES

of the

LOCHS

A NOVEL

HUNTER H. WHITE

RIVER GROVE
BOOKS

Published by River Grove Books
Austin, TX
www.rivergrovebooks.com

Distributed by River Grove Books

Design and composition by Greenleaf Book Group
Cover design by Greenleaf Book Group

Publisher's Cataloging-in-Publication data is available.

Print ISBN: 978-1-63299-687-9

eBook ISBN: 978-1-63299-688-6

First Edition

For Carson & Garrett

PROLOGUE

LEWIS OLIVER SLIPPED through the heavy door of the darkened United States Naval Academy Chapel and gave the order to go. Enough light from the moon and outside security lights seeped through the stained-glass windows for him to see his team in their dark gray tactical gear and balaclavas. His five men moved stealthily through the sanctuary toward the stairs. Unlike the chapel, the stairwell remained well lit.

Lewis knew this was the most dangerous part, when they would be the most exposed. Craning his neck, he listened for movement or voices downstairs. Based on his prior surveillance, he'd learned the navy guarded the exhibit near the base of the stairs twenty-four hours a day, but at this hour, only three guards would be on duty. He nodded to his men crouched near the edge of the steps.

After readying their weapons, his team descended in pairs. They slithered on their stomachs and stopped seven or eight stairs from the bottom. The man closest to the railing slowly raised a microthin fiber optics wire with an imbedded camera a few millimeters above the lower edge and used a small piece of tape to hold it in place.

Lewis remained at the top landing and a few yards back, with his second-in-command. He'd known Gavrie for over twenty-six years, from their time in the Russian military. That was when Lewis's name was still Dmitri Obabcov, before he emigrated from Russia to the United Kingdom and changed it. Gavrie had joined him five years afterward, and they could still grasp what each other thought with a mere look.

The camera's images of the exhibit area below the chapel danced in front of Lewis's face in the virtual headset he'd slipped on. He saw three navy guards dressed in their pressed uniforms and white gloves. Two remained stationary. One was standing at attention near the front of the exhibit, and another stood farther away, with his back to the first guard. Roaming the outer edges with a slow, uneven gate was a lieutenant he recognized.

Without removing the headset, Lewis used hand gestures to indicate the guards' positions to his team and then, with a slashing motion, instructed them to proceed. The two men closest to the bottom of the stairs pulled their weapons from their side holsters and leaped to the floor, with the other pair close on their heels.

The first guard gasped and opened his mouth, but he was unable to get a word out before one of Lewis's team raised his XREP and fired. Almost simultaneously, the other man next to him shot the second guard in the back. No loud gunshots rang out, and no blood was spilled. The compressed-air pistols emitted little sound, and the guards grunted and fell hard to the ground, their bodies spasming from the wireless tasers.

Just as Lewis had planned, the second pair targeted the remaining man, the lieutenant. The third taser shot missed this last guard and hit the large marble pillar in front of him.

The lieutenant didn't appear to have seen the intruders or heard the barbed taser shell hit the pillar near him. He ran and knelt next to one of the downed guards, then turned toward the closest of Lewis's men. Clearly surprised, he jumped up and lunged toward the invader but seemed off-balance and stumbled, only shouldering the side of the intruder's hip. The lieutenant rolled off and fell, hitting his head hard on the tile floor.

Lewis watched his team member swing his pistol back, about to strike the guard, but another fired his XREP into the lieutenant's chest. The man spasmed and writhed before he stilled.

Lewis would have preferred bullets instead of tasers. They rarely malfunctioned and provided greater certainty of a result, but the "old man," as he referred to his employer, insisted on nonlethal weapons for this part of the mission. Lewis did not agree. Nor did he agree this part of the mission was necessary or worth the risk, but he did not have to agree. He followed orders and collected his check. After he saw that the lieutenant was among the guards this evening, he knew the old man was right about using these weapons.

Lewis tore off his headset, and he and Gavrie raced downstairs, reaching the bottom just as his men finished zip-tying the hands and feet of the first two guards. They taped their mouths closed and placed cloth covers over their heads. He checked his watch. "We have six minutes."

He had to admit he loved seeing three United States soldiers incapacitated, lying helplessly in front of him. He wished he had more time to relish the scene, but he helped Gavrie quickly remove the two scanners and tripods from the thick shoulder sack he carried.

Lewis perused the exhibit celebrating John Paul Jones, whose remains rested at the center in an extravagant sarcophagus sculpted from black-and-white marble and covered in brass outcroppings of barnacles. With the soft lighting, he thought the coffin hinted at something that had been sitting at the bottom of the ocean for hundreds of years.

His team took several readings around the perimeter of the sarcophagus before scanning above and around the base, including the brass inlay on the surrounding marble floor embossed with the names of the Continental Navy ships captained by Jones during the American Revolutionary War.

"Make sure they remain secure," Lewis ordered another member of his team, Mikhail, who stood watch over the subdued guards.

"They should give us no trouble. I even smell alcohol on this one."

Mikhail chuckled, kicking the lieutenant's legs. "There was almost no need to tase him. He fell over when he charged me."

How did these people ever win wars? Lewis shook his head in wonder. He checked his watch again and monitored the others, who were taking pictures and scans of the crypt and memorabilia.

"Get a scan of that too." Lewis pointed to a plaque secured to the wall. While Gavrie repositioned the equipment, Lewis read the plaque.

> *For more than a century, the mortal remains of our first great sailor lay in an unknown grave, lost to his country. The nation is indebted to General Horace Porter for his patriotic efforts in the discovery and identification of the body.*

He sneered at the men on the floor. *Americans,* Lewis thought with more than a little disdain. *So arrogant that they honor a thief and his descendants for digging up bones.*

Gavrie stowed the equipment back in his shoulder sack and nodded to Lewis. He checked the time again, satisfied that this part of the operation had taken only five minutes and forty-nine seconds.

Within eleven minutes, the men reached their stolen SUV and casually pulled away from the naval academy grounds. They removed their balaclavas, and Gavrie turned to Lewis. "I saw nothing inside crypt. I think this was waste of time, but we must study the images to be sure."

"Understood. I will tell the old man." Lewis scratched the thick, black stubble masking his badly pockmarked face. "We still need to watch bank and wait for our chance. No need for tasers."

Chapter 1

LIEUTENANT CARTER PORTER felt dizzy and disoriented; his upper lip bled a little from where the tape had been ripped from his mouth. Rubbing his temples did nothing for the pounding in his head, and his eyes still struggled to adjust to the lights. He and the cadet midshipmen had remained bound, with their legs zip-tied and their hands secured behind their backs, until the next shift arrived.

After the intruders departed, Carter heard the other honor guards call to him and roll over to his position. They'd tried to free themselves and Carter. After a few minutes and several failed attempts, they'd stopped and just lay there. He had been half-asleep when he was jostled by one of the replacement guards and his headcover removed.

With his zip ties cut away, Carter sat propped up against one of the outer walls of the exhibit and tried not to move as a parade of investigators and bomb-sniffing dogs inspected every inch of the area. He fumbled as he loosened the wrinkled khaki tie around his neck. Then, he rubbed at the tufts of black hair jutting from the edges of a bandage on the back of his head. He wracked his brain, trying to remember who had placed the bandage there and when.

"Does it hurt much?" Gordon Booker asked, his muscular arms straining against the fabric of his uniform as he squatted next to Carter.

"Hey, Gordo. I assume you're here as the master-at-arms and not because of a bump on my head."

"Correct, but does it hurt much?"

"Not as much as the concussion you gave me from that illegal hit a few years back."

Gordon smiled. "No way, man, that hit was totally legal."

"It was *touch* football, buddy."

"Right, and my forearm *touched* the side of your head before I stripped the ball from you. It was a 'welcome to the navy, young man.'" He chortled. "Well, the extra pounds you put on since then probably could have helped pad your fall." He poked Carter on the side of his stomach, which strained against his belt.

Carter snorted in response. Over the last three years, he'd seen the scale rise to almost 215 pounds, and it wasn't muscle. Even for his six-foot-one-inch frame, it was too much. But he knew the reason, and he knew his friend knew it too.

Gordon leaned in and whispered in Carter's ear. "Damn, man, what were you thinking? I smelled the booze on you from ten feet away."

"Sorry, Gordo," was all Carter could offer. There was no reason to deny it. He had lost discipline in so many areas of his life, particularly with drinking. He knew he had guard duty, and he still thought he could handle one drink at dinner, but, as happened far too often, one drink became five or six.

"You know what's about to happen to you, right?" Gordon whispered with a sincere sadness in his voice. "The other two cadets confirmed they smelled alcohol on you too. I already would've taken you away for testing, but some guy from Homeland Security and a couple boys from CID still need to ask you a few questions."

Carter allowed his aching head to swivel to either side as he realized for the first time that the cadet midshipmen guards were no longer next to him. He didn't remember them getting up or leaving. Other than the security personnel inspecting the exhibit and the bomb-sniffing dogs checking for explosive materials, he was alone.

Not even the replacement guards remained. He had an uneasy feeling about what was to come.

Gordon stepped away as a thin man in a gray pinstriped suit and gold wire-rimmed glasses approached and introduced himself as Agent Dwayne Abrams, with the Department of Homeland Security. Two uniformed CID men stood on either side of him.

"Lieutenant Porter, we can do this someplace more private, if you prefer," Agent Abrams said.

Carter was not sure what the man meant by "this," but he didn't want to get up until he had to. "That's okay."

"Very well, then. Lieutenant Porter, you were the ranking officer on guard duty this evening, were you not?"

"Yes."

"The other guards mentioned the intruders arrived from the stairs, but none of you saw them until they reached the bottom, is that correct?"

"Yes," Carter confirmed. "After that, they were on us pretty fast and popped us with tasers. There were six or so, maybe eight of them."

The investigators nodded and jotted notes on small pads.

"The other guards also said the intruders all wore dark gray tactical gear, with hooded masks, is that correct?"

Carter lifted his hand and rubbed the bandage on his head. "Yes, I think so."

"Did they also strike you on the head?" one of the CID officers asked, pointing to Carter's bandage.

"No, I got that when I hit the floor." He wasn't going to volunteer that he hit the floor after stumbling into, and rolling off, one of the interlopers. He shifted, and the throbbing in his head intensified.

Agent Abrams tapped his pen on the notepad. "Did you see anything else that could help us?"

Feeling a little more disoriented and not sure whether it was from the taser or the alcohol, he asked, "What?"

"Did you see anything else, Lieutenant Porter?" Abrams sounded frustrated at having to repeat himself.

"Oh, sorry. No, not much. They were in and out pretty quick and looked pretty organized. After they zip-tied us, they put hoods over our heads." Carter pointed to his head but had to put his hand back down to keep from flopping over. He intended to say more, but he lost his train of thought when he righted himself.

"Lieutenant Porter!" The agent's face flushed.

"Sorry," Carter said, exhaling and slightly slurring the word. "I could still see a little out of the bottom of my hood, but only their legs and feet, for the most part. I think they may have set up something on tripods around the sarcophagus. Maybe cameras. I don't know. I have no idea what they were doing or why."

"Before you were covered, were you able to make out any discernible features? Height, weight, or markings of any sort?" The agent moved his arms as though he wanted him to use his own height and width for proportions.

Carter didn't immediately respond, and his eyes dropped to the floor. He felt nauseated and wondered if he might throw up.

"Lieutenant Porter, have you been drinking?"

"Yes," Carter said. "I did see something. When one of them zip-tied me, his shirtsleeve separated from his gloves. The man had a tattoo. I think it was manacles circling his wrist and, just above, it looked like the tops of a spired cathedral or something." He ignored the question about his drinking.

"Good." Agent Abrams scribbled in his notepad. "Did they speak? Did you hear any accents or dialects?"

"Yeah, I heard a couple of them talking. They sounded Russian or Eastern European. The one who barked most of the orders had a very deep, gravelly voice, like someone who enjoyed sipping on an exhaust pipe." He chuckled. "I only got a glimpse of his lower half out of the bottom of my hood, but he looked like a very large guy."

"Yes, good." The agent nodded, his tone subtly changing. "Well, we are still confirming this, but at the moment, it doesn't appear anything was stolen, and the sarcophagus doesn't seem to be vandalized or damaged. We haven't discovered any explosive materials or communication devices planted yet."

"Good," Carter grunted.

"Yes, it is good. Why do *you* think these intruders did this?" he asked in an accusatory tone.

"I told you, I don't know."

"If all they wanted were pictures, they could have taken a tour at any time during the day. Why do something so elaborate?"

"I don't know," he said more emphatically.

"We'll see." The agent gave a sideways glance to the other two CID officers before returning his gaze to Carter. "Do you think these men could have had any insider help?"

"Inside?"

"Yes, I mean this group invaded this institution, easily subdued three military personnel, and escaped with little trace. That would be pretty hard to do without someone here helping them, wouldn't you agree?"

Even though the inside temperature of the exhibit space was a cool seventy degrees, Carter felt a few beads of sweat forming on his forehead and more trickling down the inside of his undershirt. "I, uh, I don't know."

"Lieutenant Porter, I understand you formerly held the rank of captain, did you not?"

"Yes," Carter answered, growing more nervous. His eyes darted to Gordon, but his friend looked away.

"And this demotion," the agent flipped through his notes, "followed a charge of driving under the influence while you were on a different naval base?"

Even though the agent continued staring at his notepad, Carter felt the steely gaze of the CID officers. He knew there was no point lying. "That's correct."

"I also understand you had only a little over a year of active service left under your military contract when that incident occurred, and the navy disciplined you with a reduction in rank and a reassignment to this facility, where you served on tonight's honor guard."

"That's also correct." Carter tried not to reveal anything in his voice, but sweat rolled over his eyelids, betraying his growing concern with this line of questioning.

"I mean, getting demoted so close to the end might make me angry. What about you? Did that make you angry?"

"No," Carter said defiantly. He knew if the incident had occurred outside that naval base, the penalty could have included losing his driver's license and jail time. They could have dishonorably discharged him, but instead, they'd disciplined him and reduced his rank.

"Hmm, okay," the agent snarked. "This late-night duty is typically handled by cadets, not commissioned officers like yourself, isn't that correct?"

Carter did not answer, but the CID officers nodded.

"Why do you think the navy reassigned you here, of all places?"

"I'm sure that decision was above my pay grade." Carter smirked, blood pounding in his ears and bile rising in his throat.

"Really, you can't think of a single reason for this assignment?"

He remained silent.

"Isn't it true, Lieutenant, that you have a family connection to this exhibit?"

Carter raised his head slowly and eyed the man but still said nothing.

"Isn't one of your ancestors, General Horace Porter, honored for his distinguished service in a plaque over there on the wall?"

"Yes."

The agent flipped back to his notes. "It looks like he was a successful Civil War general who became Teddy Roosevelt's ambassador to France. Wasn't he responsible for returning and interring Jones's remains here?" He looked up from his pad. "Wow, that is certainly a hard act to follow."

Carter glared at him.

"Your wife is also in the military, correct? Major Mary Lee Porter? Already a major. That's impressive. She commands the Navy Operational Support Center in Baltimore, correct?"

"Yes, she does," Carter answered without volunteering they were in the process of getting divorced. If the man didn't know it, Carter was not about to give him more ammunition.

"Do you think the navy reassigned you here as part of the punishment, to shame you? If they did, wouldn't that make you angry? You know, angry enough to want to do something?"

Carter felt the word "something" hanging in the air and steeled himself before he answered. "No, it would not. I don't know who those intruders were, what they wanted, or why they chose tonight to break in here. I'm proud of my wife, I'm proud of what General Porter accomplished, and I am grateful and proud to serve in the United States Navy, in any capacity."

"Okay, then. So after the navy gave you this second chance, you chose to show your gratitude by drinking on duty, while armed intruders invaded the one area you were charged with guarding?"

Carter flinched. Conflicting feelings raced through him: shame for drinking and letting others down, mixed with the very real concern this man was about to arrest him for something he had nothing to do with. *This guy is unhinged!* his mind screamed, but the lingering effects from the alcohol and the taser slowed his ability to respond, and, of course, he knew the delay made him look guilty.

"You also lost a daughter a few years ago, correct? I believe her name was Courtney," the agent added.

Carter's head jerked up, his anger rising. He wanted to lunge at the man, but he restrained himself, thinking such a reaction was what the agent wanted. *He's goading me. Don't take the bait,* he told himself.

The mere mention of his dead daughter's name brought a flood of emotion. The coroner's report ultimately determined his three-and-a-half-year-old daughter died from SUDC, sudden unexplained death in childhood. He could never wrap his head around the randomness of the occurrence and the devastating finality of the result. It made no sense, and his heavy drinking started soon after her death. "You can go straight to hell," he finally allowed himself to say.

Agent Abrams appeared unaffected by the insult, but one of the CID officers whispered something in his ear, handed the agent his phone, and gestured that someone needed to speak with him.

"Would you please stay here, Lieutenant Porter?" the agent asked, but Carter understood it was not a request.

Agent Abrams and the officers stepped several paces away, and Carter noticed Gordon casually move in their direction.

Carter used the brief respite to take a few deep breaths in an attempt to calm himself. His effort was short-lived. A familiar and striking figure entered, with the same trim, athletic build she'd had when they married. Dressed in a neat, pressed uniform with her auburn, shoulder-length hair tucked into a tight bun behind her head, she strode with confidence toward him. He closed his eyes and let his chin slump to his chest.

"You okay?" she asked quietly.

"Yeah, other than being incompetent as a guard and being falsely accused," he responded, grunting as he pushed himself up into a straighter sitting position. "So, I guess Gordo called you?"

Mary pursed her lips, and he knew she smelled the alcohol on his breath. He could tell she wanted to scream and shake him. He had seen that look too many times. Thankfully, she didn't scream, which would have made his situation more precarious. He also saw the familiar disappointment in her eyes.

They had argued a lot about his drinking after Courtney died. He'd even promised a few times to cut back, but he never did. All it would take was for him to start thinking about the last day of Courtney's life and he would end up drinking himself to sleep.

The tragic nightmare of his daughter's death occurred when he was home alone with Courtney. Mary was away for a few days on duty. For him, tag-team childcare was a blessing. He loved spending time with his daughter and seeing the world through her eyes. Part of the reason he relished such time was because his own father had been away so often when he was young.

Courtney's last night was like any other. They had macaroni and cheese and watched some old cartoons. He read her a bedtime story about some silly farm animals who struck it rich after they found oil on their property. Then, he'd kissed her good night. She told him she loved him, and he told her he loved her more. After she went to sleep, he spent two hours on the computer before he went to bed. That was it. Everything was normal, until the next morning, when her skin was a sickly white-gray and he couldn't wake her up.

He tortured himself after her death, wondering if there was something he could have done. He often wondered, what if he'd checked on her one more time?

He knew Courtney's death devastated Mary, but instead of drinking, she threw herself into her military career. She never blamed him, but it didn't matter. He blamed himself. With each passing day, he retreated further into his darkening world. He had become a lost soul. Eventually, he shut down and stopped caring about practically everything. He never wanted to hurt Mary and had almost convinced himself divorce would be best for both of them. It would prevent him hurting her more, but he could tell that he had anyway.

He had also likely put the final nail in the coffin of his military career. Agent Abrams's ridiculous accusations aside, Carter had drunk too much before his shift. Prior to this evening, he had never been drunk on duty.

He berated himself. *How could I be so reckless and stupid?* He figured Mary was wondering the same thing. He realized drinking or being drunk on duty, particularly guard duty, was a more serious charge than driving under the influence. The navy could prosecute him for a court-martial offense. The only question in his mind was whether they would pursue a dishonorable discharge or an "other than honorable," or OTH, discharge. Either could affect his pension rights and benefits, and he might not be able to include his military service on his resume. His anxiety began to spiral.

"Carter." Mary gently touched his arm, obviously recognizing his internal struggle and trying to calm him. "I'll give Bobby Fredericks a call."

He nodded, remembering the name. Fredericks was the lawyer who had defended him the last time. They had paid for private counsel rather than relying on an assigned navy lawyer. "Yeah, okay. I'm really sorry," he mumbled.

She reached out and touched the bandage on his head.

He recoiled and brushed her hand away. "It's not that bad."

"I was sorry to hear about John," she offered, changing the subject. "You know that I loved him too."

"Thanks," he said, realizing this was the first time he had seen Mary since his father's funeral, about a month earlier. He had been drunk during the service and managed to slur his way through the eulogy. After the service, someone told him Mary got up and left before he'd finished. "Just one more random event that took someone I loved."

"That wasn't your fault either," Mary insisted.

"Right, just a 'carjacking gone wrong,' as the police called it." He shrugged, dropping his shoulders and rubbing the back of his head again. "You know, the only reason Dad moved here was to be closer to Courtney. He told me numerous times he felt guilty his transportation job required him to be on the road so much when I was young. He said the job cost him his marriage and a closer relationship with me, but he would not let it cost him time with his only granddaughter. Unfortunately, it was too short, wasn't it?"

Mary gave his arm a squeeze. "I know."

"I got to the hospital after they wheeled Dad into surgery," he said. "I sat in the waiting room, wondering whether I would ever see him again and thinking about the last time we were together. He had called me Carport."

His father had first jokingly called him Carport when Carter was in second grade, combining his son's first and last names. Carter hated it and would angrily remind his father that this was not his name, but his father always found it and Carter's reaction funny. Eventually, so did Carter.

"I would have given anything to hear him call me that silly name again, but he never came out of surgery." He shuddered, as if he'd experienced a sudden chill. "You know, Dad actually spent his last breaths trying to encourage me. One of the orderlies who had wheeled him in said he was very weak and could barely speak, but he whispered to him to please tell his son, Carter, something the orderly told me sounded like 'keep on!' and 'hold on!'" He shook his head, wondering why his father wasted his last few moments worrying about him. "I didn't get to tell him goodbye either."

Mary gave him a supportive pat on the arm. She'd told him numerous times she didn't blame him for Courtney's death and that it could just as easily have happened when she was home. While neither got to say goodbye, he, at least, got to tell her good night and that he loved her before she went to sleep.

Bracing himself against the wall, Carter finally stood up and straightened his uniform.

"Well, that's attractive." She pointed at his pants.

He looked down and noticed a large urine stain on the front of his green trousers, just below the edges of his uniform coat. "Great. It must be a result of the taser." He brushed the front of his trousers. "My day just keeps getting better and better. You know, it's probably a good thing you're divorcing me."

He could tell she wanted to say something, but Agent Abrams, the CID officers, and Gordon returned.

One CID man instructed Gordon, "Please see that Lieutenant Porter is given blood and urine tests before he is dismissed."

"Yes, sir." Gordon nodded crisply. "Two military police officers are on their way to escort him now."

The man turned back to Carter. "Lieutenant, you should consider yourself relieved of duty pending the results of those tests. Please be willing to make yourself available, in case we have additional questions."

Carter shrugged. *Why are you bothering? You know what the results will be.* He was glad the Homeland Security agent wasn't arresting him, and it sounded like he would be free to return to his apartment after the tests.

They stared at each other for a lingering second or two before the officers and Agent Abrams left the exhibit.

"Sorry, man." Gordon placed his hand on his shoulder. "My hands are tied, no pun intended."

"Don't apologize. You've been a good friend," Mary said.

Gordon leaned in and whispered, "Listen, man, I'm not supposed to say this, but I know you have a lot more to be concerned about with the tests. So, don't worry about that stuff the Homeland Security guy was throwing at you."

Carter furrowed his brow, confused. "Don't worry?"

"Yeah." He dipped his head. "He sweated the cadet midshipmen, too, but there is no evidence any of you were involved. He said effects of tasers can impact cognitive ability, and some people are more forth-coming if pressed soon after they've been tased. I heard them talking, and, other than these intruders trespassing on government property and roughing you guys up a bit, they're struggling to find another crime committed or a reason for any of this. Nothing was stolen, and they found nothing planted."

"Good, I guess." Carter swayed and reached out to steady himself on the wall.

"Some of what you told him sounded like it may be useful."

"Really? What?"

"The accents matched what the cadets said, but they didn't see any tattoos, like you did. The Homeland Security guy said it sounded like a Russian prisoner tattoo. Prisoners often get into gangs or orga-nized crime when they come to this country, but he was thoroughly confused, since this whole thing reads more like a paramilitary oper-ation. He's still looking for anything that links this to terrorism. Of course, those guys see terrorism around every corner, but this break-in didn't seem to check any boxes for him."

"Hmm." Carter hesitated as two military police officers appeared behind Mary.

"Major, we are here to take the lieutenant for testing," one of them informed Mary.

As they took positions on either side of Carter, one of the officers said, "You appear to have soiled your uniform, Lieutenant."

He growled. "Yeah, that's from the taser."

The officer just stared at him, and Carter realized he wasn't refer-ring to the urine stain. He meant Carter had disgraced himself and his uniform by being drunk on duty. Carter averted his eyes and studied the ground.

Mary and Gordon stepped aside, and even Carter could smell his alcohol and sweat lingering in the air as they marched him out.

Chapter 2

THE BUSTLING ACTIVITY in the lobby of the Bonnie Ness Inn made the early morning sun streaming through its large front windows seem more like a strobe light. Behind the reception desk, Hassie Douglass shielded her light brown eyes before pulling her thick black hair into a tight ponytail and tucking her blue-collared blouse under the band of her red-and-blue plaid uniform skirt.

She knew she was fortunate to have a part-time job at a luxury hotel, and her modest salary helped defray her and her grandfather's monthly expenses. She loved engaging the guests, hearing where they were from, and watching them celebrate different milestones in their lives. With its location just outside the small hamlet of Drumnadrochit, Scotland, near the midpoint of Loch Ness, the Inn's guests were typically vacationers, not business travelers.

"Staying out of trouble this morning, I hope, Ms. Douglass?" her manager, Martin Scott, asked as he strode by the reception desk.

She liked Martin. He was a sweet, short, middle-aged man with wire-rimmed glasses who reminded her of her grandfather, only a little younger and pudgier. "Only until I find my next target, sir." She smiled.

"I'm sure that's true." He laughed and shook his head. "You know, even though you were only fourteen, one of the reasons I hired you last year was your pocketful of sass. Now, I have every confidence that it will be what gets me fired one day. You're just lucky the guests love you and that I was not blessed with good judgment." He winked.

"Thank you, Martin."

"Good luck with her, Brenda," he said to Brenda Willis, Hassie's supervisor.

Brenda stood a little straighter behind the reception desk when she heard her name. "No worries, Martin." She chuckled as he ambled out of the lobby. "Don't make a liar out of me, kid." She jokingly nudged Hassie with her elbow and pushed a few strands of her bright red bangs away from her own face.

"No promises here." Hassie shrugged her shoulders and returned the grin. Brenda was over twice her age, but they got along like sisters. Then, Hassie's brown eyes flashed to a young family moving through the throng of guests toward the reception desk. The parents appeared to be in their early thirties, and a boy who she guessed to be their son, about four years old, lagged behind and tugged on his mother's dress. "In fact, I think I may have just found my next target."

Brenda rolled her eyes at Hassie before turning and welcoming the family to the Inn.

"We get to stay in a castle, Mom!"

"I know, I know," his mother said, acting like she was as excited as her young son.

Hassie smiled. She remembered the first time she saw the Inn, with its thick, gray-stone façade and large square turrets. It resembled a modern-day Camelot, even more so with the surrounding lush green hills and mountains. The place took her breath away, and she loved seeing the same astonishment and awe in the eyes of most first-time guests.

"Pssst," the boy said loudly to Hassie, while his parents spoke to Brenda.

Hassie was already walking around the desk when she heard him. "I was hoping you would talk to me."

"My dad is moving here for his job."

"Great," she replied. "We're very glad you are here and—"

"Have you seen it?" He interrupted and pointed excitedly to a framed poster of the 1934 "surgeon's photograph" of the Loch Ness Monster on the wall. "You work here, so you must have seen it lots of times, right?" His face beamed with delight and wonder.

Hassie smiled wide, put her hands on her knees, and leaned toward the bouncing boy as if she were going to whisper a secret. "I will tell you the same thing that my *seanair* told me," she said. "When I was about your age, we took a lot of walks along the shores of Loch Ness and the River Ness, and I asked him the same thing. My grandfather told me that you could always see Nessie if you wanted; it's just a matter of how badly you want to see it."

The boy seemed a little confused, but then his face lit up, evidently believing that she must have meant that she had seen the creature.

His mother looked over at Hassie, smiled, and nodded with understanding.

Hassie stood up, speaking now to his mother. "In fact, if you are interested, Urquhart Castle is only a short walk from here and is one of the best Nessie-viewing sites. We have a few brochures, and the Inn sells admission tickets."

"Can we, Mom? Can we?"

"We'll have to see," she answered.

Of course, Hassie recognized her response as mom-speak for "probably not."

The boy waved goodbye as his family lumbered toward the elevators.

A little after lunch, she saw the young boy and his mother heading toward the front entrance. His mother held his hand tightly, but when his eyes met Hassie's, he dragged his mother over to the reception desk, changing her trajectory like a tiny tugboat pulling an aircraft carrier.

"Guess what, guess what, guess what!"

"What?" Hassie laughed, rushing around the desk to him, hoping her closer proximity might reduce his decibel level.

"My mom said after lunch we could look for Nessie. Do you want to come?"

"No, honey, she needs to stay and work." His mom answered for her.

"Thank you, anyway. If you do see Nessie, please say hello for me." Hassie smiled and winked.

"Yes, we certainly will." His mom chuckled. "By the way, I'm not sure why we bothered ordering lunch. My husband had barely taken a bite when this little one announced he was finished and it was time to go."

Hassie stifled a laugh. "Well, there's a paved path on the other side of the front driveway that will take you to the shore, if you don't want to walk through the grass."

The boy frowned a little, obviously disappointed Hassie wouldn't be joining their fun, but tugged his mother back toward the front door. Hassie watched as the boy's mother had to hold on with both hands to keep her son from running off on his own.

She stood watching for a few seconds more until she heard a voice behind her that she wished she hadn't.

"Shouldn't you be behind the reception desk working?"

"Just helping a guest, Olivia." Hassie returned to the desk, not meeting the eyes of the far too stern twenty-something woman wearing a matching uniform.

Hassie got the feeling Olivia thought the two of them were competing somehow. Olivia told anyone who would listen about her aspiration of becoming the youngest deputy manager of the Inn. Hassie suspected part of the young woman's enmity was jealousy since Hassie had more fun on the job. Thankfully, Olivia's charge was limited to the Inn's restaurant, and Hassie had no interest in competing. This was just a part-time job, not a career path.

"I doubt that," Olivia sneered. "If it were up to me, the Inn would deduct from your pay all the time you spend playing while others have to do the real work."

Hassie let out an exasperated sigh, noticing the toe of Olivia's right shoe tapping on the carpet, her hands on her hips, and her mouth curled in its typical smirk. "Thanks, Olivia. By the way, isn't the restaurant open for another hour or two?" she asked, glancing at the wall clock. "I'm just surprised to see you in the lobby."

Olivia glared for another moment. "I'm looking for Mr. Scott, not that it's any of your business," she announced, turned on her heel, and marched off in a huff.

—

About two hours later, Hassie smiled broadly when she saw the mother carrying the boy, sound asleep, his head slumped over her shoulder. The mother raised her eyebrows, smiled back, and waved as she headed to the elevators.

Hassie spent most of the rest of the afternoon answering phones. Near the end of her shift, she slipped into the kitchen, hoping to retrieve a few uneaten pieces of lamb or maybe some haggis. She was careful to avoid the kitchen staff. Martin had chastised her on two prior occasions for taking food out of the trash. The food wasn't for her, but that didn't matter. This afternoon's pickings were good, and she tossed a few pieces of meat and a bone into a cardboard to-go box.

Checking to make sure nobody saw her with the box, she ducked into a short hallway leading to the storage room. The room was dark, but the light from the hallway was enough for her to reach the back exit. She slowly pushed open the door and felt the cool, lightly misting air of the alley behind the Inn.

Hassie gave a low whistle, and a mangy dog bounded up to her, whimpering and panting. She knelt so he wouldn't jump up and get her uniform dirty.

"Hey, boy!" she said, scratching the dog's head. He was a Scottish deerhound mix with a coat that was darker and shorter than most dogs of that breed. Gently patting his ribs, she thought how malnourished he looked, which always panged her heart.

The dog ferociously licked her face until she opened the to-go box. Then he barked his appreciation.

She had first seen him behind the Inn three months ago. After he returned a few days in a row, Hassie was smitten. But when Olivia saw him, she called the dog Scrounge, for its appearance and as a general insult. To Hassie's chagrin, the insulting name stuck, and other staff members used it with a derisive tone. When she did call him Scrounge, she made a point of saying it in a soft and loving way.

"Wheesht!" she scolded him. "If we get caught, we'll both be in trouble. I may not be able to save you like last time. That mean, old Olivia may not be the brightest bulb, but she knew I was the one who let you off the leash when she tied you to the back door and called the dog warden."

Hassie smiled to herself, thinking of when Olivia and Martin led the dog warden to the back alley to find only an empty leash on the door. Olivia had been embarrassed and humiliated. Martin had almost laughed out loud. Hassie already adored Martin, but she liked him even more after that. The warden had also smiled and assured them it was not a waste of his time, even thanking Olivia for calling, since the law required people to turn in stray dogs.

Out of Olivia's earshot, Martin had warned her. She recalled his words very clearly. "Hassie, I have nothing against that dog, but it's a stray and rules are rules. If the dog comes back, please do not let me catch you feeding it. Understood?" he'd implored, with a fatherly look in his eyes.

She continued scratching the dog's head and under his chin. "When you did come back a few days later, boy, I knew what I had to do to honor Martin's words." She giggled. "I can feed you, but I just have to make sure Martin doesn't *catch me* feeding you." She smiled. In her mind, she just needed to respect his words. She was grateful to the other staff members who, after seeing that the dog had returned, all agreed that nobody from the Inn would feed the dog and pressured Olivia not to call the warden, even though the mutt still clearly bothered her.

Before Scrounge barked again, Hassie removed a round lid from one of the large trash pails lining the wall. She flipped it over and dumped in the contents of the box. She knew if anyone reported seeing the dog eating from the to-go box, Martin would know it was her. Hassie observed Scrounge noisily bury his nose into the remnants of a meal that had probably cost a guest over one hundred pounds.

She was just about to return inside when she heard a female voice behind her. "Hassie Douglass!"

Chapter 3

Carter finally returned to his one-bedroom apartment a little before four a.m. The military police told him the results from his blood and urine tests could take several days and then reminded him he should make himself available for further questioning, if needed.

Sure, I need to be available, in case they need more help drumming me out of the Marine Corps. He wondered why they needed to delay the inevitable, but the navy had to go through the formalities. That was the navy way.

He was amazed Mary still seemed to care as much as she did and was handling the engagement of defense counsel. Of course, avoiding a guilty verdict would be difficult. He was guilty. If his defense counsel couldn't work some magic or, at least, get his discharge reduced to an OTH, there was a good chance the sentence could render his entire military career meaningless. It would become just an empty black hole on his resume reflecting one more thing of value he had pushed from his life.

With so much hanging over his head, he knew he should've gone straight to bed, but he didn't. He went to the kitchen. *Why not?* he thought as he poured himself a Jack Daniel's and soda. He wanted to numb the pain, trying to convince himself he didn't care, but that was a lie. He cared; he just didn't want to care. So, he drank. Settling onto his rented couch, he scratched the edges of the bandage on his head. *Nothing makes sense. How did I get here?* He pondered that question over the course of two more drinks.

—

The phone woke him a little after ten thirty a.m. He banged the front of his head on the underside of his coffee table and cursed, realizing that he must have fallen off the couch at some point. The front of his head now throbbed as much as the back.

The phone ringing interrupted a dream he had had several times that he wished was real. The dream was of the last morning of his daughter's life.

It was a warm Tuesday morning, and he, his daughter, and his dad had walked to a small neighborhood park. A few other families were there, with small children and dogs. Courtney loved playing with the dogs at the park as much as she enjoyed the swings, and Carter loved watching her play. Almost any response from the animals would cause her to giggle uncontrollably, and her laugh was infectious.

Even from his dreams, his face would feel sore from smiling and laughing. His daughter always seemed to wear the same navy-blue dress with bright yellow daisies. She loved that dress and wore it often. He had pulled her dark brown hair into braided pigtails, and she was an identical but smaller image of Mary.

In his dream, he saw his father and Courtney standing together as they were all getting ready to leave. His dad's hand swallowed her tiny hand and wrist. They were so happy.

The phone rang again, and the room swayed when he opened his eyes. It didn't help that the walls of his apartment were stark white and as unadorned as the day he moved in. He knocked the TV remote, two magazines, and his empty whiskey glass off the coffee table before grabbing the phone.

"What?" he growled when he answered.

"Mr. Carter Porter?"

"Yes. What are you selling?" he snapped, knowing that it was not anyone from the navy, since they would have referred to him by his rank.

"No, sir, this is not a sales call. My name is Tim Young. I'm with Charter Bank & Trust, on Church Road."

He remembered seeing the bank just off John Hanson Highway. Even though his mind spun, he remembered someone from the bank had left messages on his voice mail, requesting him to call. He just thought they were marketing and had ignored them.

"Sir, we have been trying to reach you concerning Mr. John Porter's account," he said. "We have not been able to reach him directly."

"Yes, he was my father. He passed away recently." Carter pushed himself onto his knees and then rolled back onto the couch, his head still swimming. "Did you say he had an account with you?"

"I'm so sorry. Yes, your father rented a safe deposit box with us. Unfortunately, the credit card he used for the rental fee was denied."

"Yeah, all of his cards have been cancelled."

"Of course, sir. Again, I'm very sorry. You are listed as a contact person. If it's convenient, you can come in to settle the account and dispose of the contents, or if you want to continue to rent it, we can set you up in our system," he offered. "I am obligated to inform you that the bank can claim it as abandoned property after eight weeks, if you choose to do nothing."

Why would Dad have a safe deposit box? He had only a modest estate, and his simple will, which left everything to me, included no supplemental asset list or any listing of a safe deposit box. He was unable to imagine why his father wouldn't have told him about it, but after Courtney's death, he had separated himself emotionally from everyone, including his father, his wife, and most of his friends.

"Uh, yeah, okay. I can come down there this afternoon and clean it out," he said and hung up.

Maybe Dad had a secret stash of cash. He laughed to himself, knowing it was impossible. His father had taken a vacation to Scotland a few months ago, and Carter knew he had saved for over a year to make the trip. He'd even sold a few things to pay for it. Carter didn't understand why it was so important for him to go to Scotland, but it had been.

He struggled to fathom anything his father had that could be valuable enough to justify keeping it in a safe deposit box. If he'd had something valuable, Carter could certainly use it. He knew his rising legal bills and upcoming divorce would sap his resources. The room still moving a little when he stood up. He relocated to his bedroom to sleep for a few more hours before he would order an Uber and head to the bank.

—

As Carter entered the bank lobby that afternoon, a trim man, probably in his mid-twenties, appeared from behind a cubicle and introduced himself as Tim Young. Carter took in his cheap poly-blend blue suit and over-starched white shirt. "I brought a copy of my father's will."

"That's not necessary, sir. You're already listed as an authorized person, with permission to access. We have your signature on file."

Carter was startled when the man presented a sample of his signature. Though it was sloppy and he appeared to have dragged the last "r," the scribble was his. Worse, he knew he must have been drunk when he signed it; and he had no recollection that he ever had.

He'd had more and more of these memory gaps, and Mary and his father had made excuses for him. He felt embarrassed, but not enough to change. "Unfortunately, I don't have a key to the box."

"We understand, sir. That is not uncommon when a family member inherits a box." The man handed Carter the current sign-in sheet, acknowledging his access to the box, which Carter signed. "However, in addition to the outstanding month's rent, there will be a three-hundred-fifty-dollar charge to open it. We have someone on site who can open the box, if you are agreeable to these terms."

Carter thought for a second and nodded. "Sure," he said, though he hadn't counted on this venture costing him money. He hoped the contents would be worth it.

It took the locksmith only minutes to drill through the outer security door. Young pulled the long metal box out of its slot and placed it on a cart. He wheeled it into one of the private viewing rooms and left Carter alone.

The box had a short lid, which opened only about a third of the top. Carter gently pulled the lid open, and his heart sank.

Empty. Are you kidding me?

He picked up the box and tilted it. Something from the back slid toward him. What he saw did not lift his spirits much. It wasn't money and it wasn't gold. Instead, inside the box was an old, worn, leather-bound book, and unless it was a first edition of *Ulysses*, he doubted the value of the book would cover the cost of the locksmith. He exhaled his disappointment and reached down to open the cover. "General Horace Porter" was written on the inside top left corner of what appeared to be a personal journal.

Great. Nothing but sentimental value. He was tempted to throw the book into the trash bin, but he thought better of it. *Dad kept this journal for some reason. It must have been important to him. But why spend money on a safe deposit box?* He checked the box again, but nothing else was there. He stuffed the leather book under his arm and called an Uber to pick him up.

—

"Hello, my name is Mike," the Uber driver informed Carter as he slid into the back seat of the black Chrysler 300. Carter inspected the journal and noticed something clipped to the inside back cover.

It appeared to be an insulated, clear plastic holder, with something thick inside.

The car pulled onto the highway, and Carter was about to unzip the plastic when he heard a large engine rev behind them. A split second later, something slammed into the side of the Uber.

Hassie's heart stopped, before turning and seeing it was Brenda. "You gave me a fright." She smiled.

"Are you feeding that mangy stray?" Brenda crossed her arms as she stepped toward her. "Kid, you need to be more careful. Olivia would love to catch you and force Martin to do something. That dog is like a pebble in her shoe."

"I know. I'm sorry, but he always looks so pitiful."

Brenda shook her head. "Leave the dog. Come help me with the housekeeping inventory. If we finish quickly, I'll let you go early."

"Yes, thank you!" Hassie exclaimed, knowing it wouldn't take long to complete that task.

Her bus wouldn't leave until five fifteen p.m., so finishing early meant she would have time for her favorite activity: strolling along the shores of Loch Ness. She cherished those opportunities, for they reminded her of the walks she used to take with her grandfather.

The two of them would search for smooth, shiny black rocks and pebbles, pretending the stones were jewels or treasure. In a way, they were. Her grandfather polished them, cut them, and incorporated them into small works of art for her. A few hung on the wall in their flat. And he decorated her backpack with them. She loved it.

Once, they found a flat, shiny black rock with glistening specks in it. The rock was so thin her grandfather didn't have to cut it, and the water had polished the stone to a high gloss. It was the perfect treasure. They took hundreds of walks along the shores and found many other stones, but never another as perfect as that one. Now, she would give anything to take one more walk with him, but he was too sick and his eyesight had deteriorated.

Her grandfather was all she had in the world. Her mother had died of breast cancer when she was six, and her parents' marriage had been short-lived. Her father had walked away, terminating his parental rights. Her grandfather later explained that her father had addictions but didn't elaborate. She had no memory of her father.

Once back inside with Brenda, she confirmed the Inn's current inventory of consumables, such as toilet paper, shampoo, soap, and other items. The time passed quickly, and they did finish early.

"Thanks," Hassie said after Brenda logged off her small laptop and dismissed her.

"Not a problem, kid. Before you go, please take these over to the maintenance department for me and let them know where we found them." She handed her a couple of loose metal washers. "I doubt they fell off anything important, but you never know."

"Sure," she told her, shoving them in her pocket and quickly forgetting about them.

Hassie clocked out and donned a light yellow slicker for her walk in the gray, misting afternoon. Almost as soon as she left the Inn's grounds, Scrounge bounded up to her. The dog hopped and jumped on something in the grass. She saw nothing but laughed when he began feverishly chasing his tail.

"Come on, you silly dog." She walked about a hundred meters and left the grassy outcropping to step onto the packed mud lining the shore.

She loved this view. There was something otherworldly about Loch Ness, particularly when the fog blanketed the distant shore. The place seemed magical, lost in the clouds. She truly felt a connection to the Loch and couldn't explain it, but a warm comfort enveloped her whenever she strolled near its waters. Perhaps it was just her imagination, but she felt love and acceptance. The feeling was intoxicating. Even though Scotland boasted over thirty thousand lochs, Loch Ness was special.

The outline of Urquhart Castle's remains appeared in the distance, and she was about to turn back when she felt a pull of something encouraging her to go just a little farther. She consulted the time on her phone; she still had a couple minutes.

Stop! She heard what sounded like a murmur.

Glancing around, she saw nobody. Sometimes, when she walked the shores, she thought she heard a voice whispering on the wind, but this was louder than a whisper. She realized no one was calling out to her. This voice was her own in her head, yet somehow, she knew it wasn't her. There was an otherness to it.

She froze. Hearing a voice in your head was never good, and she knew it. *Am I crazy?*

Be not afraid, child, she heard.

She wasn't scared. The voice was comforting, like a parent's.

Look down.

Just at the edge of the Loch, she saw four smooth, black stones. Their tiny, imbedded crystals sparkled under the water—and they were identical to the stone she and her grandfather had found a long time ago. She pulled them out and noticed how incredibly smooth they felt to her touch. *Seanair will love these*, she thought, shoving the stones in her pocket and hearing them clink against the washers. After checking her phone, she started her brisk walk to the bus stop in the increasing mist and winds. She wondered whether she had really heard the voice she thought she had, but as the wind picked up, what she really wanted was the warmth of her home.

Theirs was a simple one-bedroom, second-story flat. It was all they could afford, but the lodging was sufficient for their needs. Her grandfather slept in the bedroom, and she slept on a pullout couch in the common area, where she still could hear her grandfather's cough at night.

His coughing started a little over six months ago. As it worsened, he had lost weight. That was when his eyesight deteriorated. He'd told her he now saw only dim shapes, as if he were looking through a thin curtain in a darkened room. He recognized her voice and he could get around their flat, but he couldn't venture out on his own. Recently, she'd noticed a few blistering lesions on his neck and arm. When she asked him about them, he dismissed her concern but started wearing collared and long-sleeved shirts.

She suspected he wanted to protect her by hiding his symptoms, but all it accomplished was an increase of her pestering him to see a doctor. Given their economic status, her grandfather relied on the free National Health Service managed by the Scottish government, not the private healthcare system available to those with funds. When he finally called, he was told the soonest the pulmonary specialist could see him was in four months. That appointment was still two months away. Whether true or not, many considered private health care to be better quality, and Hassie now desperately wished she had the economic resources to afford it.

Growing up, Hassie didn't think much about money. They didn't have much, but when her grandfather became ill, she began obsessing about money. He'd taught her it was not constructive to dwell on things she could not change, but she couldn't help herself. *If only those stones were real treasure.*

Preoccupied with thoughts of their humble means, she arrived at the bus stop and hopped on. She hated the sorrow on Scrounge's face when she waved goodbye from the back row of the bus. The dog chased the bus for a little while before giving up. She felt guilty she couldn't keep Scrounge, but their place was too small, and she knew the landlord did not allow pets.

She took two buses to travel the sixty-five kilometers from the Inn to Forres. A little after six thirty, she stepped off the second bus and hiked the seven blocks to her building.

When she opened the door to their flat, it was dark. She thought her grandfather might be asleep, but she found the bedroom empty, and her anxiety rose. She flicked on the overhead light above the kitchen table and saw a note from one of their neighbors. The pulmonologist had an unexpected opening, and he had driven her grandfather to the Raigmore Hospital in Inverness this morning.

Relieved her grandfather was okay, she called the hospital and learned they were admitting him. She rushed back to the bus stop, not bothering to change out of her uniform.

Two bus rides later, she arrived at Raigmore around eight. After confirming her grandfather's room number, the woman at the information desk informed Hassie that visiting hours ended at eight thirty. She didn't care. She was concerned more about why they had admitted him, and she would stay for as long as they would allow.

When the elevator doors opened on the fifth floor, the antiseptic smell hit her. Though she had been young when her mother took ill, she remembered visiting her in the hospital. What she remembered most was that same smell, which was one of the many reasons she hated hospitals.

She gently knocked on the door of room 514 and pushed it open. She stopped. Her grandfather had wires and monitors attached to his chest, and even though he was a tall man, he seemed small and frail lying in the hospital bed asleep in his light blue gown. The skin on his bald head and face appeared grayer under the bright lights. She smiled at the small rectangular spectacles perched on his nose. He was almost blind, but he still wore the glasses out of habit. Perhaps they were a comfort, a hope that someday he might need them again.

"Seanair?" she said quietly, approaching the empty space next to her grandfather's bed in the semi-private room, grateful that he was alone for the moment.

He opened his eyes. "I know that voice. You are the *gaol mo bheatha*," he rasped, using the Gaelic phrase for the "love of my life." "I am sorry that you had to see me here, but I think they want to keep me for a few more tests."

"Hopefully they'll find out what the problem is and get you well." When she moved to the side of his bed, her heart sank. She saw many blistering lesions on his neck, chest, shoulders, and upper arms. He was far sicker than he had let her know. She started to choke up. "Did they say how long you will be here?"

"No, but their tone suggested I may be here for a little while. The doctor is supposed to come by this evening," he said, sounding exhausted. "Will you be okay for a few days on your own?"

"Sure, don't worry about me, Seanair." She glanced at the clock. It was 8:28 p.m., and she would have to leave soon. "Seanair, I almost forgot. I found some treasure at the Loch."

Her grandfather grinned, clearly knowing what she meant. "Well, put it here on the tray," he instructed, feeling for it just above his bed.

She scooped the contents of her pocket and dropped them onto the tray. Four large gold coins and two metal washers clinked noisily.

"Oh my Lord! It's gold! Seanair, it's really gold!"

Chapter 4

"WHAT THE HELL! Are they trying to kill us?" Mike, the Uber driver, screamed.

A dark green Ford Explorer swung out, preparing for another swipe.

"Yes, they are! Watch out!" Carter shouted, just as the Explorer slammed into the Uber's passenger side. The big car stayed pressed up against Mike's Chrysler, forcing it onto the left shoulder. Carter moved to the center of the back seat, fearing the side of the car was about to be ground into the steel and concrete barrier. His heart raced, and his mind spun.

"My car!" Mike slammed on the brake. The Explorer flew off and almost crashed into the barrier.

Carter had no idea whether this was road rage or something else. In either case, there was a real chance he was about to die on this freeway, and he was completely helpless. He lumbered as fast as he could into the front seat, hoping that simple act might help him control his destiny. He watched the bigger car recover and begin a U-turn into oncoming traffic. "Go!"

Horns blared, cars swerved in every direction, and one hit the Explorer's back fender, causing it to rotate and speed sideways.

"We can't sit here! They're coming back. Go!"

Mike didn't respond. He was terrified.

Carter's gut tightened when their attacker's passenger window opened and a thick, hairy arm extended, holding a compact automatic pistol. "Gun!"

Gunfire sprayed the hood of their Chrysler, and the passenger side mirror exploded.

The Uber driver stared like a deer in the headlights.

"We have to move!" Carter screamed, then pushed the driver's foot off the brake pedal and crammed his own foot on the accelerator. The Chrysler lurched forward. Grabbing the steering wheel, Carter yanked it to the right, angling away from the left shoulder.

Bullets pinged the side of their car, and a large white Chevrolet Silverado had to swerve to miss plowing into them. The move put the truck between their Chrysler and the Explorer, briefly protecting their sedan from more gunfire.

Carter used the respite to speed toward the right side of the highway. He saw an exit for Collington Road about two hundred yards ahead.

If I can get off the freeway, maybe we can survive this, he thought, weaving into the far-right lane as the Explorer raced and pulled along the Uber driver's side. More gunfire shattered the window, and Mike's head snapped to the side. Blood and bits of skull covered Carter and the dashboard.

Sickeningly, a few additional shots hit Mike's dead body, which shielded Carter. Stealing a quick look, Carter saw the large man's grinning, stubbled face.

He knew the Explorer's driver now intended to grind the Chrysler into the guardrail on the right, and there was no place for him to go. When the big car slammed into him again, the Uber car made contact with the railing. Carter felt the car tug to the right when a concrete post tore off the front fender with a jolt, but he managed to keep moving.

The exit was now enticingly close, and the two vehicles were still locked together. He tapped on the brake, and metal scraped against metal as the big car pulled slightly ahead. When the Explorer's back door reached the Chrysler's front bumper, Carter wrenched the steering wheel to the left and hit the accelerator, T-boning the larger vehicle. Keeping the accelerator pressed to the floor, his car pushed the Explorer sideways as he angled both vehicles back toward the exit on the right. He now momentarily felt he had the upper hand of control as his car, moving forward, pushed the Explorer sideways down the highway.

Carter couldn't see the road in front of him, but he got a glimpse of the exit sign through the windows of the large vehicle pasted to his front bumper, just as the enraged man in the Explorer fired wildly. Bullets cracked and penetrated the windshield. Carter ducked and waited to pop his head up until he believed they were a few feet from the exit.

When Carter did pop his head up, he saw the large man take aim at him, but before his hand tightened on the trigger, and just as Carter hoped, the driver's door of the Explorer smashed into the safety barrier separating the highway and the exit lane. The force of the crash bent the large vehicle in half, snapping the underframe. The head of the Explorer's driver met the closed car window, killing him instantly. The impact threw the huge man from the passenger seat, and the automatic pistol disappeared somewhere inside his vehicle. The steam and smoke emanating from the smashed hood of Carter's car made it impossible to see much in front of him. Not waiting to confirm whether the man with the gun survived, he kicked open the passenger front door and was about to leap out when he saw his dad's journal wedged between the back seat and the heavily dented back passenger door. He grabbed it and yanked hard, gouging a bit of the front leather cover when he freed it. Then he ran.

His left leg protested, bruised from the multiple collisions with the Explorer. He felt every single pound of extra weight as he trudged over the guardrail and into the surrounding grass and foliage. Breathing hard, he continued for almost a mile before he felt safe enough to stop and look back. Then, he pulled out his cell phone and called 9-1-1.

—

With so many shots fired, Carter's blood-soaked clothes, and a dead body in the front seat of the Uber, the police didn't treat Carter like a victim. After handcuffing him and confiscating his phone, wallet, and the journal, Detective David Schwarzbech spent the next several hours interrogating him at the Annapolis police station.

From some of the detective's questions, and from the contraband found in the sedan's trunk, it sounded to Carter as if Mike might have been supplementing his Uber income with other, illegal activities. Carter assured the police he didn't know the men who were shooting and that he had never met the driver before this afternoon. He even encouraged the detective to check his phone's call history, to confirm the last point.

At one point, they also asked him about the bandage on the back of his head. He decided not to say anything about the break-in at the Naval Academy and made up something. He didn't want to muddy the waters, and he felt like they were close to releasing him. He just wanted to go home.

Near the end of the interrogation, the police informed him the Explorer was stolen, and they had found no bodies in the abandoned vehicle.

"Have you talked to any of the other drivers on the freeway?" Carter asked.

"Yes, a few. We had several calls about the incident, and most corroborated your story that the men in the Explorer were the aggressors and the ones shooting," the detective admitted. "It's possible that it involved some type of a territorial dispute or some prior drug deal with a dissatisfied customer."

"Good," Carter said but stopped himself when he saw the detective's brows shoot up at the comment. "Sorry, what I meant was that none of that sounds like it involves me. I was there only for an Uber ride."

Detective Schwarzbech frowned. "Perhaps."

"So, given I told you everything I know, which isn't much outside of the attack, how long are you going to continue to hold me?"

The detective's frown deepened. "We're not holding you. You are free to go, but—" he cut himself off when Carter smiled and jumped out of his chair before the detective had finished his statement.

"Okay, thanks. Can I please have my stuff back too?"

"Mr. Porter, please make yourself available for the next few days, in case we have any additional questions." Detective Schwarzbech returned Carter's phone, wallet, and the journal.

Carter shrugged, left the station, and called for a taxi.

—

Returning to his apartment building, Carter noticed the clock in the entry lobby read a little after eight thirty p.m. He picked up his mail from the small postal box on the first floor. In the elevator, he thought about the large drink he would make himself. But he abruptly pushed those thoughts aside when he got to his floor and noticed his apartment door was slightly ajar and the lock hung by only one remaining screw.

"What are you saying about gold?" Hassie's grandfather sightlessly grabbed one of the metal washers. He rubbed it with his fingers and held it up to his nose. "It is not kind to try to fool a blind man." He chuckled.

"No, Seanair. This one," she said, replacing the washer with one of the coins.

She inspected the other three. They were large, shiny, and definitely old. Two of them had specks of dirt or a grainy material imbedded in them, but the other two were pristine. She checked her pocket twice more. No stones. She knew she had seen four black stones at the shore, not gold coins.

Hassie wondered how the switch was possible. She didn't believe in miracles. Her grandfather was the religious one. He had tried to encourage her in her faith and had insisted she attend Sunday school until she was twelve, but she never felt the faith he did. She had to admit there was no logical explanation for this. It was a miracle, and one they needed. She still doubted her eyes, but she knew what she'd seen in the water.

"Good Lord!" her grandfather exclaimed, holding a coin a couple millimeters from his face. "This does look like gold. Where on earth did you get it?"

Before she could respond, the door opened, and a large, square-jawed nurse in a blue uniform entered. "Visiting hours are over."

"Nancy, this is my granddaughter. The one I mentioned."

"Yes, Mr. Douglass, but I'm afraid she needs to leave now so you can get your rest."

"How is our patient, Nancy?" A short man with a shaved head and a white lab coat popped in behind the nurse.

"I have certainly felt better," Hassie's grandfather answered.

The doctor inspected the IV bag next to the bed. "Alastair, I am going to look in your eyes." He leaned over the bed and moved a small pen light from one eye to the other. "Good. We are still seeing some dilation." He straightened and removed the thin, white rubber gloves from his hands.

Hassie smiled and nodded when the doctor acknowledged her.

"You must be his granddaughter," he said, extending his hand. "Alastair mentioned you. I am Doctor Patrick Stewart. Even though I am also bald, nobody ever mistakes me for the actor. It's probably because I am taller and better looking." He laughed.

Hassie laughed politely. "Doctor, are you going to be able to cure my grandfather's cough?"

His face turned serious. "Yes, well, I am glad we were able to get your grandfather in early."

She didn't correct him about how *early* they got him in.

"I have already discussed some of our preliminary test results with your grandfather." He paused before continuing further.

"It's okay, Doctor. She needs to hear it, and please don't sugar-coat it."

"Miss Douglass, we cannot be entirely sure until all the tests come back, but based on the symptoms, I believe there is a good chance your grandfather has small-cell lung cancer, and it has metastasized to his stomach and a few other areas. The blistering skin lesions, which I am sure you have seen, are a late-onset symptom."

Hassie felt numb, suddenly unsure whether she could even move her limbs. A cold, electric shiver ran through her body.

"More recently, he has lost a majority of his vision, correct?"

She tried to speak, but her mouth was dry. She sensed her grand-father hadn't told her everything, but she wasn't expecting this. "Yes, his eyesight is much worse," she finally mumbled.

"There is a high incidence of retinal deterioration with this type of lung cancer, primarily those with a neoplasia that have suspected neu-roendocrine origins. It's another late-onset symptom."

She had no idea what he was saying or what it meant. It sounded like a foreign language, but she understood the words "lung cancer." "Can you cure him?" she asked, starting to shake.

"Miss Douglass, we are still running tests. Until we know the full extent of the cancer, we cannot propose treatment options."

"But after the tests, you will be able to treat him, right?" She grasped for hope.

"Miss Douglass, you need to understand this is already an advanced-stage cancer, and unfortunately, that limits our options." He raised and opened his palms as he spoke. "I'm sorry for being blunt."

Hassie looked at her grandfather, not sure what to say.

"We may be able to discuss certain chemotherapy or radiation treatment options soon. The surgical option is less viable, given how far the cancer has spread. Unfortunately, the radiation and chemother-apy have some serious drawbacks. They would reduce the quality of his life and have survival risks of their own, with someone your grandfather's age."

"Wait, what are you saying?"

"Hassie," her grandfather interjected, "we'll talk more after the doctor leaves."

"You will need to talk tomorrow," Nancy insisted.

Doctor Stewart glowered at her, and she exhaled loudly and left.

"Alastair, enjoy your beautiful granddaughter's company for a few more minutes, and I will be back to visit you later."

"Doctor, would it be possible for my granddaughter to stay here and sleep in the chair, if she wants?"

"Yes, she can stay. I'll let the nursing staff know." The doctor smiled, waved to Hassie, and left.

Hassie followed him out. "Doctor, please wait!" She rushed to catch him in the hall. He stopped and turned. "Would the treatment options be different in private care?" she asked curtly. "Look, I have these." She extended her open hand with the four gold coins.

He smiled and gently cupped the underside of her hand, closing her fingers back over the coins. "Miss Douglass, I couldn't accept those, even if I wanted to. You should hang on to them. I also can assure you the diagnosis, treatment, and care for your grandfather would be exactly the same in private care."

Disappointed but not deterred, she returned the coins to her pocket. "What were you really trying to say earlier?"

"What?"

"Is my grandfather going to die?" she demanded, her throat tightening.

The doctor shifted uncomfortably. "Miss Douglass, there are a number of variables and possible treatment options, but you should prepare yourself. Sometimes, a successful treatment may only mean a delay of the final stages."

"Can you cure him?"

"Let's discuss that after we receive more test results. Please, enjoy the time you have with your grandfather," he said, pointing back toward the hospital room. "We will talk further. I promise." He turned and walked away.

She had heard that tone before. She didn't like it, and she didn't like what she'd heard. It convinced her even more that her grandfather needed private care.

If I can get him to the right doctors, then they could cure him. She patted the gold coins in her pocket and knew she had to make that happen.

Chapter 5

CARTER SURVEYED THE CARNAGE inside the apartment from the doorway. His couch and coffee table were on their sides. Someone had sliced open the couch cushions and pulled out their stuffing. His three bookshelves were overturned and their contents tossed onto the floor. He leaned in and glanced to his right. The kitchen was a similar disaster.

He heard a noise from his bedroom and stepped into the apartment, the thick white carpet muffling his steps. Because his guns and rifles were stored in his bedroom closet, he removed a five-inch cutting knife from the wooden block on the kitchen counter. When he moved into the hallway, the bedroom door was mostly closed, but he could tell the light was on inside.

Shadows of feet moved behind the door. Carter steadied his breathing and raised the knife. He reared back, preparing to lunge, just as the door swung open.

"It's me, man! Don't kill me!"

Carter pulled back and exhaled. He recognized his chubby neighbor. Jerome was short, in his late twenties, with the loose hair of someone who was not military, and he was easily sixty pounds overweight. In Jerome, Carter found someone who could keep up with his drinking binges and love of *SportsCenter*.

"I didn't do this, man, I swear." Jerome stepped back slowly. "I just got home and saw your door. I came in to see if you were okay."

"Yeah, I'm fine. I wasn't here." He stepped past his friend and checked the bedroom closet. Whoever it was had ransacked the closet too, but the guns were still there.

"What did they take?"

"Not sure. My guns and TV are here, and I don't really own anything else of value," he said, scratching his chin.

"Do you know who did it?"

"No idea." He shrugged. "I know Mary wouldn't do this, and I don't owe anybody money."

"Should I call the cops?"

Carter pondered that question for a second, before shaking his head. "No. I've spent more than enough time this evening with Annapolis's finest. Besides, what would I tell them? Someone broke in, trashed my apartment, and stole nothing. They would brush it off." *Worse,* he thought, *the police might try to blame Mary.* He still cared too much to take that risk. Feeling a little overwhelmed and dispirited, he pushed his couch back on its legs, threw two of the torn cushions on it, and plopped down with a thud.

Jerome moved to the kitchen and opened the refrigerator. "Yes! They didn't steal the Heineken!"

Carter laughed when Jerome offered him one of his own beers.

"To your continued good credit, my friend," Jerome toasted.

"Well, at least until my divorce is finalized," he muttered under his breath. Just saying it aloud hurt. He didn't want a divorce, but he also didn't want to be an anvil around Mary's neck, dragging her down. She deserved better.

He tossed the journal on the table and thumbed through his mail—a few catalogs, a couple bills, and one filthy, worn letter. He wondered whether the mail carrier might have run over it before delivery. Several international postage stamps lined the upper edge of the envelope, and it had no return address. When he opened it, he noted a diagonal watermark with the name Bonnie Ness Inn on the stationery. "Jerome, listen to this." He cleared his throat and read it aloud.

"Dear Mr. Carter Porter. You do not know me, but I have paid for a first-class United Airlines ticket in your name to Inverness, Scotland. You can confirm this through the airline. Bring your father's journal and the letter. Time is of the essence. Please be careful. I cannot tell you why, but I believe that you are in danger. I assure you I am serious and this is important. Please do not reject my offering. Come soon and Godspeed!"

He turned the paper over. "That's it. There's no signature or anything else that might indicate who sent it."

It sounded absurd, but he couldn't simply dismiss the letter. Whoever sent it not only knew about the journal, which he had only discovered a few hours ago, but the postmark indicated that the sender had mailed the letter over two weeks earlier. If he had received the letter yesterday, before he learned of the journal, he knew he would have thrown it away as a crank. *How could they have known?*

"What do you think?" he asked his friend, handing him the letter.

Carter called the customer service number for United Airlines. The airline's customer service representative confirmed Carter had a credit for a ticket in his name. But the airline had no information on who had paid for it.

"I think it's creepy as hell!" Jerome said, tossing the letter back and taking a long drink of beer. "It also sounds like they may have known your dad. Do you have a journal of his?"

Carter nodded and pointed to the journal on the table. "Yeah."

"You know the person who sent the letter could be the same one who trashed your place, right?"

"Maybe, but why destroy my apartment and then pay for a luxury vacation? Why send me a letter, instead of sending an email or calling on the phone?" Carter put the letter down on the table. "No, something's missing."

"Sounds like a few pieces are missing."

"Agreed. Well, at least whoever did this only trashed my apartment, instead of the guys who tried to kill me on the freeway."

"Freeway?"

"Yeah, it was a drug-related thing involving my Uber driver. The police found some inventory in his trunk. Anyway, they rammed us and opened fire. The Uber driver took it in the head. I've been at the police station for a zillion hours, and I'm probably banned from Uber."

Jerome's eyes widened. "Really, banned from Uber? That's horrible."

Carter laughed as he uncharacteristically nursed his beer. "Yeah, that probably is the worst part."

"So, another Heineken?" Jerome asked as he grabbed himself a second.

Carter shook his head. He still had a little over half left. He turned over and over in his mind the events of the last twenty-four hours. As he sipped a little more beer, he then considered how little he had left keeping him in Annapolis. His military career was about to end in a fiery hot mess. His daughter had been gone for over three years. His father was gone, and soon, his wife. The letter and offer sounded crazy, but waiting around here for life to finish steamrolling him sounded worse.

Jerome spent ten minutes talking about three upcoming games they would need to flip the televisions channels back and forth to watch.

Carter barely listened, instead tapping something into his phone. "You know, after you finish that second, I could probably use a ride to the airport," he said. "I checked the website, and there's an eleven fifteen p.m. flight."

"Wait! You're not really going?"

"Absolutely. If I accept it, then maybe I can find out what's really going on or, at worst, settle for a luxury vacation, which I could use." He picked up the letter and the journal from the table as he stood. "Besides, I've never flown first class."

Hassie awoke in her wrinkled uniform with an ache in her hip from the chair. She had wanted to talk more with her grandfather last night, but his medications made him drowsy. She spent most of the evening watching him sleep.

Tears welled up in her eyes. He was still asleep on his back, but his breathing seemed faint, and his pale, gray skin next to the white sheets brought some of her worst fears into glaring clarity. She was terrified of the thought of losing him. She loved him with all her heart, and he was the only family she knew.

She crept out of the room to call Martin and let him know she was at the hospital and wouldn't be at work until the afternoon. He told her to take as much time as she needed. Then, she used her phone to search for local coin dealers.

After a bland cafeteria breakfast, she gently woke her grandfather and told him she would be back to see him again before she went in to work.

She headed out into the chilly Inverness morning, and it bit through her uniform. She patted the coins in her pocket several times along her journey, excited by the possibility of selling the coins and doing something to help her grandfather.

Smiling and with a little bounce in her step, she noticed how much larger Inverness was than Forres. In the distance, she could see the tops of the spires of the Free North Church of Scotland, Junction Church, and Old High Church, all towering in a row on the shores of the River Ness, like beacons to the faithful. She recalled when they were all lit up at night, they almost looked like one continuous, awe-inspiring structure. There was so much rich history that, even though she didn't live here, she felt a sense of connection to the city. She didn't know why, but she felt an ease walking its narrow streets toward the coin shop.

A few minutes later, she triggered the small jingling bell of Collector's Corner on Queensgate Street. The antique wooden door creaked as it closed behind her. She stepped toward a stocky man behind the glass display case and saw his name tag read Glen.

"May I help you?"

"I have these." She beamed, removing the coins and allowing them to clink loudly on the glass display case.

"Very nice," he said, eyeing the coins approvingly. He moved them onto a blue velvet pad and handed her a form for her to fill in her name and contact information. Then, he picked one up and inspected it. "Where did you get these?"

She fidgeted and filled out the contact information form without answering.

"Do you have purchase documentation?" he asked, closely studying the coin.

She hesitated, and he looked up at her.

"No. I, uh, found them."

"Well, you are a lucky young woman," he said. "So, these are treasure?"

"Yes, they certainly are." *That's an odd question*, she thought. *They're gold. Of course they're treasure.*

"Where, exactly, did you find them?" He lowered his head, putting on a magnifying eyepiece.

She mumbled something indistinct. She couldn't tell him the truth. He wouldn't believe her if she did.

"Where?"

"I, uh . . . found them," she replied more clearly.

His brows wrinkled. "Yes, you said that."

"I found them near our flat in Forres."

"Just on the ground?" he asked with more suspicion.

"Well, no," she said, trying to come up with a quick lie. "I found them near a burst sewage line, about a block away from our flat. It was very messy. Don't even ask me about the smell." Her hand gestures got more dramatic as she spoke. Part of the story was true. There had been a sewage line that burst in her area. "It was disgusting. As

I walked by, I happened to spot the edges of the coins under a large piece of broken line." She shrugged. "It was just dumb luck."

"Hmm. That could explain some of the extensive water and sediment exposure I see on a couple of the coins." He studied the coins again. "I hope you washed them before bringing them in." He smiled.

"Yes, of course." Hassie laughed. "The coins were in pretty nasty shape." Her lie came so easily she almost believed it herself. She was nervous and started talking faster. "I couldn't believe it. Well, I looked around for more coins, but these four were—"

"No, it cannot be!" He put the second coin down and excitedly picked up a different coin. "Amazing!"

"What?"

"One of these coins appears to bear the mark of King Philip V of Spain," he said, sounding like he was in disbelief.

"Is that good?" She leaned in closer. "Is it more valuable?"

"If it's not fake, then, yes, quite a bit. These three are very nice. They appear to be 1733 8 Escudos gold coins." He pointed to the date on the coins. "This one, however, if real, has the special mark of King Philip V. The king's mark is not part of the original coin strike. The king himself would have stamped this. In their condition, the first three, without the mark, are likely worth between eight and ten thousand pounds each. However, the one with the mark easily could be worth sixty thousand pounds or more." He held up the fourth coin. "This one is worth so much more because, if it's real, it has the possibility of being part of the fabled treasure of Loch Arkaig. Of course, the thing that makes it so valuable is also the thing that makes it worth forging."

"The Loch Arkaig treasure? Really?" She'd heard of the treasure. Pretty much everyone in Scotland had heard something about the lost treasure. She had even studied a little of that history in school. "That was the Jacobite treasure, right?"

"Correct," he affirmed. "The Jacobites tried to assassinate King George II so they could replace the monarchy with the Stuart line.

Prince Charles Stuart led the resistance and thought he was going to be the next king, but he came up just a wee bit short." Glen smiled, pinching his forefinger close to his thumb. "The assassination attempt failed, the Jacobites lost huge at the Battle of Culloden, and old Bonnie Prince Charlie had to skip his arse out of Scotland, leaving behind the Jacobites' sizeable golden treasure, which was supposed to fund the resistance."

"I know. We studied some of that in school. My teacher said the treasure was hidden somewhere in Loch Arkaig."

"That is the general consensus." He nodded. "And that is where most people have been looking for it for over two hundred and fifty years."

If these coins really were part of the treasure, she wondered how she could have found them in Loch Ness, almost eighty kilometers away. "So, you really think these could be part of it?"

"Well, I guess nobody ever thought of looking for it in a sewage line in Forres." He chuckled. "That would be a pretty fair distance from Loch Arkaig."

"Oh yeah." Hassie laughed nervously.

"Of course," Glen rubbed his chin and stared back down at the coins, "it's possible, even if originally hidden in Loch Arkaig, the treasure could have been moved, which may also explain why nobody ever found it."

"That makes sense." She liked where he was going with that train of thought, particularly if it might make her coins more valuable.

"Yes." He removed his eyepiece as he continued. "After being exiled awhile, Bonnie Prince Charlie needed funds and still salivated over the treasure he left behind. He sent Doctor Archibald Cameron to retrieve it. Cameron was captured, without the treasure, and executed by the British. Given the amount of time Cameron had been in Scotland, some speculated whether he might have retrieved the treasure but was forced to hide it again."

She could not help but smile, considering the possible value of the coins. She knew this would help her grandfather. "The treasure was all Spanish gold, right, just like my coins?"

Glen nodded. "That's right, the vast majority of the Loch Arkaig treasure was Spanish gold. The Spanish king would have welcomed a friendly ally on Great Britain's throne, so he supported Prince Charlie's efforts and sent the Jacobites seven huge casks of gold coins, as well as other gold and jeweled trinkets. Several gold coins in the first cask also bore the king's personal mark. If you really have a first-cask coin here, then it is truly extraordinary." He put his eyepiece back on and returned to inspecting the marked coin. "If this is a fake, then it is an excellent one. The crevices of the king's strike mark show the proper age and sediment accumulation."

"So, those amounts you mentioned a moment ago, is that what you would pay me for these coins?" In her excitement, she swayed from foot to foot.

He removed his eyepiece again and shook his head. "No, I cannot purchase these. Honestly, no reputable merchant can purchase these until there has been a formal inquest to confirm that the coins are treasure. If they are not, then they can be returned to you."

Feeling whipsawed, she stopped swaying and watched the man put her coins in an envelope. "No, wait!" She reached out for the coins, but he turned slightly away as he finished sealing the envelope. "You're taking them?"

"If they're found treasure, then they belong to the Crown Estate and must first be offered to the national museums."

"Wait, please. They have to go to a museum?" She wasn't sure she understood, but giving them to a museum wasn't going to help her.

"Yes, of course. Any treasure must be turned over within a few days of discovery, or else there could be significant fines and possible jail for anyone who breaks the rules. It is part of the Common Law of Treasure Trove."

Hassie felt like someone had punched her in the stomach and knocked all the oxygen out of her lungs.

"If no museum bids on them, then the Crown Estate will likely release the coins back to you and then you can sell them." He slapped a sticker on the outside of the sealed bag with her coins and scribbled something on it.

"But I found them. They're mine. What about the law of . . . you know, finders keepers?" she blurted out, grasping for anything that might stall him taking the coins.

"Yes, well, unfortunately, that is not actually a law, but I am sure it is one that has been cited by more than a few thieves." He smirked, moving the bag to a drawer under the counter.

"I didn't steal them," she fired back, leaning far over the counter and trying to see where he had placed the bag.

"Miss, again, you may get these back or be paid a reasonable value for them." He brushed the back of his hand toward her, requesting that she move back from, and off of, the glass counter. "First, I'll collect your information, and please remind me of the details of your find, so I can properly report it."

"You're really keeping my coins?" She slowly stepped back, her mouth agape.

"Yes, I just explained that."

"What happens if the museum *does* want them?" She crossed her arms in front of her.

"Then they will bid on the amount to be paid to you, the finder," he said. "They are under no obligation, but generally they try to bid close to market value. I cannot guarantee you anything, because the law makes it clear that finders have no right to compensation. But I would be surprised if the museums refuse these coins, particularly the one bearing the mark."

"But how long will it take? I'm in desperate need of funds."

"For just a few coins, it could take a couple weeks," he answered as he signed and handed her a receipt for the coins.

She blankly accepted the paper and shuffled toward the door, her shoulders sagging. Pulling the door open set off the happy jingle again.

Before stepping out, she turned to look back at Glen with a pleading in her eyes, but he had his back to her and was engaged in some other activity.

Even if they do pay me, a few weeks might be too late, and they could choose to pay me nothing.

The breeze coming through the door suddenly felt colder and damper.

Chapter 6

CARTER SETTLED INTO SEAT 5B, an oversized tan leather seat in the last row of the first-class section. This leg of the flight would be a little over seven hours. He shared part of a large armrest with seat 5A, but he was pleased that seat remained unoccupied. He stuffed his carry-on bag and backpack into the area in front of his feet.

A cheerful flight attendant named Tiffany offered him the first of several Jack Daniel's and Coke cocktails in a crystal tumbler. She used more Coke than he would have, but they were free.

He took a couple large sips of his drink and watched a few passengers board, pulling their carry-on luggage past him. He unzipped his backpack, pulled the journal out, and rested it on his lap. He took another sip of his drink, and a little splashed onto the old leather cover. Chastising himself for not being more careful, he brushed the drops off.

Carter wondered why his dad hadn't mentioned the journal before considering the possibility that he had, but that conversation had just fallen into another gap in his memory, like forgetting that he had provided his signature to the bank. He couldn't be sure, and the thought of what else he might have forgotten unnerved him. He tried to focus on something more positive and opened the journal. *Let's see what Dad thought was so important.*

He stared at the upper corner of the browned page where the name of General Horace Porter, United States Ambassador to France, was written. From General Porter's title, Carter realized when he must have written this journal. His dad had told him a few things about General Porter. He knew the general considered it a travesty that the remains of John Paul Jones were not interred in the United States and that the exact whereabouts of his remains in France were unknown. The general had used his status as ambassador to drive the efforts to find and repatriate Jones's remains, over one hundred years after the man's death.

At the Naval Academy, Carter had learned about John Paul Jones, a maritime hero and considered by many to be the father of the United States Navy. In addition, when he was a cadet midshipman, Carter was required to memorize information about Jones's life and Revolutionary War service and recite it to upperclassmen upon demand. He remembered Jones was born in Scotland in 1747 and that he died in Paris on July 18, 1792. As he flipped through the pages, he realized the journal seemed to focus on a time in Jones's life Carter knew little about.

He turned back and started with the part explaining what happened following the Revolutionary War. Jones had difficulty finding employment after the war and ultimately joined the Russian Navy, but he couldn't master their nasty politics and was relieved of command. He moved to Paris and died two years later. Since he wasn't a Catholic, the French government insisted Jones be buried in a Protestant cemetery outside the city walls. According to the journal, General Porter spent years trying to locate Jones's final resting place, since those Protestant cemeteries had long been lost to urban sprawl.

Carter felt he understood the general. The man had tremendous drive and determination—similar to how Carter used to live, before his daughter died and everything stopped.

He took a long drink and read on about the discovery of the old cemetery under some local shops and alleys in Paris. General Porter had the sad task of opening each casket until they found the corpse he was looking for in 1905. There were no identifying items or uniforms with the body—at least nothing that they initially found. So, they took the remains to the Paris School of Medicine for a confirmatory autopsy.

Loosely holding the journal, Carter stopped to wonder how they could identify a body so long after death. Suddenly, the plane dropped and the journal almost flew out of his hand. His stomach flew into his throat. He grabbed at the journal with his free hand, but he ended up slapping the back cover, which slammed the journal shut. The "fasten seat belt" light blinked on, and he heard the loud ding. The pilot came on the speaker to apologize for the unexpected jolt and encourage people to stay in their seats until they got past the turbulence. Within a few moments, the bouncing subsided, and he decided it was safe to return to reading.

The next journal entries mentioned Louis Trouver, a member of the French delegation in charge of overseeing General Porter's grave-digging efforts. Trouver arrived at the Paris School of Medicine just after they completed the autopsy. He delivered a thick, squared block of wax to the general, and explained they'd found it in a small pocket carved into the top lid of Jones's casket. Having set the lid to the side when they exhumed the body, they'd initially missed it, but Trouver found it after they removed the corpse and thought it must have been a personal effect that should return to the United States with the body on the naval envoy sent by Theodore Roosevelt.

Without taking his eyes off the journal, Carter reached for his drink, only to realize it had been a casualty of the turbulence. He saw the cup on its side in the seat next to him, along with the spilled contents and a couple pieces of ice.

Damn! He swatted his armrest. He hated to lose any of his drink and knew Tiffany wouldn't come back around until they turned off the seat belt light. His reaction surprised him, and he stopped to take a couple deep breaths. *Calm down; you shouldn't be this mad,* he told himself. Not having a drink when he expected one and knowing he couldn't get an immediate replacement created an urgency in his mind. He felt anxious and restless, and he didn't like it. Taking a few more breaths, he returned his mind to the journal, but he found it a little harder to focus on the page.

With the thoughts in his head still jumping around a bit, he forced himself to reread the part about Trouver bringing the wax block to General Porter. He could feel some of his anxiousness wane and his mind center. Then he continued reading.

General Porter described the wax as old and firm, with something encased in it. He cracked open the block and found a letter dated October 1, 1767, from a father to a son named John. Carter knew it meant the author of the letter must have been Jones's father, John Paul Sr., as Jones had added his own surname later. Carter tapped the page where it stated the letter from the wax block referenced the secret of Loch Arkaig. A simple journal note followed that indicated the general had kept the letter for further study and that he had recognized the name of Loch Arkaig as one associated with a lost treasure of the Scottish Jacobites.

After reading that last portion, Carter turned his attention to the thick zip-top holder clipped to the back of the journal. It appeared to contain the old wax block and what he believed to be the 1767 letter itself. Before reading the last pages of the journal, he carefully removed the holder. The letter inside the wax block was on old parchment. Concerned he might damage it, he returned the letter to the protective pouch and noticed two modern copies behind the wax. He took one out and unfolded it.

1 October 1767

John,

As you know, my time with you grows short, and the secret of Loch Arkaig must not depart with me. You know its purpose. The key lies at the heart of the groat and resides where your King George should rest his head. I wish we could make the journey together, mac mo ghràidh, but I am weak, and, like the young kings of the past, your nose has always pointed you towards the distant hunt. Please know your friendship is something that has always brought me a tower of pride. If I close my eyes, I can see you walking that last twenty falls toward the sea. The right choice for you, of course, requires you to leave your two friends. This is the only way for you to receive all that God has planned for you. Sometimes, our choices can leave us uncertain as to whether to move forwards or backwards, but know that the journey's end will always be at least two ells more.

Love,
Father

It sounds like a bunch of gibberish. What does any of that mean? he wondered. *Clearly, this is a private letter between a father and son, but is it more than that?*

Frustrated, he read the note a second time. After a third read, something about it sounded familiar, but he couldn't put his finger on it.

He returned the copies to the plastic folder and read the final journal entries, most of which concerned the letter. General Porter had believed "heart of the groat" pointed to an old Scottish coin, and "young kings of the past" to the son of Robert the Bruce, King David II.

The general mentioned in the journal that he had researched the reference to the groat and learned that it was minted in the fourteenth century and included the likeness of King David II. He had also learned a colloquial phrase, "not worth a groat," was still commonly used to refer to something of low value. The only other information included about King David II was that he died in 1371 in Edinburgh Castle.

The handwriting of the entries on the final page was clearly different from the rest. Carter recognized it as his father's.

His father's entries focused on Edinburgh Castle, and specifically, the tower King David II constructed as the grand living quarters for the royal family. David's Tower was in ruins now and only partially accessible to the public, but his dad also mentioned how the Scottish government used the tower to hide the crown jewels from the Nazis during World War II. His father believed his ancestor's conclusion that King David II was the key. He wrote that the reference in the letter about "where your King George should rest his head" must point to David's Tower. Carter found himself nodding with the logic of his father's conclusion.

Then it struck him. His dad's trip to Scotland had been part of a treasure hunt, not a bucket-list trip.

Good for you, Dad. He laughed. Then Carter realized that all his father's journal entries had been written prior to his Scotland trip, and he wondered how far he'd made it. *Did he go to Edinburgh Castle? Why did his journal entries just stop?* He would have loved to talk to his dad about it, or about anything.

He couldn't help but wonder whether the Porter boys might have been wrong about the importance of the letter. Jones may have wanted it buried with him because it was the last word from his father, not because it pointed to some fabled treasure. The letter sounded personal to him, but General Porter and his dad were confident it held important clues about the treasure.

Carter returned the journal to his backpack, zipped the top, and thought about the anonymous letter offering him the airline credit. It said to bring the journal and *the letter*. He assumed it meant to bring the anonymous letter, which he had. He now understood they meant for him to bring the 1767 letter. *How could they know about that letter, if I didn't know?* He shook his head and shoved his backpack under his feet.

When he heard the ding and saw the seat belt light turn off, he quickly asked Tiffany for a replacement drink, as well as a few extra mini bottles of Jack Daniel's, just in case. She cheerfully complied.

A little after one a.m., the flight crew dimmed most of the internal lights, and Carter closed his eyes and faded in and out of a light slumber. He felt a slight movement to his side, and then he felt a hand reaching into his seat area and nudging his foot off the backpack.

Hassie returned to the hospital with her head hung low. On the ride up the elevator, she shoved her hands into her pockets, wishing they were not empty. *What am I going to tell him?* She felt guilty after making such a big deal about the gold. Her hopes for offering her grandfather a private-care option all but evaporated. *I'm going to lose him.* The despair in her mind overwhelmed her as she approached his hospital room door.

She stopped and tried to steel herself. She pulled out the receipt the coin dealer had given her, acknowledging he had taken custody of her coins for submission to the Crown Estate for review.

Custody? She focused on that word. *It should have said, "We are legally stealing these from you, and it's too bad about your grandfather. Go Caley Thistle!"* She crumpled the receipt and stuffed it back in her pocket. It only made her angrier to look at it, and she knew those feelings wouldn't help her grandfather. Gently, she pushed the hospital door open.

"Seanair, it's me. You awake?" she asked, moving to his bedside.

"Yes." His voice and face noticeably brightened. "I thought you were working at the Inn."

"Yes, I will be this afternoon, but I wanted to come see you again." She lightly brushed the knuckles of his right hand to let him know where she stood by the bed.

"Then, please tell me about your treasure. What is this about?"

She let out a big sigh, and a flood of emotion washed over her. She could feel the tears starting to well in her eyes, and she hoped she could get through this without crying. "Seanair, I found a few gold coins. They are very old, and we have to wait a few weeks to find out what we'll get for them, if anything." Her voice cracked a little, and she brushed the back of his hand a little more, not telling him that they could get nothing.

Her grandfather's face brightened. "That is amazing, a true blessing!"

"It may be, but we have to wait to find out."

"Child, I know why you want this windfall, but please do not use it on me," he said, squeezing her hand.

"Seanair, please. I'd be using it for *us*." She squeezed back.

"Child, the doctors here are taking good care of me, but my fate is already sealed," he said somberly. "I should have told you sooner about my condition. I'm sorry."

"No, you cannot just give up! I need you!"

"I'm not giving up. The doctors are doing what they can, and their efforts might delay the inevitable. I hope they do, so I may have more time with you. Whether sooner or a little later, my mortal life will end. I have made my peace with that, and with God. And I know where I will be going. However, I worry for you and want to know you will be okay." He coughed forcefully as soon as he finished.

Hassie pressed the button to raise the head of the bed so he could be in more of a seated position. She handed him a cup of water from the side table, fluffed the pillows behind his head, and waited until he stopped coughing. "Don't worry about me. You know I can take care of myself."

He gave an affirming nod. "I know, but please save this new wealth, child." His voice was raspier from the cough. "It will give me comfort to know it is there for you, if needed. I have had a blessed life, even now. The biggest blessing has been you. The hardest part is not the leaving, but the thought of leaving without knowing you will be okay and knowing you have made your own peace with God." He reached out to her face, as though confirming she was still there and listening. "It's easier to say than to do sometimes, but I must trust it all to God and pray I will see you again, after this life is over." He squeezed her hand again. "So, this found gold is a blessing for you and, for different reasons, for me. It is a sign."

She had heard this talk of "a sign" before. Her grandfather never gave up trying to convert her. She was not anti-God, just an agnostic, like so many of her friends. She was scared of the finality of death, particularly when it stared her in the face. The truth was she was jealous of the kind of peace her grandfather found in his faith. He did not fear death, and he was content. She had never experienced that kind of peace and solace. The closest thing was when she walked along the shores of Loch Ness, and even then, it was fleeting.

"I understand," she finally said, even though she really didn't.

Chapter 7

HALF ASLEEP, CARTER took a moment to realize someone had nudged his foot off his backpack and moved away. Feeling the top compartment, he quickly discerned the journal was gone. He sat up in a panic.

Everyone else in the first-class section was asleep and unmoving. Looking around the side of the empty seat next to him, Carter saw a man with his back to him, clearly cradling something and slipping into a coach aisle seat about fifteen rows back. He saw only a profile of the man's face when he deftly slid into his seat holding what Carter now saw was his journal. He watched as the man then threw a blanket over his head and shoulders.

The blood rushed to Carter's face as his anger rose. He felt violated. The journal was something precious to his father, and the brazen theft of it, literally stolen from right under his feet, showed a complete lack of respect for himself and any perceived threat that he might pose to the would-be thief. Not bothering to stop to consider how the man knew the journal was in his backpack or whether he might have been the one who sent him the ticket, Carter's rage propelled him out of his seat.

The plane's cabin was dark, and the man sat two rows ahead of the back wall of a line of restrooms separating the coach sections. Most people in front of the man's row were asleep or absorbed in whatever they were watching on their personal screens. Carter figured few, if any, noticed him moving down the aisle.

The man still had the blanket covering him. Most of the seats in the man's row were empty, but the far end of the row directly behind the man was occupied by a young family, two young children and a young man, who Carter assumed was their father. All were asleep.

Carter moved quietly directly behind the covered man's seat and leaned over. Seeing a few flashes from the lower edge of the blanket, Carter realized the guy was using his phone to snap pictures of the journal.

Steadying his breathing, in one swift move Carter slipped his right hand under the blanket and grabbed the man's throat. Wrapping his thumb and fingers around the side of the man's trachea, he restricted his air. Before the man could counter, Carter hooked his strong left arm around the man's neck, protecting his other hand and squeezing.

The man reached up for Carter's arm. "Don't, or I'll crush your throat!" Carter tightened his fingers to confirm his point. His military career might be over, but he still had skills. He knew the effect of his hold. It induced panic. The feeling was comparable to being water-boarded, without the water.

"You shouldn't take things that don't belong to you," he whis-pered. Seeing the edges of the journal protruding from the blanket at the man's waist, he said, "Hand me the journal," in a hushed tone.

The man didn't move, so Carter squeezed again to prove his resolve.

The man's right hand rose slowly in surrender. He gripped the cor-ner of the journal and pulled it out, giving it a little shake as he raised it.

"Now, tell me what this is about, and you'd better hope that I believe you." Carter loosened his left-arm hold to reach for the journal.

Then, he saw a flash of metal wrapped around the man's left knuck-les rocket from under the blanket toward his face. Carter jumped back and to the right. The metal sliced into the headrest, and Carter saw it was a small but sharp triangle.

The man pulled back for another attempt, and Carter tried to squeeze the man's throat, but his sudden dodging move left him without a solid hold. He could only use his left arm to keep the man's neck pinned back.

The man dropped the journal and his right fist shot up, catching Carter on the temple. Sparks flew in front of Carter's eyes and his head ached, but he managed to keep the man pinned. Seeing the man preparing for another blade strike and no longer in a position of strength, Carter knew he was vulnerable. The man fired the knuckle knife at Carter's head. In desperation, he released the man's neck and thrust his hand toward the oncoming knife.

He missed the blade but connected with the top of the man's wrist. Though unable to stop the knife's momentum, Carter's blocking move shifted its trajectory downward.

Carter heard the sickening thud of the blade piercing the man's own exposed trachea. There was no scream, only a muffled gurgle. The blade remained imbedded in the man, with his hand tucked under his chin. Blood trickled down his neck and began to soak the front of his shirt. Carter froze for a second, feeling conflicted. He had not intended to kill the guy. It just happened, and it had happened by the man's own hand.

He looked around to see whether anyone near them had seen what happened. Nobody in front moved or appeared to be looking at them. He knew the restroom walls would have blocked the view of anybody on the other side. The small boy two seats over stirred, but his brother and father remained asleep. The boy sat up, stretched, yawned, and for a moment the boy's sleepy eyes met his. Carter stilled, not sure what the boy might have seen or what to do.

The boy offered a slight smile, curled his knees back up to his chin, and rolled his small head onto the armrest.

Carter exhaled. He could feel his heart thumping against the inside of his shirt. He hurried to retrieve the journal and remove the man's passport from his shirt pocket. It was Russian, and his name was Victor Antonov. Carter wiped his prints off the passport and returned it to Victor's pocket. He noticed half of the man's chrome belt buckle hung loosely in his lap, the mirror image of the triangle knuckle knife now imbedded in the man's own throat. *That explains how he got a weapon on board.*

Then, Carter shoved a small airplane pillow under the man's head and pulled the blanket over him, to make it appear that he was sleeping. As he did so, Carter noticed the tattoo of three cathedral spires on the man's wrist. He only got a glimpse, and he didn't want to dwell on it or leave him uncovered for any longer than he had to, but he couldn't help but notice how similar it looked to the one he had seen on the intruder at the Naval Academy. With the man's Russian name, Carter wondered if he could have been at the Jones crypt or if it was just a common tattoo. There was no way to know for sure, but he did know the man was too small to have been the leader. He started to consider the probability before he remembered where he was.

He needed to get away fast and back to his seat. Before leaving, Carter saw the man's phone on the floor with a picture of the journal's front cover on the corner of the screen. Knowing it could lead back to him, Carter grabbed the device before quietly slipping back to his seat and securing the journal.

His shirt felt damp, and it took several minutes for his breathing to return to normal. During his military service, he had seen death, but not like this. This seemed different. This felt personal, even though he didn't know the man.

He checked the phone and found pictures of the front and back covers, the first two pages, and the last page of the journal. Carter also saw the guy had already emailed the pictures somewhere. Carter deleted the photos from the phone, but he couldn't do anything about the emails sent. He knew he would have to find a way to dispose of the man's phone as soon as he could, but not on the plane.

Nervous almost to the point of paranoia, he couldn't help himself from peeking around the back of the empty aisle seat next to him to see if anyone was looking in his direction, or worse, coming toward him. So many questions raced through his mind. Was that man alone or were there others? Had he sent Carter the first-class ticket just so he could steal the journal on the plane, and how did he even know about the journal? Would the cabin crew find the body before he could deplane at Heathrow?

One thing Carter knew for sure was that he wanted no involvement with the international police.

Mary slammed her palm on the steering wheel in frustration. After dialing Carter's cell phone twice and receiving no answer, she decided to drive over to his apartment. She had just called him a third time from the car, with the same result. With the guard duty incident, the navy already had enough to kick him out of the service, and Mary hoped he wouldn't make things worse by going out and drinking. But she knew he likely had. *He's probably passed out on his couch or in some alley behind a bar.* All she had wanted to do was update him on her efforts regarding his legal defense, but now she wanted to wring his neck.

Her frustration rose to a fever pitch. She had risked a lot for him and wondered whether he even cared. A few months ago, when she had finally decided to serve the divorce papers after almost two and a half years of arguments about his drinking, part of her had hoped it might jolt him into seeking help. She told him she still cared about him, but she couldn't follow him down the road he was traveling. Instead of a jolting response, he stared at her, accepted the divorce papers with a shrug, and mumbled something about expecting her to have left him sooner than she did. That memory only made her angrier, at Carter and at herself, and she depressed the accelerator.

Arriving at Carter's apartment complex a few minutes later, her face was still flushed. She stalked into the building and stormed out of the elevator on Carter's floor. Her anger vanished, however, when she saw his damaged door.

"Carter?" she called, pushing it open.

Seeing his place was a wreck, she questioned whether it was from a drunken tantrum. She entered and confirmed the apartment was empty.

"You looking for Carter?"

Startled, Mary spun on her heel and pulled her fists up to her chest in a defensive posture. "Who are you?"

The man stepped back from the doorway. "Sorry. I didn't mean to scare you. I'm Jerome, a friend of Carter's."

She recognized the name and relaxed her posture. "Carter has mentioned you."

"You must be his soon-to-be ex-wife," Jerome said as he walked through the door, before looking embarrassed by what had just come out of his mouth.

She recoiled. "Yes."

"Sorry," he stuttered. "Anyway, I thought you might be the guy coming to fix the door. Carter asked me to watch for him."

"So, what happened here?" She waved her hand around the mess. "Is Carter okay?"

"Yeah, he's fine." He nodded and moved farther into the apartment. "He doesn't know who did it. Someone trashed the place before he got back from the police station, and—"

"What? Police station?"

"Yeah. It was crazy!" His voice rose a little in excitement. "Somebody started shooting at his Uber on the freeway."

"Yes, it was crazy," said another voice.

Mary turned toward the door and saw a medium-sized man in a light gray suit. His left hand held an open wallet containing a badge and a blue identification card.

"I'm Detective Schwarzbech," he said, rubbing his finger across the broken door latch. "I had a few more questions concerning the freeway incident, but after seeing this place, I have a lot more. I've called Mr. Porter's cell phone several times, but he never answered."

Mary looked at Jerome, then back to the detective.

"You are?" the detective asked Jerome.

"Who, me? Nobody, I'm just a neighbor." Jerome shook his head. "I was watching for a guy coming to fix the door."

"Okay, and you are?"

"I'm Major Mary Porter." She shook his hand with a firm grip. "I'm Carter's wife, but we're separated."

"So, what happened here?" He waved his pencil and started jotting down notes.

"Carter said he didn't know who did this. It was like this when he got back from the police station last night," Jerome said.

"Was anything stolen?"

"Carter didn't think so. That's why he didn't report it."

Schwarzbech jotted down a few more notes.

"Do you know whether Mr. Porter has any enemies? Someone who might do this or might have tried to hurt him yesterday?"

"Yesterday? I thought the freeway shooting was about the Uber driver," Jerome said.

"That is what we thought too, but this certainly raises several new questions." Schwarzbech's eyed narrowed as he looked at Jerome. "Where is Mr. Porter now?"

"He's not here."

"Yes, do you know where he is?" asked the officer, sounding a little annoyed. "I called the Naval Academy, and they told me he was not on duty."

Jerome fidgeted and looked over at Mary.

She could tell Jerome knew something. On one level, she appreciated his loyalty to a friend, but right now, she wanted to know where Carter was too.

"Do you know where he is?" the detective repeated.

"Me, no, not really."

Mary watched Jerome's gaze drop to the floor as he answered. She wrinkled her brow, wondering why he wasn't forthcoming. When she finally turned back and made eye contact with Schwarzbech, she shook her head no. "I don't know either. I came here hoping to see him."

"So, then, Mr. Porter is missing?" he asked, and Mary picked up on the accusation in his tone.

"He's not missing, exactly." Jerome shuffled his feet. "He sort of mentioned something about traveling."

Schwarzbech took a step closer. "Traveling? Where?"

"I really couldn't exactly say for sure. He seemed pretty upset about everything that was happening in his life, and he wanted to get out of town."

"Would you mind calling him? He may not have answered my calls because he didn't recognize my number."

"Now?"

"Yes, if you wouldn't mind," he insisted, clearly irritated.

Jerome dialed, and in a second or two, Mary heard the familiar ringtone. She walked over to the couch, bent down, and picked up Carter's phone. When she turned back around, she didn't like the look the detective was giving them.

Chapter 8

WHEN HE FELT the wheels of the airplane make contact with the runway and begin to brake hard, Carter let out a breath and thought he might just be home free. He would deplane and find a convenient place to lose the dead man's phone without incident and, more importantly, prior to the discovery of the body.

A brunette flight attendant ran by his seat to Tiffany. "The passenger in 23C is dead," she said breathlessly.

Carter gripped the armrest tightly and listened. He was impressed that Tiffany did not appear to get flustered by the news.

"I understand. It's rare, but it has happened before." She put her hand on the other flight attendant's shoulder. "The important thing is to stay calm and not do anything that might panic the passengers. Does it look like natural causes? Maybe he had a heart condition."

"No." She vigorously shook her head.

Carter sucked in his breath. The narrow walls of the plane closed in farther on him.

"It looks like some kind of a weird suicide," she explained.

He exhaled and loosened his grip. He understood why she might have thought that. With no other signs of foul play, it would look like he killed himself with his own odd knife.

"That's just great." Tiffany rolled her eyes. "Did you cover the body? Are any other passengers aware of it?"

"There was already a blanket over him. I don't think anybody saw him."

"Okay. I'll contact the terminal police and the medical director," Tiffany said. "You go back and keep passengers away from that seat. The marshals will need to remove him before the passengers in that section can disembark. They may also have a few questions for those nearest him. Understood?"

She nodded. "Do we need to restrict anybody else?"

Tiffany removed her hand from the woman's shoulder and rubbed her own temple as she considered the question.

Carter flushed and felt hot again. Staring at the ground, trying not to draw attention to himself, he desperately hoped Tiffany's next word would be no. If the authorities found the man's phone in Carter's possession, he didn't have a logical argument for how he obtained it. If they were able to find the sent email, with pictures of his journal, it would be game over. A couple more seconds ticked by, which seemed like hours to Carter. *Say no!*

"No, I think the first class and business class passengers can disembark," she said, shaking her head and pointing to the front exit door. "I doubt they would have seen or heard anything behind them."

His shoulders relaxed when the brunette rushed by him. He watched Tiffany turn and pick up a phone near the cockpit door. Her back was to him, but he could see her talking animatedly for a couple of minutes. Then he felt the plane start to pull into a gate, but it stopped short of the enclosed walkway.

"Ladies and gentlemen, it looks like they are not quite ready for us at the gate, so please stay in your seat. We will finish taxiing in and get you on to your next destination as soon as we can," the pilot informed the passengers through the speakers.

Carter suspected they were stalling until the terminal police and medical staff could get there. About five minutes later, the pilot came back on to let everyone know they were ready for them now. He asked if the passengers in the coach section could wait before disembarking, as there was a special needs passenger whom they needed to help out first.

The passengers in first and business class leapt to their feet, as did Carter. He watched Tiffany open the front exit door. Two uniformed marshals entered, spoke to her, and then headed back toward the coach section.

Carter pulled his USMC cap down over his eyes and pretended to fiddle with his backpack when they walked by. After what seemed like an eternity, she gave the signal for first class to disembark, and he was the third one off, hoping Tiffany didn't notice the sweat stains on his shirt.

He walked down the ramp and found a restroom, where he splashed a lot of cold water on his face. When he was sure nobody was watching, he placed the phone at the bottom of the sink and covered it with paper towels to stop up the drain. He continued washing his face, until the phone had been submerged for a few minutes. Satisfied, he wrapped the wet towels around the phone and discarded the package in the restroom's large trash can.

His eyes darted from side to side as he made his way to his connecting flight to Inverness. He saw nothing suspicious in the waiting area, nor on the short trip, but now he was worried about openly carrying the journal. He gripped the straps of his backpack tighter and went to the car rental booth.

After renting a small green Ford sedan, he asked the perky rental car agent in a red vest about where he might find secured luggage storage.

"I'm afraid we don't have any at the airport. The only secured luggage storage I'm aware of in Inverness is at the train station." She pulled out a map of Inverness and surrounding areas and used a pen to mark his directions to the station.

Carter thanked her and picked up the car. After departing the airport, he made several unnecessary turns along the way to see if anybody was following him. Driving on the left side of the road felt odd and required much more focus. When he felt confident that he didn't have a tail, he stopped at the train station and rented a small, automated luggage locker to store the journal, and he exited with his backpack and carry-on bag

The drive to the Inn from there didn't take long. He had considered finding a hotel closer to Edinburgh Castle, but the anonymous letter had come from the Bonnie Ness Inn, and he wanted to see how this played out. As he navigated the majestic, rolling hills of the Scottish Highlands, the sky was overcast, yet the lush, bright green terrain seemed primed for a postcard or travel brochure.

He drove by the entrance to the self-park garage behind the Inn and noticed a group huddling in the Inn's circular front driveway, some holding large cameras. When he entered the lobby holding the anonymous letter, he half expected someone to approach him. Nobody did. He went ahead and checked in. Turning away from the desk, he noticed a young woman peering out a front window toward the driveway.

She was small in stature, weighing only about one hundred pounds, he would guess. She appeared to be thirteen, but given her Inn uniform, he assumed she must be older. What drew his attention, however, was that she seemed to be hiding behind the large curtains, as if to avoid being seen by the people outside.

He wasn't sure why, but something drew him to her and told him she needed help. Perhaps it was just the remnants of the alcohol he had consumed earlier, but he could have sworn he heard a soft whisper in his head encouraging him to speak to her. It was bizarre, and he tried to dismiss it. *Whatever her issues are don't concern me or the reason I'm here*, he told himself, though his feet propelled him closer. *Just ask if she's okay.*

"Are you okay, miss?"

"No," she said, still staring out the window. "I've been betrayed!"

"Excuse me?"

"Sorry, sir," she said, turning to face him. She looked a little embarrassed, as though remembering her status. "Can I help you? Are you checking in?"

"No, I already have." He pointed his thumb over his shoulder, toward the reception desk. "It looked like you were trying to avoid the folks outside. Is everything okay?"

She pursed her lips a bit, as if she was considering whether she should be sharing personal matters with guests or whether he was trustworthy. "I found some gold coins and hoped to sell them to a coin dealer, but he elected to inform the press instead."

"Why? Were they stolen?"

"No!" She responded a bit too indignantly. "My apologies, sir."

"No worries." He chuckled. "So, why does the press care?"

She sighed and peeked back out the window. "Because they may have some historical value, in addition to their gold value. The online story came out a few hours ago and will be in the *Inverness Courier* tomorrow. The reporters flooded in within minutes and blindsided me. My manager asked them to please wait outside. I called the dealer after that, and he admitted to calling the press. They're maddening. They all keep asking me the same questions. 'Are they real? Is this a hoax? Where did you find them?'"

"That worked?" Carter asked.

"What?"

"Your manager asked the press to go outside, and they did?"

"Well, yes. He politely explained they were disturbing our guests, so the decent thing would be for them to wait outside, until my shift ended. He implied they could talk to me then."

He laughed. "Wow! That would never work back in the States. The press would follow you into the restroom to get a soundbite. Decency wouldn't be a word I would ever use to describe our press."

"Oh, we have a few rogues here as well." She smiled. "Anyway, I already told them everything I know."

Carter listened to her story about finding the coins under a broken sewer line in Forres and nodded, even though some of her body language made him wonder whether she was being truthful.

"But my shift is over in a few minutes, and I need to get back to the hospital to see my grandfather. I don't want them following me to the bus."

So absorbed in his own pain, he couldn't recall the last time he had involved himself with the problems of another. He had no idea why, but something inside continued to urge him to help her. "Can I give you a ride to the hospital?"

"That is very kind of you, sir, but no. I'm sure you are a nice person, but my grandfather would lecture me for an hour if I accepted a ride from a stranger. Thank you, anyway."

"My name is Carter. If not a ride, perhaps I can help you in another way."

"Sir?"

"It sounds like what you need is a distraction. If I can distract the reporters, then you can slip out the back and get to the bus," he suggested.

"I appreciate it, but that's not necessary."

It was clear she didn't understand why a stranger was so determined to help, but he pressed. "Does the Inn have a back exit?"

"Yes, it does, and I'm Hassie Douglass." She extended her tiny hand, and Carter shook it. "I actually arrived to work a little late today, so going out the back would allow me to see a friend before I go."

He raised his eyebrows, as if asking her whether she wanted to try it.

"I'm not sure what you are proposing, and I don't want anybody to be hurt." She gave him a wry smile.

He laughed again. "No, nothing like that. It's a simple plan. We need another person in a uniform. First, you let the reporters see you putting on a jacket or a raincoat over your shoulders."

"I have a slicker."

"Good, as long as it's not transparent," he said. "Then, pretend that you forgot something and go back. Out of view of the reporters, you give the slicker to the other person, who drapes it over their head and shoulders. I will walk out with that person and keep the reporters from getting too close. They follow us, and you slip out the back."

"Brenda would help," she murmured. "But why are you helping me?"

He thought it was a fair question. "Maybe it's just because I can." He hoped she would accept that answer, but in truth he wasn't really sure why he was doing it. He shrugged and pulled out two mini bottles of Jack Daniel's, which he had taken from the airplane, and drained the first.

"Careful with those drinks. People might mistake you for a Highlander." She chuckled.

"I think my accent might give me away." He shook his head as he unscrewed the second bottle.

Hassie walked away and returned with another female employee, who had thick red hair. The woman was older and looked nothing like Hassie, but she had the same general height and build, and wore an identical uniform.

"Hassie told me your plan, and I'd be happy to help."

After Hassie made the introductions, she said, "Thank you both for doing this. It might work. The reporter I spoke to earlier was fairly *glaikit.*"

He didn't know what that term meant, but he suspected it implied gullible or dimwitted. He smiled. "Are you both ready?" he asked, putting his travel bag and his backpack down in a chair near the entrance.

They nodded.

"Hassie, remember, after you're sure that they see you, act like you forgot something," he said.

She walked out in front of the glass door with her head up and dramatically draped her slicker over her shoulders. "Oh no! I almost forgot my purse," she mouthed and came back inside.

Carter tried not to laugh at her overacting.

"You're a real friend, Brenda," she said, hugging her and handing the slicker to her.

"Good luck, kid," Brenda said, pulling the slicker over her head and shoulders. "I can see the ground and where I am stepping, but I cannot see far beyond that," she told Carter. "You'll need to guide me, and we can head toward the surface parking lot."

"No problem." He wrapped his arm around her shoulders as they walked out together. Before the two had even reached the curb of the driveway, six or seven reporters rushed them.

"Can I have just a quick word with you, Miss Douglass?" a thin, square-jawed reporter shouted.

"Gentlemen, Miss Douglass has nothing to add to her prior statements," Carter announced without slowing. "She thanks you for your interest, but please let her pass."

As he expected, the reporters did not respect his request. They followed and fired more questions. Mostly, he heard a jumble of discordant, Scottish-accented noise.

"Are you okay?" he whispered to Brenda as he nudged her and encouraged her to pick up the pace and stay ahead of the reporters.

"Yes, just don't let me trip."

After a couple minutes, Carter glanced over his shoulder and saw Hassie walking in the opposite direction. He also saw a light blue Audi approaching her from behind and slowing down. Maybe it was because of what happened on the Maryland highway or on the airplane, but his alarm bells went off. When the Audi stopped, the passenger door opened, and a man got out, Carter went into emergency mode.

"Change of plans! I think Hassie may be in trouble. You make a fast break for the surface lot and try to draw the reporters. I'm going back to help her. You go first."

"Oh, okay, now?" Brenda asked, obviously confused and wondering what in the world had happened.

He raised his voice enough for the reporters to hear. "Yes! You go on ahead and hurry. I'll catch up."

Brenda lifted the slicker but still shielded the side of her face from the reporters and started to jog. As he suspected, the reporters did not care about him. They followed her.

He waited a second and then he ran flat out, feeling his extra pounds. Once he got close, he waved his arm, trying to get Hassie's attention. He saw the girl's bewildered expression, but it turned to surprise when the young man from the Audi reached out and grabbed her arm.

Carter pushed himself to run harder and got close enough to hear the man speak.

"Miss Douglass?" the man asked, still holding her elbow.

"Hey!" She turned and pulled away.

Breathing hard, Carter grabbed the man's shirt and spun him away from Hassie. The man looked at least ten years younger than Carter and about three inches shorter. Carter raised his right fist, intending to drive it through the man's protruding jaw. To his surprise, both the man's arms shot straight up under Carter's armpits, then around him in a tight bear hug.

"Run, Miss Douglass. You're in danger!" the man yelled.

The ringing of her desk phone in the Navy Operational Support Center office jarred Mary back to the present. Carter's issues made it hard for her to concentrate on anything else. She was relieved the caller identification did not indicate it was the Annapolis police, but her relief was short-lived. It was from the CID.

Oh yeah, Carter's intoxicated-on-duty charges.

She hit the speaker button. "This is Major Porter."

"Yes, this is Detective Inspector Chuck Reynolds with CID." The man's voice boomed through her office.

"Yes, sir." She knew Chuck but offered no sign of recognition. As far as she was concerned, he was nothing but a pompous, self-absorbed jerk who believed every woman admired the cut of his uniform as much as he did. He had flirted with her before, not caring about the ring on her finger. He had harassed more of her friends than she could count. For all the talk about how progressive today's military was, in many ways, she knew it was still an old boys' club, and he represented the worst of that club.

"I'm calling about your boy."

"Are you referring to Lieutenant Carter Porter?" she asked, trying not to show her irritation with his disrespect.

"I'm referring to the possibility of an Article 112 proceeding. His EIG urine test came back. Your boy failed. His other tests showed positive markers for CDT and PEth, suggesting a long-term, heavy alcohol abuse, but I bet you already knew that."

She remained silent. There was nothing to say. The results were not a surprise, but they still felt like a gut punch. She hated that Chuck had been the one to deliver it.

"Detective Reynolds, Lieutenant Porter has engaged Bobby Fredericks, a civilian defense counsel, and—"

"Mary, Mary," he said, with a syrupy tone. "Please, it's Chuck. And that may not be necessary."

Mary felt the back of her neck get hot. She wanted to demand this piece of garbage show her respect and refer to her by her rank. As a major, she could have handed him his head on a platter for such insubordination, but something about his cocky tone gave her pause. She needed to find out what he really wanted.

"If you're on speaker, please pick up," he requested.

She hesitated but lifted the receiver. "What?"

"Look, the best Carter could hope for is a de-escalation to an Article 15 resolution, instead of a full-blown court-martial."

She remembered the navy had used an Article 15, nonjudicial punishment for Carter's last infraction.

"Otherwise, your boy could be looking at up to three years in the brig, along with a dishonorable discharge."

"I understand the possibilities." Her fist tightened. "Again, we have engaged civilian defense counsel."

"Oh, it's more than a possibility. With his prior disciplinary action and these test results, it's an absolute certainty."

"Thanks for your opinion," she snapped. "You have permission to contact our defense counsel. I have provided you with his name. I'm now hanging up."

"Wait, don't!"

"What?" She raised her voice, exasperated.

"Listen, are you familiar with Article 46 of the Uniform Code of Military Justice, part of the Rules for Court-Martial?"

"No, of course not. Why would I be?"

"Well, under that rule, the defense is entitled to request and obtain access to all evidence, including the urine and blood samples. That allows the defense to conduct their own tests."

She was puzzled by the direction of this conversation. "Okay. I'm sure our counsel will request them."

"I'm confident that he will. However, there can be issues if the original samples are lost."

"Lost?"

"Yes, if the samples are lost *after* the defense counsel requests them, then that could be an Article 46 violation, which could disallow the original test results. In turn, that likely would lead to a dismissal of the court-martial proceeding."

An uneasy flittering erupted in her stomach. *Why is he telling me this?*

"If, however, the samples are lost *before* defense counsel requests them, like today, for example, then that would *not* be an Article 46 violation. There is less of a presumption of misconduct, and the court-martial can proceed with the original test results. It may be illogical, but that is the navy way." He giggled a little. "Anyway, if we admit our test results into evidence and there is no ability for the defense to retest them, then it is pretty much of a *fait accompli*. Of course, even with a retest, his chances are miniscule, but he would have a chance."

"What are you telling me?" She slapped her palm on her desk harder than she intended and it stung.

"Me? I'm not telling you anything." He chuckled sadistically. "I'm simply suggesting it would be bad for you if the samples were lost *before* your counsel asked for them, and it would be very good for you if the samples were lost *after* such a request."

"So, are the samples lost?"

"Well, that is an interesting question. You see, I submitted a written request for the samples this morning and there is a record of the request; but wouldn't you know it, there is no record of my receipt of those samples. At least, not yet."

She knew exactly what that meant. He had the samples and could claim they had already been lost, before Bobby could request them. "What do you want, Chuck?"

"Me?" Mary could hear the sarcasm in his voice. "Nothing. I just want everyone to be happy. I want you to be happy. I want Carter to be happy. And, of course, I want to be happy."

She wanted to wretch. Reporting him for this would accomplish nothing. It was her word against his, and she noticed he carefully avoided directly stating his intent.

"Our office can get hectic, and some evidence can get lost. I hate to admit it, but it has happened."

I bet it has, you worm. Mary's blood boiled. Before this, she had struggled with what was the right answer for Carter. She still cared for him, but he was guilty. She had smelled the alcohol on his breath. Discharge might not be the worst thing for him. He could get help without the scrutiny of military eyes watching him. He could start a new life. She wanted that to be his choice, not a choice made by this cretin. She thought men like Chuck were the true disgrace to the uniform.

"So, listen. On a totally separate note, I am planning a small dinner party on the day after tomorrow at my place around seven p.m. I hope you can come. It'll be an intimate affair."

She could feel herself starting to shake with rage. *Yeah, right, an intimate affair.* There it was, the *quid pro quo*—if she slept with him, maybe, they get Carter's charges dropped because of the "lost" samples. Of course, he offered no guarantee, not that it mattered to her. She would never cheat on Carter, even now and even if blackmailed.

The shirt collar of her khaki uniform felt like it was choking her, and perspiration formed on her upper lip. If she said no too quickly, he would make sure the samples were lost before Bobby could request them. She knew she needed to buy some time and figure out what to do. She was accustomed to thinking on her feet, analyzing changing circumstances, and adapting to overcome obstacles. Now, she was not sure what to do.

"Well, I certainly have a lot to think about."

"I hope to hear from you soon about the dinner." Then he hung up.

She slammed the receiver down twice. *Why do I care more about Carter's future than he does? And where the hell are you, Carter?* her mind shouted.

Chapter 9

"ARE YOU OUT OF YOUR MIND? I'm helping her!" Carter yelled, startled by the young man's response.

The man still hugged Carter tightly under his arms, pressing his head up under Carter's chin. Off balance, Carter stepped backward and pushed one of the man's arms down, hoping to create a little distance and gain the advantage. Frustratingly, the man immediately raised his other arm and took a step forward. Carter tried again but suffered the same result.

With the man's arms so high under his armpits, Carter couldn't easily get a grip or swing his arms. As soon as Carter lowered one of the man's arms, the other shot up. With every step back, the man matched it. This strange struggle continued in a circle. Carter had trained for many fighting styles, but he had no idea what the young man was doing. This battle was like trying to remove a giant squid attached to his wetsuit.

"Do you know him, Miss Douglass?" the man yelled to Hassie, who had watched the strange scene from a distance.

Initially, Hassie didn't answer. Carter saw she was transfixed on the odd back-and-forth. Finally, Hassie laughed. "Yes, I know him. But I have to ask, are you two *dancing*?"

"Let go, you idiot!" Carter demanded and stopped moving.

"Yes, I know him," she repeated and stepped toward the man. "Who are you?"

The man loosened his hug and released Carter, now extending his hand. "No hard feelings." The man puffed and wiped a few beads of sweat from his forehead across his closely cropped black hair. He also waved to the driver of the Audi, who had exited the vehicle but stopped and returned when it became apparent that there was no danger.

He had a firm grip, and Carter had to admit the young man had spirit. "What's this about?"

"Sorry. I'm Royce MacArthur," he said, turning to Hassie. "Miss Douglass, I urgently need to speak with you inside. I think you're in danger."

Her brow furrowed, but she pointed behind her. "Okay, there's a back entrance through the alley."

They entered the alley, and Hassie laughed as Scrounge bound up and jumped on her.

Carter noticed the Audi following them into the alley, but the driver stayed in the car when they reached the Inn's back entrance.

"That's my friend, Robert. He gave me a ride." Royce waved to him again.

"Okay, sport, what's this about?" Carter asked as soon as the three stepped into the storage room and the heavy door closed behind them.

"Miss Douglass, I came to warn you."

"Warn me about what?" She raised her palm to her chest. "And please, call me Hassie."

"I'm the deputy principal of Right for Scotland or RFS," he said, handing her his business card.

To Carter, the card looked cheap and nondescript. It simply read Right for Scotland in green block letters, and underneath, J. Royce MacArthur, his telephone number, and address.

Hassie knitted her brow and had a bewildered expression, clearly not recognizing that organization.

"Really, you don't know RFS?" he asked, surprised and a little disappointed.

"I'm sorry, but what does this have to do with me?" she asked.

"Well, RFS is the current successor organization to the Jacobite movement and cause," he said, as if that explained it all.

Carter had heard of the Jacobites from the journal, but he didn't know much about them. He'd also seen brochures for Jacobite-themed tours at the airport and in the lobby.

"As you probably know, the Jacobites wanted the Stuart clan to supplant the British monarchy hundreds of years ago." Royce started to pace but continued talking. "RFS is less concerned with restoring the Stuart line to the throne. Instead, we fully support Scotland as an independent, sovereign country with its own monarchy. BREXIT helped us gain support, since many in Scotland didn't agree with the United Kingdom's election to leave the European Union."

"Why is this relevant?" Carter asked, mildly annoyed. He removed and downed another mini bottle of Jack Daniel's.

"You're a soldier from America, right?" Royce said with a hint of admiration. "I guessed by your haircut and your military cap." Usually, Carter considered it an insult to be called a soldier. Marines were more than that. He thought about correcting the guy, but this kid seemed easily diverted, so Carter just nodded. "Yeah, sort of."

Royce smiled. "My grandfather was in the Royal Scots Dragoon Guards. That was a huge honor. I wanted to join the Scottish army, but they wouldn't take me. I have a slight arrhythmia. They thought it might slow me down or become a health risk, but it wouldn't have. In fact, I can even control it, a little. Make it skip if I want. That was part of the reason I joined—"

"How does this relate to a danger to Hassie?" Carter let more of his annoyance slip, but he quickly tried to dial it back. "Please, just tell us why you're here."

"Sorry, I get distracted," Royce apologized and smiled nervously.

"It's about the gold coins Hassie found. They could be part of the Jacobite treasure."

"Yes, I know that," she said. "The coin dealer told me. Unfortunately, he also told the press."

"I know. The public is captivated by the lost Loch Arkaig treasure."

The Loch Arkaig treasure from my journal? The thought hit Carter like a mallet. The still air in the storage room suddenly felt much warmer to him.

"People have searched for it for centuries, and RFS has been at the forefront of the recent efforts. For us, it means more than just the gold. The treasure is a symbol of hope for Scotland's undying desire for freedom and independence," Royce said with reverence.

"But the gold would be nice too, wouldn't it?" Carter asked, swaying a bit from the alcohol.

Royce frowned and shot him a glance.

"I understand the symbolism, but why would that endanger me?" Hassie asked.

"Because, unfortunately, we aren't the only ones searching for the treasure." Royce's expression softened, and the excitement in his voice rose, like a child describing everything he just got for Christmas. "RFS recently discovered one of the best clues to the treasure in over a hundred years. We located an encrypted communiqué to Prince Charles Stuart from Doctor Archibald Cameron in 1753, shortly before Cameron's capture by the British. The prince had sent Cameron to Scotland to retrieve the gold, still believing the Jacobites could help him become king. Of course, Cameron failed to return with the gold."

Royce stopped talking when Carter tried to lift the top metal chair off one of several stacks in the storage room. The chair under the one he grabbed also lifted when he pulled, but it quickly separated and fell with a loud clank onto the tile floor. "Sorry," Carter said, setting the chair down. He slumped into it and threw his arm over the stack.

Royce stared at him blankly for a moment. "Anyway, in the communiqué, Doctor Cameron acknowledged what many of us had long suspected. He had recovered the gold from Loch Arkaig. Still in Scotland but fearing his imminent capture, he sent the treasure to be hidden again."

"Did it say where?" asked Hassie.

Carter heard the big dog scratching at the door and barking, obviously wanting to be let in.

"That dog," Hassie muttered. She smiled and shook her head at the back door, then turned to Royce. "Sorry, please continue."

"Thankfully, no, he didn't expressly say where, or else the British might have found the treasure long ago. Doctor Cameron neither stated where he sent the gold nor the name of the person he had entrusted it to; but he did offer a few clues."

"So, that was good, right?"

"Yes and no." Royce shrugged. "We discovered the communiqué about four months ago. We were searching for records relating to Prince Charles Stuart. After extensive searches of the records in France, we decided to search some of the British ones at the National Archives in London. We came across a letter addressed to Prince Charles Stuart among the possessions of a suspected Jacobite sympathizer. The Jacobite was captured by the British before he made it out of Scotland to deliver it. To the casual observer, the letter probably offered little more than a weather report for Loch Arkaig, but we recognized certain Jacobite codes. And the letter was signed 'LGL,' which we recognized as the acronym for the 'Less Gentle Lochiel.' It was a nickname Archibald Cameron sometimes used."

"Less Gentle Lochiel?" Carter asked. He leaned the chair onto its back legs and caught himself before falling over backward.

"Yes, Archibald's father was sometimes referred to as the Lochiel, which was derived from the name of the area where they resided, near Loch Eil. His two sons, Archibald and Donald, served in the Jacobite army. In addition to being a medical doctor, Archibald was a brilliant strategist and a respected fighter. He was promoted through the ranks much faster than his older brother, and some suggested Donald must be the 'Gentle Lochiel,' which, of course, would make Archibald the 'Less Gentle Lochiel.'"

"There are worse names to be called." Carter chuckled.

"I suppose." Royce shrugged. "After we found the letter, we made the mistake of informing the press. We were so excited. We even stupidly bragged that with this letter, along with RFS's comprehensive historical records, we now had a pretty good idea of whom Doctor Cameron had entrusted with the treasure."

Now interested, Carter leaned forward. "Did you tell the reporters who or where?"

Royce shook his head, grimacing as if physically pained. "No. We knew the who but not the where. We told the press, as a bit of a tease, that we would explain everything to them after we found the treasure." His voice cracked. "We were arrogant and foolish, and it cost a life."

"But were your assumptions about the treasure correct?"

Royce took a couple breaths and squared his shoulders. "We never had the chance to pursue the leads after that. Our office was broken into less than thirty-six hours after the news story came out. They murdered one of our members. Then, they burned our offices down. There was no question the news story triggered the break-in. RFS lost all of its physical records in that fire. Worse, we lost my friend Christopher Yates, who was there when the men broke in."

"I'm so sorry," Hassie offered.

"Thank you. He was a good friend. Before working together at RFS, we were schoolmates at the University of Highlands. I studied marine science." Royce lowered his head.

"Did the police catch the people responsible?"

"No, not yet. RFS didn't have security cameras or other protections, which might have helped the authorities. Why would we? RFS is primarily a politically active historical society."

"Do you know what they were after?" Carter asked.

"Yes, we believe they wanted information concerning one of our eighteenth-century Jacobite members. He was a gardener."

"A gardener?" Hassie asked. "Why?"

"Because that is who we believe Doctor Cameron entrusted with the gold. His name was John Paul Sr."

Carter's heart was in his throat. His head spun, and he slowly pushed himself up and out of the chair, trying to absorb all Royce was saying.

"We collected most of the records we had on Mr. Paul in one place. The authorities confirmed the fire started from a large amount of accelerant used in that area. That's how we knew the break-in and the murder were tied to our news story."

"Are you talking about the father of John Paul Jones?" Carter asked.

"Yes. His son, John Paul Jones, played a prominent role in your early war, did he not?" Royce tilted his head. "Did you know Scotland was very supportive of the colonies' battle for independence?"

"Yes, he did, but I can't say that I was aware of Scotland's role in the war," Carter said, now wondering whether Royce might know anything about Jones's letter.

"We suspected Mr. Paul may have been involved, but until we found Doctor Cameron's communiqué, we didn't know for sure. It made sense. As a gardener who cared for many prominent estates, he would have had access to a host of possible hiding places. Nobody would have looked twice at a gardener with boxes and digging tools."

"Do you have any thoughts on where he might have buried the treasure?" Hassie asked.

"No, not really. On one hand, knowing it was Mr. Paul is a helpful clue, but on the other hand, him being a gardener who had broad access to so many properties means the treasure could be in a lot of places." He shrugged his shoulders. "But that's not why I'm here."

"You think those people who murdered your friend may come after me?" asked Hassie.

"If they think you have information about the treasure, then they may come for you. They've already killed once."

"But I don't know anything about the treasure," she insisted. "I just found a couple of coins." She leaned against the door and repeated her story about the ruptured sewage line.

Carter eyed her. For some reason, his gut instinct still signaled she wasn't being completely honest.

"I read about your find."

"I don't know anything more or why the reporters are still following me."

"Let's hope they're the only ones following you," Royce said.

"How long will it take for things to blow over and for Hassie to no longer have to look over her shoulder?" asked Carter.

"Hard to say. Either until the rest of the treasure is found or Hassie convinces everyone she knows nothing more."

"Maybe the murderers will find the treasure soon," Hassie said.

"I hope not. I would hate to reward evil. If they do find the treasure, there is a good chance they won't publicize it. They would melt the gold or sell it on the underground market." Royce scowled. "That would be a tragic loss of history."

"Then, where does that leave us?" asked Hassie.

"Again, we need to convince people that you don't know anything, or we need to find the treasure and publicize it, which is what RFS wants, in any case." Royce paced a little more as he talked. "It's possible that your discovery might help advance the search efforts, starting with considering how and from where the coins could have ended up in that line. Even though we lost so much in the fire, I think RFS's involvement and support remains critical to any search efforts. I hope you agree."

"For a modest share of the claim for RFS, I'm sure," Carter retorted.

"Of course, for a share." Royce sounded defensive. "RFS would benefit, and we have a rightful claim to it, or at least a portion of it."

Carter tossed the mini bottle of alcohol he finished and chuckled. "Good luck with that claim, my friend."

"King Philip V contributed most of that gold, and the king did not give it to any one person. He gave that gold to support the Jacobite cause. *Our* cause. We have a claim."

Carter didn't know why he egged on Royce, but he did. "You know, I almost signed up for a Jacobite boat tour. Perhaps we owe them a share too."

"We?"

"We?" Hassie asked, turning to Carter.

"Hassie, you might as well include us," said Royce. "If you don't, RFS could tie up your claim in the courts for years. As the successor to the Jacobites, RFS has a rightful claim."

"You should have been a lawyer, buddy," Carter said.

"Why, because of the persuasiveness of my arguments?"

"No, because lawyers tend to annoy me, and they always end up costing me money." He snorted.

Royce's face reddened.

"So, Hassie, I have a question about where you *said* you found the gold coins." Carter noticed the alcohol added more indictment in his tone than he intended.

"I have questions too," a Russian-accented voice behind them said.

The already darkened storage room dimmed even more for a moment when a hulking figure blocked the light from the kitchen hallway. A black balaclava covered most of his face.

Two things caught Carter's attention: the semiautomatic pistol with a silencer-extension on the barrel in his hand, and the familiarity of the man's gravelly Russian accent.

Hassie froze when she saw the large man with a gun.

"I tell old man that girl knows nothing, but since I find her here with soldier, I may be wrong and will enjoy confirming," he said, moving like a cat from the shadows.

Her skin crawled. She watched Carter move toward the large man, but he swayed and stumbled into the stack of chairs.

"Easy, soldier." The stranger redirected his gun toward Carter. "This not hill you want to die on, I think."

Carter straightened, embarrassed by his failed action.

"I know what you think, soldier, but you are too far away to challenge without being shot." He positioned himself with Carter and Royce on one side and Hassie on the other.

"You were at the chapel, weren't you?" Carter asked with a tone of disbelief. "I recognize your voice."

"You remember me." He raised the gun toward Carter's chest. "This is good; and this gun is not taser."

"You know this guy?" Royce turned to Carter with his mouth open.

"No, but he and a few of his friends broke into the Naval Academy Chapel a few days ago."

"Hah, very good." The man laughed, moving toward Hassie.

She turned and started to run for the exit, but she heard a muffled shot and the wood paneling above the door splintered. Hassie froze in terror. She watched the big man's hand move like lightning, whipping the gun back toward Carter and Royce.

"Do not try again or next bullet goes through back of head." He nudged closer to her.

Still paralyzed, her eyes darted back to Carter and Royce, desperately hoping one of them could do something.

"Your drive on freeway. Impressive." The man taunted Carter.

Carter furrowed his brow, as if something was slowly dawning on him. "That was you too?" he sputtered. "You weren't after the Uber driver. That show was for me."

"You smarter than you look." The big man nodded at Carter.

"Then I'm sorry I didn't kill you when I rammed your car," he shot back, and Hassie thought he was trying to rattle the man.

"This I know."

"If you wanted to kill me, why didn't you do it at the chapel?"

"Not kill you. We still needed what your father gave you and what you took from bank. Now, I take girl, and I need you give me journal and letter."

Take girl, Hassie's mind shrieked, but her legs refused to move.

"Journal?" Carter asked, purposely sounding confused.

"Do not test me, soldier. Victor sent pictures of a few journal pages from plane before he died," he said with an icy resolve.

Hassie had no idea what Carter or the man were talking about, but she was grateful, for the moment, that his focus was directed at Carter.

"Well, flying can be dangerous."

Hassie noticed Carter taking a tiny step toward the man.

"Perhaps, but being stupid, I think, is more dangerous. Stop moving. Where is journal?"

"I don't have it with me."

"This I know. I already checked your bags in lobby."

"Yeah, your friend, Victor, convinced me carrying the journal around may not be wise." Carter looked over at Hassie. "Now, just let her go and I'll get you the journal."

Hassie felt her insides shivering, and she desperately hoped the man would agree to Carter's offer.

"No. I take girl to confirm she knows nothing. You bring me journal, and maybe you get girl back." He laughed sadistically. "Do not make me wait long." He wrapped his large, muscular arm around her shoulders and pulled her close.

She resisted until his arm tightened like a boa constrictor. Her eyes went wide. She could barely breathe.

"Enough, girl. Now you put hands in these," he said, dropping a thick, plastic zip tie with two large hoops into her hands.

Pleading to Carter and Royce with her eyes, she slipped her small hands into the handcuffs.

"Good, now use teeth to pull tab in middle and tighten around wrists."

With tears welling in her eyes, she gently bit onto the plastic tab and pulled, tightening the bands. She stopped when they were snug.

He growled. "Hold up hands."

Without taking his eyes off Carter and Royce, he grabbed the tab with his free hand and yanked it hard.

"Oww!" she screamed.

Royce lunged.

Helpless, Hassie watched the Russian whip the gun in Royce's direction and pull the trigger. The bullet slammed into his shoulder and Royce fell onto the floor, writhing.

The man jerked the gun back to Carter.

"No, please!" Hassie begged.

"You son of a—" Royce yelled, before a second shot blasted his kneecap. He rolled to his side, grabbing his knee.

Hassie cringed at the sight and felt helpless.

"Now be quiet or next one goes in your *head*," the man said. "Then, these two no longer worry about your claim to treasure." He laughed. "Where is cell phone?" he asked Hassie.

"It's in my skirt pocket," she stammered.

The big man kept his eyes locked on Carter as he removed her cell phone.

"Nice and warm." He tossed the phone to Carter. "I text you in one hour. No police, or you get girl back in pieces. Bring me journal and letter, and maybe girl live."

"Understood," Carter replied. "Do you need her cell number?"

"No, I have it already."

He already has it. That's not good. She implored Carter with her eyes to do something, anything. *Please don't let him take me.*

When his eyes met hers, she saw an almost imperceptible shake of his head, suggesting that there was nothing he could do at the moment.

"Do not move," the big man ordered Carter. "We leave. Be smarter than father and you live. Your father not so smart, now dead."

"What?" Carter reeled, clearly confused by the man's comment.

"What about my father?" His second inquiry sounded angrier, and Carter made the mistake of taking another step toward him.

The man fired the gun again, but this time the bullet sparked off the hard floor only millimeters from Carter's foot.

"Be smart, get journal," the man barked before refocusing on Hassie. "Come, girl!" He yanked her by the ponytail and backed out of the exit. Except for a quick glance over his shoulder, he kept his eyes on Carter until the heavy door closed.

"If you scream, I put bullet in your head and leave you in that trash pail," he instructed Hassie, both of them still facing the now closed exit door and gesturing toward the row of large trash cans lining the outside back wall.

She felt his hot breath through the cloth covering his mouth, and it sent chills down her spine. *Where is he taking me? He's going to kill me.*

With his vice-like grip on her ponytail lifting her almost onto her toes and the other hand holding the gun, the man spun her around like a doll. They turned away from the door and were about to walk out of the back alley, when she felt the rush of fur fly past her.

Scrounge slammed into the man, clamping his teeth onto the wrist holding the gun.

The man stumbled backward, releasing Hassie.

Off balance, Hassie tumbled to the ground, unable to break her fall with her wrists bound.

"Stupid dog!" he shouted, punching Scrounge and slamming his foot down on the back of Hassie's knee, keeping her pinned.

"Oww!" she shrieked.

The dog winced but bit harder on the Russian's wrist.

He shook the dog from side to side. His foot ground Hassie's knee into the pavement, and she screamed. Scrounge held on until the man jerked his wrist, pointed the barrel toward the dog's chest, and pulled the trigger.

The bullet sliced through Scrounge's chest cavity.

"No!" Hassie screamed.

Scrounge landed close to her. He tried to stand, but his front two legs buckled, and his lower jaw slapped the pavement.

She reached for him, but the man fired two more bullets. One hit the dog's front leg and the other pinged off the concrete. "Stupid dog!"

"Scrounge!"

He whimpered and tried to crawl to her, but he couldn't lift himself. His claws scraped and slipped before he coughed and collapsed.

Her mind reeling from the brutality and loss, Hassie reached out to touch Scrounge with her bound hands, but before she could, the man grabbed her ponytail and lifted her back onto her feet, yanking her away.

Seeing the growing pool of blood around Scrounge, she cried. Her knee radiated pain and slowed her walk, and the big man practically dragged her by the hair.

The blue Audi that Royce had arrived in remained parked near the end of the alley, with Robert in the driver's seat, his eyes wide and mouth slack.

"Help!" Hassie screamed, but the man pressed the barrel of the gun to her temple and told her to shut up.

"Get out of car!" he ordered Robert as he hauled Hassie closer to the car.

Almost catatonic, Robert didn't move. Only when the two reached the driver's side window did Robert break eye contact and try to start the car. He pushed the starter button over and over.

Hassie heard the Audi's motor fire up, and the large man pumped a bullet through the window and into Robert's skull.

Hassie thought she might throw up.

He yanked Robert's body out of the running car, retrieved the key fob from the dead man's pocket, and popped the trunk.

"Let me go!" she screamed, kicking at his legs.

"Shut up, girl!"

The stark reality of her situation hit her. If she got in the trunk, she knew she was dead. "No, please!"

In a desperate attempt, she clasped her bound hands together and swung as hard as she could for the bridge of his nose. Her tiny fists missed and hit his cheek.

"You have spirit, little one," he said, throwing her into the trunk and slamming the lid shut.

Chapter 10

INSTINCTIVELY WANTING TO run after Hassie, Carter had to stop himself, knowing that he first had to make sure Royce was stable. Racing over to the downed man, Carter felt conflicted and guilty. Maybe if he were younger, or maybe if he had not drunk so much, he could have lunged when Royce did and taken his chances. But the opportunity had come and gone. In that split second, he second-guessed himself, which he had done more and more since Courtney died. He knew that second-guessing was not a luxury afforded to a military officer; it could get people killed.

Royce moaned when Carter touched his shoulder. "Hang in there, buddy," he said, noticing the young man's pale face. His shoulder wound didn't look too bad, but his knee was a bloody mess. Carter wrapped a spare tablecloth firmly around his leg and moved Royce's hand to his injured knee. "Keep pressure on the wound, to stem the bleeding."

Royce didn't answer, and his eyes seemed glazed. Carter was concerned he was going into shock.

Their heads had jerked toward the door when a dog yelped, followed by Hassie's scream.

Royce finally pushed Carter's hand away. "Go after her! He's going to kill her."

Carter leaped to his feet and ran to the exit. He shoved the door open, not sure what he would find on the other side or whether he might catch a bullet for his effort. He sucked in his breath at the sight of the alley. To his immediate left was a large pool of blood. He was relieved to see it was coming from a wounded dog and not Hassie. He believed if the dog wasn't dead already, it would be soon. Ahead, Robert's bloody corpse lay on the ground. Even from this distance, Carter could tell the man was dead.

Near the end of the alley, the Audi was backing out, and for the briefest moment, Carter locked eyes with the big man behind the wheel. Though the man still wore his face covering, Carter saw the smile in his eyes, like the Cheshire cat. What concerned him most was that he didn't see Hassie in the car.

"He's taken your car, and I think he's murdered your friend," Carter yelled.

"Robert? No!"

"I'm sorry."

"You need to leave and go get the book, or whatever that guy wanted," Royce said, gritting his teeth.

"Yeah, right. But before I leave, I'll go find some hotel staff and tell them you need an ambulance."

"Tell them to call the police as well."

Carter frowned and shook his head, reminding him that the Russian guy had said no police.

Royce waved him off. "Carter, that guy shot me and killed Robert with a handgun. There's no way to avoid police involvement," he explained, his speech slower and more deliberate.

Carter sighed. "Okay, you're probably right." He nodded. "Maybe if the police can find that Audi quickly, we can end this without putting Hassie's life in any more danger." Then he added, "Listen, just tell the police what happened, but don't mention me or the journal. If the police cannot catch that guy quickly, then I have to be in a position to make the trade without a police presence. Agreed?"

"I cannot lie to them."

"What?" Carter asked, not sure whether Royce had heard him or whether shock and blood loss was impairing his senses.

"I'll not lie to the police. I'll tell them that the man shot me, he shot Robert, and he kidnapped Hassie. But if they ask me directly, I will tell them about you and your book." Royce winced and then looked Carter in the eye. "Understood?"

Exasperated, Carter closed and rubbed his eyes. "Well, for Hassie's sake, please don't volunteer more than you have to."

"Just go, get that book he wanted."

Carter was amazed at how composed Royce was. He had taken two bullets and still cared more about Hassie than his own wounds. *He would've made a good Marine.* Carter turned and ran out of the storeroom, down the hall, and through the kitchen. Within a few seconds, he found an Inn guest phone just outside the kitchen and called the front desk.

"Reception," a far too chipper female voice answered.

"We have an emergency. I heard someone scream near the kitchen, and when I went to investigate, I found a man bleeding in the storeroom. He said that he had been attacked. His knee is bleeding a lot, and I think his shoulder may be hurt too. The man said that the guy who attacked him also kidnapped one of your Inn staff and murdered someone in the back alley."

"Wait, what? Are you serious?"

"Yes, very serious," Carter said, with more urgency. "Please call for an ambulance and the police now. This is not a prank. If you have any Inn medical staff, please also send them back to the storeroom."

"Oh, okay, sir," the woman sputtered, a nervousness creeping into her voice.

"Please do it now."

"I will do it straightaway. Thank you, sir. What is your name, sir? Are you a guest with us?"

Carter hesitated before answering. "Uh, no. I was just here to make a, uh, delivery. Please hurry. I'm going to go check on him and wait for the ambulance." He hung up and ran toward the garage.

Hassie breathed so hard she wondered if she might hyperventilate. Her heart was beating in her throat. She had never experienced claustrophobia, but she did now. The dark trunk felt like a moving coffin. As terrifying as the abduction was, this part was worse. She was frightened of what he would do to her and thought of the possible horrors to come.

Knowing she didn't have much time, she patted her hands around the walls of the trunk. On a side wall, she felt a metal plate with screws at the corners. The top edge of the plate protruded a little and felt sharp. She rubbed the zip ties back and forth against it. Each turn of the car slammed her head and shoulder against the trunk walls. Ignoring the small cuts forming on her wrists, she heard a few of the plastic strands fray. She persisted until the bands snapped and she felt the ties fall away.

Searching in the dark, she next patted around the interior of the trunk seeking anything she might use as a weapon, but found nothing. Her eyes finally began to adjust to the dark, and near the trunk lock, she saw a tiny glowing circle attached to a thin cable. It took her a second to realize it was an emergency release. She moved her hands along the cable and latch, trying to figure out how it worked.

After what seemed like an eternity, the car slowed and jerked to a stop. She yanked down on the cable latch, but it didn't open. Panicked, she yanked harder. Nothing happened. The car lurched, and her face slammed into the latch.

Is it broken? she wondered, rubbing her sore cheek and checking the latch again. That is when she saw it: a tiny, faint arrow sign pointing up. *I need to yank the cable up, not down, if I get another chance.* A bead of sweat ran down the side of her nose.

When the Audi sped up, she felt dispirited and let out a long, frustrated breath. She shook her head hard to clear the fears and negative thoughts from her mind. *Stay positive. Be ready for next time.* She rolled her knees up under her stomach and pressed her back against the trunk lid.

Several minutes passed, and she was about to straighten her leg to clear a cramp when the car began to decelerate. She hoped it was slowing for a stoplight and not more stop-and-go traffic. Then the car came to a complete stop.

It's now or never. She pushed the cable up hard and popped the latch. She knew this would alert the driver, and she launched herself, but the car moved slightly before she was out; she stumbled and shoulder-rolled on the pavement then jumped to her feet and ran, with her hands flailing like a running swan.

The sounds of screeching tires and honking horns overwhelmed her senses, and one car in oncoming traffic swerved to avoid her. Glancing around, she recognized a few familiar cathedral outlines. She turned and sprinted toward Falcon Square. Hassie was across the busy street screaming for help before she ventured a glance behind her.

She saw the big man slam the trunk and climb back in, while other drivers punched on their cell phones and honked their horns.

As she watched the back lights of the Audi speed from view, Hassie finally caught her breath and her heart started to slow, hoping that she was safe, but deep down, knowing she wasn't.

Mary waited for over ten minutes in the small entry area of Bobby Fredericks's law office. No receptionist appeared to work in the office, which had cheap simulated wood-panel walls and a call button for clients to push.

"Hello, Mary," Bobby said, inviting her back. "Carter couldn't join you?"

"No," she said, trying not to stare at his unfortunate comb-over perched on top of his pear-shaped head.

When he'd represented Carter before, Mary only recalled him wearing two different suits—one a three-piece brown suit and the other a charcoal gray two-piece. Today he wore the brown suit.

"I would say that it is nice to see you, but that would sound oddly self-serving." He gave her a half smile.

She settled into one of the conference room chairs. "Have you received Carter's blood and urine test results from the CID yet?"

"Yes, I glanced at the results. They're not good, but we'll request the samples so we can do our own testing," he said. "Given Carter's prior disciplinary action, they're not likely to go easy on him."

"I understand."

"Even with our retest, there's no guarantee that the results will move the needle."

"Bobby, what if those samples went missing?" she asked, uneasily. "Would it matter *when* they were lost?"

He gave her a puzzled expression. "Yes, that is possible."

She suspected it was true, but she didn't want to take Chuck's word for it.

"Are the samples missing?"

"I'm not sure. Please request them soon."

"Will do," he said. "If we are stuck with the prosecution's test results, we can still try to challenge the chain of custody and lax lab practices, but it's an uphill battle. On a separate note, I will need a retainer of seven-thousand-five-hundred dollars."

"Really?" she said, surprised that it was three times the retainer they'd paid for Carter's prior charge.

"Yes, this will be a harder case."

She wrote a check, realizing his fee reduced their checking account to a little over four thousand dollars.

"Since you are still married to Carter, they cannot require you to testify, and anything you tell me is privileged." Bobby cleared his throat before continuing. "Is Carter working on his drinking? A twelve-step program, perhaps?"

"No," she admitted sadly. "That's one of the reasons we're divorcing." She had begged him to talk to someone or attend an AA meeting, but he always refused. She used to wonder why he couldn't see what she and others around him saw. It took her a long time to learn that alcoholics didn't see the world like everyone else. They saw the world through the bottom of a glass, distorted and wrong. When she would press, he would just shut down and shut her out. His silence kept them from talking about Courtney, and it kept them from moving on together.

"I'm sorry. If the case goes against us, then it may be helpful to argue that Carter is an addict who is trying to do something about his problem. If we argue that he is an addict but has done nothing about it, then that doesn't help."

"I'll need to discuss that with him, but I doubt he'll admit that he has a problem, much less an addiction."

He ran his hand through the hair above his ear. "I'm sorry. I've known some addicts. Sometimes they have to hit rock bottom before they find the will to change."

"Yes. I hoped Carter would change to save our marriage, but I was wrong."

"Well, not all hope is lost. We'll do the dance and see where it leads," he said. "I just wanted to be honest with you about the challenges we're facing."

"Thank you, Bobby."

"No problem. When will Carter be available to talk?"

Mary pursed her lips. "Unbeknownst to me, he elected to travel overseas."

"What?" He sat up straighter in his chair. "When will he be back?"

"I don't know. He must report back in four days or he'll be AWOL. I have no idea why he went or when he'll be back. You'll need to proceed and do the best you can without him."

"Okay," Bobby said hesitantly. "Are you sure he wants to fight this and hasn't already given up?"

"Yes, I'm sure," replied Mary. "He asked me to engage you." *Actually, I'm the one who suggested this engagement and Carter only gave his tacit approval, but I can't allow him to give up, even if he already has.*

"Good. I don't want to be the only one in court fighting for the defendant. That rarely works out well."

"Bobby, there is one more thing," she said. "The day after the navy relieved Carter of duty, he was involved in a shooting. He wasn't the one shooting. He was in an Uber when someone shot at them on the freeway. The driver was murdered. The Annapolis police are investigating."

Bobby listened, wide-eyed, and Mary was glad that he didn't request an increase in his retainer.

Chapter 11

CARTER RETURNED TO the Inverness Railway Station. Once again, he felt disappointed by its appearance. He expected a dimly lit station with a train engineer hollering next to a giant black beast, billowing steam, but instead the station was bright, clean, and modern. Most of the trains bore the yellow and blue colors of ScotRail.

He quickly retrieved the journal from the storage locker and tucked it under his arm. The unfamiliar ringtone of Hassie's phone chimed from his pocket, but only twenty minutes had passed since Hassie's abduction.

"Hello?"

"Carter!" Hassie said.

"Hassie? Are you okay?"

"Yes, I got away. I'm scared he may come back. I borrowed this phone and called because I wanted to make sure you didn't go to meet that psychopath."

After what she had just endured, her concern for him was touching. "Where are you? I'm at the train station. I'll come get you."

"Thank God. You're close. I'm in Inverness too, in Falcon Square by the unicorn."

"Unicorn?"

"Yes, it's near the center of town." She provided him with directions and instructed him to look for the huge obelisk with a giant bronze unicorn on top of it.

Based on her instructions, Falcon Square was just around the corner, and he should be able to reach her in less than a minute or two. He thought about returning the journal to the locker but decided to hang on to it as he rushed back to his car.

Driving on the other side of the road seemed particularly challenging with the narrow, winding streets and the multitudes of people lining the sidewalks and milling around what appeared to be the city square. He spotted Hassie hiding behind the giant obelisk. She poked her head around the side. Carter honked, and she ran to the car.

"You okay?" he asked when she jumped into the passenger seat.

"Yes, please go now."

He noticed her voice sounded much higher pitched and tried to calm her. "It's okay. You're safe now. I'm amazed you escaped." Carter pulled away and continually checked the rearview and side mirrors.

"I know he would've killed me. I know it. I saw him . . ."

He saw the horror reflected in her face and the tears streaming down.

"It's okay. You escaped and that's what's important." He wanted to focus her mind on something more positive and asked her to tell him about her escape.

After recounting how she got out of the trunk, she asked, "How is Royce?"

"His shoulder isn't too bad, but his knee is pretty ugly. He should be at the hospital by now."

"That maniac murdered his friend and left him on the ground. It was ghastly." She buried her face in her hands.

"I know. I saw the body. It was."

"Scrounge tried to protect me, and he shot him. He just shot him." She choked up again.

"Scrounge?"

"My dog. Well, he's not really *my* dog. I feed him scraps behind the Inn when the manager isn't looking. His name is Scrounge." She wiped away a tear. "Did you see him? Is he . . . dead?"

He didn't want to cause her more pain, but he decided she deserved the truth. "Yes, I saw him. Even if he's still alive, I don't think he will be for long. He was badly hurt and bleeding out when I left."

"I need to go back and check."

"No. That guy may try to grab you if you go back."

"I cannot just let him die alone!"

"Hassie, the dog may already be dead. Please don't go back until it's safe." He pressed the phone into her hands. "Now, you should call the police."

"I agree. Then we'll help Scrounge," she said.

"Tell the police that you escaped and are safe. Royce already will have told them about your abduction."

Nodding, she started to dial but froze. "No!" she screamed.

"What?" Carter asked, braking a little. He pulled over and stopped near a small, modern-looking kilt and clothing shop.

"A text message from him," she said, her voice quivering as she held up the phone.

Carter saw a picture of an elderly man in a hospital bed. "Is that your grandfather?"

"Yes, he's very sick."

"What does the message say?"

"It says, 'Bring me journal and girl. Do not call police.'"

"Don't worry, we are not turning you over to him." Carter looked her in the eye as he said it. He pulled back onto the road and drove toward the outskirts of the city. He exited the highway onto a dirt road, making sure that he stopped where the trees would largely obscure the view of their car.

"Okay, but what about my grandfather?" She shook her hands in frustration. "What does that guy want from me? I don't know anything."

"Let's call the police."

"You saw the message. No police. Besides, this isn't the United States," she snapped.

"Meaning what?"

"Meaning that not every citizen is issued a gun when they're born, like they are in America. People aren't allowed to carry handguns. Most police don't even carry guns. My grandfather has an old shotgun, but he had to register it."

Carter understood. In a gun-restricted society, a sociopath like the man they encountered could kill a lot of people. "Well, maybe if everyone had guns, it would be a fairer fight and men like this would think twice before casually swinging his gun around," he said, though not entirely sure why he was arguing. "Also, to clarify, not everyone in America has a gun at birth."

"Really, you have no guns? I thought you were a soldier."

"Yes, I do. Unfortunately, they're back home. And a gun out of reach is as useless as an unloaded gun."

"So, what about my grandfather?"

"Can you move him to a more secure site?"

"I don't think so. There is no other NHS hospital nearby. He's frail. He has cancer and is almost completely blind," she explained as she called the hospital.

From the half of the conversation he could hear, he assumed she was speaking with a nurse, and he patiently waited for her to hang up.

"She said that my grandfather was sleeping and she didn't want to disturb him, unless it was an emergency. He has *not* received any visitors today, and she just checked and there was nobody in his room now, not even another patient." She seemed pleased to hear that he was still there and alone in the room.

"That's good news, but he, or someone, was able to get in and take that picture of him without the nursing staff seeing him. We have to be careful." Carter rubbed the stubble on his cheek.

"Okay, but we have to do something," Hassie said.

"I agree." Carter stroked his chin. "Let's call Royce and see how he's doing. Maybe he can call the police and let them know you escaped and are safe." He paused. "Just to be safe, don't tell him where you are so, if asked, he won't have to lie to the police. I doubt he would anyway. We need to avoid doing anything that could put your grandfather's life in greater danger, but we need to call off the police search for you. If we're stopped, I don't want to be arrested as your kidnapper."

"Okay, that makes sense." She nodded as she dialed Royce's cell phone number from his business card. "I hope he's okay. Thank you too for your help, Carter."

"You're welcome." He realized he was sincere. Though he'd questioned his motivations in the beginning for helping her, he liked her spirit and bravery—and he didn't want to see any harm come to her.

"Royce, I'm so glad to hear your voice." Hassie hit the speaker button. "How are you? Carter and I were both worried about you."

"Hassieeeee, is that really you?" Royce asked, slurring his words.

"Yes, I escaped and I'm here with Carter. Unfortunately, the man who abducted me is still out there," she said.

"Thank God! I was afraid he'd kill you—"

"I'm okay. How are you?" she repeated. "And which hospital are you at?"

"I'm feeling grrrreat at the moment. I'm at Raigmore."

"Thank you for coming to warn me, and thank you for risking your life to try to stop that monster."

"Of course. You know, I don't have so many friends that I can afford to lose one," he said.

She smiled, obviously touched.

"Royce, why do you sound different? Are you drunk?" Carter asked.

"Carterrrrr! No, I don't really drink, but they gave me a shot of something to prepare me for surgery. They should be coming to get me now."

"Royce, we are so glad you are going to be okay. If you can, we need to ask you for a favor. We need you to tell the police that Hassie escaped and is safe. And do not mention me. In fact, it would be better if you called anonymously, not mentioning your name, either." Carter stared at the phone, waiting for a response. "Royce?"

"Yessss. I will remem . . . bem . . . bemer."

Carter raised his eyebrow. "Royce. This is important! We're not in a position to call the police. We need you to do it."

"Okay, and I'm very glad that you're both okay." He giggled. "Hey, that rhymes."

"No, that doesn't rhyme," Hassie said. "You just said 'okay' twice."

"Oh, okay. I did?"

Carter thought he heard a sadness in Royce's response.

"Royce, can you call the police as soon as you hang up with us?" Carter pushed.

"They willll be glad that you are okay too."

"Yes, they will," Carter said. "So, please call."

"I will and—" The call abruptly terminated.

Carter and Hassie stared at the phone, then at each other.

"I think he'll call," Carter told her. "He's a strong guy, and he's only involved because he cared about your safety."

She nodded. "I still can't believe what he did for me."

"Yeah, he really is a friend." Carter smiled.

"So, do you have the journal that the psychopath wants, and what is it?"

"I do, and most of it concerns the repatriation of a dead body and a letter," he said.

Confused, she asked, "Is that why he wants it? And a letter from who?"

"John Paul Sr."

Her eyebrows shot up. "Wait, the person Royce mentioned?"

"Yes, the same, but don't tell him about it."

"Why?"

"So far, that Russian guy is focused on you, because you found the gold coins. And on me, because I have the journal. Let's not give him another target in a hospital bed. For now, keeping Royce in the dark keeps him safe." Carter raised his eyebrows, waiting for her to agree.

"I understand, but you should understand that I owe him. He tried to save my life."

"Yes, he did." He nodded.

"So, what about my grandfather?" she asked.

"If we can't move him, then we have to either give the Russian guy the journal or we find a way to take the fight to them," Carter said. He preferred a good offense to being stuck on defense.

"If you give them the journal, will it be over?" She had an aura of childlike hopefulness.

"No." He immediately held up his palm in apology for his bluntness. "Sorry. Unless they find what they want quickly after we give them the journal, I think they will likely still come after you for what they think you may know. They already have."

Her shoulders sagged. "So, what are you thinking? How do we take the fight to them?"

He handed her the letter inviting him to Inverness.

"This came from the Inn," she said, touching the watermark on the stationary. "Do you know who sent it?"

"No, but this is why I came to the Inn. I hoped that whoever sent it might show themselves when I arrived—and the Russian guy showed up."

"So, you think the Russian sent you a first-class plane ticket?" she asked, bewildered.

"I don't know, but I doubt that he personally sent it. Something tells me that he is more likely the muscle, not necessarily the brains. Before he abducted you, he mentioned an 'old man.'"

"So, any ideas?"

"Not yet, but on the plane, I noticed something there." He pointed at the top right corner of the letter.

"I don't see anything. It's just a blank area."

"Hold it up to the light."

"Oh, I see some indentations."

"Yeah. To me, it looked like someone may have written something on the page just above the one they used to write this letter."

"Hmm." She hunted through the center console and removed a small pencil. She gently rubbed the lead across the indentations, revealing some letters and numbers. *BNIWF671*.

"It looks like code. Any thoughts?" he asked.

She scrunched her brow as she studied it. "Actually, I do. I think this is for the Inn's Wi-Fi. The password for each room is *BNIWF* plus the guest's room number. So, this code would have been used for someone in room 671."

"Excellent!"

"How does that help us?"

"Can you access the Inn's guest records?" he asked. "Specifically, can you see who was in room 671 around the time the letter was postmarked, maybe a few days before and after?"

"It's absolutely against the rules, but yes, of course." She gave him a crooked smile. "I don't have access myself, because I am only a part-time staff member, but I've seen enough full-time staff members log in to know how to do it, and even know a few of their passwords."

He smiled. He liked this girl. "Can you do it remotely?"

"I think I can on my phone." She smiled back.

He showed her the date on the envelope. "If you can, access it without using your identification. If the people behind this are monitoring things online, it would be better that they not see your name in the search, which might let them know we are on to them. Can you do that?"

"Maybe." Hassie paused, thinking for a moment. "I'll use Olivia's name and password." When prompted by the Inn's secure website, she typed in some characters and then made a thumbs-up sign. "It looks like Mr. Andrew Lennox checked into room 671 four days before that date and departed two days after."

"That sounds like our guy. Did he leave an address when he checked in?"

"Yes, an address near Murlaggan, not that far from Loch Arkaig."

"Great, Loch Arkaig." He clapped. "It definitely sounds like we're on the right track."

"I guess. You think we should go there?"

"Not us, just me. We need to find a safe place for you. Then, I need to sneak into your house and get your grandfather's shotgun. After that, I'll go have a chat with Mr. Lennox."

"That could be dangerous."

"Yes, which is why I need the shotgun."

"Carter," she started with a questioning tone, "you sound like your mind is made up, but I'm not sure about this."

"I'll be careful, and remember, I do have training." He pointed to his USMC cap.

"I understand, but it's just that this feels wrong. I can't explain why, but it just feels like a mistake."

"Hassie, one thing I learned a long time ago is that it is better to advance than retreat," he said, taking her phone.

"What are you doing?"

"We need to buy some time and protect your grandfather. So, I am doing something that I do very well." He gave her a smile. "I'm playing dumb." He typed a text to the Russian.

Who's that in the pictures? You have the girl, and I have the journal. If you hurt her, I'll burn the journal and then I'll find you.

He showed her the message before he hit send.

The response came back quickly.

Do not play games or girl's grandfather will pay price.

He frowned and typed, *I have the journal but not the girl, and you gave me her phone. Remember?* He hit the send button.

I no longer have girl. I think girl already contact you, but if not, she will soon. You tell me when you have girl. Don't make me wait long.

He showed her the response and she shuddered.

"I think we have what we need for the moment—a little more time. Now, we need to make good use of it." He put her phone in his pocket and then tapped on the steering wheel, considering whether to press her on something that had been bothering him. "Hassie, I need you to tell me something."

"What?"

"Where did you really find those coins, and please don't tell me that baloney story about a broken sewer line."

Hassie was genuinely surprised. "You don't believe me?"

"Nope. Maybe it takes one to know one, but I think your story is a load of high-grade manure. So, come clean. Where did you really find them, and are they part of the treasure?"

"I don't know whether they are part of the treasure." She looked down and felt embarrassed at being called out.

"Where did you find them?"

"You're right. I made that part up. You would never believe the truth."

"Try me. I need to know what you know—now."

She took a deep breath and then told him about the quiet voice that directed her to the stones in the water. She mentioned them looking identical to one she found with her grandfather years before. At last, she told him about pulling the gold coins out of her pocket at the hospital, like some kind of magic trick.

He stared at her.

"What? It's the truth."

"Well, I don't sense any deception. The story is pretty fantastic, but you really believe that is what happened, don't you?"

"It's not what I believe; it's what happened," she shot back.

"I certainly understand why you made up the other story. It's easier to believe, and it served to direct attention away from where you really found the coins, which is good."

She appreciated his support but doubted whether he believed her. "I guess."

"Have you heard this voice often?"

"I knew I shouldn't have told you." She crossed her arms. "And no, I have not. The only times I thought I heard anything was near Loch Ness. Usually, it was just a general feeling, rather than any specific message, but this time was different. The voice was clear, and it directed me. It sounded like my voice in my head, but it wasn't me. It had a separate spirit all its own. It wasn't evil. I'm sure that it was trying to help me."

"So, a friendly ghost in the Loch led you to the coins."

"I never said it was a ghost," she fired back before closing her eyes and exhaling loudly. "Believe me, don't believe me, that's up to you. But it's the truth."

"Okay. I'm sorry. I don't mean to antagonize you. I'm on your side. I'm just trying to understand," he said. "Were there any other black rocks besides your four? Perhaps it was a trick of the light and maybe there were more."

"No, I looked. The four sat alone. There was nothing else around, and it was *not* a trick of the light."

"Okay, okay." He held his hands up, then started the car and pulled back onto the highway. "Please use your phone and check for a hotel around here. Nothing fancy. Actually, the dumpier, the better." He handed her the phone.

She nodded, then typed and swiped on her phone. "How about the Lucky Loch Hotel. There is no website for it, but the travel site states that it has eight rooms and that there is generally capacity." She chuckled a little. "The 'generally capacity' comment usually means it's a dump and someplace to avoid." She gave him the directions from the travel site.

The two rode in silence for a little while before a nondescript sign came into view.

—

What she saw when they pulled into the hotel's dirt driveway was a standalone building with chipped brown paint, plain and run down.

"I don't think the Inn will have any competition from this fine establishment," Hassie said with a smirk.

"Heck, it looks better than some of the barracks I've bunked in."

Hassie stayed in the car while Carter reserved two rooms next to each other. He told her that he'd paid in cash, just to be safe.

"Look at this," he said, handing her a handwritten receipt. "I saw no computers, so I think this place may be off the grid, which is perfect for us at the moment."

After Carter pulled the car around to the back, he made sure to shield her from view until she got to her room.

"If you're still going to my flat to get the shotgun, could you grab a few things for me? I've been wearing these clothes for two days."

"Good idea. These are the only clothes I have." He chuckled. "My bags are still in the Inn's lobby, unless the Russian stole them."

"Well, you are about the same height as my grandfather. You are welcome to borrow what you need from his closet." She offered him the key to her flat and gave him directions and their flat number.

"I'll leave shortly," he said.

"Carter, let's agree on something. If your plan doesn't work, then we give them the journal and hope they'll be satisfied with that, right? We cannot put my grandfather's life at risk."

"Agreed, but you know that may not end it. They may still come after you. As long as we have the journal, we have a bargaining chip. We should try to delay giving it up if we can, but if we have to go that route, we will."

"What should I do while you are gone?" she asked.

"Please stay here. Don't go out or call anyone on the hotel phone. Just stay out of sight, please." Smiling, he removed his USMC cap and put it on her head. He pulled it down a little over her eyes. "The longer you stay hidden, the more the Russian might believe that you already went to the police or just ran away before I had a chance to tell you about your grandfather. Maybe that will be enough to scare them."

"I want to go see my grandfather, but I know that wouldn't be safe right now." She pushed the cap up on her forehead. "I really should go see if Scrounge survived. If he's dead, I want to give him a burial by the Loch. I promise that I'll stay out of sight."

"Look, I understand, but no. Don't go to the hospital or to the Inn," he insisted. "You know they're watching both."

"But I—"

"No. As soon as it's safe, I'll go back with you. I'll even help you bury your dog."

She could see that arguing was fruitless. She wanted to do right by Scrounge, and she felt the pull of Loch Ness. The last several hours had been so overwhelming, and she longed for the comfort she found there. Even if they were watching the Inn, she knew that she could slip in and out of the back without anyone seeing her. "Okay, I won't go," she lied.

"Good. I'll take your phone. That guy expects me to have it. I'll also hang onto the journal. I think it is best if we keep you and the journal separated for the time being. If you see or hear anything suspicious, call me or run."

Hassie nodded and determined she would head out to check the alley behind the Inn after Carter left. She had to find Scrounge.

Chapter 12

CARTER FELT HUNGER PANGS when he arrived in Forres, a little before eight p.m. He had not eaten anything since he was on the plane. He also desperately wanted a drink. At a local pub, he wolfed down a sandwich and a dark ale. He thought about ordering something stronger, but decided against it. He still had a long night ahead. Thinking Hassie might be hungry too, he got another sandwich to take back to her.

When he got to Hassie's apartment complex, he noted that it was not well lit. He circled the complex twice looking for anyone watching the building. To be safe, he parked three blocks away and walked.

Two men and a woman were hacking at an exposed part of an underground pipe with a sledgehammer about a block away. He could have sworn that he heard one ask whether the others saw any gold yet. The scene made him smile. *I'll have to let Hassie know what her little white lie has wrought.*

Pulling down a new cap he'd purchased at the pub, he walked by the building, then circled back and entered from the opposite end. He rounded each flight of stairs cautiously. The corridor leading to Hassie and her grandfather's flat was quiet and empty. The hall light closest to their flat was out, making the area around their door dark. He checked to his right and left before slipping the key in and opening the door. A light was on in the flat's bathroom, providing enough light for him to see.

An old break-action, side-by-side shotgun hung on a wall in the living room, coated with a thick layer of dust. He shook his head at the relic. He removed the weapon and opened it to confirm it wasn't loaded. That was when he realized that he had forgotten to ask where her grandfather kept the shells. *An unloaded shotgun won't be much help*, he chastised himself. Methodically, he searched through the drawers nearby. No luck.

He scanned the shelves, mostly filled with cheaply framed photographs of Hassie and her grandfather, as well as a few ribbons and certificates celebrating some of Hassie's academic achievements. From there, he moved to the bedroom. He rummaged through the chest of drawers, not finding any shells, but he did find Hassie's clothes and a few of her grandfather's shirts that should fit him. The pants he found were too small, so he would have to make do with the blue jeans he wore.

Finally, he slid open the small closet's accordion door. In the back corner of a shelf, he saw an old box of shotgun shells. He brushed away the spiderwebs from the back of the box and pulled it out. One of the sides seemed ready to come off in his hands. He gently shook the box; it felt like it was about two-thirds full.

On the closet floor, he found a small travel bag, which he used for the clothes and the shells. He looked around the flat a little more to find anything else that could be helpful. He spotted a pink backpack on the kitchen table, which he assumed was Hassie's. Several small rocks and sequins glued onto the backpack formed an "H." He removed the journal from inside his tucked shirt and shoved it in.

As he was about to leave, he stopped at the sight of something he recognized. His gaze locked on the bottle of Jack Daniel's Black Label by the kitchen window. It looked nearly full.

He wanted a sip. Needed it. But more than that, he wanted the whole bottle. *I can take it, let Hassie know, and give her money to replace it.* He hesitated, knowing that if he took it, he would have more than a sip. *I should just leave it and walk out.* He stood for what seemed like hours before striding over to the shelf, grabbing the bottle, and taking two quick sips. He stuffed the bottle in the travel bag and left the flat.

Before heading to the car, he checked the perimeter one more time. All he saw was the people banging away at the sewage line.

—

On his way to Murlaggan, Carter noticed a car's headlights a couple hundred meters behind him. He slowed a bit, and they slowed a bit. He sped up, and they sped up. His senses went on full alert until the headlights turned onto an intersecting road. Carter pulled onto the shoulder and stopped. After twenty minutes, the car had not circled back, and he continued to Murlaggan.

It was now a little after eleven p.m., and Carter parked over three hundred meters from the address they'd gotten from the Inn's records for Andrew Lennox. He was surprised it was not an office building or a compound. The place didn't look like an evil lair of someone with killers on his payroll. Instead, Carter saw a nice two-story farmhouse with bright white stone and a long, sloping roofline surrounded by several acres of cultivated land and a large fence confining several dairy cows.

He advanced toward the downstairs corner window with the shotgun under one arm and Hassie's backpack strapped over his shoulders. He steadied his breathing and knelt under the windowpane. Peeking in, he saw a man sitting in a den chair in front of a small fire. The man had his back to the window, and Carter saw he had a thick mane of gray hair.

The old man.

Slowly moving around the perimeter, he checked each window. There was no way to know whether anyone was upstairs, but the old man was the only one downstairs. As he approached the back door leading into a kitchen, he heard the cows mooing and chuffing behind him. He reached for the door handle. Surprisingly, it turned, and the latch clicked open.

With the shotgun readied on his shoulder, he moved in and crept toward the den. He swept the gun from side to side, ready to fire at any sign of danger.

In the small hallway, the flickering shadows from the den's firelight played on the walls. He stepped in, expecting to see the back of the old man's head resting in his chair, but the chair was empty.

His mind reeled and pulse raced. Wondering whether the man had moved to the couch, he inched in that direction.

"That is far enough, laddie."

Carter felt the barrel of a shotgun press to the base of his skull.

"Now, please toss your gun on the couch and turn around slowly," the man ordered.

Damn! He closed his eyes, tossed the gun, and turned. He saw a thin, elderly man in his seventies. His skin looked weathered from a lifetime of working outdoors. His eyes were not filled with malevolence and hate, but confusion. This man did not recognize him at all.

"Those dumb cows are better than guard dogs. As soon as they see anybody near the kitchen door, they assume it's me coming to bring them a treat or a salt block." The elderly man chuckled.

Carter felt off balance. None of this added up. This man, the farmhouse, the cows—none of it made sense. "Andrew Lennox?"

"Yes." He crinkled his brow. "How do you know me, and why are you breaking into my house in the middle of the night, with a gun?"

"I'm sorry," Carter said. "I think I made a mistake."

"Yes, you made a large mistake." Lennox bobbed the shotgun barrel.

"No, I mean I thought you were trying to kill me." Carter raised his hands in surrender.

The man stared at Carter for a moment. "Son, I don't even know you. Why would I want to kill you?"

"Did you send me a plane ticket recently?"

"Good Lord!" Smiling, he lowered the shotgun. "Are you Carter Porter?"

"Yes," Carter stammered.

"Well, I'm not sure how you found me. If you think that because I sent you that expensive ticket I must have lots more money lying about, I can assure you I do not."

"No, sir. I'm not here to rob you. I thought that you might be involved with some bad people, but obviously I've made a huge mistake."

"What were you intending, lad?"

"Over the last couple days, people have tried to kill me and others near me." He slumped and sat down on the couch. "Sir, I'm battling an enemy of unknown origin and strength. I mistakenly assumed that you were involved. Thank you for not shooting me. If the situation was reversed, I doubt that I would've shown the same restraint."

"Well, I considered shooting you, but a couple of things made me reassess whether you really were a threat," Lennox said with a lilt in his voice. He pulled up a wooden chair and sat across from Carter.

"Really?" Carter was surprised. He was a Marine and found it hard to believe that someone would not have considered him a clear and present danger. "What things?"

"First, your shotgun looks like it hasn't been fired or cleaned since the Great War. It might have been a greater threat to you."

Carter nodded sheepishly. Given his military background, the condition of his weapon was embarrassing. "I'm almost afraid to ask, but what was the other thing?"

"Your pink bedazzled backpack. It would make my granddaughter jealous." Lennox laughed.

Carter smiled and glanced over his shoulder. He had not considered how ridiculous he must look. "Fair points, both. Again, I'm sorry. This was a terrible mistake."

"Mr. Porter, I tried to warn you that I thought you might be in danger. Please know that the danger is not from me," Lennox said. "Is this all about the journal and letter?" he asked as he tossed his shotgun onto a padded chair.

"I believe so."

"What is the journal? Why is it so important?"

Carter screwed up his face. "Sir, you mentioned them in your letter. That was why I took it seriously. In fact, you sent that letter over a week before I even knew either existed."

He smiled and nodded as though he understood.

"How did you know about them?"

"I didn't know. I had instructions to find you, mention a journal and letter, and send you a ticket," he said. "I am neither a poor man nor a wealthy man. I could afford the ticket, but I did not want you to misconstrue my generosity as an invitation to become my ward. That is why I gave it anonymously." He grinned.

Okay, now we are getting somewhere. "Can you tell me who told you to contact me?"

"I can, but—" He paused, frowning and rubbing his hand through his thick hair.

"Please, sir. There are lives at stake, and not just my own."

He nodded. "My beautiful wife, Laura, told me to do so."

"Your wife? Can I speak to her? Is she upstairs?"

"I wish you could, but she passed away over fourteen months ago. It was unexpected, and I was thankful she did not suffer."

"I'm sorry for your loss. So, she told you to do this over fourteen months ago?"

"No, son, she told me that a few weeks ago."

Carter stared at him in disbelief, but the man was not joking.

"I know it sounds unbelievable, but it is the truth." Lennox smiled.

Carter agreed, the story sounded unbelievable.

"The last anniversary Laura and I celebrated was at a nice hotel on Loch Ness, the Bonnie Ness Inn. It was wonderful."

Carter leaned back and listened.

"After Laura passed, grief and loneliness overwhelmed me. I went back to that Inn on what would have been our next anniversary. That first evening, I walked the shores of the Loch Ness, just as Laura and I had. That is when I felt it for the first time. In my grief and agony, there was a presence, a warmth and a comfort. It lifted my spirit, and it helped me to see beyond my own pain. I cannot explain it."

Carter could not help but compare how similar Andrew's description was to Hassie's. The man didn't sound eccentric, even if what he said did. "So, this presence, you believe it was your wife?"

"Well, I didn't know what it was at first, or whether it was just my imagination. I made another trip to the Loch a month later. The next time, not only did I feel it, I actually saw my wife," he said, with complete wonder and gratitude. "She was young, and she stood in her wedding dress holding a bouquet of flowers. She looked as real as you do now. She was breathtaking."

Carter wondered whether the man was simply delusional from his grief, but he sounded cogent. "Did she speak to you?"

"Well, yes and no. She stood and smiled at me. Then, I heard a voice. It was my own voice, in my head, but somehow, I knew it was another speaking. It had to have been her. She knew my very thoughts."

"Sir, again, I'm sorry for your loss. I know, better than most, what it's like to lose someone close."

"Thank you. That actually was another reason I didn't shoot you. I saw the pain in your eyes. It was like looking into a mirror."

Carter was unsure how to respond. "Again, thank you. But how did this vision of your wife lead to me or the journal?"

"This voice, my wife, told me to find you and tell you to bring the journal and letter. She also told me to warn you of danger. I didn't know what any of that meant, but when a force of nature, much less my beautiful wife, commands me to do something, I do it or die trying."

"This voice mentioned me by name?"

He shook his head. "Not at first. I had to ask for a more precise name, since the only name mentioned sounded so odd."

Okay, so maybe it wasn't really about me. "So, what was that first name?"

Lennox looked down, as if trying to remember. "It was 'Carport.' The name made no sense to me, so I asked for a fuller name. That is when I heard Carter Porter and that you were from someplace in America that I was not familiar with. I searched your name on the internet as soon as I returned to my hotel room."

Carport? That's impossible!

Hassie had only intended to lie down for a few minutes after Carter left, but she awoke almost three hours later, according to the small plastic clock near the bed. She stretched and rubbed her eyes. She wrote a short note, letting Carter know where she was going and assuring him that she would be careful, and slipped it under his door.

Knowing that the Inn was over five kilometers away, she wished that the room had a small refrigerator or something with some bottled water, but it didn't. She was pretty sure that she had spied a vending machine outside the front of the hotel.

She crept through the cool misty night, trying to heed Carter's warnings and stay out of sight. Thankfully, she didn't see anyone near the front of the hotel or any movement from inside, but the vending machine only had sodas.

She got two bottles of Irn-Bru for her journey. She enjoyed the fizzy orange bubblegum-tasting drink sometimes, and it was second only to whiskey in popularity in Scotland. Without a bag to carry them in, she stuffed them into one of the large pockets of her skirt. For the most part, she stuck to the road but had to dart into the brush when she saw the headlights of an approaching car.

An hour later, she saw the Inn in the distance. She stayed in the shadows and hiked through the tall grass before entering the alley.

The back of her neck tingled when she saw police barriers and yellow tape. The remnants of a large blood stain and the drag marks on the pavement by the back door made her stomach tighten.

She had to know whether Scrounge was alive or dead and followed the scrapes of blood to the edge of the tall grass. She quickly moved forward, spreading the tall grass with big arm movements and scanning the ground as she lumbered through.

The bristles cut her calves and shins through her thick blue socks. She found nothing and considered venturing into the Inn to find Brenda. She knew Brenda was working a double shift and would know whether someone had already disposed of Scrounge.

A sound caught her attention. The gurgling moan came from farther up the hill than where she had been searching. She pushed through the tall grass and was about to take another step when she nearly tripped over him.

"Scrounge!" she cried out, dropping to her knees.

His fur was wet and matted with blood, rain, and dirt. He raised his eyebrows but was too weak to lift his head. She wrapped her arms around him and cried. The entry and exit wounds on the side of his chest were huge, gaping holes. They looked so painful, she didn't dare touch them. She was horrified at the way his paw just hung off his front leg.

She felt utterly helpless, wiping the tears off her cheeks. She would not leave him here to die alone. She would stay and then find a nice spot, with a view of the Loch, to bury him. If she had to, she would use her fingernails to dig.

"I'm here, boy."

The dog tried to maneuver closer to her but whimpered with each movement and labored with each breath.

"Be still, boy. I am with you, and I will not leave you," she said, using a soothing tone.

In the middle of the cold, wet field, she felt a warmth wash over her, as if her grandfather were wrapping his arm around her. More than that, she felt a comforting presence, similar to what she had felt before, but stronger. The voice in her mind was louder and clearer than she had ever heard it.

Bring him! Bring him unto me now!

Chapter 13

BRING HIM UNTO ME NOW! the voice repeated.

Hassie understood. She needed to take Scrounge to the shore.

She had never been a spiritual person. That was her grandfather's department; but she now faced a reality that she could never have imagined. It was not a question of whether to believe or not believe. This voice and presence were real, and it would be crazy to deny it.

From a sea of dark despair, she was offered a thread of hope, and she grabbed it with both hands. Squatting down, she tried to pick up the animal. With her slight build and the dog's wet bulk, she failed and fell hard to the ground. Twice more she tried without success. The front of her blouse and skirt were filthy. She was already panting but no closer to the shore. Scrounge whimpered from her efforts, which tore at her heart, but she knew this was the only chance Scrounge had to survive.

"You're just too big, boy." Sitting on her knees, she wiped at her face with her dirty hands and considered her options. She came up with only one, and it would cause Scrounge much more pain.

"Sorry, boy. I really am," she said as she lay down and pressed her back to the dog's side. He whimpered when she used her shoulder to turn him to his side so she could get under him. Gritting her teeth, she rolled him onto her back.

With the full weight of the dog on her, she could barely breathe. Slowly, she shifted her knees up under her stomach and pulled the dog's front legs over her shoulders. Scrounge's damaged paw scraped the ground as she maneuvered, and he squealed.

"I'm sorry," she whispered, trying not to cry.

Using one hand to brace herself and the other to hold onto Scrounge's good leg, she slowly stood up. Her thigh muscles strained, and she remained heavily stooped as she started walking toward shore. The poor dog's back paws dragged on the ground. He rested his head on her shoulder, and his breath bathed her neck.

The trek took several minutes, and she stumbled to her knees a few times. When she finally felt the soft, wet soil of the shoreline beneath her shoes, she was puffing hard, and Scrounge felt limp.

She gently lowered him onto his side. Thankfully, she saw his ribs moving up and down.

"What now? Please help him!"

Empty both of your bottles and place them upright near the water.

The instructions made no sense to her, but she didn't question them. She emptied the bottles and watched the fizzy drinks drain and bubble in the mud. She planted the empty bottles by the water's edge and returned to Scrounge's side.

His breathing became more erratic, and she knew he could not survive much longer. "Hang in there, boy." Out of the corner of her eye, she swore she saw the bottles disappear, just for a second. *It must have been some trick of the light,* she told herself, because she could now see the bottles clearly were in the same spot.

Return for the bottles.

What was the *point of that?* Hassie wondered.

She sucked in her breath when she bent down to pick them up. A dark liquid filled each bottle, and a grayish, gelatinous substance plugged their tops. She saw no disruptions in the mud around the bottles other than her own shoe prints. The transformation to suddenly full bottles was like magic.

Take these bottles, child. One is for your Seanair. Give it to him as soon as you arrive, waiting no more than a minute or two. Also, make sure that he drinks at least half of the leigheas fala, *and preferably all of it.*

Hassie picked up one of the bottles. The liquid was a dark red color. *Can this really help my grandfather?* she wondered, slipping it into her pocket.

Yes.

Hassie recoiled. *Wait, you can actually hear my thoughts?*

Yes, child.

The air was electric. She knew that she should be afraid, but for some inexplicable reason, she was not.

This other bottle must be for Scrounge, correct?

Yes. Pierce the seal and feed it to him. Roll him onto his back. Make sure he looks into your eyes, and pour it slowly into his mouth.

"I understand," she said aloud.

The dog moaned when she rolled him onto his back, but he didn't resist. She used her thumb to poke through the seal, and the top crackled, as if she had cracked a crème brûlée. An unmistakable smell of iron and blood hit her, but she scooped up Scrounge's head and looked into his eyes.

He placed his good paw on her arm while she poured the liquid into his mouth. In the moonlight, the liquid had a pinkish tint and was the consistency of tomato soup.

"Drink it, boy."

Scrounge's eyelids were little more than slits, but he held her gaze. After what seemed like an eternity, she heard a weak swallow. Stronger gulps followed, and a light steam emanated from his fur.

She had no idea what to expect, but what happened next was beyond her wildest hopes. Scrounge flipped over and let out a loud, triumphant bark. He panted and bounced up and down, as if he were a puppy. He jumped onto her, smothering her face with licks.

"You're really okay!" She laughed. She took the dog's injured front paw in her hands. There was no sign of injury, not even a scar or any fur missing where he had been shot. She hugged him and rubbed his sides. Blood and mud still matted his fur, but he had no wounds, not even a mark. She had witnessed a miracle.

Thank you! How is this possible? she asked in her mind as she hugged him again.

Your love helped to save your friend, child.

On the long drive back, Carter replayed the conversation with Andrew Lennox. He knew he was too old to believe in ghost stories but wondered how the man had known his childhood nickname. It rattled him.

He felt guilty for having told Hassie that his hard-charging plan to confront the old man was the best option to help her, but nothing about his trip to Murlaggan had improved their situation.

Still twenty minutes from Inverness, he called Hassie's room but got no answer. After the second attempt, he worried she wasn't there, and he knew what that meant. Either the Russian had tracked her to that hotel or she had broken her promise and gone to see her grandfather or check on that dog. At least he had the journal.

He considered going back to the hotel, but the Russian could be there and Carter would be walking into a trap with his only bargaining chip.

Part of him was angry Hassie may have broken her promise to him, which he had made for her own safety, but given the other possibility, he sincerely hoped that she had left voluntarily. *Hospital or Inn?* Either way, he needed confirmation and would have to check to know. He remembered Hassie telling him she thought she could check on the dog and stay out of sight. *Inn first*, he thought.

The clock on the car's dash read 3:52 a.m. when he saw the Inn. He drove by the alley but saw no signs of her. He parked in the garage, got out, and removed the bottle of Jack Daniel's from Hassie's backpack. *I may need this.* He opened the top and took a healthy drink.

He slung the pink pack around his shoulders and inspected the alley. Relieved it was empty, he took another swig and felt the burn down his throat. Following the bloodstains, he walked to the tall grass.

"Hassie," he called in a loud whisper but received no answer. He checked around the edges of the grass for another minute or two before sighing heavily. Then, through the cool breeze, he could have sworn he heard a murmur. He spun around, but nobody was there. He couldn't be certain, but he thought he heard someone encouraging him to come to the shore. He took another small drink, chalking up what he'd heard to his imagination, but still headed toward the shoreline.

His concerns turned to darker thoughts. *Where could she be? Did the Russian have her?* A wave of guilt washed over him, and his gaze dropped to the ground in front of him. *Did I put Hassie in danger by leaving her alone?* The possibility that he might have put her in harm's way was overwhelming.

He now cared for this young girl who, in some ways, reminded him of Courtney. Those guilty feelings mixed with the burn in his stomach morphed into anger at himself.

He tripped and fell over the small rocks littering the shore and slapped the packed mud. He sat up, grabbed the bottle, and took another swig. His head spun. *Do something!* his mind screamed with an impotent rage. He removed Hassie's phone from his pocket and swayed as he typed out a text message to the Russian.

If you hurt her, there is no rock you can hide under that I won't find you! Just after he hit the send button, he closed his eyes and took a few deep breaths so he could focus on what he should do next. When he opened them, he noticed a faint light just a few meters from him and gasped.

Carter's heart was in his throat. A glowing halo surrounded her.

She said nothing. She just stared at him as if looking straight through him. The image before him wasn't Hassie; it was Courtney, and she was wearing her blue dress with yellow daisies.

He knew that this was not a dream, and it was not a delusion. She had dimension, and he couldn't see through her. She looked real enough to touch. More than that, she looked perfect.

Carter began to sweat profusely, the alcohol exited through every pore. Part of him was afraid that if he moved, she would disappear. Finally, mustering the courage, he put the bottle down and crawled toward her.

"Courtney," he called to her, still disbelieving his eyes. He reached out to touch her arm, but grabbed only air. He fell onto his chest. His daughter was gone. She had simply evaporated into the night, like someone had switched off a lamp light.

"No!" he screamed. He frantically felt around the ground where she stood. There was nothing. He looked in all directions, but she wasn't there. He was alone again in the empty darkness, hearing only the gentle lapping waves of Loch Ness.

He flipped to his back and cried uncontrollably. It was amazing how quickly loss flooded back. Devastating images seared his mind. He saw himself standing over Courtney's bed, viewing her small, oxygen-deprived body.

Stop! Get those thoughts out of your head! He couldn't go through all that again. He had not been strong enough to do it the first time. Tears welled up, and he felt disoriented, almost like he was walking down stairs in the dark and missed the last step—that sick feeling of falling through empty space, completely helpless to stop it.

He rolled onto his hands and knees and crawled to the Jack Daniel's bottle. Alcohol was the only thing that numbed his pain. *I'll drink it all if I have to.* He took his first drink but stopped when he thought he heard a female voice calling his name.

"Carter!"

Still on his knees, he slowly turned, and a large figure barreled into him, pushing him onto the pink backpack. "Ughh!" he grunted. The force knocked the bottle from his hand. "What the he—" A slobbering tongue lapped his face.

"Let him up, boy." Hassie laughed.

"Hassie!" he yelled, jumping to his feet and embracing her in a bear hug. His relief that she was unharmed lifted a guilt so heavy, he almost started to cry again.

The reaction seemed to startle her, and it took a second for her to return his hug. "I thought you would be mad."

"I was, for a moment, when I called your room and got no answer, but I was more afraid that the Russian had found you." He released her, wiped his eyes, and noticed she was filthy and smelled like wet dog.

His gaze landed on the fallen Jack Daniel's bottle. He rescued it from the mud and took another long drink. He started to wonder whether the vision of Courtney might have been the alcohol and guilt after all.

"You didn't get my note?"

"I never went back. When you didn't answer, I couldn't risk it." He took another sip. "I hoped that you'd come here, looking for that stupid dog."

She put her hands on her hips. "Scrounge is great."

"Is this the same dog?" he asked, teetering as he bent down to inspect it. "I see blood, but I don't see a mark on him."

"His recovery was pretty miraculous."

Carter sensed that she wanted to tell him something but was holding back. He was not sure whether to press.

"Scrounge tried to save my life, didn't you, boy?" She bent down and scratched the dog behind his ear.

At that moment, Hassie reminded him so much of Courtney and how his daughter used to play with the smaller dogs in the park. If only for that moment, the memory filled him with a joy he had not felt for a very long time, almost a giddiness. "Please forgive me," Carter playfully mocked, lifting his palm to his chest. "This dog has certainly earned *his* blood stripe." He thought for a second, and a wry smile crossed his face. "In fact, I think Scrounge deserves a more formal acknowledgment of his heroism."

She eyed him, clearly not sure where this was going.

With a buoy of his spirit, Carter knelt in front of the dog and raised the square bottle like a royal scepter. "By the power granted to me by nobody on this continent, and with no ability whatsoever to affect the legal status of anyone involved, for displaying courage beyond measure in a profound effort to save the life of Hassie, I hereby dub thee Sir Scrounge, Honorary Knight of the Round Table." He then gently tapped the bottle on each of the dog's shoulders.

Scrounge barked his approval.

Hassie giggled. "Wow, nobility," she said, patting the dog. "Don't let this go to your head, boy."

He barked again.

"He will definitely need to work on his table manners." She laughed. "He normally just eats out of the top of the trash pail."

"That is a fair point, my queen." He laughed. He often referred to his daughter as his queen or the queen of his heart. He didn't intend to say it to Hassie; it just came out, but it didn't bother him. "I must correct this grievous error," he announced, as if pained by some tragic mistake. Again, he held up the Jack Daniel's bottle.

"By the power granted to me by nobody on this continent, and with no ability whatsoever to affect the legal status of anyone involved, for displaying courage beyond measure in a profound effort to save the life of Hassie, I hereby redub thee Sir Scrounge, Honorary Knight of the Round *Pail*." He again gently tapped the bottle on each of the dog's shoulders.

"Much more appropriate, I think." She laughed. "It is a very strong name. It may be a *little* long, but he'll grow into it. On a separate note, is that my backpack?"

He chortled. "Yes, I needed to put the journal in something inconspicuous, so I chose a pink bedazzled backpack."

"Well then, brilliant!" She smiled. "I'll need it back."

"Understood. It didn't go with my outfit anyway."

"So, were you right? Was Mr. Lennox behind all of this?"

His smile turned into a frown. "No, you were right. The trip was a mistake. He was just a lonely old man who missed his dead wife. He isn't involved." He elected not to share the ghost story with her. Of course, after seeing Courtney, he might have to reconsider Lennox's story.

"So, you remember our agreement, right?"

Carter nodded. "Yes, I'll give up the journal, but not you."

"Well, we may be able to move my grandfather after all," she said, tapping her pocket.

"Really? When?"

"Later this morning, I hope. I'll have to go to the hospital to arrange it. I promise I'll be careful. Maybe you can surrender the journal right after I move him."

He was about to ask her if she really had to go to the hospital, when he saw a man approaching, holding a flashlight.

"Get down," Carter ordered.

They crouched just below the top of the grass ridge. "I think somebody's over here," they heard the man say.

He heard the approaching man's Russian accent as he spoke into a phone. His medium build made Carter think he wasn't the one who had abducted Hassie, but he was heading straight for them. In a few more steps, he would be on top of them.

Chapter 14

"I SEE NOTHING YET. Is he in Bonnie hotel?" the man asked and stopped.

"No, I am inside hotel and we monitor hotel cameras. I saw image from garage and outside, moving toward shore," Carter heard the deep, gravelly Russian voice respond over the phone's speaker.

Then Carter heard a second male voice from the man's phone, a voice he didn't recognize. This one had a British accent. "He's close to your location."

The man slowed to scan the area, and he was only five or ten meters from where they crouched.

Good, they don't know she's here. He saw panic in Hassie's eyes. *If the man comes close enough without detecting us, I could strike. I would have the element of surprise.* He pulled off the backpack and handed it to Hassie.

She mouthed, "What now?"

He gestured that he would engage the man but that she should get ready to run. Carter could tell she was terrified, but she nodded.

"Can't be sure, but he may really think we have girl." The gravelly Russian voice on the phone laughed. "We get soldier first. He has journal somewhere. Girl can wait. She will come for grandfather or call police. We monitor police calls. If she calls, we grab her. We know anonymous call to police said the girl escaped, and that call came from hospital, so probably grandfather. We will get her."

Carter gave Hassie a nervous look. Calling the police was no longer a good option. He thought the last voice on speakerphone sounded like the large Russian and wondered how many more there might be on the grounds. It was clear that the Russian had received Carter's earlier text and, at least for the moment, didn't believe Hassie was with him.

The man holding the phone continued his approach, and they pressed themselves up against the mud and grass barrier. Scrounge remained quiet, huddled at Hassie's feet. Soon, there would be no way to avoid detection, and Carter prepared to act.

For a second, he thought his eyes were playing tricks on him. The change took only a blink, but the distortion was unmistakable. Carter felt as if someone had pulled a thin curtain of water between them and the man, like looking up at the water's surface from the bottom of a shallow swimming pool. At the same time, he felt a warmth wash over him—a comfort. The atmosphere seemed quieter. He could no longer hear the wind.

Only four or five meters away, the man stopped and turned back toward the Inn.

"Do you see him?" the British voice asked.

"*Nyet*," he responded.

Carter thought about lunging now. With the element of surprise from behind, he knew that he could easily take the man.

"He must be there. We tracked the girl's phone from Murlaggan to your location. He didn't even stop at the other hotel," the British voice urged.

They're tracking Hassie's phone? How could I have been so stupid? Carter berated himself. *I led them right here, and they know about the Lucky Loch Hotel.* He realized Hassie's decision to break her promise to him had probably saved her life, at least for the moment. His stomach knotted.

As the man turned toward them, he saw the butt of a pistol extending from his coat.

The man raised the flashlight and swept it across the grass, over the top of their heads. He took two quick steps forward and stopped.

He now stood only a meter or so away, and Carter wanted to lunge, but something held him back.

Stay.

The voice was his, but he knew he hadn't thought it. He didn't move.

The Russian looked right at him, but he didn't make eye contact, react to them in any way, or pull his gun—it was as if he didn't see them at all.

Carter couldn't comprehend it. He still thought about lunging for the man's gun, but he stayed put. He tapped Hassie's shoulder, pointed to his own eyes, and waved his hand in front of them, indicating that the man didn't see them. Then he shrugged.

"Keep looking for him there. He is near," the gravelly Russian voice ordered.

Carter watched Hassie close her eyes and whisper something. He thought that she might be praying, but the words her mouth formed were, "Is this you?" and "Are you preventing him from seeing us?"

She nodded and crinkled her brow a little, as if something confused her, then she smiled and mouthed, "Thank you."

He didn't know what she was doing, but he didn't have time to ponder it or ask her about it. The man was almost upon them. Carter stood, readying himself to fight. If the man really could not see him, then he easily could knock him out.

No, Carter Porter. Be still. Carter felt the words more than heard them. He wasn't entirely sure whether he had heard anything.

"I go back to garage to look for soldier's car," the gravelly Russian voice on the speaker said.

"Understood," the man in front of them replied, stepping over the grass embankment.

Carter backed up as the man hopped down. He let the Russian pass, but the man turned and walked toward Hassie. Carter was afraid he was going to walk right into her, and his mind snapped.

No, Carter Porter!

Whether it was the alcohol, the concern for Hassie, or the anger over what these men had done, he was filled with a sudden rage that he could no longer control. He jumped up and felt a jolt of cold wind. The watery curtain was gone.

He swung the Jack Daniel's bottle at the back of the man's head. The bottle connected with a hideous thud. It didn't break, and the man didn't fall.

"Ahh!" The man grabbed his head and twisted around. His eyes were glassy, but they met Carter's.

He can see me. Carter reeled back to hit him again, but the man slumped and fell sideways into the mud.

He wanted to tell Hassie to run, but she and the dog were gone. *I hope she knows not to go back to the other hotel.*

Carter grabbed the man's holstered nine-millimeter pistol. He patted the guy's pockets and found two spare magazines and a set of car keys. *This should slow them down.* He tossed the keys into the Loch. He was tempted to shoot the man, but he couldn't murder an unconscious man. In addition, he knew that with no silencer on this gun, the noise would draw attention and he didn't know where the other Russian was or how many more were around.

His rage waned and gave way to concern for Hassie. She had the backpack and the journal, which made her a double target. Since he still had her phone, he had no way to contact her.

A sudden warmth washed over him again, and to his astonishment, Hassie and Scrounge appeared not five meters away from him. Like a magician's trick—one second he saw nothing, and the next a girl and her dog appeared.

He heard the crackle of the man's speakerphone again. "Gavrie, what did you say?"

"Where did you go?" Carter whispered to Hassie.

"I've been here the whole time." She shrugged in confusion as she mouthed her response. "I saw you."

Impossible. They were gone. It made no sense, but he forced himself to refocus. They needed to get to his car and leave.

He grabbed the speakerphone. "I see him," Carter said in his best Russian accent.

"Repeat! Gavrie, repeat!" the British voice requested.

"I see him," he repeated. "He is at ruins of big castle. He has something in hand. May be journal. Come now!"

Two men raced out the front of the Inn, and a larger one came from the garage. All three ran in the direction of the ruins.

Carter and Hassie waited a few seconds before they and Scrounge sprinted for the garage. He didn't feel better about their chances until they reached the corner of the Inn. Carter hoped the large Russian had not left someone behind. He crept up to the second floor of the garage before signaling to Hassie that it was safe.

She opened the back door of his car. "Go on, boy."

"Wait," Carter said.

"We can't leave Sir Scrounge."

"He'll be okay here, and he'll slow us down."

She stood there, holding the back door open.

Carter rolled his eyes. "Okay, get in and hurry."

Hassie smiled and jumped in with Scrounge.

As soon as he closed the driver's side door, the overpowering aroma of wet dog hit him. His eyes teared up. "Dang! That smells worse than Plebe Summer at Annapolis. It's like a punch in the face." He smiled and cracked all four windows. He pulled out Hassie's phone and typed a text.

The girl knows nothing, leave her out of this. I'll leave the journal someplace public and text the location. After that, the girl, her grandfather, and I are finished. I know you're tracking the phone, so I'm turning it off.

He showed it to her, and she nodded her approval.

He sent the text, removed the phone's battery, and pulled out of the garage, leaving the headlights off.

Near Merchiston Park in Edinburgh, a thin, almost emaciated man in his late fifties sat behind his oversized gilded metal-and-glass desk. With all the prominently displayed Incan and Mayan artifacts, Avery Darrow's office looked more like a museum.

Smiling, he picked up a lucite deal toy from the corner of his desk and gazed at it. An investment banker had given him the mini tribute to memorialize Darrow Health Technologies' first acquisition of a major competitor, Orion Pharmaceutical Ltd. It was the only work-related tribute he allowed in his office.

Avery had learned early that in the pharmaceuticals industry, being best was not as important as being *first*—first to patent and first to market. Even if their drug was not as effective as a later competitor's, the first entrant commonly dominated the market. At the time, Orion was about to be first with a late-stage cancer drug, and preliminary reports suggested that Orion's drug was better than the one DHT was developing. But Orion desperately needed capital, following certain unexpected reversals.

Avery had swooped in and acquired the company for a fraction of what it would have cost only a few months prior. Orion's drug became the first to market, but under the DHT flag. This one transaction had helped Avery's company leapfrog into a leadership position in a multibillion-dollar industry.

He returned the deal toy to its place of honor on his desk. He kept it as a reminder of what it took to succeed in a kill-or-be-killed business. In the case of Orion, all it took was a targeted computer virus and a small plane crash that killed Orion's top research scientists to nudge them into financial instability.

That small crash was the first time he had ordered an actual killing, but it wouldn't be his last. It was also the first time that he had engaged the services of Lewis Oliver. He knew Lewis was a dangerous man, but his services were like potato chips; it was hard to stop after only one. Avery sometimes wondered whether he, personally, would have the strength to kill. He always thought he could, but he chose to outsource the duty because of time constraints and the greater certainty of results offered by a professional. Relying on Lewis, however, meant the man had compromising information on him, and that bothered Avery. He scratched the back of his hand, as he often did whenever his anxiety rose. The hand bore the scars to prove it.

Father would not have approved of the use of such extreme measures, but then again, he never had to face what I did. He recalled how shortly after his father's death, industry "friends" had swooped in like vultures. His father had put his own blood, sweat, and tears into founding DHT. *They brushed me aside and carved up DHT, stealing some of our best personnel and over a third of our market share.* His feeling of helplessness had diminished long ago, but his feeling of rage remained strong. He never forgot those who smiled to his face while they drove a knife in his back. When he rebuilt DHT, he swore that he would never be that vulnerable again.

A soft buzzer on the intercom sounded a little after nine a.m., bringing Avery back to the present and alerting him to his guest's arrival. Then, his assistant ushered in Darrell Wilson.

"Darrell, it's wonderful to see you," He greeted his guest with a vigorous handshake.

"Always a pleasure, Avery," Darrell responded, pushing his ample girth onto the overstuffed leather couch.

Avery noticed he wore the eighteen-karat gold Rolex he'd given him as a "gift" six years ago. It was worth it. Paying a few thousand pounds in political contributions and gifts to the right officials allowed him to exact concessions worth millions.

Avery knew that Darrell was the right government official. As a principal of the Crown Estate Scotland, he was responsible for administering and leasing thousands of hectares of Crown Estate land and waterways. That the CES owed little accountability to the people of Scotland, nor received meaningful oversight from Parliament, also meant that the favorable lease terms Avery obtained would never be challenged.

"Darrell, DHT needs another five hundred hectares contiguous to our existing leased acreage." He handed Darrell a plat showing the proposed location.

"Yes, I reviewed your application," Darrell said, putting on his glasses as though trying to look smarter than he was. "That acreage includes river frontage and access."

Avery nodded. "As you know, we use a variety of crops in our pharmaceutical lines, and yes, the river access would allow us to more efficiently move our harvested traditional, as well as genetically altered, grains to our testing facility up north," he explained while hiding his true intent. *I need that frontage for additional security for the T-Farm.*

His massive farming operation was a perfect cover to hide his covert and illegal onsite drug-testing facility. Only a handful of people knew the T-Farm, as they called it, existed. He scratched the back of his hand. *With that frontage acreage, we can more easily dispose of certain evidence in the river.*

"That makes sense." The chubby man nodded in unison with Avery. "But leasing costs are higher per hectare for river frontage," he added sheepishly.

"Now Darrell, you're not trying to take advantage of an old friend, are you?" Avery stopped nodding and gave him a hollow smile.

"No, sir, never." He shook his head and started to stand up, obviously fearing that he had offended his host.

Avery gently put his hand on Darrell's shoulder to reassure him and to encourage him to remain seated. "Please just tell me what you think you will need."

"Well, your other acreage is leased for two hundred pounds per hectare. We could easily request five hundred for the river frontage acreage, but I think the board would accept three hundred."

I would have paid ten times that amount, but I still have to put on a show for this fool. "Thank you, my friend. Your efforts are always appreciated." Avery patted his shoulder before withdrawing his hand. "That amount would be acceptable, and you know that I will express my gratitude in other, more tangible ways after the lease is signed."

"That is not necessary, Avery. I'm just trying to enhance value for CES."

Avery knew the man had to say this, but naturally Darrell expected a generous gift. "You are truly a credit to CES."

The men chatted for a few minutes before Avery escorted him out. As he watched him leave, Avery smiled. *Thank the heavens for useful idiots like Darrell Wilson.*

Chapter 15

FOR THE THIRD TIME in less than twenty-four hours, Carter registered at a new hotel. The Red Regency Hotel was located on the outskirts of Inverness. All the rooms opened onto a small white-gravel parking lot. He occupied room 134, and Hassie took room 138.

After grabbing three hours of desperately needed sleep, he showered and put on a button-down shirt. As he dressed, he thought about seeing Courtney. He had experienced many alcohol-induced sights, but never anything like that. She had seemed so real. The vision haunted him.

He picked up the room phone and called the car rental company. Fearing the Russian might have placed a tracking device on his rental car, he had parked it almost two kilometers from the hotel last night. He made up an excuse and told them that he needed a replacement vehicle, requesting that they deliver it to him at a pub in town.

He stepped out and lightly rapped on Hassie's door. At first, he heard nothing. *Would she have snuck out again?*

Pressing his ear to the door, he was glad to hear Scrounge panting on the other side. *She wouldn't have gone anywhere without that dog.* He knocked again.

"Just a minute," Hassie called out. She opened the door, wearing jeans and a thick pullover.

"I still can't believe this is the same dog," he said, patting Scrounge. He examined the bathed dog further under the room's lights. "I see no marks. It's amazing."

"It's more than that," she corrected him. "It's a miracle, just like the miracle of that man not seeing us on the shore." She placed her hand over her heart. "I say that, and I have never uttered anything like that in my life, but it's the truth."

"Truly amazing," he repeated, still inspecting the dog and only half listening to what Hassie said.

"Carter, last night, just before you hit that man with the bottle, did you hear anything odd?"

"No, not really, other than what we overheard the Russians saying" he answered quickly, without thought. He had certainly seen something unusual, but he didn't immediately recall the urging he felt to remain still and not attack the man. "Why?"

"No reason," she responded, before changing the subject. "Well, maybe Sir Scrounge just needed a good bath."

"He does clean up well." He turned to her. "So, you said you could move your grandfather this morning."

"Yes, I think so."

"Good. Remember the text I sent to the large Russian. I'm still pretending that I don't know where you are."

"Do you think he believed you?"

"Not sure, but I'm hoping it might buy us time for you to move your grandfather," he said. "You also need to be very careful at the hospital. I'm sure they're watching your grandfather's room, so don't go directly there, and be ready to abort if you see anything suspicious. Are you sure you have to go to the hospital at all?"

"Yes, but I'll be careful. I have a plan."

He noticed that she glanced over at her bedside table and what appeared to be a soft drink bottle when she said it.

Carter shrugged. "Okay, but tell as few people as possible where you are moving him, preferably not the hospital administrators, and try to sneak him out." He scratched his chin as he thought about it. "We also need to coordinate the surrender of the journal. If I contact the Russian the moment you feel you and your grandfather are safely out, then they may be confused and choose to focus on getting the journal instead of pursuing you or your grandfather. We'll use the exchange to draw them away."

She sat on the corner of the bed and looked down. "After that, will it really be over?"

"No," he said, not intending to be harsh. He pulled over one of the two chairs next to the room's small table and sat facing her. "Look, I don't think so and I doubt you do either. I still have the man's gun from last night. If I can get some answers from whoever shows up for the journal, then there is still a chance we can end it."

"Is the gun really necessary?" She frowned.

"You know what these men are capable of, and giving up the journal is no guarantee they won't come after you. We must be prepared."

She shifted in her seat on the bed.

"I'm sorry. We have no good options. Getting some answers from them will be our best chance to end this."

She slowly nodded. "I understand, but this sounds a little like your earlier plan."

He shook his head. "No, not exactly. I'm putting the journal out there, just as we agreed." Before she could argue with him, he pressed his plan further. "So, where is a populated area, maybe a market or café?"

"Around here, maybe the Café Victoria in the Victorian Market. It's on Queensgate." She gave him a questioning look. "Why?"

"I need a public place for the exchange. And I need to scout out the area in advance so I can find the best place to watch someone retrieve it."

"Since we cannot use my phone, how should I contact you once I move my grandfather?"

"Call me at the café, but don't use real names. I'll let the wait staff know I'm waiting for a date. Her name is . . ." He raised his eyebrows, waiting for a response.

"Olivia."

"Olivia. My name will be John." He smiled. "If you have to leave a message, either tell him that you are on your way, which will be our signal that you and your grandfather are safe and moving. Or that you are running late, which will be the signal that you and your grandfather are not safe."

"Okay, but why the two messages?"

"I need to know your situation. If you're not safe, I'll hang on to the journal to trade."

She nodded in understanding. "You still haven't really told me what's in it."

"That's right, I haven't, and I don't think I should." He tightened his jaw and gently patted Scrounge's head next to where Hassie was already patting him. "I don't want any of those men coming near you or your grandfather, but if things go wrong and they grab you again, it will be better for you if you don't know what's in it. That way, we still have a bargaining chip."

Her expression turned more sullen. "Okay. I just want this to be over."

"I do too." He stopped patting the dog. "Now, what's my name?"

"Carter."

He shook his head. "No, Olivia, what's my name?"

She smiled. "Oh yeah, sorry. John."

Hassie entered through the back of Raigmore Hospital at a little after ten a.m. Following Carter's advice, she avoided large waiting areas with far too many prying eyes. She was nervous, but she knew she had to do this.

Checking around the first corner on the ground floor, she watched for any bad people. She didn't know what any of them looked like. The large Russian had worn a mask and it was so dark on the shores last night, she was not even sure she could recognize the man Carter hit. She tried to spot anybody who didn't belong. Of course, other than hospital staff, she realized nobody really *belonged* in a hospital.

An older man wearing a pressed suit and a hospital identification badge sauntered toward her in the hall.

She stepped in front of him. "Excuse me, sir. Can you tell me where I could find the laundry?"

"What?" He stopped.

"The laundry?" She repeated but tried to quickly explain when she saw his brows furrow. "My younger brother is three, and he lost his green binky. We think the orderly might accidentally have taken it with the bed sheets. Please, sir, he's very distraught."

"Well, that is important. My daughter had a binky she slept with until she was eight." He smiled. "The laundry is on the basement level. It should be at the end of a long corridor, near the loading dock. If they give you any trouble, just tell them that I said it was okay. My name is Peter Roseland. I'm in the administration office."

"Thank you, sir. You have been uncommonly kind." Without thinking, she leaned in and gave him a hug.

He stepped back, breaking her embrace, and chuckled. "Well, we guardians of the binkies must stick together." He smiled again and wished her good luck before continuing on in the opposite direction.

She located the laundry, and only one person questioned why she was there. They backed off when she mentioned Roseland's name. She searched for and found what she was really after: a set of hospital scrubs and a surgical scrub cap. In a restroom, she slipped the scrubs on over her clothes, tucked her hair under the cap, and now looked like any other hospital personnel. To complete the disguise, she grabbed an empty clipboard. Patting the Irn-Bru bottle in her pocket, she headed for the stairs.

Exiting on the fifth floor, she kept her head down and marched with purpose toward her grandfather's room.

"Excuse me, madame," Hassie heard a Russian-accented man say to one of the nurses.

Her heart stopped. He sounded like the man Carter had hit with the bottle.

"Yes, sir," the nurse responded.

"I must go downstairs for cigarette and to make call," he told her. "I do not want to miss relatives when they come to visit Mr. Douglass in room 514. I wish to surprise them. I have traveled far after I hear my uncle sick. If he has visitor in next thirty minutes, please call me at this number?" He handed her a paper slip.

"Yes, sir, of course," the nurse agreed. "No, sir, I cannot accept that," she said when he tried to hand her a banknote.

"Please, this very important."

Hassie didn't see whether the nurse accepted the money, as she stared down at the clipboard until she heard the sound of the man's footsteps heading toward the elevators. When she turned around, she saw a large bandage on the back of the Russian's head.

Not knowing for sure how long the man would be downstairs, she rushed to knock on the door of room 514 and opened it. "Mr. Douglass, are you awake?" she asked in a deep voice, quickly closing the door behind her.

She winced. Her grandfather looked so frail. Blisters covered many of his skin lesions. He looked worse each time she saw him, and she knew, with a certainty, that if he stayed, he would die here.

"Seanair, it's me." She rushed to the far side of his bed and grasped the hand not attached to the IV.

"Is that you, child?"

"Yes."

"Thank goodness. I was afraid you were someone coming to stick me with needles or, worse, that you were Nurse Nancy coming in to give me a sponge bath." He chuckled. "I must admit that I fancied the idea of a sponge bath until I had one from her. I think she uses steel wool."

She smiled, then remembered that she needed to feed him the leigheas fala within moments of her arrival. "I have something for you, Seanair. It will make you feel better. I need you to drink all of it quickly." She punctured the bottle's gelatinous seal with her thumb.

"Of course, child. What is it?"

"I was told it's a leigheas fala."

"Really?" her grandfather chortled.

"You know what that means?" she asked, surprised.

"Yes, it's Gaelic for a blood cure." He shook his head, still chortling.

Is it really blood? She was a little grossed out, but blood or not, she hoped it would work.

"It doesn't smell good, but please drink it all." She put the bottle in his hand.

Her grandfather smiled. "I hope some slick vitamin store salesperson has not conned my unsuspecting granddaughter out of your hard-earned money for some advertised cure-all."

"Please give me a little more credit than that, and please just trust me, Seanair." She cupped his hand holding the bottle and nudged it upward.

"Of course, child. I trust you with my life."

"Please hurry," she urged. "I love you." *Please let this help him,* she prayed.

He drank his first tentative sip, followed by a much stronger gulp. Suddenly the hospital room door burst open, surprising him. He jumped and pulled the bottle away from his lips.

"Mr. Douglass, it's time for your—" Nancy stopped. Her hand shot out and ripped the bottle out of his hand. "Mr. Douglass, you know that you're scheduled for more blood tests this morning and are not to have anything by mouth." She tilted her wrist and poured the remaining contents of the bottle out in the bedside sink.

"No! Stop!" Hassie cried. The bottle still seemed to have been pretty full.

"You know, these fizzy drinks are not good for you right now and can interfere with the proper absorption of certain medicines."

Hassie watched in horror as the last drops fell into the sink and down the drain. "No!"

"Oh, you shouldn't be in here," she said, as though noticing Hassie for the first time. "It's time for Mr. Douglass's bath. You'll need to step out." Her tone was sharp. "And where did you get those scrubs?"

"I was cold, and one of the orderlies loaned them to me," Hassie stammered. *What do I do now?*

"Okay, well, please step out." She pointed toward the door.

"It is okay, child. It will just take a few minutes and you can come back. I didn't have much of your drink, but I am feeling better." He offered her a warm smile.

She was confident that he just said that to be nice. Despairing, she left the room and collapsed against the wall.

"What in the world!" Nancy exclaimed before swinging open the door. "Tell Doctor Stewart to come immediately!" she shouted to one of the other nurses.

"Is my grandfather okay?"

She could see her grandfather putting his hospital gown back on and pushed her way into the room. "Are you okay?"

The nurse grabbed her arm. "I'm not finished, and the doctor is on his way. You should wait outside so that you do not upset your grandfather."

"She is not the one upsetting me." He sounded stronger and his voice more resonant than Hassie had heard in many years. "We can finish the silly bath later."

"That's fine, Mr. Douglass, but Doctor Stewart will be here shortly."

Maybe it was her imagination, but Hassie thought his skin looked pinker and healthier. She pulled away from the nurse and asked, "Do you feel better?"

"Yes, much," he said, surprised. "I can inhale without coughing, and my joints feel stronger." He clenched and unclenched his fists. "I can see some shapes and a little more light. Except for my sight, I feel like I could bound out of bed."

"That's what I hoped for." She laughed in amazement, then leaned in and whispered. "Seanair, we need to leave the hospital, now."

"What? Leave to go where?" he asked loudly.

"No, you cannot leave! The doctor will be here soon." Nancy glanced out the door as she spoke.

Hassie bent closer and whispered again. "Seanair, there is too much to explain, but we're in danger and we have to leave now. It concerns those coins I found."

Doctor Stewart walked briskly through the door. The nurse said something to him and pointed. "See for yourself, Doctor."

"Mr. Douglass, I'm just going to lower the top of your gown so I can see the lesions."

"What lesions?" Hassie asked after he pulled the gown down to her grandfather's stomach.

"This is astounding!" The doctor touched several areas on her grandfather's shoulders and arms, shaking his head. "All of the lesions have not only improved; they're completely gone. There's not even any scar tissue." He took out his stethoscope and asked her grandfather to inhale. "Just impossible."

Hassie knew that the transformation wasn't impossible. She was terrified that he had drunk too little of the remedy, but it had worked. *Except for his sight, the leigheas fala has miraculously healed him.* "Doctor, can my grandfather go home now?" she asked, more as a demand than a question.

"We should run more tests and X-rays. I hear no restrictions in his breathing. It's incredible, but we need to understand why." He seemed to listen more intently through the stethoscope. "There is no precedent for this."

"My grandfather needs to leave. Can he go?"

"We really should do more tests," the doctor mumbled.

"I am feeling much better. Could I return another time for those tests?" he asked.

"Well, Alastair, we cannot hold you here against your will," the doctor answered. "You're not a prisoner, but I would strongly recommend that you stay."

Nancy returned with the phlebotomy kit. She wrapped a rubber banding around Alastair's forearm and drew some blood.

"At least that will be the last needle stick for a few days." He grinned.

"Please, let us get some X-rays before we discharge you. The discharge papers could be completed in about thirty minutes." The doctor was clearly disappointed they were leaving.

Hassie worried that the X-rays could take too long, and the Russian could come back at any moment.

As if sensing her tension, her grandfather offered a compromise. "Doctor, if the X-rays can be done immediately and we can leave straight from there, then yes."

"I'll call down to the imaging department right now to make sure they can get you in and out," the doctor assured him.

"If they can't, then I will come back another time. I also want to say that you and your staff have done a wonderful job."

"Thank you, sir, but I know that we cannot take all the credit for these amazing results." The doctor scribbled notes on his medical chart.

"Well, all the glory goes to God, of course, but He generously shares credit for the good that is done."

—

Hassie and her grandfather proceeded to the first floor for X-rays. She decided to call Carter from a hospital phone in the X-ray area. Since her grandfather was feeling so much better and they were leaving soon, she hoped Carter could let the large Russian know that he was surrendering his journal. It might entice the one smoking to leave.

The young man who answered the café phone informed her that there was a person matching John's description sitting at one of the tables, but he could not allow customers behind the counter to use the phone. She asked the worker to inform John that Olivia was on her way and would be there shortly.

As soon as her grandfather emerged from the X-ray area with his discharge papers, Hassie pushed his wheelchair toward an exit. Only then did she tell him about the abduction, the threats to both of them, and explained that they were not returning to their flat.

They'd almost reached the exit when she heard a man's voice behind her.

"Hassie Douglass! Stop!"

Chapter 16

CARTER WISHED HE could have spoken to Hassie directly, instead of just receiving the message from the waiter. She had stuck to her part of the plan, and now he needed to stick to his, whether he liked it or not. He would offer the journal and lure them in. As he patted the pistol in his pocket, he hoped that the large Russian would show himself.

Even though he had agreed to this plan, he hated to risk the journal. It was part of his family's history and of great value to his father. He felt as if he'd failed his father by veering off onto this path.

When he'd read the journal on the plane and learned of his dad's involvement, a part of him hoped he might follow in his father's footsteps and continue this hunt, as a way to honor his dad. Since Courtney died, he had felt disconnected, as if her death had severed some magic wire connecting his life and purpose to the world around him. He was truly adrift, not only because he had lost his daughter, but also because he had lost his connection to his family. He felt the journal and quest had offered him a new chance, but he couldn't abandon Hassie.

Before the young waiter who delivered Hassie's message returned to the counter, Carter stopped him.

"My date said she would be here shortly, but I still need to go and pick up something. Could I leave a few things here to hold this table?"

"Sir, we're not busy. There will be plenty of tables when you return."

"Understood, but I want to reserve *this* table." The table was just outside the entrance to the café and would be easy to monitor from a store in the covered market. He reached into his wallet and removed a fifty-pound sterling banknote.

"I, uh . . ." The waiter looked nervously from side to side.

"Please take it and watch the table for me. I'm leaving a couple items so I don't have to lug them." Carter extended his hand with the banknote.

"Thank you, sir," the waiter said, taking the money. "I'll watch your things." He handwrote "RESERVED" on the back of a postcard and placed it on the table.

"Thanks." Carter removed the modern copies of John Paul Sr.'s letter, stuffing one in his shirt pocket and the other in his wallet. He placed the journal with the original letter, encased in wax, on the table, and draped the sweatshirt he'd bought at the market over the back of the chair.

"What does your date look like, so I can keep an eye out for her?"

Since there was no date, Carter thought quickly and described a beautiful woman who resembled Mary.

"This Olivia sounds like a fine, bonnie catch." The waiter winked. "You should work hard to keep her, right?"

The man's compliment stung Carter. He was right. He should never have lost Mary. He should never have let it happen. She was still the same woman he'd fallen in love with, and they had been perfect together. He was the one who had changed. He started to dwell on these negative thoughts and then perceived that the waiter expected a response.

"I'm trying." He offered with a weak smile.

The waiter nodded and returned to the counter.

Carter inserted the battery in Hassie's phone, turned it on, and heard a chime. He closed his eyes and took a deep breath. There was a return text from the Russian.

Give us journal and letter, if you want this to end.

Carter felt a modicum of relief that the message did not mention Hassie. He texted back.

The journal and letter are on a reserved table just outside the entrance of Café Victoria in the Victoria Market. You better hurry. I'm not waiting around. Again, the girl, her grandfather, and I are finished.

He stood up, waved to the waiter, and walked to a small store across the market walkway to watch and wait.

—

Carter positioned himself in a souvenir shop across the wide corridor from the café. Standing behind a window display, he had a clear view of the table and the journal, but he could feel his heart racing, and his skin felt prickly.

I need a drink, he thought, wiping the sweat from his brow. His head hurt, and it was increasingly difficult to stand in one place and focus. *Why didn't I buy a drink, just one? Where is the big guy?* he wondered, patting the pistol in his pocket.

He checked the time on the phone. It had been thirty-six minutes since he sent the text, and his eyes darted to each person who passed. He worried if he looked away, he would miss it.

Just then, someone rushed toward the table, but it wasn't the large Russian. A young teenage boy slammed into the front of the table and reached across toward the journal. He righted himself and raced off with something in his hand.

Carter saw that the journal was no longer on the table and bolted after the boy.

The boy was fast and had a lead. He darted left at the first intersection of the indoor market.

As Carter rounded the corner, the boy was almost forty meters ahead. *I'm going to lose him in this huge mall.* He pushed himself to run faster.

Near the next intersection, the boy leaned right and looked back over his shoulder. Carter watched a young mother pushing a stroller and a man tugging the hand of a toddler behind them round the corner, coming in the opposite direction.

The boy tried to make a running leap over the stroller, but the toe of his tennis shoe caught the metal strut, and he somersaulted over and onto the ground. The stroller tipped over on its side. The infant rolled onto the cold, tile floor, screaming.

"My baby!" the mother shrieked, rushing to it.

The father, who was about Carter's size, let go of his daughter's hand and ran over, shoving the boy face-first back onto the floor.

Carter raced up.

"You could've killed my child!" the father screamed, grabbing the boy's arm and flipping him onto his back.

"I was running from him!" he said, pointing at Carter.

Still firmly holding the boy's arm, the man gave Carter a dagger look.

"He stole that book from me," Carter quickly responded before turning to the woman scooping up the baby. "Is your baby okay?"

The mother hugged the infant tightly, and the baby's screams subsided. She nodded to Carter that her infant was fine.

The father ripped the book from the boy's hand and then eyed Carter, confused. "He stole a *Bible* from you?" The father held out the leather-bound book, the covers of which had a coloring similar to his journal.

Carter stared in disbelief. "Son of a—" he yelled, turning on his heel. *The boy was a decoy*. He ran back toward the café.

He reached the table and saw the waiter on the ground, rubbing his jaw.

"I'm sorry."

"What happened?" Carter demanded.

"From the counter, I saw that boy hit the table and push your book into the chair. Then, I saw you run after him. I came over to pick up your book, when a large man grabbed it out of my hand and slugged me in the face. I'm sorry."

"It wasn't your fault." *It was mine.* He helped the waiter to his feet. "Did you see where the guy went?"

"Yes, through that exit," the waiter answered, gesturing at a nearby door.

Carter jogged to the exit, but he saw nothing. The large Russian was gone, and so was the journal. *Damn!*

"Hassie, stop!" the man ordered.

She turned, preparing to scream, if necessary, but saw Royce hobbling out on some forearm crutches and with a large white plaster cast covering most of his leg.

"Royce!" She squealed and ran to hug him.

He winced when she wrapped her arm around his bandaged shoulder, but the show of affection clearly touched him. "Thank you. The NHS doesn't let you stay very long after surgery. So, they want to make sure I can maneuver on these crutches before they toss me out later today, or maybe tomorrow. I can't use the underarm crutches because of the shoulder wound," he explained, exhausted and uneasy on his feet. "The shoulder still hurts, but not as bad as the throbbing in my knee."

"Sorry about the hug," she said, "but I'm so glad you are okay. And thank you for calling the police to let them know that I escaped."

"Yes, I'm amazed I remembered." He laughed.

"You were pretty gone when we spoke to you." She giggled. "I'm also glad you remembered to make the call anonymously. We now know that the Russian guy is monitoring police calls."

"The police said my call confirmed what had been reported by other eyewitnesses who saw you escape from the trunk and run from a large, scary-looking guy in a mask. However, the police said they cannot close the file or go much further with the investigation without speaking to you directly."

She nodded. "I can't do that yet, particularly if they are monitoring police calls. Now, come meet my grandfather."

Royce moved clumsily on the crutches.

"Seanair, this is the man I told you about," she said.

"Yes, my granddaughter told me of your heroism. I am in your debt, sir." He extended his hand in front of him. "I am Alastair Douglass."

Royce took his hand. "You owe me nothing, sir. I only wish my efforts had been more successful. However, from what I hear, Hassie needed no savior. She freed herself."

"You discount your own courage. And, as the history of humanity has recorded, we all need a savior. I thank you again."

"You're very welcome, sir." He smiled at Hassie.

"Are you recovering well from your injuries?" Alastair asked. "If not, Hassie may have something to help."

"Yes, I will be on crutches for several weeks, but I should be fine."

"Can we offer you a meal?" Alastair asked.

"Seanair! Remember, we need to leave quickly and are not returning to our flat. It's not safe." She began to slowly push the wheelchair again.

"Where's Carter?" Royce asked.

"He's delivering the journal to the Russian guy."

"Carter is giving up his journal?"

"If he can extract some information from them, he will, but if he cannot, then yes, he will give up the journal and the letter; but we really need to go," she said, explaining that one of the Russians was at the hospital.

"What letter?" Royce asked.

"Royce, I'll tell you what I know later, but we have to leave."

"You know that they may still come after you, even if Carter gives them what they want," he said in more of a clinical than an emotional tone.

"Royce!" she exclaimed sharply, closing her eyes and exhaling to calm her growing irritation. "I'm sorry. You're right. There's still a risk, which is why we cannot return to our home yet. Carter didn't share his entire plan with me, but I think he intends to confront whomever shows up for the journal. I fear his plan is reckless."

Royce shook his head. "The man does appear to have a streak of impetuousness about him. That can be beneficial in some instances, but it could also get you killed."

She pushed her grandfather a little faster toward the exit door, and Royce followed along.

"Do you and Alastair have a place to stay?" he asked. "I have an extra room."

"That's very kind, but we have a hotel room. We need to wait there for Carter to return."

"Okay, do you have a car?"

She stopped, realizing that she had not thought about transportation. It was too far to walk and the bus was too public. "Actually, no, we don't."

"Great. Let me offer you a ride. A friend was visiting and is about to leave, after I return from my crutches walk. He can drop you by your hotel."

"That would be brilliant." She leaned in to hug him again but stopped herself. "Thank you, Royce. You're a good friend."

Avery tapped the mute button on his phone headset when he heard the familiar light knock on his office door. His executive assistant entered. She had worked for him for the last twelve years, and he could attribute the longevity of her career to one thing: her discretion. He made sure she did not have access to the deepest secrets of the company but she still had learned enough. She knew his personal schedule and that he kept two sets of DHT accounting records. That would be enough to blackmail him, if she so chose, but he knew that she would never cross him. She had seen too many of his enemies and competitors disappear or meet with tragedy to think it all must be coincidence, and, to her credit, she never asked him about it. Understanding fear and greed were powerful tools, he paid her generously.

"Yes?" he asked as she approached the side of his desk.

"Sorry, sir, but Doctor Elizabeth Thresher is on the line, and you requested that I interrupt you when she called."

"Of course, good, thank you," he responded with a slight excitement in his voice. He quickly ended his other call, but he waited for her to exit before he clicked over.

"Doctor Thresher, I received your report on my Incan quipu, and I want to thank you for your diligent efforts," he began with a syrupiness to his voice. "I must admit that you came highly recommended, and you have not disappointed."

The truth, which he would never share with her, was that she was his fourth choice. The first expert only offered a limited review of the wooden base of the quipu but insisted that he was incapable of interpreting the knotted strings. The next two refused without even seeing his artifacts. To increase his chances, he doubled his proposed price for an expedited review and a confidential report to fifty thousand pounds, before he discreetly reached out to the professor of pre-Columbian studies at the University of Bologna, who focused almost exclusively on the Mayan and Incan cultures. She jumped at his offer.

"Mr. Darrow, I should be thanking you," she responded with an elated Italian accent. "The specimens you sent me are five of the most well-preserved examples of Incan quipu I have ever seen."

"Wonderful. Your report was quite helpful," he said. "Please summarize it."

"Yes, sir. Even though the Inca had no written language, they did use quipu, like yours, for a variety of purposes, but predominantly for communicating amounts," she said, as if teaching one of her classes.

Avery knew all this, but he let her continue.

"Once the early Conquistadors arrived and learned that they were a form of communication, the Roman Catholic Church ordered that they be destroyed. Such artifacts were declared to be a form of idolatry or cursed, or both," she explained. "They burned and shredded most of the quipu, destroying so much history."

"Yes, it was tragic, which is why I want to make sure that these are properly preserved and, ultimately, studied by the brightest minds." That was a blatant lie, of course. He would never allow anyone he could not control to see or study them.

"That is wonderful to hear, and I'm honored to have made your list, sir," she said.

"Your report suggests that some, like mine, may have included more than number and date information. Can you elaborate on that element?"

"Yes, in addition to their suspected use in everyday transactions, it is our understanding that the Inca used some in rituals. Many experts believe that the ritual quipu included syntax, making them literary."

"And you do believe that mine are literary ones, correct?"

"Well, before I discuss yours, I need to explain the basis for some of my conclusions. As I am sure you are aware, there is quite a bit of academic speculation regarding how to interpret any non-numerical syntax, and whether any such interpretation is even possible."

Avery had learned this last point only too well, which is why the second and third experts declined to even try. "Based on your report, you believe that you are able to translate the quipu, even though many of your colleagues refused to try?"

"With some qualifications and a few educated assumptions, as articulated in my report, yes, to a degree."

"I understand. There must always be assumptions. Now, what about mine?" he pressed. He had read her report, but he wanted to hear how strongly she asserted her conclusions.

"In my opinion, yours appear to be literary quipu. This is further evidenced by the attempt of their creators to preserve them by attaching each to a sturdier wooden base. Each of yours include references to

Pacha Kamaq, who was an adopted Incan god of creation," she began. "The first three are in amazing condition and are incredible finds, but the last two are truly extraordinary. These last two describe a different, unknown quipu, the quipu *of* Pacha Kamaq, which, if it existed, would be of incalculable value."

Avery's pulse quickened, but he said nothing and let her continue.

"I cannot say with certainty what this other quipu is. Is it one made by Pacha Kamaq himself? Is it a quipu transcribing the word of Pacha Kamaq? Or is it something else? I don't know, but your two supplied some additional information about its physical appearance."

"Please go on."

"Well, it wasn't from the quipu itself, but some of the carvings on the wooden base of one of those quipus not only depicted the symbols for Pacha Kamaq but also gold and jewels. This suggested to me that this other quipu being described was not fashioned from camelid fibers, but was fashioned out of gold and jewels," she continued in a clinical tone.

"A golden quipu. That would be interesting, wouldn't it?"

"Such a quipu would have to be something of tremendous importance to the Incas. In addition, this Golden Quipu of Pacha Kamaq would purportedly hold some dangerous but sacred truths. I believe that much of what your quipus describe are rituals for handling it and limiting the access to it to a chosen high priest."

Avery tried not to gasp. He'd heard of the possibility of a golden quipu from his first expert, but Thresher had gone further in her analyses and opinion than he could have hoped. She also confirmed what he had always believed since first acquiring his quipus. "And your thoughts on the dangerous but sacred truths?"

"Unfortunately, I cannot say what these truths are, but your quipu suggest that they could change the world and perhaps even time."

"I wish they offered more answers than questions," Avery said.

"I agree. One of the questions I have is why they chose to elevate Pacha Kamaq in this manner."

"I saw your footnote about the focus on Pacha Kamaq being curious to you," he affirmed.

"Yes, the Ichma people of Peru worshipped Pacha Kamaq as their creator god, but the Inca merely adopted and accepted Pacha Kamaq as part of the Inca's pantheon of gods when they conquered and assimilated the Ichma. Most scholars believe that the Inca revered their god, Inti, more than Pacha Kamaq. However, the fact that they would devote such a sacred and special quipu to an adopted god is extraordinary and curious. As I mentioned, this Golden Quipu would have been something of immeasurable value to the Inca, and your quipu may change our fundamental understanding about the priority of their deities," she added.

He smiled. This woman clearly had been worth what he'd paid her, but for the moment, she had served her purpose.

"Mr. Darrow, I could make a career out of the study of your quipu. With further study, more information might be revealed. Would it be possible to—"

"No. I have already scheduled certain physical testing to accurately date my artifacts." He scratched the back of his hand as he offered this additional lie. "There might be a later opportunity for you to study them further."

"Yes, sir. Thank you."

"Of course, once we find the Golden Quipu, you may have an opportunity to decipher it as well," he added.

Doctor Thresher giggled. "Well, I can certainly dare to dream, but please understand there may be no Golden Quipu. It's possible that the references were metaphorical, not literal. We cannot know without a lot more study and hopefully additional source materials."

"Understood, Doctor, but I can dare to dream too," he said, finishing the call. He would do more than dream, because he knew a few things that the doctor did not.

I know the Golden Quipu exists. I've known it since I obtained those five quipus and the first expert mentioned the Golden Quipu,

Avery thought. Since then, he had devoted himself to finding it. He had spent years and no small amount of money searching.

The early records from South America were scant and unhelpful. It was only after he focused his search on Spain's expeditions that he discovered the truth.

Avery had secured a sixteenth-century ship's manifest listing a gold-and-jeweled native creation resembling a harp. The object was delivered to King Phillip II. Other ship records suggested that some of the crew believed the item to be cursed and did not want it in their cargo.

Avery found only a few other references to the mysterious golden artifact in the records of the Spanish royal family. He learned that the royals refused to display it publicly, out of fear of the Church, which had banned all native artifacts. The artifact's reputation as something cursed grew, and the last reference to it that Avery could find was almost two hundred years later, during the reign of King Philip V.

Even though King Philip V's reign lasted almost sixty years, Avery learned that there were periods where the man suffered from a host of mental issues. These included some manic episodes that could be violent, involving biting himself and, on at least one occasion, believing he had been turned into a frog. As a result, the allegedly cursed golden artifact of the natives took on even more importance. The disturbed king was terrified of it, but he could not simply destroy it without fear of looking weak, since none of his predecessors had done so. Avery surmised from other Spanish documents that the king found his opportunity to relieve himself of the cursed item by including it among the contributions of gold offered to the Jacobites. But Avery also knew with certainty that this item must have been the Golden Quipu and that it must now be part of the lost treasure of Loch Arkaig. *The treasure and the Golden Quipu will be mine.*

Chapter 17

HOW COULD I HAVE BEEN SO STUPID? Carter berated himself. He had lost his journal, obtained no answers, and failed to keep Hassie and her grandfather safe. He still had two copies of the letter and recalled from the journal notes that his father believed some of the clues pointed to David's Tower. Carter had not planned this next move, but he was angry and didn't know what else to do. Since the Russian now had the journal, he assumed that was where the Russian would go, so he would too.

I'll find either the treasure or the Russian. He hoped he would find the Russian first, wondering whether the man really could have been involved in his father's death.

An hour into the drive, he remembered Hassie's phone was still on, so he pulled out the battery. When he stopped for gas, he borrowed a phone and called Hassie's room.

"Is it over?" she asked excitedly.

"No, he got the journal and letter," he told her. "He got away before I got any answers."

"So, what now? My grandfather is with me, but we can't live in this hotel forever." He heard the disappointment in her voice.

"I'm heading to Edinburgh Castle," he informed her and explained why.

"Do you know what to look for there?"

"No. I'll look for clues, but I'll also look for the Russian. Since he has my journal, he'll show up there. I know it."

"Carter, I'm not sure about this."

"Sure about what?" He was confused. He was doing this to help her as much as anything. "The only way this whole thing ends is to find the treasure first or to find and stop the people chasing you."

"I know, and what you're saying sounds logical, but . . ."

"But what?"

"It just feels wrong."

"What do you mean, wrong?" he asked with growing irritation.

"I can't explain why, but I just feel like you should come back here. We can decide what to do next. My grandfather thinks we should try going to the authorities in person rather than calling them."

"No," he shot back a little more forcefully than he intended, which also drew a questioning look from the gas station attendant who had let Carter use the phone behind his counter. Carter gave him an apologetic smile, turned his back to the man, and lowered his tone almost to a whisper. "You told me that the police cannot sufficiently protect you against men like this, and reporting it now would bring you into the open. David's Tower is our best course."

"Okay, maybe you're right, but it just feels like when you went off with the shotgun."

"Well, I have more than an old shotgun now." He patted the handgun tucked in his back waistband under his shirt and softened his tone. "Please, stay there with your grandfather and be safe. I'll let you know what happens."

"Okay. You be safe too, and I hope you are right," she said.

I hope so too, he thought, suddenly less sure of his convictions.

"Do you have it?" Avery asked as soon as he heard Lewis answer his cell phone. He was always careful not to use any names in their telephone conversations, which might implicate him or DHT, but he had to know whether the big man had acquired the journal and, more important, the letter.

"Yes. I bring it."

"Excellent!" Avery exhaled with a satisfied grin. With the records his men had stolen from RFS, he was confident they would be able to decipher the letter's riddle, but he needed the whole letter. Victor's journal pictures only described a couple of excerpts.

"But there is problem," Lewis said.

"Problem?" His grin faded.

"Yes. Another still wants this item, and he and his phone are on way to Edinburgh. What are instructions?"

Avery's grin returned. *Of course he's coming here. The journal notes point to David's Tower.*

"Sir?" Lewis asked.

"Is he traveling alone?"

"I believe so."

"Interesting." Avery scratched the back of his hand, working through this new development like an equation. "When you drop off the package, my assistant will have a ticket for you. I think you will enjoy seeing this attraction, and you might even run into your friend there."

"I understand. If I do, would you like to meet him?"

Avery understood what Lewis was asking and thought for a second before answering. "No, not this time, but you can offer him my personal condolences." Avery snorted. "I want you to see this attraction soon, while you can. It is very old and could collapse at any moment."

This last statement clearly surprised Lewis, and the big man was silent for a moment. Avery could almost hear his hesitancy, but he felt no need to explain himself, particularly over a phone call. Lewis didn't need to understand why he gave the order; all he needed to know was that he must destroy David's Tower without any questions. The other thing Lewis needed to appreciate, and Avery was confident he did, was that if he didn't do as ordered, he would find someone else and then go after Lewis. "Do you understand?" Avery said, a little irritated for having to ask.

"Yes. Understood."

"Excellent. My assistant will meet you in the garage to retrieve your item and provide you some tickets, as well as some helpful information about the attraction," he explained. Based on a quick online search he conducted while they spoke, Avery found what he believed would be perfect: a ticket for the special tour of David's Tower at Edinburgh Castle, beginning in two hours. Before Lewis would arrive for the exchange, Avery needed to collect the other "helpful information" for Lewis, including schematics, drawings, and pictures of different views of the castle and the tower. With Lewis's extensive training with explosives, that's all he would need to accomplish the task.

Carter reached the Edinburgh city limits a little after three p.m. Finding the castle was not difficult, since it was the most prominent part of the city's skyline. The imposing twelfth-century structure sat atop Castle Rock, a volcanic plug situated in the middle of the city.

Not entirely sure what he needed to look for when he got to the castle, he decided a tour made sense. He parked in a public garage about two kilometers away and briskly walked the cobblestoned street toward the George IV Bridge. Brightly colored storefronts lined the narrow street, reminding him of a scene from *Harry Potter*.

He stopped in a small shop advertising tickets for Edinburgh Castle. The last guided tour of David's Tower was at four p.m., and a fee of one hundred pounds promised a "one-of-a-kind" tour that allowed the participants to don hardhats and traverse down the inside walls of the Half Moon Battery, surrounding the remnants of David's Tower.

"Sir, it's three forty-five p.m.," the clerk said. "This is a premium ticket and you may end up missing the first part of the tour. We have several times available tomorrow, if you would prefer."

"No, I'll try to hurry."

The clerk nodded. "To enter the castle, you must pass through some metal detectors, but the line moves rapidly." He provided Carter with a map of the castle and used a pen to circle the locations where his tour was to begin and make scheduled stops, so he could catch up if he arrived late.

He left the store and began jogging to the bridge, when it struck him and he stopped. *Metal detectors. The gun!* They would arrest him if he tried to go through with a handgun.

Carter raced back to his car and hid the gun and spare magazines in the glove compartment. *If I bump into the Russian, at least he won't have a gun either.* He ran at a faster clip toward the castle.

He was panting when he passed through the metal detectors at 4:32 p.m. Consulting the map, he headed to the first circled location. The stone masonry, the arched halls and doorways, and the thick stone façade all looked impeccable. Unable to enjoy the magnificent view, he rushed by the entrances to the Scottish National War Memorial and the National War Museum, and past several cannons positioned along the top level of the Half Moon Battery.

Not finding his tour group at the first circled location, he descended a level and found about fifteen people surrounding a plump, balding man wearing a starched white shirt and a dark-green-and-yellow kilt.

His oversized name tag indicated that his name was Chester. He nodded to Carter when he joined as he continued informing the tour group how David's Tower, in its glory back in the fourteenth century, used to be over twenty-five meters high, but the tower's remains now stood only eight or ten meters, almost all of which were below ground level and encased by the battery.

As the guide led them to the next location and prattled on, Carter followed but only half listened. He focused on the crowds, searching for the large Russian and seeking out any clues from the letter on the walls and furnishings. His ears perked up when they reached the king's bathroom suite and Chester pointed to where the government hid the Scottish Crown Jewels during World War II. He explained how some jewels had been hidden in a hole in the wall, and a crown concealed under an ancient toilet.

Could they have hidden the Jacobite treasure in the tower walls? he wondered, but quickly surmised how difficult it would be to know without tearing down the whole tower.

When the tour group made their next stop at the site of the infamous "black dinner" of 1440, at which the Sixth Earl of Douglas and his younger brother were murdered in the presence of the king, Carter continued to consider what it would take to hide something in the stone walls of such a large hall. He checked for any areas that looked like someone might have chiseled out the stone masonry and replaced it, but he saw nothing to indicate that.

If it were me, I would place the treasure in a corner and build a new wall in front or around where I hid it. It would be faster and easier. He looked for walls or jutting stoned areas that were newer or different than the surrounding walls. He scanned the individual rooms and nooks to see if any were smaller in area than they should be, but the rooms were all uneven and most of the stone masonry appeared consistent. *Perhaps I'll see something when we look at the outside portion of the tower walls.*

The tour group moved on. "Now, for the next part, you all will need to wear special equipment," Chester announced.

Carter hoped this would be when they got to walk down into the space between the inner walls of the Half Moon Battery and the outside walls of David's Tower, below the castle vaults. He believed this part of the tour would offer the best chance to inspect the tower's walls and possible hiding places for the treasure.

A few metal posts and retractable nylon belts restricted access to a dark entrance ahead. Carter peered through the opening and saw some narrow metal spiral stairs. A tall, slender, red-haired man introduced himself as Theodore, and Chester informed the group that Theodore would be guiding them on the final part of the tour.

"Thank you all for coming, and I will now leave you in the capable hands of Theodore. Those metal stairs are not good for a large man in a kilt, or more accurately, they would not be good for anyone who might have to follow me back up." Chester cackled. "As you see, Theodore had the good sense to wear pants today."

Theodore waved and smiled, obviously having heard this joke many times before. He then handed out individual vests with reflectors and hardhats with a small miner's light to each of the tour members, encouraging them to test their lights. "Even though there are some scaffolding lights along the stairs, once we reach the bottom area, it will be dark and you will need your headlamps."

Carter smiled. *I bet they could have installed plenty of lighting down there, but they thought the darkened underground cavern and miners' lights would be more fun for tourists and justify the expensive ticket price.* He tested the headlamp on his hardhat.

"Hold on, Theodore," someone called from the stairs. Another man wearing a similar uniform ascended. "My group needs to come up before we can let yours go down," he said.

"Running a little behind today, Reggie?"

"A woman bumped her head on something and briefly lost consciousness. Nobody saw it happen, but we confirmed that there was no debris around her to suggest falling rocks or a safety issue. The medical staff brought her up on a stretcher a few minutes ago. Now we need to get the rest of my group out."

"Everyone, please step back so we can let the prior tour come up first," Theodore stated loudly and waved his arms in the direction he wanted them to move.

Carter stepped back and observed as the first of several tourists exited the stairs.

"Are you afraid of heights?" a woman next to him asked, sounding nervous.

"No, not really. You?"

"Heights terrify me. I knew that we would be going down some spiral stairs, but I didn't realize how high it would be. I'm not sure I can do this," she said.

"I'm sure you'll be fine." He turned to face her. "Just stay close to the others and try not to look down beyond the next step or two. If you can, focus on the railing and the wall."

"I'll try," she responded without confidence. "When it's our turn, would you go in front of me?"

"No problem," he offered with a smile and turned back to see Theodore standing by the doorway to the metal spiral stairs.

"Okay, everyone, it's our turn," Theodore announced. "I'll go first, and you need to follow single file behind me. Our lovely assistant site manager, Vivian, will go last," he explained, pointing to an attractive young woman.

As soon as Carter stepped onto the first narrow metal stair, it creaked under his feet. Completing the slow-moving trek down took several minutes, and the nervous woman behind him touched his back with almost every step down. The outer walls of David's Tower appeared largely flat and nondescript, offering no discernible hiding place for the treasure.

"Does everyone have his or her headlamp on?" Theodore asked when Vivian reached the bottom.

"Theodore, before we move to the first excavation site, we have a special announcement."

Theodore gave her a befuddled look. "Really?"

"One of our guests, Mr. Carter, is joining us today on his fortieth birthday. Let's all wish him a very happy birthday, or as we say in Scotland, *Là breith sona*," she said.

With a little encouragement, the group clapped and repeated as best they could, "Là breith sona!"

Since he was only thirty-three and it wasn't his birthday, Carter was slow to perceive that the group had directed their gaze at him.

Then he felt sweat forming on his forehead. Nobody here should have known his name, not even the woman scared of heights. "Thank you, but how did you know this was my birthday?" he stammered.

Vivian laughed. "Your friend, the big man with the accent. He said he was supposed to be on this tour with you but mistakenly bought a ticket for the prior tour. He saw you in line and asked me to announce it when we got to the bottom, and he would wait and listen from the top of the stairs."

I missed him, talking to that woman. He knows I'm here! Carter raced to the bottom of the stairs and looked up. He saw nobody at the top. What he did see chilled him to the bone. Attached to the bottom of three or four of the metal stairs were small blinking lights connected by some wires to a clay-like material.

"Get down!" he screamed, jumping off the last stair to the ground, covering his ears and opening his mouth. A split second later, the stairs exploded in a deafening and fiery blast.

Chapter 18

CARTER'S EARS RANG, his head pounded, and dirt filled his nostrils and covered his face. Violent coughs forced their way out. He tried to open his eyes, but they hurt and all he saw was darkness. He felt around with his hands, unbalanced and disoriented. His heart rate spiked with the terrifying and lonely feeling.

When his mind cleared, he remembered the blast, followed by an equally frightening collapsing of walls and stone around him. He also recalled a sense of falling before his shoulder and head slammed into the ground. It felt like he had fallen a kilometer, but it was probably more like five meters.

He pushed himself onto his knees, but when he tried to stand up, something large blocked him. He heard moaning and crying from someone nearby, but he couldn't see them. Worse, he couldn't help them.

This reminded him of battle and the confusion and helplessness soldiers often felt after a battle plan went horribly wrong.

Remember your training. Calm your breathing! He wiped away the dirt from his eyes and nose with the inside of his shirt. Thick dust filled the air, and he could hardly breathe without coughing.

Opening his eyes a little wider, he now saw a few small streaks of light. He realized that those were from the headlamp of his hardhat, which had fallen a short distance away. He crawled over and grabbed it. Even though the deafening rumble of rocks had subsided, he still heard large pieces of rock breaking off and falling.

The light from his headlamp revealed a large hole above him, where he had been when the bomb went off, close to the place the bottom of the stairs used to be. Only the last few metal stairs were visible; the rest were twisted under tons of rock. Seeing the devastation above, he knew that falling through the floor had probably saved his life.

Vivian's head and shoulders were visible, extending out and over the edge of the hole. Her eyes were open, but they had an empty, vacant expression. He estimated that a metric ton or two of rock had crushed her below the chest. He shuddered at the thought of her mangled corpse and remembered that six or seven other tour members had been to the right of her and were likely dead as well.

It feels just like war. All this pointless death. Why? None of it made sense to him. They could have just killed him if all they wanted was to eliminate a competitor for the treasure. *Why would they destroy the treasure's location and possibly the treasure itself?* he pondered.

They wouldn't, unless they had already found and removed what they needed. The destruction of the tower was simply to remove all traces of their activity and to eliminate me. He slumped as he exhaled.

He had lost. He had lost the journal, the treasure, and the opportunity to find the Russian and end the threat to Hassie and her grandfather. That last realization pained him more than the throbbing in his shoulder and his head. Unless he did something fast, he would lose his life down here.

"Hello! Can anyone hear me?" he called out, erupting into a coughing fit. He heard fracturing and scraping of rock above him. Some dirt and flooring beneath Vivian began to crumble. A few more rocks fell through the hole near her head.

Okay, yelling is a bad idea. His heart pounded in his ears. *Don't panic! Control your breathing. Assess your surroundings.*

He heard a groan from somewhere to his side. His shoulders and knees protested as he crawled around the jutting rocks and two more bodies, but they had no pulse. Rounding another rock pile, he saw three people. One was an elderly woman lying on her back. The other two were on their knees, patting a large gash on the woman's head.

"She's still bleeding!" a younger woman leaning over her said.

"You need to keep the cloth pressed firmly on the wound," Carter instructed. "Try not to move her head. She may also have a spinal injury from the fall."

"Okay." The young woman looked up at him with a pleading in her eyes. "This is my mother. She injured her head when we fell through the floor."

Carter recognized the other person as Theodore. "This woman needs medical attention, now."

"I know, I know," Theodore repeated blankly but didn't move.

Suspecting the man may be in shock, Carter grabbed him by the arm. "Theodore, listen, she needs medical attention."

As if waking from a bad dream, he jerked his head up. "Yes, she does, but look at all the rock above us. We are now twenty meters down from where we entered the stairs, maybe farther. They won't be able to dig us out until they believe it's safe up top, and I have no idea how long that could take."

Carter knew he was right. Getting to them from the surface could take several hours, if not days. He wondered how much oxygen was in this space. "The stairs are not an option. Is there another access to this area?"

Theodore's headlamp swept around. "Well, I've never actually been here before."

"Wait, this was your first time as a guide down here?"

"Oh, mercy no." He waved his hand dismissively. "I've guided this tour a hundred times, but we are not where we're supposed to be. We fell through the floor into this chamber or tunnel area."

Carter glanced up. Maybe it was his imagination, but to him, the hole above them appeared to be growing, and that wasn't good.

"If we get out of here alive, we'll be famous. People always suspected that there were tunnels under the castle, perhaps even leading back to the Royal Mile," Theodore said. "This is a historic find, but I cannot tell you anything about this tunnel."

"Please do something!" the young woman pleaded. "My mother needs help."

Carter leaned forward, almost nose-to-nose with Theodore. "We need to see whether this tunnel leads out so we can get help."

The guide seemed less convinced. "Sir, I told you, I don't know where this tunnel leads. It could be part of a maze, and you could get lost down here forever."

Carter noticed he said "*you* could get lost," not *we*.

"Theodore, you and I need to try," he said. "If the authorities are able to dig down here soon, then these two can be helped that way. If not, then we need to find another way out of here and bring back help for them. We can't just sit here."

Theodore's gaze darted from side to side and up and down, everywhere except at Carter.

"Theodore, I could try it alone, but we stand a much better chance if we go together." He gently grabbed the man's arm, getting him to look in his eyes again. "You know the general area and topography better than I do. I need you."

"What about her?" He pointed to the young woman.

"She needs to stay with her mom, Theodore." Carter made sure to use Theodore's name whenever he could. From his military command training, he knew calling the man by name would make a personal connection, and creating a common goal could help build trust in a time of crisis.

Theodore nodded slowly, but he looked like he might throw up.

"Which direction should we try?" Carter asked.

Theodore looked up at the hole again and the remaining stairs before pointing back in the direction Carter had come from. "That direction would be more toward the Royal Mile."

The two men crawled past where Carter had originally fallen, to where the tunnel should continue, but some of the recently fallen rubble and stone blocked the way.

"Theodore, I think we can get through, but we'll need to move some rock first."

They spent the next several minutes moving small rocks and dirt away. More than a few times, stones and rubble would fall to replace what they had just removed.

Carter's head hurt. The air felt thin, and he could feel it in his muscles.

"We're going to die down here," Theodore mumbled, rocking back and forth on his haunches.

"Stop!" Carter backhanded Theodore's shoulder—not hard, but enough to get his attention. "Focus on moving the next rock."

Finally, a small opening at the top of the blocked area widened. Carter could smell cleaner air on the other side. "Come on," he ordered as he crawled through the opening and into a wider space.

Theodore followed him and then pushed himself up onto his feet.

"At least this hole will provide some more air for that woman and her mother," Carter said, breathing hard from the exertion. The air in this tunnel wasn't filled with dust and particles assaulting his nostrils with every breath, but it was still old and dank.

The top of the tunnel was a little over two meters high, but the dim lights from their headlamps showed it narrowing ahead and the ceiling sloping down.

Carter's headlamp started to flicker. "We should hurry."

Lewis strode into a private dining room in the back of The Kitchin in Edinburgh. Avery waited at the table with a jeroboam of 2009 Philipponnat Clos des Goisses.

"I took the liberty of ordering some brill, oyster, and caviar, followed by an entrée of North Sea red mullet," he said as Lewis took a seat next to him.

He would have been satisfied with a cheap bottle of vodka and an overcooked steak, but he was here because Avery had ordered him. He never understood why his boss took the unnecessary risk of meeting in a public place, but he paid the bills and gave the orders.

A waiter filled Lewis's glass with the champagne and left the room.

"I understand there was a disturbance at the castle." Avery rolled his hand in the air as he said the word "disturbance," as if he trying to think of the proper word. "The bloody press is making it sound like the murder of William Wallace, instead of just rearranging a few bricks. Ridiculous!" he hissed. "Still, I monitored the media reports, and it sounds like the blast destroyed much of the Half Moon Battery, all of David's Tower, and resulted in approximately sixty casualties."

Lewis could hear the pleasure in his boss's voice with regard to the last part. "Did the press mention any suspect parties?" he asked, knowing that he had left no traces. The only person he'd spoken to was that female tour guide. *She is under a mountain of rock, with soldier.*

"No, my friend. Early conjecture is that it may have been a radicalized Irish group, though they could not speculate on what message they intended to send with the bomb." He snickered.

"Sir, may I ask question?"

Avery shrugged.

"Your experts say treasure may be worth between two hundred and seven hundred million pounds. This is a lot, but—"

"But why go through all this for something that may only be worth a fraction of what DHT makes?"

"Yes. It is no difference to me. You pay me well. I am just . . . curious." Lewis took a drink of water, leaving the expensive champagne untouched.

"You are perceptive, my friend. Yes, the gold would be nice, but it alone would not justify this cost and risk. No, what I am after is something that is with the treasure, the Golden Quipu."

Lewis had heard him use that term a couple of times. He assumed it was part of the golden treasure or a name for the treasure itself. He had even used the term once himself and remembered how confused the soldier's father had looked when Lewis demanded the journal and the Golden Quipu.

"Its value cannot be overstated, and thanks to you, we are one step closer to finding it," Avery said. "I have people poring over the RFS records, as well as the journal and letter you recovered. We will find it soon. I know it."

"Sir, journal stated treasure was at castle, which is now rubble," Lewis mumbled into his glass.

Avery smirked. "Do not worry, my friend. I may be many things, but I am not a fool."

He raised and shook his hand. "This I know, and I mean no insult."

"Of course not." Avery let out a small chuckle. "Please just do what I ask, and let me worry about everything else."

He knew the old man was no fool and surmised that he must already have removed what he needed from the tower.

"So, was the soldier among the casualties?" Avery slipped an oyster in his mouth.

"I believe so, yes."

"Good." He sniffed his champagne before taking a sip. "Have you located the girl yet?"

"The girl? No, did you still want her?" Lewis asked, bewildered. "It sounded like she knew nothing."

Avery was lowering his hand to put his champagne flute down but stopped. "Yes, I want her. Did I cancel my prior order?" His tone turned stern, and he stared coldly at the large man and set the flute down.

"No, sir, you did not." Lewis fidgeted.

Avery softened his tone a bit. "Think about it. This peasant girl mysteriously finds four gold coins from our treasure around the same time she joins up with the soldier, who has our letter. That sounds like more than coincidence, wouldn't you say?"

"Yes, it is very coincidence." Lewis nodded.

"Find her!" He pounded his fist on the table, almost knocking over his champagne flute.

"Yes, sir."

"Find out what she knows." He leaned forward toward Lewis. "It may help us. She should be easier to find with the soldier gone."

"Perhaps, yes. Unfortunately, the soldier had girl's phone, and he is at bottom of rock pile," Lewis explained, trying to manage his boss's expectations. "She will turn up. We are looking, and we monitor police calls."

"You can still use her hospitalized grandfather to bring her in, right?" Avery leaned back in his chair.

Lewis squirmed. "There has been another complication. Girl's grandfather no longer in hospital."

"What? Did he die already?" Avery's brow crinkled.

"No, hospital discharged him." Lewis rubbed the side of his neck.

"They discharged him? I thought he was about to die."

"Yes, this is what hospital records said."

"So, did they release him to hospice care?" Avery asked, clearly confused.

"No, it appears he had a sudden, unexpected healing," Lewis answered quickly. "Records of hospital say that doctors cannot explain. Nurse's notes call it miracle. Records also noted that the grandfather's last blood test may be tainted because grandfather drank something he was not supposed to before test, some drink the girl may have brought him. They discharge him before Gavrie—" Lewis stopped talking when he saw all the blood had drained from Avery's face. The man was terrified. Lewis had never seen the old man like this, but something had shaken him to his core.

Chapter 19

THE SMELL OF DRY ROCK permeated the air in the tunnel. Carter and Theodore had been walking for at least an hour, but they had no idea if they were any closer to an exit. Parts of the tunnel had cratered—probably due to earthquakes—and the cracked and separated ground slowed their progress. A few times, they had to stop and clear blocked portions.

Theodore talked incessantly, mostly about the history of the castle. Carter knew that the guide's annoying chatter was just the man's coping mechanism to deal with the terror of the situation and the fear that the tunnels could collapse or that they might die down here, alone and in the dark. Carter didn't try to stifle him, particularly after his own headlamp started to flicker and Theodore panicked.

Carter reassured him it would be okay. "But let's turn off your light, to preserve it until we need it."

Theodore's hand shook a little as he reached up and turned off the light. "That makes sense, I guess. I'm pretty sure my headlamp had a full charge before we started. Some of the guests' headlamps don't always get recharged until they run out."

Carter's light lasted a little less than another hour before it went out, and Theodore immediately flicked his on. The two continued for another three hours in the dark tunnels.

They'd encountered four forks, forcing them to decide which direction to go. Each decision could have meant the difference between finding an exit and dying. They'd chosen alternate directions, going right and then left, believing this would help them continue in the same general direction. Using a small rock, Carter marked the first fork with the number "1" and the second with the number "2."

Only half listening to Theodore, Carter tried to figure out how the Russian had bested him again. He figured the Russian had injured the woman on the earlier tour as a distraction so he could be the last one from his tour to come up and plant the C4 under the stairs. *He also asked Vivian to do the birthday thing only after we reached the bottom, making sure everyone below died; but how did he know I would be here?*

"These are old tunnels, but it's widely believed that the military excavated other tunnels to travel unmolested to the castle," Theodore prattled on.

So many questions swirled in Carter's mind, but he finally returned to the bigger one—why had the Russian destroyed David's Tower? Deep down, he already knew the answer. *He wouldn't have unless he'd already removed what he needed. He intended the bomb to remove all traces. All of this was for nothing. The treasure is gone.* He sagged. He wasn't sure he could feel any worse, until he heard Theodore.

"No!"

"What?" Carter asked, stepping around him.

There was a fork in the tunnel ahead, but this one had the number "2" clearly emblazoned on the wall.

"Damn!" Carter slapped the rock wall. The last one and a half hours had served only to travel in a big circle.

Theodore's headlamp flickered, and Carter thought if they did not get out soon, they would soon be in complete darkness, with no hope of ever getting out.

"We're going to die down here," Theodore blubbered

Carter couldn't allow him to continue his rant. *In extreme situations, you have to maintain the hope that you will survive, even if it's not logical.* He had seen many instances where people who believed they would not survive allowed their belief to become a self-fulfilling prophecy. Likewise, he had seen countless examples of people who maintained a positive outlook in certain-death situations and used it to propel them to find a way to make it through and survive. A positive attitude could be more important than any weapon a soldier could bring into battle.

"We're not going to die!" Carter growled. "This is a setback, nothing more. This is why I put the numbers by the forks. If I hadn't, then we may not have ever known we traveled in a circle. Now we know which tunnel we should take. We'll go down this one, and if we come to more forks after this, then I will use a lettering system to mark them so we can distinguish them as forks that tree-branched off of this one," he said. "Theodore, do you understand?"

The guide slowly nodded.

"Theodore, I need you to look me in the eye, and I need to hear you say it."

"Oh, okay," he said, regaining some composure. "I understand."

They traveled in silence for another thirty minutes before Theodore's headlamp flickered again. Carter saw something ahead when they rounded a turn—a small mound. Even though shadows covered most of it, Carter saw human bones protruding, and it stopped him in his tracks.

"The bones are too small to be an adult. They look like a child's bones," Carter said, examining the pile.

Next to the diminutive skeleton, a small set of bagpipes and a broken lantern lay strewn and covered with soot. The ground nearby had separated, creating a drop-off of a little over a meter.

"I think the kid broke his leg falling off the drop-off." Carter pointed to the child's broken femur. "The soot and charring suggest the lantern may have burned him after the fall."

"Oh my! This is the Edinburgh Piper Boy!" Theodore announced gleefully.

"You know this kid?"

"No, of course not. I always thought the story was a myth." He shook his head, but his voice turned more buoyant. "According to legend, hundreds of years ago, the people of Edinburgh discovered a web of tunnels they believed connected the Royal Mile to Edinburgh Castle. Enlisting the assistance of a small boy, they tried to map the tunnels by sending him in with his bagpipes."

"They sent a boy, alone, into these tunnels?"

"Yeah, that's the story. He played as he walked so someone on the surface could follow the music and chart the surface course of the tunnel." Theodore pointed up. "After a while, the music stopped. Searches were mounted, but they never found the boy. Some castle tour guides say they can still hear the ghostly sound of the boy's bagpipes at night, rising from below the castle. I really thought it was just a myth."

To Carter's surprise, Theodore took his phone out.

"They will never believe me without pictures." He giggled.

That's a good sign. He wants the pictures to show people when we get out. "We need to keep moving. So you will have the chance to tell everyone of your discovery."

"*Our* discovery. We'll be famous."

"You can have all the credit, Theodore. I prefer to stay out of the papers. Let's keep going." Carter moved forward.

After another fifty meters, they made a sharp right turn, and Carter saw a pile of loose stones and dirt sitting in the middle of the tunnel. The wall next to the pile was convex, as if something huge had hit it from the other side. As they approached, Theodore's headlamp went out, plunging them into complete darkness.

"Don't panic," said Theodore. "My phone has a flashlight, and it still has most of its battery life."

"Good," Carter said, wishing he had not left Hassie's phone in the car.

Theodore turned on the flashlight feature.

"Wait. Please turn it off for a second."

As soon as he did, Carter saw a few tiny pinpricks of light emanating through the cracks in the sidewall again, and he also thought he smelled diesel fuel.

Theodore flicked his light back on.

"I think this is our play," Carter announced, feverishly removing some dirt from the curved portion of the wall. He was surprised to see modern bricks after a little scraping. A few bricks were loose, and he pushed them out.

On the other side was another tunnel with a paved road, overhead lights, and a stronger smell of diesel.

The hole was too small for them to wriggle through, and they couldn't loosen more bricks by hand.

"Hello!" Theodore yelled.

No response.

Carter picked up a large stone from the pile and knocked out more bricks. When he had enlarged the hole enough, he crawled through and stood up.

"We're really going to survive, aren't we?" Theodore asked as Carter helped pull him through the hole.

"Our odds have certainly increased." Carter brushed some of the debris off his shoulder. "A vehicle must have broken that and pushed in the wall," he said, pointing to a broken and bent section of guardrail.

"I'm glad it did. This must be the military transport tunnel. There should be a guard station at the end." Theodore pointed into the distance. "We really are going to be famous."

"Seriously, just make sure they send back help for the two women. You can have all the credit for finding the lost tunnels and the bagpipe boy." Carter turned and made eye contact with Theodore again, making sure it registered. "I'm only in Scotland for a couple days, and I don't want to spend it with reporters and government officials."

Theodore seemed giddy at the prospect of taking all the credit.

After a few minutes of walking, they saw military personnel milling around a red barrier arm extending across the tunnel road.

"You saved my life, Mr. Carter, and I don't even know your first name. Thank you."

"You're welcome. My name is . . . John. It's John Carter," Carter said, not wanting to give him his real name.

Several guards rushed to surround them. Theodore explained their situation and showed them his Edinburgh Castle identification. Then he asked them to send medical personnel to help the survivors.

In the chaos and confusion that followed, Carter slipped around the security barrier and left. His journey and search for the treasure was over. He had failed Hassie and he had failed his father. One thing he would not fail at, however, was locating a liquor store. He had to tell Hassie that she and her grandfather would have to remain in hiding for a while, and he didn't want to do that sober.

Avery had been silent for over forty minutes. He paced back and forth, muttering and rubbing the back of his hand. His dinner sat cold and untouched.

"Is there a problem with the food, sir?" a waiter asked.

Neither Avery nor Lewis responded. After an awkward pause, the waiter quietly backed out.

"How could they have it already?" Avery muttered. "It's not possible." What Avery knew, but few others did, was which important historical figure had owned his five quipus when he died. That person had become as obsessed as Avery, and because of his obsession, much of the world knew Juan Ponce de León.

When Avery had purchased the artifacts with an anonymous preemptive bid through an agent, the sellers had not understood what they had, which was fine with him. The auction listed the items as acquired by Ponce de León in 1509, when he was still the governor of Hispaniola. The sellers had associated them with other unrelated artifacts Ponce de León collected among his travels. Avery had learned from other obscure sources and diaries that Ponce de León had acquired these quipus after he heard rumors about the rejuvenating powers of a mythical elixir of life.

Ponce de León had been fascinated by the prospect of a fountain of youth and had tortured many natives, which ultimately led him to the five quipus in a temple of one of the high priests. The fact the high priest chose to die rather than reveal the secrets they held convinced Ponce de León, even more, that the quipus must hold the key to finding this life-giving prize, even though he was never able to decipher them.

Since Avery learned those five quipus actually pointed to the Golden Quipu, he concluded that the Golden Quipu, with its "dangerous" truths, in fact, must have been the basis for the stories and legends of a miraculous fountain of youth. But until Lewis told him about the girl's grandfather, he didn't know whether the Golden Quipu would ultimately direct him to a place, like a spring, or whether it provided a secret recipe for a rejuvenating substance. Now he knew it must be the latter.

"Sir," Lewis offered, "if they already had treasure, why did soldier go to castle?"

"I don't know; maybe he was trying to throw us off the trail." Avery shook his head. "After all, we destroyed the tower to dissuade them from pursuing their search further."

"Perhaps, but we have journal and letter now," he said, sounding unconvinced.

"Exactly. We have them. Why would the soldier have given them up so easily?" Avery vigorously rubbed the back of his hand as he spoke.

Lewis shrugged. "To save girl and her grandfather."

"Or, because he no longer *needed* them."

"So, what now?"

"They haven't gone public with the treasure, other than the four coins, but if they have it, why not?" Avery wondered aloud.

"Because, I think, either they do not have treasure yet or they have it but do not want to make public because, like us, they do not want to lose it to government."

Don't jump to conclusions. All might not be lost, Avery thought, taking a long breath. *It's possible there could be other reasons for the girl's grandfather's sudden cure, but I need to know.*

To cover all bases, Avery would have his people continue to scour that journal and letter for clues, in case the treasure was still out there for the taking. If his fears were valid and this girl already had it, then he also needed to locate her fast. One way or another, the Golden Quipu would be his.

His back stiffened with a new resolve. "Get me every hospital, doctor, and medical record that exists on that girl's grandfather. Find her and her grandfather. Find them now! When you do, take the grandfather to the T-Farm."

"Yes, sir. We have strong network of scouts and computer people. We find them soon," Lewis assured him.

Avery raised his voice. "Get moving!"

"Understood." Lewis pushed his chair away from the table and stood. "I find and bring grandfather to T-Farm. What about girl?"

"If she's with him, then bring them both. If not, take him and make sure you leave a way to communicate with her. We can use him as bait to lure the girl, just like your original plan."

"Understood." Lewis wheeled around and forcefully pushed open the dining room door; it banged against the doorstop as he charged out.

Chapter 20

THE CRUSHING WEIGHT of his failures ground Carter down, leaving him feeling as if he had failed at life. It was almost too much to bear. He purchased three bottles of premium Irish whiskey before he left Edinburgh, and he still had almost a third of the Jack Daniel's bottle he had taken from Hassie's flat remaining. By the time he arrived at Inverness, he had finished the rest of the American whiskey. His vision blurred, he had difficulty recognizing any street markings or staying in the correct lane, and he could no longer remember the name of his hotel. Fortunately, at this late hour, nobody else was on the road.

Thinking he saw something familiar, he made a sudden U-turn and quickly sensed that it was a mistake. In trying to make a turn back, he lost control and the back tires slid. The front of the car popped up over the curb, and a stop sign appeared in front of him. His mind floated like a raft on a fast-moving river. Then, he felt a jolt and the pole disappeared under his front bumper. Not understanding what had happened and frustrated by the car's sudden and unexpected slowing, he pressed the accelerator down. A loud scraping sound ground in his ears, and he felt something pulling on the undercarriage. He pressed harder on the accelerator and finally felt the car jolt forward and off the curb.

He managed to get the car back onto the road and wondered why the vehicle seemed to pull hard to the right. He rolled down the window to let in some cool night air, but several dashboard-warning lights popped on and smoke rose from under the hood. With his foot still firmly pressing down on the accelerator and unable to see through the windshield, he tried to keep the car pointed straight. Within a few moments, the road no longer felt paved and the car bounced before slamming to a stop. Carter shot forward, and the airbag exploded into his chest and face.

"Owww!" he yelled. He was enveloped by white, as if swallowed by a giant marshmallow. Disoriented and smelling a thick, smoky gunpowder odor lingering in the air, he sensed something pointy sticking him around his ear. Looking around, he discovered what jabbed him were broken and bent stalks of grass. As the airbag deflated, he saw that all sides of the car were covered by a forest of tall grasses.

Maybe I can back out of here. He thought, but the car engine sputtered and died. His further efforts to start the car failed, but he kept trying until he spied Hassie's cell phone on the floor in front of the passenger seat.

He drunkenly laughed some more, grabbed it, and fumbled a bit before plugging in the battery and dialing a number he knew by heart.

It was a little after seven p.m. at the Navy Operational Support Center when Mary's phone rang. Seeing that it was an international number, she picked up.

"Hello," she said, closing her office door.

"Maarrrr . . . ," Carter slurred.

She recognized that drunken voice immediately. She had heard it too many times.

From her own experience, as well as what she had heard from other spouses or former spouses of alcoholics, calling exes or soon-to-be exes and blathering incoherently was what alcoholics did after they got sloshing drunk. Usually it accomplished nothing other than convincing their former lovers why they were absolutely right to leave the relationship.

"Carter? Where are you?" she demanded. Whenever he drunkenly called, she always worried he was either calling from jail and needing bail money or calling from a ditch somewhere. She could never predict when he might go off the rails again and she would get this call. The anxiety was too much to live with. "Where are you?"

"Mary, I miss you," he slurred. "I'm in a big field somewhere. My car broke."

That answers one question. He's in a ditch. "Whose phone are you on?"

"It's Hassie's phone. She's like thirteen, maybe older. I knighted her dog and—" He started coughing before finishing his nonsensical ramble. "Oh yeah, I probably shouldn't use this phone or talk long, because they may be tracking it."

"Who's tracking it? The police? Did you steal a girl's phone?"

"Nooo." He let out an intoxicated laugh, as if that were a silly question to ask. "The guys who kidnapped her. She got away, but they're still chasing her and me. They're really, really baaad guys."

"Wait, what?" She stood up from her desk, squeezing the phone so hard she was surprised the plastic handset didn't crack as she tried to take control. "Carter, stop!"

"What?" he asked, confused.

"Where are you, right now?"

"I'm supposed to be in Inverness, I think."

"Scotland?"

"Yeah. Hassie and I got a couple of rooms at a dumpy hotel to hide. It's the Regency Red Hotel or Red Regency Hotel or something like that; I can't find it. Do you know where it is?"

She bent down and scribbled the words "Inverness" and "Red

Regency" on a notepad before she continued. "No, I don't. Now, who is after you and this girl?"

"Some Russian guys. They killed the Uber driver and blew up a *castle*." He emphasized the word "castle" as if it were hard for him to believe himself. "They're really baaad."

Mary hardly knew what, if any, of Carter's story, to believe. His tale sounded like drunken nonsense, but she'd heard about the murder of the Uber driver. She had no idea what the references to a castle and a girl's dog were about, much less why anyone would be chasing him. "Carter? Are you still there?" she asked, not hearing him for a few seconds. She knew she needed to obtain as much information as she could before he passed out or hung up.

"Yup."

"Are you safe?"

"I failed, Mary. The treasure is gone, my dad is gone, and I almost killed a guy with some loud dairy cows."

Most of what he said after that was unintelligible babble, making it harder to believe any of it. She heard something about a journal, a treasure, a big Russian, a dog, and somebody tracking his phone. When he mentioned seeing Courtney by Loch Ness, however, she heard the pain in his voice, and an electric spark filtered down her spine.

"Courtney was so beautiful, Mary, just exactly like she was. I could have reached out and touched her. She was real," he said as his voice cracked.

If he started crying, Mary knew that would be the end of this conversation, and she tried to redirect him. "Carter, are you safe?"

"Sort of. I'm in the car, but I don't know where I am."

"Listen to me." She made a chopping motion with her hand as she spoke. "Don't drive. Sleep it off."

"I need to pull the battery out of the phone; they may be tracking me," he said in a manner that made her wonder whether he heard what she'd just said. Then she heard some sounds of rubbing against the phone's mic, which she assumed was his hand fumbling with the phone, probably turning it over to take off the battery panel.

"Carter!" she yelled.

"What?" she heard him ask after more fumbling sounds.

"Stop drinking tonight and sleep it off. When you wake up, find your hotel, and call me from a hotel phone." Hearing no response, she kicked her trash can in frustration.

"Yup, I'm pulling the battery out now."

"No, wait," she shouted. "Don't pull it out y—" The call ended. *Damn!*

Carter forced his caked eyelids open, his head pounding. The sun streaming through the top of the car's windshield not covered by grass pained him. His shoulder, knees, back, and cheek ached, and the front of the steering wheel looked melted. Dirt, dust, and a little blood covered his ripped shirt and jeans. He felt sick, then opened the door and threw up in the tall grass. His forehead glistened with sweat, but the cool morning breeze felt good. For a minute, he couldn't remember where he was.

He grabbed Hassie's phone and battery and stuffed them in his shirt pocket. He shoved the pistol and extra magazines in his jeans pocket and pulled his untucked shirt over the protruding handle. Still feeling the effects of the alcohol, he was challenged by the effort it took to traverse through the tall grass on the uneven ground. He stumbled and fell three times, adding a few more tears to his clothes.

When he finally made it back to the road, he looked back at the tall grass covering all but the top of his car. *I'm going to need another story for the rental car agency.*

—

From the lack of activity on the streets, he guessed the time was a little before seven a.m. Finding an open bakery, he bought four fresh scones and two large bottles of water. He wondered what the proprietor must have thought about this filthy and disheveled American, but the middle-aged woman said nothing and cheerfully accepted his money.

With a little food and a lot of water, his mind cleared, but his head and body hurt. As the sun rose, he began to recognize a few landmarks that he'd missed in the dark. He was only three kilometers from the hotel.

About an hour later, he limped through the hotel's parking lot. Not bothering to clean himself up in his room first, he knocked on Hassie's door.

She opened the door and squealed. "You look terrible!"

He saw an elderly man sitting at the side table working on a breakfast of square Lorne sausage and streaky bacon, and was surprised to see Royce in the other chair.

Hassie introduced Carter to her grandfather.

"Your grandfather looks good," he told her.

"Yes, except for his blindness, he's doing fantastic." She beamed.

"It truly was a miracle blood cure that she gave me. I thank God for the extra time I will now have with her, even if I cannot see her lovely face." Alastair smiled, squeezing Hassie's hand.

Carter didn't know what he meant by "blood cure," but he assumed the man was just being a doting grandfather.

"Hassie told me you are a soldier and that you sacrificed a lot to help her. Thank you."

"I wish I could have done more, sir."

"Nonsense, son. I am in your debt. It is your willingness to act that is important, not always the result. Remember John 15:13: 'Greater love has no one than this, that he lay down his life for his friends.'"

Carter knew that quote, but he preferred the one from General George S. Patton: "No bastard ever won a war by dying for his country. He won it by making some other poor dumb bastard die for his country." "Well, I would never forgive myself if anything happened to Hassie," he said before turning to Royce. "Wow! I wasn't expecting to see you here, buddy. How's the leg?" He patted Royce's good shoulder.

"The leg's doing better." Then, gesturing toward Hassie and her grandfather, he continued, "I ran into them leaving the hospital and coordinated their ride. I brought them some breakfast this morning so they wouldn't have to venture out." He brushed from his shirt some of the dirt that had fallen off Carter's arm when he patted him. "You do look awful, by the way. Were you at the castle when the bombing happened? The authorities think it may have been an Irish militant group."

"Yes, I was, but it wasn't the Irish. It was the Russian who shot you in the leg. He destroyed David's Tower and tried to bury me and my tour group under it."

Hassie covered her mouth. "That's horrible! I told you not to go. We all were so worried about you when we saw the reports on television."

"It was horrible, but a handful of us survived."

"Reporters interviewed a tour guide," she said. "His name was Theodore something. He said that the cave-in resulted in his finding some previously hidden tunnels under the castle and the remains of the Edinburgh Piper Boy. He said he led a group of medical personnel back through to rescue a woman and her mother."

Theodore the Lionheart, he thought, smiling and shaking his head. "Yeah, we got pretty lucky with the deeper tunnels."

"So, you really were there?" she asked.

"I was, and I even managed to hang on to your phone," he said, removing it and the battery from his shirt pocket. A folded, damp, and dirty piece of paper also fell out of the pocket and fluttered to Hassie's feet. "Don't use the phone until we know it's safe," he reminded her.

She picked up the paper. "What's this?"

He had almost forgotten. "It's a copy of a letter from John Paul Sr. to his son, John Paul Jones, written in 1767. It only came into my possession recently, after my father died, but it's been in my family for a long time. My father believed that something in the letter would lead to the Jacobite treasure," he said with a defeated tone.

"Why didn't you tell me about the letter? I mentioned John Paul Sr. to you when we first met, but you said nothing," Royce asked with more than a hint of accusation.

"Two reasons. First, I wasn't sure I could trust you. Second, I wasn't sure about your dubious claim to a share of the treasure."

"May I see it?" Royce requested.

Hassie looked to Carter, who shrugged. "Go ahead. I doubt it matters anymore. The treasure is gone." He plopped down on the corner of a bed.

"How do you know?" she asked.

"General Porter's journal notes about the letter state that the 'heart of the groat' and the 'young king' referred to King David II. My father's notes concluded that David's Tower was the place where a king should rest his head, as referenced in the letter. It all made sense. The treasure or the key to finding the treasure was in the tower. Thanks to our Russian friend, that is now a pile of rubble." He lowered his head and massaged his temples.

"So, the treasure is gone and not still in the rubble?"

"The man who did this is heartless, but he's not stupid. He, or whoever he works for, would have removed everything they needed before they destroyed the castle."

"Now that they have your journal and the treasure or the key, when do you think my grandfather and I will be safe?" Hassie asked.

He'd been dreading her question and arched his aching back before answering. "Unfortunately, it's uncertain at best. I'm so sorry. I hoped that I could confront the people behind this and end it for you, but I failed."

Royce seemed pensive, studying the copy of the old letter.

"So, I guess your claim to a share of the treasure is pretty worthless," Carter said to Royce. "At least we can dispense with the lawyers and an extended lawsuit." He laughed, but nobody joined in.

"Well, if you're giving up, then Hassie and I will take your share of the treasure." He smiled, not taking his eyes off the letter.

"What are you talking about? The treasure or the key is gone. Even if we knew where they took it, I'm not sure one pistol would be enough to challenge them," he said, reaching down to pat the gun in his jeans pocket, but it was gone. *Idiot! It must have fallen out when I tripped in the grass.*

"I don't know if the treasure is gone, but I do know that the treasure or key was *never* in David's Tower." Royce sounded certain.

"That's where my dad said it was, and it's where they hid the Scottish Crown Jewels during World War II. How can you be so sure it wasn't there?"

"You said that you went on a guided tour, but obviously you didn't listen to what they said, did you?"

"Well, I was about forty minutes late for the tour." He felt his face reddening. "Why?"

"There are *two* reasons," Royce responded. "First, in 1753, when John Paul Sr. would have hidden the treasure, Edinburgh Castle was a British stronghold. A Jacobite loyalist wouldn't have hidden the treasure—and the last remaining hopes for the cause—in the midst of their enemy."

Carter was unconvinced. "Well, it would have been the last place the British would've looked."

"Unlikely. The Jacobites would've needed quick access to it."

Carter shrugged.

"The second reason is the most compelling. In 1753, John Paul Sr. would never have heard of David's Tower, much less been able to direct his son there."

"What are you talking about? It was built in the 1300s."

Royce nodded. "Yes, that's correct. King David II built it as part of the living quarters for Scottish royalty. You were also correct when you said that the Scottish government used the Tower to hide Scotland's jewels from the Nazis."

Carter nodded, as if Royce were helping to make his argument.

"But in 1573, Sir William Drury destroyed most of the Tower as part of the Lang Siege. A year later, the Half Moon Battery was constructed on top of the remains. It wasn't until 1912, when an archaeologist rediscovered the remnants, that anyone knew that part of the Tower had survived. Until then, few had even heard of David's Tower for almost 350 years."

Carter's jaw dropped.

"So, John Paul Sr. would never have hidden a treasure there or used clues to direct his son to a place he had probably never heard of or knew existed," he said.

Carter was dumbfounded. Royce was right. The treasure or key was *never* at David's Tower. *Before I got involved, I assumed that General Porter's and my father's studied opinions and conclusions about the letter should be given deference, instead of putting in the work and reaching my own conclusions. A classic leadership mistake.* He could almost see some of his old instructors at the Academy shaking their heads at him in disappointment.

General Porter was wrong, Dad was wrong, and I was wrong— again. He now wondered whether his father might have discovered his mistake after visiting Scotland. *Perhaps that was why he never added any more journal notes.* Carter noticed Royce was looking at him, waiting for some response.

"You're right. The treasure or key was never there." He nodded with respect.

Hassie nodded as well.

"Why would they have blown it up, if it had nothing to do with the treasure?" Carter wondered aloud.

"Well, they had your journal notes," Hassie interjected. "If they knew that you believed the treasure or key was there, then destroying it before you could confirm that it was a false lead might prevent you from searching further. You might just give up, if you survived at all."

"Maybe, and it would've worked," he agreed. "It's just hard to comprehend the level of evil it took to kill so many innocent people, just to throw us off the trail."

"I like that you used the word *us*," Royce said. "I also like the theory about the letter pointing to King David II. His likeness is on the groat, and as the son of Robert the Bruce, his story and history would have been well known in Scotland, even during John Paul Sr.'s time."

"If it is not too much trouble, could one of you read the letter aloud?" asked Alastair.

Royce did as Alastair requested.

Hearing the letter read, Carter once again felt there was something familiar about it. The thought needled him, just on the edge of his memory.

"Any thoughts?" Hassie asked.

Her grandfather laughed, a hearty and healthy laugh.

She chuckled. "What is it, Seanair?"

"Sometimes only the blind can see."

"Sir?" Carter asked.

"I think I know where the letter is directing you. Mr. MacArthur is correct. It was not David's Tower."

Mary tossed her canvas carry-on bag into the overhead bin above her coach-class seat. The ticket had drained another $2,200 from their savings account.

Unlike Carter, she formally requested a leave from the navy, and she received one for a week. She set her flight return date in six days.

Carter creates some drama, calls for help, and I come running. It's the same toxic pattern, she scolded herself. Even though she had initiated the divorce proceedings, she still had feelings for him and couldn't abandon him. They had shared a life and, for a time, a beautiful daughter.

She slid into her seat, thinking about his drunken call. Only getting bits and pieces, he had said something about a treasure, a young girl, and blowing up a castle. His words still made no sense. She was tempted to call the police or Interpol, but she decided not to, since it all may have been part of some drunken delusion and she did not want to increase his troubles.

A flight attendant asked for her order, and she considered ordering a stiff drink, but she requested a Diet Coke. Alcohol had caused enough problems in her life.

If nothing else, maybe I can convince Carter to return and make some effort to salvage his military career and preserve his freedom. If not, then others will decide his fate. She wasn't sure whether she would succeed, but she would try.

Chapter 21

SCROUNGE DRANK FROM the hotel room toilet, then loped out and put his head on Carter's knee.

"You really know, Alastair?" Carter asked, rubbing the dog's head.

"Please read the third sentence of the letter again."

"'I wish that we could make the journey together, *mac mo ghràidh*, but I am weak, and like the young kings of the past, your nose has always pointed you toward the distant hunt,'" Royce read.

"In that one sentence, the author mentioned the young kings of the past, a nose, and a distant hunt, as well as a Gaelic reference." Alastair lightly tapped his nose. "That is the only time Gaelic is used. Why there?"

"I see it!" Hassie exclaimed.

"What is the Gaelic word for nose?" Alastair asked her with a knowing grin.

"It's *sròine*," she answered, smiling.

"Correct, and for Urquhart Castle?"

"*Caisteal na Sròine*." She giggled. "The word *sròine* means nose or nostril, which makes Urquhart Castle the *Castle of the Nose*." She hugged her grandfather's shoulders. "Seanair reminded me of that shortly after I began working at the Inn. It always struck me as funny."

"It's compelling," Royce said.

"There's one more thing," she added. "The Inn has several brochures about Urquhart Castle and its history. Unlike Edinburgh Castle, Scottish royalty never lived there. The only known Scottish monarch to have ever visited was King David II. He used it once as a hunting lodge."

Royce clapped. "It would make sense. English soldiers destroyed most of Urquhart Castle in 1692 to prevent the Jacobites from using it as a stronghold. When John Paul Sr. acquired the gold, it still would have been accessible to the Jacobites, and English soldiers would not have given the ruins a second glance."

"You've convinced me." Carter held up his hands in surrender.

"So, Urquhart Castle it is," Royce agreed.

"One problem." Hassie held up her finger. "I've been several times, and there is no treasure, just some empty rooms and ruins."

"I understand, but you weren't looking for treasure or clues," Carter said.

"No."

"Your perspective might be different this time, and with Royce's knowledge of Jacobite history, he might spot something as well."

"What about the Russian?" Alastair asked. "Don't put my granddaughter in danger."

"I'll be with her, and I won't leave her, sir. I promise. The Russian thinks I'm dead, and he's not looking for Royce. We can scout the area before Hassie gets out of the car." He looked at Royce with eyebrows raised, waiting for him to confirm.

Royce nodded.

"We won't take any unnecessary risks," Carter added. "We'll also take the dog. He's already shown his willingness to protect her."

"Seanair, I don't want us living in fear. We need to find the treasure and end this so we can be safe. You're healthier now, and we have a lot to look forward to."

He nodded slowly. "I will wait here and pray for you all."

"You're going on a trip, boy," she said to Scrounge, who barked in response.

"Hassie, you know that we cannot keep a dog," her grandfather reminded her.

"I know, but this is probably the first time he's ever slept indoors. It's like a vacation for him."

"I know you believe you are doing this dog a kindness, but exposing him short term to an easier life could make it harder for him to return. Unless one of your friends is going to adopt him, he will have to return."

She turned pleadingly toward Royce.

"Sorry, I can't." Royce shook his head. "I'm finishing my degree in marine science, and once I get a permanent position, I may have to travel a lot."

Hassie turned to Carter with pouty, puppy-dog eyes.

He laughed. "I'm only here for a couple days and my future looks uncertain after that. I'm in no position to adopt a pet. Sorry."

"Well, we still have today." She patted the dog.

"We can use my car," Royce announced. "I borrowed it, since I needed an automatic transmission to be able to drive in my leg cast."

"Okay, I need to take a shower and call the rental car agency for another replacement," Carter said, not bothering to explain. "We can leave after that."

Hassie arranged the food they had gotten for her grandfather's lunch and, if necessary, dinner, on the side table and explained to him what was there and where it was on the table.

"Seanair, we'll call you when we're done." She hugged him.

"Be careful, child." Alastair hugged her back. "I'll be here."

She shut the door to the hotel room. When she reached the car, Royce said, "Your grandfather loves you a lot."

"Yes, we're all each other has. Well, except for Sir Scrounge here." She smiled and reached down to pat his ribs.

"Did you really name him *Sir Scrounge?*" Royce asked, then sniggered.

Before she could explain, Carter's hotel door opened.

"Do you think you'll need that?" she asked, seeing the shotgun hanging on Carter's arm.

"It's better to have a weapon and not need it than to need it and not have it."

"You'll have to leave it in the car. They won't let you enter with it," Royce said, hobbling on crutches to the driver's side of the Zafira.

Carter placed the shotgun in the back of the small minivan, covering it with a thick blanket, while Hassie and Scrounge jumped in the back seat.

"Want me to drive?" Carter asked.

"No, but thank you." Royce swung his leg cast into the driver's seat. "This is a borrowed car. I cannot let someone else drive, particularly someone who's been drinking."

Even though she had only known Royce for a short time, Hassie could tell his last statement was made without intending insult.

"I was just offering." Carter waved his hand dismissively, hopping in the passenger seat. "Besides, how do you know I've been drinking?"

"You reeked of alcohol when you arrived. And I saw vomit stains on your shirt." Royce rolled his eyes. "You remind me of my friend's five-year-old son. Finding his wife's chocolate cake destroyed, his father asked him if he ate it. Chocolate cake covered the boy's face, hands, and hair, but he vigorously claimed his innocence. It was all his dad could do not to laugh."

Carter clenched and unclenched his jaw, and Hassie could swear she saw the back of his neck redden. As far as she was concerned, Carter deserved what he got for asking such a stupid question, and his reaction told her he thought so too.

"You should throw that shirt away. Those stains are not coming out," Royce added, pulling onto the road.

Carter clicked on the car radio and turned up the volume, earning a sideways glance from Royce.

"So, what are we looking for when we get there?" Hassie asked.

"Any place large enough to hide a treasure or for anything that might correspond to something in the letter." Carter pointed at the copy he'd pulled out to read again.

"That makes sense. The letter mentions a key, so it may not be the treasure at all."

Royce nodded. "So, we really don't know what we are looking for, but we hope we'll know it when we see it."

"Three sets of eyes are better than one," Carter parried.

"I've certainly heard of worse plans." Royce smiled.

"I think that may be the closest to a compliment you'll get from Royce." Hassie giggled.

"Knowing Carter, that may be true," agreed Royce, and they all joined in a lighthearted laugh.

"Wow, luck is on our side," Hassie said, pointing to a car backing out of a space at the onsite parking area. "Tourists usually have to park in a remote lot, away from the castle."

"We'll leave the car running," Royce said as he and Carter jumped out to scout the area, leaving Hassie and Scrounge in the car.

She nodded, smiling at Carter's less-than-stealth disguise of a cap pulled down over his eyes.

After ten minutes, they returned.

"We hit a good time. Two tour groups just left, so not many people are in the exhibit now. Nothing looked suspicious," Carter assured her.

Royce turned off the car, and the trio, along with the dog, made their way to the visitor center. A scale model of the castle in its glory days sat near the gift shop, and they spent forty minutes inspecting it and chatting about possible hiding spots, until Hassie noticed a few patrons taking too much of an interest in their conversation.

"Let's go out and look around," Hassie suggested.

Royce and Carter agreed, and they ventured to the actual ruins, walking past an ancient trebuchet. Several acres of lush green grass surrounded the castle and extended to the shore of Loch Ness, but to enter the ruins required crossing a concrete walkway over a dry moat. She pictured the drawbridge that used to be there and gazed up at the guard tower connected to the large arched stone entrance.

Initially, they focused on the castle's residence and master chambers areas, where a king would have rested his head, but the remaining structure was incomplete, and none of them saw anything noteworthy.

"Where to next?" Royce asked.

"I hoped that something would jump out at us."

"There is still more to see," Hassie urged.

Carter nodded. "Let's check out Grant Tower. There's a reference to the word 'tower' in the letter."

"It's hard to miss. It's that huge, square structure over there, down from the guard tower." Hassie gestured, and they made their way over.

"British attacks destroyed the roof and upper levels of the tower," Royce explained.

They followed the signs to the two levels they were allowed access to. Hassie's shoes scraped on the reinforced metal grating that had been installed on the area that was safe to walk. She looked through one of the barred windows and surveyed the grassy area behind the tower and the large, bushy trees by the shore of the Loch, a short distance away.

"You know, compared to Edinburgh Castle, this is a lot more of a fixer-upper, even after the bombing," Carter whispered.

After another hour, Hassie could tell that Royce was getting tired and Carter was slowing down.

"Anything?" she asked, discouraged.

"Not yet. Royce?"

He shook his head.

"I was sure this was the right place. Everything pointed here." She stamped her foot.

"I agree, but we're just not finding anything," Royce said.

"I did too, but I was also pretty certain about David's Tower." Carter frowned. "I'm not ready to give up. Let's go take a look at the outer walls. At least I won't have to pay a ridiculous tour fee to check these out."

They walked along the edge of the outer wall of the guard tower, toward Grant Tower, and Royce grabbed Carter's arm as he was about to step off the paved sidewalk. "We are only allowed on the sidewalk and paved areas."

"I just want to look," Carter said, gently removing Royce's hand. "Hassie, doesn't Sir Scrounge need a bathroom break about now?" He winked.

She nodded and smiled. "You know, I think he might. We wouldn't want him going in the castle or on the sidewalk."

Carter turned to Royce. "You stay here and try to distract anyone who gets curious."

Royce shook his head, and hobbled back toward the entrance.

If the exhibit personnel caught them, Hassie knew they wouldn't get into serious trouble. They casually strolled in the grass, toward the tower.

She felt Scrounge pull hard on the leash. "I think Sir Scrounge really does have to go." She laughed. "What are you expecting to find out here?"

"Not sure. I just wanted to check all sides."

"Thanks, Carter. I'm really grateful that you and Royce are here, trying to help," she said.

"Don't thank me yet. For all we know, I may be leading us astray." He smiled.

Something told her he wasn't. Perhaps it was just a gut feeling, but as soon as Carter asked whether she and Scrounge should come out behind the tower, she could have sworn she heard something in her head say yes.

Scrounge bounded up, lifted a leg, and relieved himself on the outer wall of the castle.

She checked around to make sure nobody had seen the dog desecrate the tower. Nobody seemed to notice them. She could no longer see Royce and assumed he had moved back inside.

When the dog finished, Carter and Hassie inspected the outer walls, being careful about where they stepped.

"Look." She pointed to a spot on the wall about two meters off the ground.

Carter turned.

"It looks like someone chiseled the word *Benson* there, and it looks like it's been there for a very long time." She turned to Carter, and his lower jaw hung open. He appeared dumbstruck. "What?" she asked.

"I'll be damned!" Carter slapped a fist into his palm. "That's why that old letter sounded so familiar," he added, almost mumbling.

"What?" Hassie repeated with more urgency. "What is it?"

"Hassie, get Royce!"

"Why?" she asked, a little frustrated that he hadn't explained why he was so exhilarated. "I don't think he'll come out on the grass."

"Then tell him that you and he were right. The letter pointed here. Drag him if you have to." He pulled out his copy of the letter with a huge grin as she started back to the castle entrance.

Lewis insisted on hourly updates on the search for the girl and her grandfather. He monitored the news on the castle bombing. Most of the reporting still blamed an Irish fringe group and mentioned only three survivors—a male tour guide and two women—but the interview of the guide disquieted him. He mentioned a fourth survivor, an American named John Carter who had a birthday to remember.

Damn! He slammed his palm on the table. He knew that survivor was Carter Porter, not "John Carter." Lewis picked up his phone and called one of the few non-Russians working for him.

Percy was British and one of the best computer hackers available. Lewis could accomplish a lot through blunt force, but on occasion he needed someone like Percy. Any hacker could break into a system and steal a few credit card numbers, but Percy was an artist. He could be in and out without the target knowing that he had breached their system. Not only could he steal information, he could plant some without leaving a single electronic fingerprint.

"Have you checked girl's phone?" Lewis barked.

"Yesterday, when it pinged on the road to Edinburgh. Afterward, you told us not to worry about the phone. Why?"

"It may not be under pile of rock," he said. "Check now."

Lewis stewed for almost two hours before Percy called back.

"The last phone ping was at 12:34 a.m. this morning, in Inverness. We already had assets in the area. They located Porter's abandoned car."

"Where?" Lewis demanded.

"It was half buried in some high grass. There was some kind of accident, as if someone might have run the car off the road. It was badly wrecked, and we also found Gavrie's pistol in the grass."

He didn't understand who would have run the soldier off the road. *Is there another player involved?* "What happened?" he asked.

"Not sure. Nobody has filed a police report, and we saw only the tire tracks from the abandoned car. It may have been a one-car accident, but we don't know."

"See if soldier or girl registered in any hotel nearby."

"That won't be necessary," Percy said. "We searched the rental car company online. We confirmed that Porter called them about a wrecked car. He asked for a replacement car to be delivered in town, not at the Bonnie Ness Inn, which the agency had listed in their records as his hotel. The agency also noted that his call appeared to come from a hotel named the Red Regency Hotel."

"Excellent," he said. "Find out room number and text to me address and directions."

"Yes, well, that hotel is ancient, and none of their files are accessible online. We would have to manually check their records onsite to confirm."

Lewis smiled. "I will confirm when I get there."

—

Lewis picked the lock of the door for room 134 in less than a minute. He entered quietly, but the room was empty and the bed untouched. A heavily soiled shirt lay bunched up in the corner. He checked each of the drawers. Except for a couple button-down shirts, they were empty. He moved on to room 138's lock and nudged the door open.

"I thought you were going to call me first. Did you have any luck?" the elderly man asked.

"I would say yes, good luck, Mr. Douglass."

"Who the devil are you?" Alastair demanded, fumbling for the hotel phone.

Lewis slapped him hard across his cheek and ripped the phone out of his hand.

Alastair lifted his arms over his head, but they were no defense against the three palm strikes from the Russian that left his upper lip bleeding.

Lewis relished the smell of fear from helpless prey. When Alastair crumpled in his chair, Lewis called Avery. "I have grandfather. Girl not here." He listened and nodded. "Understood. Gavrie will take him to T-Farm." He hung up and turned back.

"Hey, old man." He kicked his leg. "Where is granddaughter and soldier? You said you expected them to call. Where they go?"

"You're the man who abducted her."

Lewis said nothing.

"She is far away and not coming back." Alastair straightened up defiantly.

"Be still and this will not hurt much," Lewis said, removing a small syringe from his coat pocket. He flicked off a rubber tip cover and tapped the syringe a few times.

Chapter 22

CARTER SMILED WHEN he saw Royce hobbling toward him on crutches, with Hassie and Scrounge at his side.

"What did you find?" Royce asked, uncomfortable being out on the grass.

Carter pointed to the name on the wall. "Hassie spotted that."

"That name was not in the letter." Royce furrowed his brow.

"I know," Carter said reassuringly. "Something in that letter sounded familiar to me, but I couldn't put my finger on it."

"Now you can?" Hassie asked.

"Listen, Plebe Summer was the commencement of my time at the Naval Academy. They teach you how to salute, march, and other things."

Hassie and Royce glanced at each other, confused.

"As a plebe, I had to memorize and spout back to upperclassmen certain information about important naval figures, including John Paul Jones. We not only had to memorize the names of the ships that John Paul Jones captained for the Continental Navy but every ship that he ever served on before that, along with additional facts regarding those ships."

"Why?" asked Hassie.

"I don't know, it's a navy thing. That's not the point."

"So, the Benson was a ship?" Royce asked.

"No!" He held up his hand, frustrated.

Now Hassie's eyebrows furrowed.

"Plebe Summer was a long time ago, which is why it took me a while to remember. The very first ship Jones sailed on was the *Friendship*. He was very young and still lived in Scotland. The captain of that first ship was named Benson. Benson!" Carter repeated the name and pointed up to the chiseled name.

Hassie grabbed the letter from Carter and read it aloud again.

"Now, notice the word 'your'? That word prefaces the word 'nose,' which led us here, to this castle. The word is also used three more times—'your King George,' 'your friendship,' and 'your two friends.'"

Royce still looked dubious.

"Just hear me out, buddy." Carter put his hand on Royce's good shoulder. "Jones's first three ships in order were the *Friendship*, the *King George*, and the *Two Friends*. Jones's father died long before Jones made it to America. Those first three would have been the only ones Jones's father would have known. In fact, Jones was still on the *Two Friends* when his father died. According to the letter, the *Friendship* brought his father a tower of pride. That ship was captained by Benson." Carter again pointed to the chiseled name on Grant Tower. "Remember, he wrote this letter to his son, intending it to be something that only his son would understand."

Now Royce's jaw dropped. "You make a very compelling argument, and I agree with your logic. However, if you're correct and Mr. Paul chiseled that name on the wall, what now? Though the castle is in ruins, I don't think they will let us knock down walls."

"I don't think we'll have to," Hassie said. "The letter also says, 'If I close my eyes, I can see you walking that last twenty falls toward the sea.' So, I think it means we should walk about twenty paces toward the water."

Carter nodded. "There's a lot of water around here, so the exact bearing from this wall is a little unclear, but it should be somewhere out there." He gestured to the grassy area between the tower and Loch Ness. "Look for something related to those ships."

Royce stepped out from the wall to the left, Hassie to the right, and Carter in the middle. "There's a lot of overgrowth. So, look carefully," Carter called out as the three continued to fan out.

"Hey," Hassie shouted a few minutes later. "I see something chiseled on this garden stone."

Carter raced over and helped brush away some grass. Etched on the rock was a length of chain, with the middle link bent and broken open.

"My God! That's it!" Carter cried.

"That's what? That's not a ship. It's just a broken chain," she challenged.

"The *Friendship* was a merchant brig that sailed between England and Australia. However, the *King George* and the *Two Friends* were slave ships," he explained. "The picture of a broken chain was a symbol used for freed slaves."

Hassie looked at Royce, who shrugged.

"I misread the part of the letter talking about the need for Jones to leave his two friends to receive all God has planned for him," Carter admitted, as much to himself as the others.

"How so?" Hassie asked, then read that part aloud: "'The right choice for you, of course, requires you to leave your two friends. This is the only way for you to receive all that God has planned for you.'"

"Jones was an amazing sailor with a storied career. But learning his history at the Academy colored my perspective. When I read that passage before, I read it as something written by a father who could see his son's destiny of greatness at sea and encouraged him to leave his family and friends to fulfill that destiny. But I was wrong. John Paul Sr. was proud of his son's sailing on a merchant brig, but obviously he wanted his son to leave the slave trade. This letter was written by a father who was trying to save his child's soul before he died," explained Carter, bowing his head.

Royce chimed in. "That makes sense. Scotland was a leader in the abolitionist movement and outlawed owning slaves around 1758, even though other elements of the trade were permitted. That would have been only nine years before he wrote that letter."

"Did Jones follow his father's advice?" Hassie asked.

"Eventually, yes." Carter lifted his head and nodded. "By the time he sailed on the *Two Friends*, Jones was the first mate, which would have entitled him to share in the lucrative profits of that ship. Jones's father died in 1767, shortly after writing this letter. When the ship made port in Jamaica the next year, Jones had become so disgusted by the slave trade that he left the ship and his share of the profits."

"If my grandfather were here, he would quote Mark 8:36: 'What good is it for a man to gain the whole world, yet forfeit his soul?'"

"So, where do you all think we should we go from here?" Carter asked.

Royce took out his copy of the letter and started to laugh. "I think I know."

"Really?" said Hassie.

"I think Carter is absolutely right about the importance of the word 'your' in the letter. 'Your nose' directed us to this castle. 'Your friendship' directed us to that wall with the name Benson. 'Your two friends' led us to this stone. That leaves 'your King George.'"

"Right, and Carter said that was the name of the first slave ship."

"Yes, but it was also the name of a real person—a person who was the king when this letter was written. King George III," Royce explained.

"Okay?" Carter knitted his brow.

"Look at the last sentence of the letter." Royce read it out loud. "'Sometimes, our choices can leave us uncertain as to whether to move forward or backward, but know that the journey's end will always be at least two ells more.' Jones's father was a true Jacobite. He would've hated King George. Remember, they tried to assassinate King George II but failed. King George III succeeded him in 1760. Where should *your* King George rest his head?" Royce asked before answering his own question. "Not in the royal suite of a grand palace. For a Jacobite, the proper place for him to rest his head is two ells straight down." He pointed to the ground. "An ell is about a meter in distance."

"Six feet under." Carter smiled. "That makes sense."

"Yes, it does."

"We can't dig here now; too many people. We'll need to come back tonight."

Avery drove his metallic black Bentley Mulsanne through DHT's expansive crop fields where genetically altered corn and wheat were grown and tested. Few field workers even looked up as he drove by.

All employees of the farming operations knew of him and the off-limits area on the northeast side. Tall, electrified fences and hundreds of mounted cameras surrounded the area. A large, single-story, metal-frame building and a multilevel garage sat inside. Foliage netting stretched above and across the structures, making the facility invisible to anyone who might fly overhead. What could not be seen by anyone on the surface, however, was the state-of-the-art, three-story, underground genetic testing facility directly below the metal-frame building.

At the gate, security personnel checked not only Avery's security card and identification, but also required him to exit the car so they could check the inside and trunk. Avery had insisted on these standard security protocols, without exceptions. After passing through, he drove a short distance to the garage, where personnel directed him to a parking space near what appeared to be a nondescript service elevator. He dialed a randomized security code and submitted to a retinal scan before the elevator pinged and allowed him to get on to travel down.

Avery was told Alastair Douglass had still been unconscious when he arrived but that he should be waking up soon. He quickly headed toward Examination Room B, which he understood held their new patient. A trim man with short, straight black hair and a wheatish complexion greeted him outside the examination room.

"Mr. Darrow, I was about to call you," Dr. Naj Aggarwal said.

"Doctor, do you have the results?"

"Preliminary results, sir, but yes."

"Good," he said, directing the doctor into a small consultation room.

"Sir, our findings are as fascinating as they are puzzling. We believe that the patient orally ingested a drug of some kind. As a result, a material percentage of it would have been diluted and destroyed by stomach acids before the remainder would be absorbed through the stomach lining."

"Get to the point. What did you find?"

"Whatever this drug was, it appears to work via a short-lived two-pronged attack. The first prong supercharged the lymphatic and immune system, immediately enhancing the production and effectiveness of T cells, B cells, and phagocytes."

"In layman's terms, please, Doctor, and hurry."

"Yes, sir. All of these help a body fight infections, germs, and foreign bodies."

"And the second prong?" Avery asked.

"The second prong is even more amazing and less understood. Somehow, it has the ability to reboot the damaged cells so that infections, diseases, and malformed or invasive cells—such as cancer cells, for lack of a better description—are reprogrammed from within," Dr. Aggarwal said with a childlike sense of wonder.

"Reboot, like a computer?"

"Sort of. Like a computer, when you reboot, most codes revert to their default settings. That is what this prong appears to do at the cellular level. It resets the cells. Combined, these two prongs explain why the observed effect on the patient was immediate. Blistering lesions, for example, would completely disappear before your eyes. According to his medical records, the patient had myriad problems affecting various organs, tissues, and muscles, even cancer, which had metastasized in his brain. With the exception of his vision loss, they all appear to have been cured, at least for the moment," he finished, sounding awed.

Avery nodded with a distant gaze, as if it were exactly what he had expected to hear. But he wasn't pleased. *That all makes sense if they have the Golden Quipu.*

"Even more, this substance has the ability to trigger and reboot certain stem cells," the doctor added.

"What?"

"His medical records indicate the patient had his appendix and gallbladder removed, but they appear to be regrowing." Dr. Aggarwal shook his head. "In fact, it is very possible that his eyesight would have already been restored and the organ regrowth complete, but the narcotic your men used may have suppressed or countered some of the drug's efficacy. We can't know for sure, because we have no explanation for how or why this worked."

Avery shook his head in disbelief. *They must have found it, and it truly is an elixir of life.* He vigorously rubbed the back of his hand. "Can you reverse engineer it?"

The doctor shifted from one foot to another. "We need to do more testing, and I would still need a clean sample of the substance itself. We do not know what mutations and reactions occurred when it interacted with this patient's system." He nervously flattened his bushy eyebrows as he spoke. "Without a sample of the substance, there are just too many variables. I also need a larger baseline of patients. Without these, our efforts to reverse engineer could take decades."

"That is unacceptable, Doctor."

"There is another complication, sir," Dr. Aggarwal added, averting Avery's glare. "This drug appears to be rapidly disappearing from the patient's system. It's almost like it has a natural kill switch."

"Is that bad?"

"Not necessarily." He shook his head. "But we have concerns for this patient. We do not know how much of the mystery drug he consumed or whether there might be a critical volume that must be consumed," he said.

"Why? Why is that a concern for Douglass?"

"Sir, this drug is extremely potent, but it may act in a manner similar to antibiotics." The doctor shrugged, as if that explained everything.

"Meaning?" Avery sighed, irritated he had ask.

"Sorry. If someone stops taking their antibiotics as soon as they feel a little better, instead of completing their entire prescription, the infection could come back more aggressively and resistant to that antibiotic." The doctor reluctantly looked up at Avery as he explained. "We don't know, but we're afraid that could happen with our patient. His blindness was one of the last symptoms of his cancer, but it was not cured, even though everything else was. Perhaps it was because of the narcotics your man injected or maybe an incomplete dose. We don't know." Dr. Aggarwal shoved his hand in the pocket of his lab coat and clinked something metal, which served only to irritate Avery more.

"You seem to be avoiding something. More specifically, what does that mean?" His eyes bored through the doctor like a hot knife through soft butter.

"Mr. Darrow, we cannot know for sure until the drug has run its course and completely disappeared from the patient's system. Will his cured status stabilize and remain, or will his diseases and ailments return? If they do return, will they return as quickly as the drug cured them, like a tidal wave? If that happens, it will kill Mr. Douglass."

"Your medical opinion?" Avery barked.

Dr. Aggarwal fidgeted, then rushed through his conjectures. "I strongly fear the latter. We already see a few signs of deterioration in some organs, and the regrowth of his appendix has all but ceased. We estimate that the drug should be completely gone from his system within a couple of hours. If there is a faster deterioration, we may need to put the patient in a coma to reduce brain swelling from the onset of symptoms, which could kill him. Of course, even comatose, his other returning ailments could kill him."

The doctor took a small step back, probably expecting Avery to explode, but he didn't.

Instead, Avery stopped rubbing the back of his hand and smiled. Not a smile of joy, more like the smile of a hungry shark about to bite into a wounded sea lion. *A drug can have two basic functions. It can cure or cause harm. A drug with the ability to cause every prior ailment or condition to reappear could provide the basis for an extremely powerful bioweapon.* His smile broadened.

Whether the secrets of the Golden Quipu offered a miracle cure or a harbinger of death, he didn't know yet, but he began to calculate the potential profits from either and both. "Thank you, Doctor. Can I see our patient now?" he asked with an eerie calm.

"Yes, he's waking up." The doctor nodded, led Avery to the room, and opened the door for him.

"Mr. Douglass, can you hear me?" Avery observed the cold, dazed man as he came out of his induced slumber.

"Where am I? Who are you?" Alastair yanked at the restraints locking his wrists to the bed.

"You're in a medical facility. I'm your host." He leaned over the bed's railings.

"Why have you taken me?"

"Mr. Douglass, may I call you Alastair?" asked Avery with a fake charm that did not sound natural.

"No."

"Very well." He straightened back up. "First, we are fascinated by your inexplicable cure, and we need to study it."

Small beads of perspiration appeared on the elder man's brow.

Your body will always betray your true feelings, Avery thought, baring his teeth. *He's truly afraid, and he should be.*

"Let me go!" Alastair demanded, pulling at his wrist restraints.

"My Russian associate said you told him that your cure came from something your granddaughter gave to you, a leigheas fala." He patted the elder man's wrist restraints, taunting him. "I do like that name, by the way."

The sweat on Alastair's brow grew. He looked scared and confused, obviously trying to remember when he would have provided that information and wondering what else he might have told them. "I don't know what you are talking about," Alastair said, his voice cracking a little.

"Come, come, Mr. Douglass. Lies do not become a man of your years."

"Release me!"

"I'm sorry, but I cannot do that *yet*." He loved giving his prey hope that they might escape, when there was really no chance whatsoever.

Alastair grit his teeth. "What do you want?"

"Many things. Let us start with information. Where is your granddaughter and Carter Porter?"

"To the devil with you!" Alastair spat in Avery's direction.

"Then, let me try a different tack." Avery coolly leaned in to whisper into the old man's ear. "Did they find the treasure at Urquhart Castle?"

Alastair recoiled. He quickly tried to right himself, but the damage was done.

Avery just shook his head, a part of him wishing this could have been a little more challenging. His own experts had suspected the letter he obtained from the soldier might point to Urquhart Castle, but they weren't sure of other clues in the letter yet. Alastair's drugged answers to Lewis's questions were not helpful. He'd peppered the man with questions about where he, his granddaughter, and Carter found the treasure, but Alastair just annoyingly repeated, "Not at David's Tower."

Avery wondered how this old man could have resisted the effect of the drugs. However, seeing his startled reaction to the mere mention of Urquhart Castle gave him more answers than his own drugs did. Normally that would have bothered him, but what he found more disturbing was the confirmation that they had beaten him to the treasure.

How could they have already obtained the Golden Quipu and uncovered its secrets? This man and his granddaughter, and even the soldier, are peasants.

He wanted to dismiss the notion of anyone beating him, but he could not reject the evidence lying in the bed in front of him. Nor could he dismiss his own medical experts' conclusions on the inexplicable cure. *They must have obtained it and somehow deciphered its secrets. There is no other explanation.*

"Thank you, Mr. Douglass. You have been most helpful." Avery smirked. He hated the feeling of being behind, but he knew that the game wasn't over. He had the girl's grandfather. He knew his experts' belief about Urquhart Castle had been correct. And very soon he would possess the Golden Quipu, the leigheas fala, and the gold.

"No, you will not harm my granddaughter!" Alastair raged, which only made Avery grin as he watched the feeble old man fight helplessly.

In a move that surprised even himself, Avery reached down and grabbed the blind man by the throat, squeezing hard enough for Alastair's eyes to go wide and his thrashing to cease. Smiling, Avery let the quiet terror of the moment sink in.

Through his orders to men like Lewis and the doctors at the T-Farm, he had controlled the fate of many men, but this was the first time that he'd *actually* held someone's life in his hands. He was not the physical type, but he had to admit he liked this very much. He felt a rush of adrenaline flood through him. The feeling of complete power over another was intoxicating. *I could do it; just squeeze a little harder.* But he stopped himself. He knew he still needed this man, at least for now.

"What happens to you and your granddaughter will depend on whether she gives me everything I want," Avery hissed and released the elderly man's throat. He turned on his heel and left to go to his office.

As soon as he got back, he called Lewis. Avery still held a smile on his face from the that last moment with the blind man, and he could tell his heart rate remained elevated from the exhilaration.

Chapter 23

CARTER SAW THE QUIZZICAL LOOK on Hassie's face when she used Royce's phone to call her grandfather. She quickly hung up.

"Everything okay?" he asked.

"Yes, I'm sure it is," she said. "No answer, but he may be taking a nap or in the bathroom. I'll try again after we get to Royce's place."

The rest of the way to Royce's rented semidetached duplex, they rode in silence.

Royce pulled into the driveway and opened the car door. "The shovels are in a shed, in back."

They started to follow him, but Carter watched as Hassie stopped and stared at the cell phone, almost as if she were afraid to call.

Carter gently took the phone. "I'm sure he's fine, but let me give it a try," he said. "If no answer, then we'll jump in the car and head back. Deal?"

"Deal." She nodded. "Thanks."

Carter hit return dial, and someone answered on the first ring.

"Alastair, this is Carter," he said.

Silence.

"Alastair, can you hear me?"

"I hear you fine," a gravelly Russian voice responded. "I missed your call earlier, but I knew you would call back."

Carter gave Hassie a grave look. Her face darkened and she grabbed onto his arm.

"Where is Mr. Douglass?" Carter demanded.

"He is not here, but he is in safe place. Is girl with you?"

"No, I have no idea where the girl is." He held his finger to his mouth, hoping Hassie wouldn't say anything that could be overheard. "You already have what you want—my journal and the letter. Now let the old man go."

Hassie squeezed her eyes closed, and her fingers dug into Carter's arm.

"We do not have what we want. We think you have treasure we want. Now, we have grandfather."

He did not like where this conversation was going. "We don't have the treasure."

"If you play dumb, we send you old man in pieces."

Carter's stomach churned and knotted. He worked through possible responses in his head, but he could visualize each one making the situation worse. He said nothing.

Royce hobbled back and opened his mouth, but Carter held his finger up again.

"Bring us Golden Quipu, a sample of leigheas fala, and rest of gold. We bring you grandfather. This is good trade, I think, at least for girl."

Carter noticed that he did not say anything about delivering Hassie too, but he didn't have to. For some reason, he knew she would still be a target, and regardless of what they promised, they did not have to honor their bargain.

"You want a Golden Quipu and a fala?" Carter asked before he could stop himself. He didn't want the Russian to think he was playing dumb, but in this case, he was dumb.

His stomach sank again, and he feared he had made a huge mistake.

"You play dangerous game, soldier. Talk to girl. Golden Quipu was with treasure and looks like large golden harp with jewels. Girl knows this. You know this too, I think."

He wasn't going to argue, but he had no idea what the Russian was talking about. He needed to buy some time. "Let Mr. Douglass talk."

"You should listen better and talk less. Grandfather not here, but he is in safe place. Not so safe if you refuse."

"It will take some time." Carter consulted his watch. It was almost seven thirty p.m.

"You have two hours."

"We need at least twenty-four. We can only retrieve what you want at certain times, to avoid security personnel." He looked at Hassie and Royce for support, but they both shrugged, not sure what Carter was agreeing to. "There is a lot of gold."

"Understood." He paused a moment. "You have twelve hours. Turn on girl's phone. Text me when you have it. If longer than twelve hours, there may not be much left of grandfather."

—

Carter slumped into one of Royce's kitchen chairs as Hassie berated herself.

"It's my fault. I never should've left him alone," she said, fighting back tears.

"No, Hassie, I think it's my fault." Carter stooped even farther in the chair. "After the Edinburgh Castle bombing, I thought I'd lost everything. I got drunk, crashed my car, and I think I may have used your phone to call my wife." He stared at the ground. "I was stupid, and I'm so sorry. That may be how they tracked us to the hotel."

She was quiet for a long moment. "If it was, you didn't do it intentionally, Carter, and you've tried to help us."

"Thank you, Hassie. We'll get your grandfather back," he said, though he had no idea how. He still blamed himself, but her forgiveness was an incredible act of generosity.

"He's old and can't defend himself." She quivered and covered her face with her hands.

"Carter, exactly what did the Russian demand?" Royce asked.

"Besides the gold, he wants something with the treasure called a Golden Quipu. He said it looks like a golden harp with jewels." He tapped his temple as if trying to recall the other item. "He also said he wanted a sample of something he called the leigheas fala."

Hassie's back straightened, but she said nothing.

"He thinks we already have the treasure and this other stuff. He also thinks that Hassie knows about it." Carter raised his palms in question. "Hassie, do you know about a Golden Quipu?"

"No, I've never heard of it." She shook her head.

"Royce, what about you? Is it part of your Jacobite history?"

"No, I've never heard of it either." Royce shook his head as well. "Is that fala thing supposed to be with the treasure too?"

"He didn't say, but I guess so." Carter shrugged. "Have you ever heard of it?"

"No, it means nothing to me." Royce shook his head again.

"Hassie?"

She paused and screwed up her face a little, as if not sure how to respond. "Yes, I've heard of the leigheas fala, but I'm not sure you will believe me."

Her answer surprised Carter, and apparently Royce too.

"It's an old Gaelic term meaning a blood cure."

"A blood cure, like what your grandfather mentioned?" Royce asked.

"Yes, it's a liquid, something to drink. Someone gave it to me, but I really don't know what it is. It was red, like a vegetable juice, and it smelled really bad."

"Do you have any more of it?" Carter asked.

"No," she said, then told them about the disembodied voice or spirit who filled two Irn-Bru bottles with a liquid that this voice called leigheas fala. She described how it miraculously cured Scrounge and even though he only took a couple of sips, it cured her grandfather of everything except his blindness. "I don't have any more of it."

Carter tried to hide his skepticism, but Royce's expression did not.

"I promise you it's true. Even the doctor called it a miracle," she insisted.

"That's a lot to take in, but I saw the dog. He was at death's door. Now, there's not a mark on him," Carter said. What she said sounded unbelievable, but he knew that it sounded no more unbelievable than seeing his dead daughter. He did not share that with them, knowing they would have said he was delusional or just drunk.

"You're right. When they wheeled me to the ambulance, I saw the dog bleeding out," Royce said, now bending down to inspect Scrounge.

"I don't know what it is. I prayed for help. The voice answered and helped me, Sir Scrounge, and my grandfather."

Carter was not sure he believed all of it, but he was in no position to challenge her. "Do you think you could request more of it?"

"I can't promise, but I can try," she offered. "I can do it while you're digging. I'll take Sir Scrounge, so it'll be just as it was before."

"Do you have any bottles of Irn-Bru?" Carter asked Royce.

"A few in the refrigerator." He indicated with his thumb the refrigerator behind him. "I guess, to quote Sherlock Holmes, 'Once you eliminate the impossible, whatever remains, no matter how improbable, must be the truth.'"

"If we're going with fictional detectives, I would choose Scooby-Doo. In fact, much of my life has been guided by vintage Hanna-Barbera cartoons," Carter joked and poured out the contents of two Irn-Bru bottles into the sink.

"That certainly explains a lot about you." Royce laughed as he grabbed and emptied a third bottle. Then he poured a bottle of V8 juice into it. "Just in case the mysterious spirit doesn't answer you, Hassie," he said, "does that look like your leigheas fala?"

"That's a good idea, but I think the red was a shade lighter." She added a little tap water into the top and shook it. "The leigheas fala was thicker and smelled worse, but the color is closer now."

"Okay, it's only eight p.m.," Carter said. "There may still be

tourists at the castle, so we need to be very careful. I would've preferred we wait until much later, but we don't have the luxury of time."

"We still need to get the shovels and picks from the shed," Royce
reminded him.

"Thank you both," Hassie looked at each one as she said it.

Carter dug into his small satchel and pulled out his last two miniature bottles of alcohol he still had left from the plane. He cracked open
the screw top of one.

Hassie's mouth dropped. "What's that?" She pointed angrily to the
bottle.

"It's just a little to calm the nerves," he said defensively.

"Please don't. We need you."

"Yeah, but it's just . . ." She turned her back on him, and he glanced
at Royce, who shook his head at Carter in disappointment.

He was about to say something else but stopped. Suddenly, for the
briefest moment, he could visualize himself in a mirror, and he didn't
like what he saw. *How many times have I offered that excuse for my
drinking? Even now, after I've hurt this girl and put her and Alastair's
lives in danger. What is wrong with me?*

Then, he did something he had never done for Mary. He screwed
the top back on a full bottle of alcohol and returned it to the satchel.
"Okay. I won't."

Royce nodded. "Good. We should go now."

"Thank you," said Hassie when Carter set the satchel down on the
table and stepped away.

Royce stopped as they walked to the car. "Listen, they have Alastair,
and they know about the leigheas fala, so they may also know about
Urquhart Castle. This could be a trap."

"If they think we already have the treasure, they should wait for us
to bring it to them; but you're right, we shouldn't assume anything."
Carter nodded.

Hassie agreed, jumping into the back seat.

"Of course, you know why you shouldn't assume, right?" Carter asked, trying to lighten the mood.

They both stared at him.

"You know the old joke. When you *assume*, you make an *ass* out of *U* and *me*."

Royce gave Hassie a sideways glance and started the car. "Well, mate, I don't know how anything that you do or assume could make an arse out of me, but I think we can all agree that you are an arse." He chuckled.

"No argument." Carter laughed. He had to admit, there was a lot about this young man that he liked.

Dr. Aggarwal shouted orders at the medical personnel scrambling around Alastair's bed. At times, it was hard not to just stare in awe. The elderly man's body withered and decayed right in front of them, like something from the end of the old movie *The Picture of Dorian Gray*. It was sickening to watch but impossible for the doctor to divert his eyes.

Alastair's skin turned sickly gray and his arm and leg muscles sank and atrophied. His chest heaved with each breath. Blistering lesions popped up everywhere, and he suffered violent spasms. The medical staff had no idea what to do.

"Mr. Douglass, can you hear me?" Dr. Aggarwal asked.

No response.

He knew he was losing his patient. "Give him the propofol, now!" he barked, hoping to induce a coma and slow the brain swelling.

The nurse attached a small bag to the IV, and the old man's restless writhing subsided.

A short time later, Dr. Aggarwal paced outside Avery's T-Farm office, running his fingers through his unwashed black hair. *We did everything we could*, he told himself, but he feared that might not be enough to avoid Mr. Darrow's wrath. He lightly tapped on the office door and entered.

"How is our patient, Doctor?" Avery asked, looking up.

"Sir, we had to induce a coma. The recurrence of so many symptoms caused brain swelling. We'd hoped the coma would allow us time to treat his other symptoms. We tried everything." The doctor wiped the sweat from his eyebrows. "Unfortunately, it was not enough, and fifteen minutes ago, Mr. Douglass lost all brain function. The onslaught of so many medical issues was just too much for the frail body to weather."

Avery squinted and rubbed the back of his hand. "Can you keep him alive?"

It was an odd question. "Mr. Darrow, the patient is brain dead. Mr. Douglass is on a ventilator, which permits his heart, kidneys, and certain organs to continue to function. I wanted to speak with you before we removed the ventilator."

"Have you obtained all the blood and tissue samples you need?"

"Yes, we took several samples and biopsies. The most valuable were those taken when the patient arrived. Cancer and related complications riddled the samples we collected a few minutes ago. It is hard to believe that they were taken from the same patient." The doctor ran his hand through his hair again. "Can we remove the ventilator?"

Avery said nothing for an agonizing few seconds. "The death of the girl's grandfather is a setback, to be sure, but I know my plan could still work," he mumbled to himself as he punched his fist into the palm of his other hand.

"Sir?"

"No, Doctor. Keep the patient on the ventilator, and make sure he will be ready to move in a few hours."

"Move?" the doctor asked, confused.

"Yes. We are going to exchange our patient for the leigheas fala and an instruction manual for creating it. In short, we will trade a worthless corpse for the greatest treasure in human history," he said, sounding almost ebullient.

Perspiration covered Dr. Aggarwal's forehead.

"For my plan to work, Doctor, we need our patient to appear to be alive. Do you understand?" he asked, eyeing the man without blinking.

Wiping his brow, Dr. Aggarwal thought about how he had long ago given up any ethical or moral illusions about his work at the T-Farm. DHT paid him too much to pass up. He'd deluded himself into believing that he was advancing medicine without the constraints and delays of laws and regulations. They could test and modify new drugs in real time. Scientists learned as much from a drug's failure as they did from its success. Of course, there were cruelties, and many test patients suffered and died. At times, he still struggled with violating the first rule of the Hippocratic Oath—*do no harm*. He realized that Mr. Darrow still waited for his response, and there was only one acceptable answer.

"Yes, Mr. Douglass will be ready to move."

Chapter 24

AFTER COLLECTING SHOVELS, flashlights, and other tools they thought they might need for a night dig, Carter, Hassie, and Royce drove to the Inn. For almost an hour they drove back and forth until they saw no other headlights on the road. A little before eleven p.m., Royce pulled off the road closest to the part of the shore Hassie had directed them to. Even though lights surrounded the Inn, the shoreline was dark.

"Okay, you get out and do your thing," Carter said. "Royce and I will head to the castle and start digging. If you see anything suspicious, run to the Inn and make as much noise as you can."

"Agreed, and I'll have Sir Scrounge," she responded, rubbing the top of his head.

"The bravest of all the canine knights." Carter chuckled.

"He is indeed." Hassie smiled. Then she handed the bottle of diluted vegetable juice to Carter. "Let's leave this one in the car. If my prayers are answered, I don't want to confuse them."

The air was cool when she opened her door, and Carter felt a light mist coming through.

"I still wish we could all stick together," Royce said.

"I know, but we discussed it. You need to start digging, and I don't know how long this may take, if it happens at all." She waved them off. "And I want the circumstances to be as close to the same as before."

"If you succeed before us, then come to the castle. Be careful on your approach, just in case. If we succeed before you do, we'll come back here or look for you at the Inn," Carter said.

"Agreed." She turned, and Carter and Royce pulled away.

—

The two men pulled into the parking lot at Urquhart Castle. Carter thought the ruins looked almost ghostly at night. The few security lights mostly pointed inward, not out at its perimeter or behind Grant Tower.

Royce let the car idle for a little with the headlights off as they watched for any movement. Carter saw nothing, not even a security guard.

"It all looks pretty quiet. You see anything?"

Royce shook his head. They got out and started to unload their gear. "I've never done this, you know—trespassing and damaging property." Royce looked out at the castle grounds.

"It's for a good cause."

"That's the only reason I'm doing it." He let out a heavy sigh. "We need to keep an eye out for the police. If we're caught, there will likely be some stiff fines and a night or two in jail."

Carter stifled a laugh. Given the risk of running into the Russian here, and his court-martial back home, a couple nights in a Scottish jail didn't sound too bad.

Royce took longer to navigate the uneven ground and thick grass on crutches. He insisted that Carter bring a shovel for him and intended to help, whether Carter wanted him to or not.

"Point your flashlight down, not around, if you need it. We don't want to draw any attention," Carter suggested when the two men met at the stone with the broken chain symbol.

Royce turned his flashlight off and used the little moonlight slipping through the clouds overhead.

Carter was thankful the misting had stopped. He first excavated the surface, roughly in the shape of a large rectangle. The rainy conditions had kept the first meter of dirt saturated, but he found digging was more difficult after that.

Royce had to wait until Carter dug deep enough that he could lower himself into the hole. He braced his cast against the side so he could deliver a harder jab into the soil without falling over.

Carter knew Royce was doing his best with the pick, but he made scant progress. Although Royce was not yet supposed to put any weight on his bad leg, he helped loosen some of the packed soil.

When they had made it a second meter down, Carter felt his shovel hit something solid. He cleared the dirt around it and saw the edge of a log. "Thoughts?" he asked, puffing and wiping his sweaty face.

"No idea, but there seems to be another one." Royce tapped his pick on a small exposed piece of a second log.

"The logs are tilting toward each other." Carter pointed.

"What does it mean?"

"I wonder," Carter muttered. He cleared more dirt along the first log until he reached the edge of the hole.

"Shouldn't we keep digging down and around those logs?"

"First, dig a little farther to the side of your second log and see if you hit another log, and let me know if that one is angled too."

Within a few minutes, Royce found a third log. "Yes, I found one, and it is angled inward, like the other two."

"Hah! My friend, I think we have a wagon wheel." Carter laughed, slapping Royce on the back.

Royce looked unconvinced. "That would have to be the world's biggest wagon."

"Sorry, I meant, we have a hub and spokes. It's a wagon wheel design."

"Is that good?"

"I think so, but it depends on what we find at the hub." He shrugged. "If you bury something small, you risk never finding it again unless you dig in the exact same spot. The deeper you bury, the greater the risk. The hub and spoke design would allow you to be off by several meters and still find a log, or in my analogy a spoke, to lead you home."

"That makes sense, I guess."

"Any markers you leave on the surface, like a garden stone, could be moved or destroyed. As long as you know the general area, this design is very useful." He continued to dig a small tunnel toward the hub.

Even though he didn't complain, Carter was sure that Royce was glad to have a rest, particularly given his condition. Carter dug on his hands and knees along the log until almost all of his body was in the miniature tunnel he'd created. Then, his shovel clanged against something.

"What did you hit?" Royce asked.

"Not sure yet." Carter backed out. "Hand me a flashlight." He waited to turn it on until he extended his arm into the tunnel to conceal the light from the surface.

Royce bent down. "It looks like a stack of rocks. Did we hit more ruins?"

"I don't think so. It's like a miniature pyramid. See how it tapers up at the top. All of the logs intersect here, at the hub." He pointed to the small rock structure, which was about a meter squared.

"So, you really think that's it, and not just more ruins?" Royce rubbed his forehead, leaving behind a streak of mud. "You know, for someone to use this design would require a lot of effort. Wouldn't all of that digging and logs draw attention?"

"Probably, unless you had a ready excuse, like being a gardener."

"Maybe, but that pyramid is not a mountain of gold," Royce said.

"No, but it could be the key to finding the treasure."

"That's right, the letter referred to a *key*." Royce nodded enthusiastically. "I hoped we would find the treasure."

"Yeah, me too." Carter smirked and lightly clapped Royce's shoulder again. "C'mon, let's see what we found."

"Wait!" Royce grabbed Carter's arm and pointed toward the parking lot. "That's not good."

Over the top of the edge of the hole, Carter saw blue and yellow flashing lights. He watched the police car pull into the parking lot and stop next to theirs. Two officers got out. One inspected the car, then crossed the concrete walkway bridge into the castle. The other walked around the perimeter, in their general direction. Carter's pulse quickened. There soon would be no way to miss them or their huge hole.

The two men crouched back down in the hole. Carter sucked in his breath and held it, hoping the man would not turn their way. His mind raced through options, but few were available.

Carter stole another peek over the top of the hole. The officer was heading in their direction, but he was looking back over his shoulder toward the entrance and the other officer. Carter picked up a small rock from the hole. *If I can throw this against the castle wall, behind the officer, maybe he'll head back the other way to investigate.*

He pulled his arm back and readied to throw, when gunshots shattered the quiet night. The echoes off the stone ruins made it hard to tell where the shots had come from. But after the fifth, he could tell they'd emanated from the entrance of the castle, where the first officer had gone.

Hassie placed the empty bottles of Irn-Bru upright, close to the water's edge, just as she had done before. She waited for an hour, but the bottles sat untouched and unchanged. She paced back and forth along the shore, with Scrounge prancing by her side. The cold breeze off the water swept across her face, and discouragement set in.

Finally, she knelt down in silent prayer. *Are you here?*

A comforting warmth washed over her.

Yes, child, I have always been here.

"Please, I need more leigheas fala for my grandfather."

I gave you leigheas fala for your grandfather. I can see your heart, child. I know why you are asking for more. I am sorry, but I cannot give it to you for that purpose.

"Please, my grandfather's life depends on it!" she pleaded.

That is not true. I know of the false bottle that you brought with you. It is no sin to deceive, if used to prevent the commission of an evil.

"I know, but they could kill my grandfather." Her eyes watered.

Child, I do not refuse you out of spite. The leigheas fala is a precious gift. It was bestowed to me, along with the awesome and sometimes painful responsibility of deciding when to use it. When you offer the leigheas fala with love, it has the power to work miracles.

"I know. It worked miracles for my grandfather and Sir Scrounge."

Child, if I provide you the leigheas fala for a ransom, the men you give it to would contaminate it into an unspeakable evil. I have seen their hearts, and it saddens me. Countless numbers would suffer and die. I cannot allow that, and I cannot allow you to be a part of that. Even though your motives are pure, your actions would contribute to moral and physical evil on a global scale.

Hassie recoiled, as if she had been punched in the gut. She hadn't considered why they'd demanded it, only that it was part of the ransom. Her grandfather would never want her to give them a tool for evil, even to save his life. She was uncertain of what to do. "Are you sure?"

Yes, I am, child. I sense that you are wondering what your grandfather would want. That is right and just to consider. Your grandfather would forgive you because he loves you, but he would never forgive himself for all the pain and death that would result, simply to spare his life. You know this to be true.

"I know you're right, but I'm so worried about him that part of me still wants to give them anything they ask." She held her palms open as she spoke.

I understand that more than you know. Unfortunately, I now must ask you to do something that will not ease your burden.

Hassie didn't understand.

For what your friend John must do, he needs two strong legs. I need you to give him the leigheas fala.

"John? Do you mean Carter? 'John' was just a pretend name he used."

No, not Carter Porter. I mean your friend Royce. His name is John Royce.

John? she wondered, looking over to see that one of the two Irn-Bru bottles was full. "Please don't ask this of me," she begged. "I'm not sure I can do it. I know they would use it for evil, but I also know that it could help free my grandfather, and once I have it in my hand . . ." She stopped herself. "Please don't ask me to do this. I'm just not sure I'm strong enough."

I am sorry. You are one of the few who heard my call and answered. I wish that meant an easier life for you, but that is not always true. I need you to do this. I know you are strong enough. Your heart is pure and your colors are bright. I am confident that you will make the right choice.

Hassie picked up the full bottle and stared at it, then she and Scrounge ambled toward Urquhart Castle.

In time, you will understand, child.

As she walked, Hassie was not sure what she would decide. She knew the right choice was to give it to Royce and that the kidnappers would corrupt it into an evil, but it also could save her grandfather. She had never faced a temptation or choice like this. *It's not fair.*

No, child, it is not fair, but I know you will do right.

As she approached the castle, she heard gunshots and instinctively dropped to a knee.

Mary sipped her third cup of coffee in the food court at Heathrow Airport. The airline had delayed her connecting flight to Inverness. While she waited, she called and texted the cell phone number Carter had used to call her, but there was no answer.

Where are you? she thought in frustration, but also with concern. She couldn't help but wonder whether he was really in trouble or if what she'd heard on the phone from him had just been drunken babble. When he drank, he could do some stupid and even reckless things, but for some reason this situation felt different and her anxiety rose.

She could not allow her anxiety and negative thoughts to consume her, so she tried to distract herself and use the time to search online for hotels near Inverness. She located a few references to the Red Regency Hotel, but no website. If she did not hear from Carter by the time she arrived, she knew that she would head there first.

She felt the vibration of a text but laughed when she saw who sent it. It was from Chuck.

Mary, I guess you are running late for dinner tonight. Let me know if you can still make it and I will shove your dinner in the oven to keep it warm.

She had all but forgotten about his lame extortion, and now, for the briefest of moments, she allowed herself to fantasize about all his appendages that she would enjoy breaking, one by one. *This isn't helpful, and don't let him win by wasting any more of your time.* She tried to focus on more constructive thoughts. She texted him exactly where he could shove his dinner and put her phone back in her pocket.

When he'd first made his unethical and illicit proposal, she hoped that she would have had time to turn the tables on him, perhaps capture him on a recorded line and get him to incriminate himself. Of course, everything had gone sideways again when Carter drunk-called her. Now, she was just too tired and too angry to pursue her counterattack. Chuck might actually follow through on his despicable threat, but when faced with two awful choices, she had to go with the least awful one. Not that his proposal was even a choice.

She did have to make a "least-awful" choice when she served Carter with the divorce papers, and that had felt like she was breaking off one of her own limbs.

She pulled her phone back out of her pocket and tried calling Carter again.

Chapter 25

THE OFFICER CLOSEST to Carter and Royce dropped to a crouch after the first gunshot and whipped around.

A split second before the officer's flashlight washed over them, Carter saw something shimmering roll between them and the officer, as if a thin curtain of water drew closed. Unlike the last time he'd seen this protective sheet, this time he was sober. He felt a sudden warmth. He also felt safe, like when his mother had wrapped her arms around him in his youth. With all that happened around them, such feelings made no sense, but neither could he deny them.

The officer showed no indication that he'd seen Carter and Royce, yet they were impossible to miss. The officer jumped up and ran along the back wall, toward the castle entrance. Three more gunshots echoed, and Carter watched him pull his handgun and return fire, before rushing around the corner and out of view.

"I thought police didn't carry guns," Carter squatted back down and whispered.

"They must be ARV," Royce whispered back.

Carter raised his eyebrows, waiting for the explanation, which he knew would come.

"The ARV are the tiny fraction of officers, maybe a couple hundred, who are allowed to carry guns."

"That's all?"

"That's all who carry guns, and that is generally sufficient." Royce nodded. "Who are they shooting at?"

"Not sure, but I suspect our Russian friends." Carter peeked out again over the top of the hole. "If so, then I'm glad these officers have guns."

After several more shots, three motorcycles fired up and screamed out of the castle entrance. The two officers yelled something, ran back to their car, and gave chase, leaving Carter and Royce alone in the dark. The shimmering distortion had disappeared.

"I'm guessing we would have met the business end of the Russians' guns if we had hauled up any gold. They were just waiting," Carter said, realizing how lucky they were. "I'm rarely this happy for the police to arrive, but they probably saved our lives."

"Carter, I hate to think this way, but do you think Alastair told the Russians we were here?"

"Not sure, but I wondered too." He slowly nodded. "If he did, it wasn't voluntary. They also have my journal, so they may have figured out the clues."

"Yeah, maybe."

"Okay, I think they're gone now, but they or the police may return. We should hurry."

"How did that officer not see us?" Royce pointed back toward where the officer previously stood.

Carter was about to tell him that he had seen that illusion before, but he saw Hassie and Scrounge bounding toward them from the water's edge.

"Thank goodness you two are okay. I heard gunshots, and I was afraid they were shooting at you." Hassie waved as she approached the hole.

"We didn't know there were three armed men in the castle. As soon as the police arrived, they opened fire. They escaped on motorcycles and the police followed them," Carter explained.

"Who were they?"

Carter looked at Royce. "We don't know, but we think it was the Russians, waiting to see what we dug up."

"I hope the police catch them." She leaned over the hole. "So, did you dig up anything? Any luck with the treasure?"

"Carter found a small rock structure, and we were about to see what was inside." Royce pointed to a small side tunnel.

"Right, and we need to hurry." Carter crawled back into the tunnel.

"Did you have any luck with that fala thing?" Royce asked, leaning on the handle of his pick.

She showed him the bottle in her hand. "Sort of." She paused and took a deep breath, before continuing. "Royce, is your name John?"

"Yes, it's John Royce MacArthur." He laughed. "Royce was my grandfather's name. I always wanted to follow his example, but I wasn't allowed to serve. I've gone by Royce since I was young. My parents still call me John. How did you know? It's not on my card."

She nodded, staring at the bottle. *You know what you have to do. Just do it*, she told herself, kneeling down and handing it to him. "This one is for you. Please drink it all," she urged, turning her head to the side.

He accepted it with a puzzled expression. "For me? Why?"

"The spirit told me that for what you must do, you need two strong legs." Her voice quivered.

"Really? You heard those words precisely?" he asked, his eyes wide.

Hassie tilted her head, confused. "Yes, those exact words. Why?"

"Well, I thought I heard that same phrase. One of the officers looked right at us and didn't see us. At that moment, I heard a whisper. I could have sworn I heard a faint voice say that for what I must do, I needed two strong legs," he said, still wide-eyed.

Of course, none of this surprised Hassie. She was only surprised that he was surprised.

The muffled sounds of Carter moving in the small tunnel drew her attention, and she watched rocks fly out over his legs.

"So, I should drink this?" He held up the bottle.

"Yes, please break the seal with your thumb and drink it all quickly." She bobbed her thumb. *Before I change my mind.*

He broke the sugary seal, peered in, and sniffed, then quickly pulled the bottle away from his face, with a sour expression. "You know, this is all too weird for me, right? This stuff could have anything in it. There could be toxins, bacteria, or other impurities, which could make me sick." He sniffed it again. "I mean, if anybody other than you had handed me something that looked so gross and smelled like fish blood and told me to drink it, I would have laughed. My mind is telling me not to, but another part of me is telling me to drink it."

"Royce, please just drink it," Hassie pleaded. "It was meant for you."

He looked up at her from the hole, and their eyes locked.

"Well, between the part of my mind saying do it, my friend telling me to do it, and some mysterious voice saying I need to do it to have two strong legs, that makes three to one in favor." He smiled.

She offered a weak smile in return.

He lifted the bottle to his mouth and gulped the fluid, stopping to catch his breath halfway through. Then he drank the rest.

She gave him a thumbs-up sign.

"Thank you." He handed her the empty bottle.

"You're welcome, but this gift was not from me."

"Oh, yeah."

"So, what did it taste like?" she asked, accepting the empty bottle from him and returning it to her pocket.

"It had a strong iron taste, like blood. Honestly, I tried not to think about it. I just hope I don't develop a craving for it, like some vampire from *Twilight*," he joked.

"Well, if you do, I can promise that Carter and I will be on Team Royce," she bantered.

He laughed. "You probably shouldn't make any assumptions about Carter."

"That's right, he said not to assume." She nodded.

"Yes, he said you shouldn't assume and he's an arse." He smiled, pointing down at him.

She laughed. "Do you feel any different yet?"

"Actually, I do. I can feel a heat on my knee, and my shoulder no longer throbs." He looked down at his cast. "Let me try something." He put more weight on his cast-covered leg, then balanced and rocked on it. "I feel no pain at all. This is incredible! It feels great."

She nodded and crouched down when she heard a slight tinkling of metal and saw something slip out the bottom of his cast and pants leg, onto the top of his shoe. "What's that?"

"I think those may be the surgical staples from my knee." He picked the bent staples off the top of his shoe.

"Are they supposed to fall off?"

"No," he said, unbuckling his pants and yanking them down over his cast to his ankles.

"Whoa! What are you doing?" She stood up and back at the unexpected sight of him in his stark white briefs.

"Sorry, I forgot myself. Please turn around." He covered himself with his hands until she turned. Then, he grabbed a small garden trowel. "I need to see my knee. I feel no pain at all." He hacked at the cast and used the edge of the trowel like a knife. The top part of the cast began to crack, and he used his hands to push one side and pull on the other. The crack widened and spread down the length, allowing him to split the rest of it open. He flashed his light on it. "Nothing, not even a scar," he announced excitedly. "It feels perfectly normal. In fact, I used to have a scar on my shin from a childhood accident on a metal slide. That's gone too."

He pulled his pants back up, informing Hassie, and she leaned back over the hole. He reached up under his shirt and patted the bandage on his shoulder. "This is truly a miracle." He laughed. "You should find a way to bottle that stuff. It would be worth a fortune."

Yeah, I think somebody else already thought of that. Hassie grinned.

"I found something," Carter announced as he slowly wriggled his legs and torso backward out of the tunnel. He stood and showed them an old, round, heavily rusted metal container. "What did I miss out here?"

"Quite a lot, actually. Hassie gave me some of that leigheas fala stuff. It really works." Royce did a couple half squats to prove the point.

"Wow! You should find a way to bottle and sell that stuff." Carter smiled in amazement.

"Great idea. I wish I had thought of it." Royce chuckled.

"That's not gold." Hassie pointed to the muddy metal object. "I think it may be an old tinderbox. It looks a little like the one we have on a shelf at home."

"I think you're right, and it is old." Royce reached over and touched the side of it.

Carter placed it outside the hole, and he and Royce pulled themselves out.

The box looked hand hewn and uneven. Someone had hammered the top lid in place. The age and rust sealed it even tighter, but Carter pried off the top with a trowel.

The three peered in, and Carter brushed some dust away. Inside, they found a small wooden box with the letters "JP" chiseled into the top.

"That must be for John Paul." Royce nudged Carter with his elbow.

The wooden box had no hinge, but a thick yellow wax coated the entire circumference where the top connected to the base.

Carter used the smaller blade on his pocketknife to pick at the wax, which was old, brittle, and chipped away easily. "This looks like the same kind of wax used to seal the journal letter," he told them, sliding the top up and off.

Inside, Hassie saw a cloth bundle and gently removed it. She spread it open, and in her palm were two very old coins and a small, folded piece of parchment. "Not much of a treasure."

"Those are old groats." Royce inspected the silver coins.

From what Hassie could see, the coins were unevenly round. Each had a cross shield on one side and the profile of someone wearing a crown on the other.

"That's King David II." Royce pointed to the figure on the coin.

Hassie carefully unfolded the parchment, noting that it was dated prior to the journal letter, and she began to read it aloud.

"'14 August 1766.

"'John,

"'Our cause has suffered greatly, but it is not dead. As long as those who are loyal maintain the fire in their hearts, there shall always be hope. You must not allow the Loch Arkaig gold to fall into the hands of King George's loyalists. Keep it safe until the day when our voices and our swords are ready to rise up again. On that date, in victory, we shall restore the rightful king to the throne.

"'The gold is safe, inside a cave on the small island in Loch Ness. The entrance is near the water's edge, on the side of the island closest to the shore of the Loch. To see the entrance, you must first tame the great beast.

"'Like one of God's angels, the great beast has watched over the gold and protected our cause. I have left the key for you. It will reveal the great beast for only a few minutes. Recall how you must hold and use it. I showed you when you were young. When used, you will have only a short time to find the entrance before it will disappear from view again.

"'Use care and do not to touch the great beast. Your touch will be like poison to it. Give thanks to the great beast. Its nature is pure, and we would be lost without it.

"'Love, Father.'"

"Great, more riddles." Carter sighed. "Did you see a key?"

"You've seen everything that I have. This is all that was in the box." She held up the cloth with the two coins.

"Well, at least part of this riddle is easy to solve," Royce said with a little optimism in his tone. "There is only one island in Loch Ness. It's Cherry Island, a crannog island, located about twenty kilometers to the south, near the mouth of River Oich."

"A crannog?" Carter asked.

"Yes, it's not a natural island. It's a man-made creation constructed hundreds of years ago by building up tree trunks and rocks. There used to be a small castle on it in the fifteenth century, but it's barren now."

"Is it hard to get to?" Hassie asked.

"Not if you have a boat. I have an inflatable raft at home, but at most, it only holds two people."

"We still have to find the key, right?" She returned to Carter's question.

"The key must have something to do with these coins. Why else would they be in the box?" Carter leaned in closer. "It looks like one of the bars of the cross on each of the coins has been sanded down into a small groove from one edge to the center." He showed them.

"I don't think that is part of the original design." Hassie squinted as she studied it. "I've seen a few before."

As Carter flashed his light over the coins, Hassie noticed a tiny hole, almost miniscule, at the end of the groove, where the bars of the cross shield intersected. She asked him to flip the coin over and realized the tiny hole pierced King David II's eye on the obverse side.

"No, I don't think that hole is normal, either," said Hassie.

"What does it mean?" Royce asked.

"No idea." Carter shrugged.

Hassie took both coins and rolled them in her palms before stacking them. "The coins feel like they fit together along the grooves. Here, see for yourself." She handed them back to Carter.

"You're right." He held the two together with his index fingers and thumbs. "And when we align the grooves, they form a small hole on the outer edge of the coins."

"With that hole on the edge, it almost looks like a whistle." Hassie smiled.

"Maybe." Still holding the coins together with this thumbs and index fingers, like a tiny sandwich, he blew into the edge hole of the coins, but it made no sound. "Well, that proved uneventful." Carter chuckled.

They looked at each other, not sure what to do next.

Then Royce turned his head, as if he'd heard something, and then back with a puzzled expression. "I think you may have been holding them wrong."

Carter handed him the coins, and Royce used his dirty shirt to wipe off the edge that Carter had just blown into.

"Are you afraid of catching something from me, after all we've been through?" Carter lifted his hand to his heart in mock offense.

"I've heard about you American sailors, and there's no telling where your mouth has been." Royce smiled.

Hassie and Carter laughed.

"Okay, I'll give you that one." Carter held up his hands in surrender.

"I can't tell you why, but I think you are supposed to hold the coins like this." Royce clasped his palms as if in prayer and held the coins between his upper palms and his slightly spread index fingers. The fipple was on the outer edge, and he almost reverently lowered his chin onto the inside of his thumbs and placed his mouth just over the fipple.

"Really?" Carter laughed again, watching Royce's elaborate maneuvering.

"Here we go." Royce pursed his lips and blew.

A loud, piercing whistle vibrated on the air.

"That made a huge difference! How did you know how to hold it?" Carter slapped his shoulder.

Royce opened his mouth to answer, but his eyes went wide and most of the blood drained from his face.

Hassie saw his reaction and turned toward the Loch. She saw it too, but couldn't believe it.

Once again, two groats reveal me.

She heard the booming voice in her head, but this time, she saw who spoke.

Lewis's car sat in a wooded area two hundred meters behind the Red Regency Hotel. He trained his powerful binoculars on the hotel room doors, watching for movement and to see whether the girl and the soldier returned. He turned up the volume of his earpiece for the listening devices he'd planted in their rooms. He had left the room doors closed but unlocked, hoping whoever returned might wonder if someone was still there and pause, making it easier to see them.

The vibration of his cell phone on the passenger seat disturbed his quiet surveillance. He thought it might be Avery calling again. Lewis said nothing when he was told earlier the grandfather had died. He was less confident than Avery that their planned exchange might work with a corpse, which was the reason he had sent Gavrie and two others to Urquhart Castle without telling Avery. Until they saw the girl or received new orders from Avery, his men were to watch, not engage.

"Алло," he answered in Russian, still peering through the binoculars.

"It is me," Gavrie said in Russian.

"Speak," Lewis continued, still in Russian.

"We watched him at the castle, but the police showed up. An officer surprised one of our men, and he fired," Gavrie rattled off quickly.

"The officers had guns and fired back. We escaped before more of them showed up."

Lewis cursed through gritted teeth, suspecting which of his men it was. "Did you see the girl?"

"No, only the soldier and another man," Gavrie responded.

"Was the soldier arrested?" He knew the soldier's arrest would not be good for them. Their plan would not work with police involvement, and they would lose the treasure.

"I don't think so," Gavrie said. "The police chased us. I'm not even sure if the other officer saw him digging behind the castle."

"What did he dig up?"

"Nothing that we saw," Gavrie said. "Should we return to the castle?"

Lewis thought for a second. If his own men forced Porter into police custody, Avery would blame him. "No, not if the girl isn't there. Do not go back. Check with Percy to see if she had any credit charges online. Find her. The girl is now the key."

"Understood," Gavrie responded.

"Make sure that idiot who fired first is not with you when you return."

"He will not be. He had an unfortunate and fatal accident," Gavrie assured him. "The police stopped to address the dead man while we got away."

Lewis assumed that the "accident" involved a bullet from Gavrie's gun into the side of the man's head. "Excellent."

Chapter 26

THE HALF-MOON PROVIDED enough light to see something that defied explanation. Carter flinched, almost falling backward into the hole. Royce and Hassie remained motionless and stared.

A massive beast floated at the water's edge. Most of its thick torso was submerged in the dark waters, but its long neck stretched almost five meters in the air. Its head hovered over the shore as a river of water poured off its neck onto the rocks. Its black skin glistened and sparkled like diamonds. It had a snout like a horse, only much bigger and longer. A small shock of short, wavy, pinkish whiskers populated its head, and a similarly colored enlarged dewlap hung under its chin. With its mouth slightly agape, the rows of large, sharp teeth were visible. If it so desired, the beast could bite any of them in half. Terrifying and breathtakingly beautiful, this creature was truly majestic.

"It's a plesiosaur!" Hassie said.

"Actually, it's too big," Royce corrected her. "A plesiosaur would only be three to five meters in length. It looks more like a giant Elasmosaurus, which could grow to be fifteen meters or longer. However, they primarily inhabited North America during the late Cretaceous period. It truly is most curious," he explained, leaning forward to get a closer look.

Carter almost laughed at Royce for being so clinical in this moment.

"Yeah, the most curious part is not that our large friend exists, but that it appears to be on the wrong continent." Carter smiled sarcastically.

Royce shot him a glance. "I was simply making an observation. Marine biology is my field of study, after all."

I am glad that you consider me a friend, Carter Porter, the great beast said. *I mean you no harm.* Again, Carter heard the clear, booming, and present voice of the beast in his head, and by their reactions, he assumed that Royce and Hassie did too.

"I thought you were only a spirit I could hear speaking through my voice. How are you communicating?" Hassie asked aloud.

Carter wondered the same, having heard the beast's voice in the same way in his own voice.

You all have so many different languages. Sadly, this often serves only to isolate and separate you. I am blessed with the ability to hear your hearts. I call to all who walk the shores of Loch Ness, but very few hear me over the sound of their own thoughts and desires. There are some whose hearts have hardened and cannot hear me at all. Most simply dismiss what they hear as their imagination. Hassie Douglass was one of the few who heard and responded, the great beast said.

As it spoke, Carter felt the beast's dark, piercing eyes looking straight through him. It could read his mind and knew his innermost, desperate desires. He felt exposed, almost naked, in its presence. "So, you know my thoughts?"

Yes, of course, Carter Porter.

"I always thought the Nessie stories were myth; but you're real and nothing like what I imagined." Hassie stood in awe.

Please do not call me that.

"Do you mean Nessie?" she asked.

Yes, please do not call me that.

"Would you prefer the Loch Ness Monster?" Carter asked, hearing Hassie's nervous response and trying to deflect attention.

Lowering its head close to Carter's face, the beast stared into his eyes. *You will call me a monster at your peril, Carter Porter.*

He shuddered. The beast was not enraged, but stern, like a parent disciplining an unruly child. Carter had disappointed this creature in some way, and he felt guilty. "I'm . . . I'm sorry," he stammered and took a step back.

The name Nessie, or more offensive variants, is simply an effort to name me after the place I reside. To name someone based on where they reside is to diminish them. It devalues them by attempting to define them. I am far more than this place, and I can assure you that I have been here longer than Loch Ness.

Carter had no idea what to say. When faced with awkward moments, he often opted to say something stupid. "My wife was born in the state of Maryland, and her given name is Mary."

That is not the reason she no longer resides with you, is it, Carter Porter? The great beast chastised him again.

It was unnerving and humbling to face a presence who had the ability to shine a light on the darkest corners of his mind. Part of Carter wanted to run and hide, but he couldn't. Filled with an overwhelming sense of shame, he avoided the beast's stare.

Thoughts of so many horrible and selfish choices he had made over the last few years flashed through Carter's mind, in reverse chronological order. He couldn't control it, but the images in his mind finally stopped when he saw himself standing over Courtney's bed, looking at her lifeless form. His heart shuddered, his eyes welled up, and his knees buckled.

"We have no desire to offend you, but most people do refer to you as Nessie or the Loch Ness Monster," Royce stated.

The beast looked at Royce, and its expression softened.

What most people call you does not define you, unless you let it. I will not allow it to define me, and neither must I accept it. By informing you that this name offends me, I have given you a choice. Knowing it offends me, you now can choose whether to continue to call me by

*that name or not. The choice you make will be one of the many things
that define you.*

The beast turned back to Hassie.

Child, you know this better than most.

"Me? Why?"

*The name originally given to your canine friend was a name of deri-
sion. With Carter Porter's assistance, you changed it into a name of love
and strength, Sir Scrounge, Honorary Knight of the Round Pail.*

She smiled and scratched the top of Scrounge's head. "Yes, I
understand."

Royce stifled a snort before speaking. "Again, we have no desire to
offend you. What should we call you?"

*John Paul, the man who wrote the letter you hold, had a young
son.*

Carter listened and looked up, recognizing the reference to John
Paul Jones.

*Long ago, he brought his young son to me for the first time. The
child was four. Before his father used the groats to reveal me, the boy
saw me approaching through the waves. Sometimes young children
can see past the distortion of light I use to shield myself. He squealed
with delight, pointed, and said, "Fiogry."*

"Fiogry? What does that mean?" Hassie asked.

*In truth, I believe the child conflated two Gaelic words, "fíor
grian," meaning true sunshine. It was just something that the young
boy uttered, but he did not say it with anger, fear, or hate. He said it
with the love and the pure joy of an innocent child. It made my heart
swell. I am Fiogry.*

Carter, Royce, and Hassie looked at each other and nodded.

"Fiogry it is." Royce smiled.

"You said that you have been here longer than Loch Ness," Hassie
said. "Can I ask you what you are?"

*Like each one of you, the Lord of lords created me from the orig-
inal light and colors.*

"The Lord of lords?" Hassie brushed a few strands of hair from her face.

Yes, child. The Lord of lords, or as I sometimes refer to Him, the Lord of light. He goes by many names, in many religions and in many languages.

Hassie looked like she was almost afraid to ask another question, but she did. "What did you mean when you said that you were created from the 'original light and colors'?"

The original light is the love of the Lord of lords. As for the colors, all living creatures emit a color. A person's color can change, just as their mood can change, but their color usually defaults to what is most natural for that person.

"What's my color?" Hassie pointed to herself.

Child, your color is bright yellow, with a few tinges of brown. This means that you are a student, eager to learn and achieve your goals. It also suggests that only now are you experiencing an awakening of the spirit, which is what allowed you not only to hear me but also to have a willingness to respond.

That elicited a warm smile from Hassie. "Thank you."

"What about me?" Royce chimed in.

John, your color is forest green. You are a natural healer, and you are a friend to nature and to the natural world. You have a strong heart.

"Thank you. I understand that you are a healer too."

Carter could not know for sure, but he thought Fiogry grinned at that.

Yes, I am an incarnate healer. As such, my colors include all the bright colors of the rainbow.

Fiogry turned to Carter. *You have not asked about your color, Carter Porter. Your color is normally red, reflecting a passionate and self-sufficient person, but you have darkened and created a fog on your color. This discoloration stems from an anger that you cannot let go. The anger is what has fueled your vice and the fog. I have seen it countless times. I call it a fog of stupidity, because you have chosen this path and stubbornly refused to turn back. This fog dulls your mind and dulls your heart. It distorts the choice of right and wrong, preventing you from realizing your full potential. You risk turning your color dark gray.*

"Dark gray?" Carter ran his dirty fingers over the top of his head, choosing not to respond to the "fog of stupidity" comment.

Yes, those with a dark gray color are holding on to negative feelings. They represent an unforgiving spirit. When your color shifts into dark gray, I cannot help or protect you. That level of anger or hate would prevent you from hearing me. My voice would be only an empty scream into an abyss. Sometimes, bursts of anger can push someone into that dark spectrum, until their anger subsides. For those who live with anger or hate, however, this color begins to permeate their very soul, and the nature of their color can permanently change. I am deeply concerned for you, Carter Porter.

"Great! Now I'm being lectured to by a New Age dinosaur with pink highlights," Carter muttered sarcastically.

I may be many things, Carter Porter, but I am not New Age. What I tell you gives me no pleasure. I am truly worried for you.

Once again, Carter averted his eyes.

Hassie raised her hand, as if she were trying to get a teacher's attention. "What do you mean that you cannot help those with a dark gray color?"

My greatest blessing is the ability to help and heal. I can bend light to shield and protect not only myself, but also those who are in need, as long as they stay out of that dark gray spectrum of color. I shielded you and Carter on the shore until his anger drove him into that spectrum. Then I could no longer protect him.

Carter remembered when he'd attacked the man with the Jack Daniel's bottle. Anger and rage had filled him, and at that moment he could no longer see Hassie. When his anger subsided, he was able to see Hassie and Scrounge again. It was strange, but now he understood.

"You also can project images, can't you?" Carter asked. "Like my daughter, Courtney."

Yes, images from your memory and what your heart wants to see most. Even though the image brought you pain, it also brought you joy. Sometimes the things that can bring you the most joy can also bring you pain.

He again saw Courtney standing next to him. This time, he just stared and didn't reach for her. "Thank you. She died three years ago."

"Your daughter is beautiful," Hassie offered. "I'm so sorry."

"You can see her too?"

She nodded. "She's wearing a little blue dress with yellow flowers."

Yes, Carter, they also can see her, because I am allowing it.

Courtney smiled and looked up at her dad, and he smiled back.

Would you all like to see what Sir Scrounge wants to see most of all? Fiogry asked.

"The dog?" Royce smiled.

"Absolutely!" Hassie exclaimed.

As if on cue, Scrounge barked. A tiny blue bird appeared in the grass. He lunged at it, but the bird disappeared. The dog pawed through the grass, and it took him a second to realize that the tiny bird had reappeared, perched on his tail. Scrounge barked again and feverishly chased his tail in circles.

Royce and Hassie laughed hysterically, and soon Carter joined them. The scene was ridiculous.

"Poor Sir Scrounge." Hassie shook her head, still laughing.

Honestly, it always seemed a little mean to me, but Sir Scrounge so loves chasing that little bird, even knowing that he will never catch it.

The little bird evaporated. Likewise, the image of Courtney faded and disappeared. Scrounge slowed and stopped spinning, panting loudly.

"You're hurt," she said, gesturing to the large sunken area on Fiogry's side and back.

Carter noticed several other deep gashes and scars across its neck and body. Hassie reached out to touch one of the scars, but the massive beast recoiled with the agility of a snake—so fast, it surprised him.

Please do not touch me, child. The oils in your skin will corrode and damage my outer layer. Once that happens, the fresh water of Loch Ness can further damage my flesh and organs. It is quite painful and could be fatal.

"I'm sorry." Hassie stepped back.

Only then did Carter remember the warning in the letter not to touch the great beast.

"Can't you use the leigheas fala to heal yourself?" she asked.

Carter noticed two small tube-like extensions coming from either side of the beast's shimmering dewlap, and he deduced that this must be what Fiogry used to secrete the blood cure.

No, child. The leigheas fala is a gift I can use to heal others, but it is not for me.

"That seems so unfair." Hassie shook her head. "To be given a gift of healing that you cannot use for yourself? Have you ever asked the Lord why you can't use it, or, for that matter, why you must live in an environment that is so dangerous and harmful to you?"

No, child. It is not for me to question the Lord of light, nor for you, Fiogry responded.

"Perhaps not," Hassie acknowledged.

Hassie, to be a part of this world means that you must also experience the risk and pain of this world. The Lord of light once experienced all of the risk, pain, and suffering of this world, as well as the world that has been and the world to come. Why would I question an opportunity to follow His example, even if mine may only be the tiniest step?

Carter could not help but feel that part of Fiogry's explanation to Hassie was directed at him and his efforts to escape this world through alcohol.

Hassie paused for several seconds, obviously considering Fiogry's answer, but her expression reflected that she still had so many questions. "Okay, you may have had no choice regarding a life in the water and the risks that it brings, but if human contact holds such danger for you, why don't you avoid humans? Why do you call to them and invite that danger? Why call to me?"

I have the ability to bend the light, and I can use this to help shield me from the dangers of unwanted physical contact. I must risk some contact with humans, however, in order for me to use the leigheas fala for its intended purpose. Healing and the ability to help others are precious gifts, and I am grateful for them. I also required your assistance to bring the cure to those who needed it.

Carter took a few steps forward, wanting to be closer to the beast, until Scrounge ran in front of him. He almost tripped, before stopping, smiling, and bending down to pat him.

"Yes, but is it really a gift if—"

Child, the Lord of light provides each of us with different gifts and talents, as well as different challenges. If we only focus on the challenges, or worse, forsake the gifts given to us by focusing on why the Lord did not grant us certain other talents or gifts, then we will fail. We will fail to appreciate all that we have, we will fail to use the gifts and talents we possess to their fullest, and we will fail to find our true purpose in life. We will fail the Lord.

Royce stepped around Carter and inched closer to Fiogry, careful not to touch the beast or give any impression that he might. "How did you injure your back?"

That injury occurred over fifty of your years ago. Like yourself, there was a man named John. He drove his sea vessel on Loch Ness for some kind of speed competition. He hit me with tremendous force. As I mentioned, my outer layer protects me from the corrosive elements of the water, but if breached, the water will quickly dissolve my tissue and organs. If unabated, it can consume and even destroy me. If I am able, I must surface and hold the injured area out of the water until it crusts over. For small scratches, this scarring may take only a short time. The injury from that vessel was extensive and the intrusion of the water swift. I am thankful to have survived. I now give motorized water vessels a wider berth.

"John Cobb!" Royce snapped his fingers. "I saw a video of him trying to set a speedboat record on Loch Ness back in the 1950s using a jet-propelled boat. He died when his boat hit something, but nothing was visible. It was a mystery, and the authorities ultimately concluded the boat must have hit some kind of freak wave or extreme change of currents."

It was not a freak wave.

"Couldn't you have avoided the boat?"

Perhaps, but the vessel was moving very quickly. The light I bend does not prevent objects or people from making physical contact if they get close enough. I had approached it because I had wondered if the driver, John, might be the one.

"The one?" Royce asked.

Yes, I had hoped that he was you.

"Me? I wasn't alive in the 1950s." Royce furrowed his brow.

No, you were not. John Paul, who wrote the letter you hold, was a kind and gentle soul. He asked me to protect the treasure he hid in a cave, under the small island, until either he or John returned to retrieve the gold for the Jacobites. I agreed. Since his colors left his mortal body, I have waited for John to return.

"I assume that he meant his son, John Paul Jr., whom we call John Paul Jones," Carter interjected.

"Carter, you shouldn't assume, and you're an arse." Royce laughed.

Carter smiled and shook his head.

I suspect that you are correct about who he intended, Carter Porter, but I based my promise to him on the actual words used, not on words that he may have intended. Words are powerful, and they have meanings. I promised to help protect the gold in the cave and to wait for John to come, on behalf of the Jacobites. In short, I waited for you, John Royce MacArthur. Fiogry turned to face Royce.

"You've been waiting for me?" Royce was awestruck. "I'm honored, but you should know that RFS is primarily a volunteer historical society."

Yes, I have, and yes, it is.

"But you gave me four of the gold coins from the treasure, didn't you?" Hassie interjected. "You projected the image of a black stone I previously found with my grandfather over each of the coins in the water, right?"

Yes, child. Those coins had fallen from the boxes before they reached the cave. You asked for help. I offered it in the way that I could, and in a way that you would know it was one of my wonders, and not merely your own luck.

"Weren't those coins still part of the treasure?" Carter asked.

Yes, but I was asked to help protect the gold in the cave, not all of the treasure.

"Oh yeah, words have meaning." Carter tapped his finger on his temple.

Yes, they do.

"Of course, you could have just told us where the treasure was hidden," Carter challenged.

Some knowledge must be earned, not given. In addition, things must occur in their proper order, or not at all. I could not have told you or Hassie earlier without violating my promise. You three needed each other, and I sincerely hoped it would lead you all to me. For that same reason, I could not tell your father, Carter Porter, when he walked these shores.

"My father?"

Yes, I briefly wondered if perhaps he was the one. Your father's name was John, he possessed John Paul's letter, and he came for the treasure; but he was not here for the Jacobites.

"My father!" Carter exclaimed, as if finally understanding the answer to a question that had eluded him. "That's how you knew to tell Lennox to invite me to Scotland and told him a nickname that only my father knew, right?"

Yes. Since your father knew that special name for you and he so loved you, I believed it was safe to use, at least for purposes of encouraging you to come. I hope that did not pain you.

Carter laughed and shook his head. "No, it's fine. It was just a silly childhood name. As you said, a nickname doesn't define you, unless you let it," he said, before adding, "In truth, I would have loved to have heard my father say it to me one more time."

I am glad. Now, John needs to go to the small island in the Loch.

"The small island!" Royce whooped, slapping his head.

"Yes, you already told us that there was only one island, Cherry Island," Carter reminded him.

"The reference to the 'small island' did not just describe its size; it described its relative size in relation to another island."

"But there's only one island, right?" Hassie asked.

"Yes, there is only one island now, but when the letter was written, there were two," Royce explained. "I can't believe I forgot there was a second. It was named Eilean Nan Con, also called Dog Island, because the owners once maintained hunting dogs on it."

"What happened to it?" Carter asked.

"When they constructed the Caledonian Canal in 1830, it raised the water level of Loch Ness a few meters and Dog Island slipped beneath the waves."

Royce's knowledge of such history amazed Carter.

That is correct. You will need to go to the small island, and you will need two strong legs. Please tell no man what you three have seen here, nor the wonders that you have experienced. I ask this to protect you, and to protect me.

The creature backed away from the shore and disappeared from view. They heard a splash but saw nothing on the waves.

After landing in Inverness and still not being able to reach Carter, Mary made her way to the Red Regency Hotel, arriving a little after one thirty a.m. She entered the small and dimly lit hotel lobby. What little furniture was there was dingy and faded. Heavy black scuff marks stained the white linoleum floor in front of the wooden reception desk. Mary rang the bell chime and waited. After two more chimes, she heard some rustling from a small office behind the desk. The office door opened and an impossibly old man wearing a red vest shuffled out.

"Welcome to the Red Regency. Are you checking in?" the man asked with a yawn.

"My husband already checked in. I just need a key."

"What is your name, and what room is your husband in?"

"My husband's name is Carter Porter, but I don't know his room number."

The clerk eyed her a little suspiciously. "Yes, we have a guest here by that name, but I cannot give you his room number. The guest must provide it to you."

"Please, I can show you my identification." She handed her passport to him.

"Yes, ma'am. I'm sure you are his wife, but we do not have you registered as a guest. Therefore, I cannot provide you with his room number or a key. I'm sure you can understand," the clerk tried to explain, picking up his desk phone. "I'm calling his room and will ask if he can add you to the guest list."

The clerk's smile turned to more of a puzzled look. He hung up and dialed a second number. "I'm sorry, ma'am. There is no answer. That is as much as I am allowed to do."

She realized that she was not going to get him to change his mind, but she got an idea from the bank of slots behind the clerk's desk. Each slot was numbered and corresponded to the rooms of the hotel. "I understand. It's not your fault. It's my husband's. Could I leave a note for you to give to him, to let him know where I will be?"

"Of course, but you will need to leave two notes."

"Two notes?" she asked.

"Yes, your husband reserved two rooms."

Two rooms? she wondered, but hid her surprise. "Oh, that's right. I forgot about him getting the second room. He hates to work in the same room he sleeps in," she lied. "I'll jot down two notes, since we're not sure which room he is in."

She folded the first note and handed it to him. She watched him place the note in the 134 slot, while she pretended to write the second. As he turned back, she folded the second note. "You're very kind." She handed it to him and watched him slip it in the room 138 slot. She gathered her bags and left the lobby.

Back in her car, she turned it on and pretended to be doing something on her phone until she saw the clerk shuffle into the office. She backed away and pulled around the side of the hotel. No other cars were parked near Carter's rooms, which she found curious.

She got out of the car and stepped back into the damp night air. Even though nobody was around and the parking area was dark, Mary could not help but feel like she was being watched. The tiny hairs on the back of her neck tingled. She looked from side to side as she approached the door. *It's just your imagination*, she told herself, lightly knocking on the door.

No response.

She knocked a second time before testing the door handle and felt it turn in her hand.

"Carter?" Mary whispered as she slowly pushed the door open.

Chapter 27

HASSIE, ROYCE, AND CARTER stared at the open water of Loch Ness, having difficulty comprehending what they had just seen. None of them spoke for several moments, until Carter heard the faint sound of a police siren.

"We need to go." Carter returned to the hole and picked up the shovels and tools.

The three trotted back to Royce's car and quickly got on their way.

"Can we toss this now?" Carter lifted the Irn-Bru bottle with the vegetable juice and prepared to pour it out the window.

"No!" Hassie squealed. "We still need it. Fiogry would only give me leigheas fala for Royce, not for the ransom of my grandfather. She believed those men would use it for evil, and I believe her. So, we still need that bottle."

"Hassie, I never would have accepted—"

"Royce, what I gave to you was meant for you. It was as much my choice to give it to you as it was Fiogry's, and it was the right choice. My grandfather would never forgive himself if we contributed to something that could cause so much harm to others, even to save him. We'll find that quipu thing, and we will give the Russians the vegetable juice. Hopefully, that will be enough."

Royce drove for a while before he broke the silence. "Hassie, you referred to Fiogry as 'she.' Is it because you heard your own voice in your head?"

Hassie smiled a toothy grin. "I hoped someone would pick up on my use of the gender pronoun. No, it's because Fiogry is wise beyond measure, possesses amazing power, and does not demand public glory for all her accomplishments. Of course, she's a 'she.'"

Royce laughed. "Okay, that works for me."

Carter just smiled. "She was a very impressive 'she.'"

Another car's headlights approaching about two or three kilometers ahead ended any further banter. But it wasn't the headlights that gave Carter pause; it was the spinning, colored lights on its roof.

Royce turned off their headlights and pulled off the road, to a spot hidden from view of the approaching car.

Carter sucked in his breath until he saw the car pass in the opposite direction and heard the blaring siren fade.

When they returned to the highway, Royce drove five miles per hour under the speed limit, to Carter's annoyance.

"Please hurry," Hassie urged. "We still have to find the treasure and retrieve the quipu thing."

"It wouldn't serve us well to get pulled over for speeding," Royce retorted.

Carter waved to Hassie, indicating that Royce was probably right.

"I've been thinking. In addition to my raft, we're going to need a dry suit or a well-insulated wetsuit and scuba tank," Royce said.

"That's true. If the top of Dog Island is now underwater, the cave entrance could be six or seven meters deep. The water in Loch Ness is around five degrees Celsius. Hypothermia would be a risk within minutes without a suit," she said.

"I have a wetsuit, scuba tanks, and regulators in my shed," Royce informed them.

"Really?" Carter asked, surprised.

"Yes, to study marine life, you occasionally have to get in the water," he said in a matter-of-fact tone. "I hope to get a position with one of the large fisheries after I graduate. My role with RFS doesn't provide a salary."

"Any chance you have a wetsuit for me?" Carter asked.

"No. I just have the one, and it wouldn't fit you. I may have an extra bathing suit, if you're going to join me in the raft. It will only accommodate two."

Carter turned toward Hassie. "I think we should try to stick together as much as possible; but unless you see it differently, I think Royce and I should go in the raft, and you and the dog should remain in the car with the engine running. The Russians are still after you, and if they find us while we are in the middle of the Loch, we would be easy targets. If you see anything suspicious, you could hit the gas and get out of there. You could also honk the horn to warn us."

Hassie agreed.

—

After reaching the duplex, Royce and Carter rushed to collect the equipment from the shed. "When I was getting certified to dive, I was taught that redundancies are your friends and could save your life if something fails," Royce told Carter as he stuffed two scuba tanks and extra goggles and regulators into a large mesh satchel.

"The navy taught me the same thing." Carter nodded. As he was about to leave the shed, he spied a ball of thick nylon cord. *This could be useful*, he thought, grabbed it, and followed Royce to the car. They loaded everything in the back and soon headed toward the Loch.

—

They parked close to shore at the southern end of Loch Ness.

"There's Cherry Island." Royce pointed to an island about one hundred fifty meters out. A thin fog had slipped through the small trees inhabiting the island, giving it the appearance of floating on a dark cloud.

Small docks littered the shore not too far from them, but everything was dark and still.

Carter plugged the air pump into the car's lighter and jumped out to inflate the raft.

Royce put on his wetsuit and checked his gear one more time. One tank was a standard silver eighty-cubic-foot tank with enough oxygen to last about an hour, and the second yellow one was thirty cubic feet. "Since this will be a shallow dive, I can use almost all the air in the tank searching and won't have to worry about decompressing when I come up, but I brought a smaller tank in case I need more than an hour underwater," Royce advised as he pulled the raft toward the shore.

Wearing only a borrowed bathing suit and a T-shirt, Carter felt the cold breeze blowing off the cold water creep into his joints. To distract himself, he tried to focus on the steps he needed to accomplish to finish inflating the raft and loading the equipment into it. "Do you know exactly where Dog Island is supposed to be?" Carter asked, feeling the wetness seep through his tennis shoes as he helped lower the raft into the water.

"Yes, there should be a metal pole and small flag to mark the top of the island. They put it there as a warning to boats, since what used to be the top of the island is now a shallow bar." Royce pointed to the flag flapping above the water. "There it is."

"How are you going to bring up all that gold with just a small raft?" Hassie handed Royce the small scuba tank.

"We're not," Carter stated flatly.

Royce turned to him. "We're not? Then what are we doing here?"

"We need to find that Golden Quipu thing and maybe a handful or two of the gold as proof that we have what they want. We can give up the location of the treasure if we have to, but let's just focus on what we really need: to free her grandfather. Agreed?"

Royce shrugged. "It's okay with me, but it's Hassie's call."

Hassie nodded. "Do you have the two groats?"

"Yes." Royce patted a small waterproof bag, which he stuffed into a mesh bag attached to his waistband. He tossed a thick plastic oar into the raft.

Carter eased into the raft first, and a little water splashed in when Royce hopped in. Carter's teeth chattered. "I'll paddle," he volunteered, hoping the exertion might warm him.

The fog was dense, and he lost sight of the marker several times, but he paddled in the right general direction. As they closed in, he saw the painted metal pole and the small blue flag. He let the raft drift up and tied it to the marker pole with part of the cord.

Royce slid the bulky scuba tank onto his back, rocking the raft, and Carter grabbed the sides to steady himself.

"Have you ever cave dived?" Carter asked.

"No, only open water diving. Why?" He strapped the tank belt around his waist.

"I have once. It can be disconcerting," Carter said. "It really isn't something you are supposed to do alone, particularly at night."

Royce frowned. "Really! You're raising this now? We're here, and you know that we have to do this for Hassie and her grandfather."

Carter felt he should be the one diving, but that wasn't possible without a wetsuit. "I'm sorry, and you're right. Just be careful down there."

"Thanks, I intend to be," Royce said, fitting the goggles onto his face. He removed the two groats from the bag and handed them to Carter. "It's time to call our friend." He left the extra diving flashlight, goggles, regulator, and small tank in the boat, but kept a flashlight and the small pry bar in the bag. "I'll be back for these other items, if I need them."

Carter saw a small, oddly shaped blue-and-red tag attached to the lip of the mesh bag, which he wondered about but didn't ask. He secured the items behind him, holding the two coins between his palms, and blew.

From nothingness, Fiogry appeared only a few meters in front of their raft.

Once again, two groats reveal me.

In the water, Carter believed the beast seemed even bigger. She could have easily swamped their raft if desired, but she remained still and calm.

John, I will not hide the entrance of the cave from you, and you should be able to find it more easily now. It is on the side closest to shore, Fiogry said.

"Thank you." Royce rolled over the side of the raft and turned on his flashlight. He placed the regulator mouthpiece between his teeth and blew hard. Before slipping beneath the water, he smiled at Carter and gave him a thumbs-up.

"Take this with you." Carter handed him the remaining coil of nylon cord attaching the raft to the marker pole. "Tie this around your waist. When you find the cave entrance, give the cord a single tug. If you get into trouble, give me two or three hard tugs."

Royce pulled the mouthpiece out. "Carter, you don't have a wet-suit. There won't be much you could do if something goes wrong."

"I just don't want you to feel like you are alone down there."

"Thanks, but I will be alone down there, except maybe for Fiogry. That said, depending on how heavy the quipu is, I might use this to let you haul it up." He tied the cord around himself, then he replaced his mouthpiece and quietly slipped below the surface.

Royce had told Carter that the water of Loch Ness remained murky to pitch black, due to the high peat content of the surrounding soil and the near constant rain and runoff. Still, he was surprised how quickly Royce's flashlight disappeared in the water. He couldn't even see the bubbles from Royce's scuba tank.

He was alone except for Fiogry, but he felt a warmth wash over him again. His teeth stopped chattering. Even in the foggy mist, Carter knew that Fiogry saw right through him. Its pink dewlap shimmered almost to the point of glowing in the dark.

Carter, your soul is troubled.

"I'm just worried for my friend."

You are, that is true, but that is not the main concern troubling you, is it? That is not what caused you to create a fog around your color, Fiogry pressed.

"Yeah, the fog of stupidity."

Correct. It is a fog of stupidity. It distorts your thoughts and, worse, it distorts the choices you make. It can make truly awful choices appear acceptable, if not desirable. It leads you down a path that you would have once called inconceivable and, yes, stupid. The farther you travel that path, the harder it becomes to turn around, retrace your steps, and start on a different path.

He averted his eyes.

Carter, many of your life choices have put you on a dangerous path. You need to turn around.

"You know what started me on this path," he said, staring down at the water lapping at the side of the small raft. "It's not a path that I want to be on, but I can't go back to the place where it started. It's too painful." A sense of anger crept in. *Why would you even suggest such a thing?* he thought.

I know the pain you feel, Carter. I, too, have lost those whom I loved. I once wished that the gift the Lord of light gave me included not only the ability to heal the sick and the broken, but also the ability to take away their soulful pain. Then, I reminded myself of the glorious gift that I had received and that the Lord is the only one who can cure soulful pain.

"I wish you could take my pain away. The desire not to feel that pain is part of what led me down this path."

I understand much better than you know, but that desire is no excuse. I ask you, though, what if you could start again? What if you could go back in time, before Courtney was born? What if you still maintained the full knowledge of what the future held for you, Mary, and for Courtney? You would know the death, pain, and the tremendous loss that awaited you. In an effort to spare yourself that pain, would you have chosen not to have had Courtney? Would you have chosen to have never known and loved your daughter, even for the brief time that you did, in order to not feel the pain of her loss?

The question hit him like a sledgehammer to his heart. He would never have made such a choice. Those few years with Courtney were the most magical of his life. Until she entered his life, he had never understood the concept of true, unconditional love. When she was born, this tiny life had joined his and Mary's, and it transformed them both. They loved her before she could even communicate or love them back. Even when she was old enough to speak and sometimes defy them, they loved her with all their hearts until the day she died.

"No, of course not!" He would never consider the possibility of never knowing her. "But . . ." *I should have been able to save her*, he thought, unable to verbalize the rest.

Carter, you blame yourself for things that are not your fault. Some things are within your control to change, and others are not. What happened with your daughter was not within your control. It was simply Courtney's time. One day, it will be your time as well. When that day comes, consider what you will want to see when you look back upon the choices you have made in your life since her passing.

Fiogry's arguments were not exactly new to him. Mary and his father had told him similar things, but he had tuned them out. He could not say why, but Fiogry's words resonated in his heart. His eyes welled up. "Will I see her—" A single, hard tug on the nylon cord cut him off before he finished his question.

Darkness surrounded Royce. Even with his powerful flashlight, visibility was only a meter at most. From the raft, he'd followed the marker pole down to the former top of the island about three meters deep. Once he moved in the direction of the shoreline, he became disoriented. Though he was in the open water, the sheer blackness created an uneasy, claustrophobic feeling, and he lost where he was and which way was up.

Just take deep, even breaths, he told himself.

Progress was slow as he scoured the bottom and edge of the former island, but from the moment he lowered himself below the surface, he felt something guiding him. He was not sure whether it was Fiogry, but something urged him forward and deeper.

After almost ten minutes, he was six meters deep and descending. This edge of the island was steeper. He noticed a small grouping of rocks jutting out from the thick brownish kelp, dancing with the soft current. His flashlight washed over the area to an emptiness behind the kelp. He tore away the growth to reveal a hole a little more than a meter in diameter.

This has to be it. He finished clearing the kelp and gave a single, hard tug on the nylon cord. He hesitated for a moment, looking into the downward angling tunnel. With the scuba tank on his back, he would have barely enough clearance in the tunnel, and if he got stuck, he wouldn't have room to turn around. His heartbeat quickened.

Just take deep, even breaths. Hassie needs this.

Gently grabbing the sides of the tunnel entrance, he pulled himself in. He glided almost all the way into the hole but felt the top of his scuba tank bump up against the roof. He used his hands to pull himself farther downward. Then the tunnel turned back upward. His buoyancy carried him up this part of the tunnel, which expanded as he rose.

The tunnel leveled off and emptied into a small chamber about ten meters in length and two meters in height. He could have stood up in the cave had it not been filled with water. He suspected that air had once filled the cave, but now cracks in the soil above must have allowed it to flood after the island sank. His air bubbles filled the sagging ceiling, and many escaped into the cracks.

That's not good. Who knows how long before this whole ceiling collapses? He thought about the weight of the water pressing down on Dog Island. *Just take deep, even breaths.*

He checked his dive watch. He still had almost forty minutes of air left. He saw ten, maybe fifteen wooden crates stacked in the corner of the chamber. The wood appeared weak and corroded. Some had been stacked on top of others, and the crates on the bottom had collapsed. Their spilled contents glistened under the beam of his flashlight. The sheer volume was stunning. Estimating how long it would take to remove all this with his tiny raft, he almost laughed. Carter was correct. They just needed the Golden Quipu and one or two handfuls of the gold for now.

He kicked his flippers and moved closer to the crates, but his motion stirred up a lot of silt and debris in the chamber. Particles swirled everywhere. The already darkened water became a thick cloud. He could see nothing and worried that he might have trouble finding the exit again. With visibility barely beyond the end of his nose, he had to feel along the walls until he reached the first crate.

The crate had a latch and rusted padlock on the front, and Royce used the small pry bar to separate the hinges from the old wood. Trying not to stir up more debris, he lifted the top. He had to hold his flashlight no more than a few centimeters away from the contents he inspected or else the flashlight was useless. Inside were thousands of gold coins, plates, and other trinkets. He searched but found nothing that looked like a harp.

He moved to the second and third crates, finding more of the same. It was impossible not to disturb the silt as he checked upward of seven crates. He found only mounds of gold, silver, and other treasures.

Royce's watch indicated that he had fifteen minutes of air, but his progress was too slow. He was not sure he would have time to finish searching them all before his air ran out. With the debris in the water, he was concerned that he might miss a crate.

Just take deep, even breaths.

Royce's movement in the small chamber had another effect. A few chunks of the ceiling fell. At first they were not big, but they were large enough to get Royce's attention. *That's not good.*

He forced himself to focus on and open the next crate and then the one after that. He worked slowly and methodically, afraid that he would miss a crate in the cloud of silt if he moved too quickly. When he opened the top box on the next stack, he sucked in a deeper breath on his regulator. Lying on the top was an incredible sight. The object had forty or fifty thick strings of gold intricately knotted at different lengths, with embedded rubies, emeralds, and diamonds. Matted and held in place by a thick golden base, the piece resembled a gold-and-jeweled harp—and was stunning.

He could tell the base had been hand-hammered. He brushed his fingers across the borders that were rounded and displayed delicate etchings and intricate designs. He had never seen anything this beautiful or valuable. Gently lifting the harp-like object out of the crate, he realized it was heavy, weighing ten or twelve kilograms. He gently put it back down and grabbed two handfuls of gold coins from the last crate, stuffing them into his mesh bag.

Next, he removed the wooden lids from two crates and placed the Golden Quipu between the inside frames of the lids, giving a little protection to the artifact inside. Thankful for the cord, he untied it from his waist and used it to tie the two lids together. Given its weight, he hoped Carter could pull it up, but at the moment, holding on to it helped keep him anchored to the floor. He checked his watch and saw he had approximately ten minutes of air left.

Time to leave, he thought, feeling more nervous about the stability of the ceiling of this small cave as more chunks fell.

He was about to feel his way toward the cave exit when the two lids slipped out of his hands. With the sudden loss of weight, he shot up and banged his head and shoulders into the sagging ceiling. A huge section of ceiling collapsed in front of him, almost hitting his face as it came down.

Panic ensued. Disoriented, unable to see, and terrified that the whole roof was about to come down, his survival instinct forced everything else from his mind. Royce kicked hard toward where he believed the exit was, only to be jerked to a stop. Looking down, he saw that the loose cord attached to the lids had wrapped around his arm.

The Golden Quipu! He couldn't see the lids that enclosed the artifact below him through all the silt, but he tugged hard on the cord. Nothing moved. *They must be under some mud that fell.* He heard a rumble above him. *It's all going to come down!*

His heart still racing, he unwound the cord wrapped around his arm and followed the other end toward the cave exit. Believing he might barely survive, he internally thanked Carter for making him bring the silly cord. As he reached the lip of the tunnel, he turned, braced his flippered feet against the wall, and gave one more tug on the cord attached to the two lids. He pulled with everything he had. First, he felt a slight movement and then a release as the package came free and hurled toward him.

Unable to see through the muck and afraid the wrapped lids might hit him, he turned as the rest of the ceiling over the crates collapsed in on itself. A massive wave of displaced water hit him, slamming him against the side wall of the chamber. His ears popped and throbbed, and the force knocked the goggles off his face. Frantic, he grasped for his goggles on top of his head. If he lost those, he would never be able to find them. He snatched one of the straps before they slid off. Slipping the goggles back onto his face, he cleared the dark water with a tilt of his head and a hard nasal exhale.

Part of the cave exit had been blocked by the cave-in, but he believed the remaining hole still provided enough of an opening for him to get through. He glanced down and saw that the corners of the lids holding the Golden Quipu had dug into the side of the tunnel. More sections of ceiling fell and more displaced water rushed by him as he grabbed the edge of the package and pulled himself into the tunnel.

The collapse and rushing water had another adverse effect. The size of the tunnel seemed to be shrinking, and his scuba tank banged harder against the roof. The bulky Golden Quipu package under him slowed his progression, and he was still a couple meters from the bottom of the tunnel before its path would turn back upward.

Royce grabbed onto the end of the cord and gave it two hard tugs, hoping that Carter would get the message and start pulling.

Initially, he could feel the cord tighten and the artifact start to move under him. Just as he and the package were about to reach the lowest part of the tunnel, the ceiling at the bottom of the tunnel collapsed, trapping him and the Golden Quipu inside.

Chapter 28

"CARTER?" MARY WHISPERED AGAIN, stepping into the hotel room. Her senses were on high alert. The door was unlocked. Even when he drank, Carter was a freak for security. He wouldn't have left it unlocked.

She flicked on the bedside lamp, illuminating the room. The bed was empty. She saw no luggage, and the chest of drawers contained only a couple of shirts, which she didn't recognize. No toiletries or Dopp kit were in the bathroom.

Is this even his room? Nervous she might have wandered into a stranger's room, she reached for the door handle to leave just as the door burst open, hitting her in the shoulder and knocking her onto the floor.

Though startled, she had the presence to roll, grab the edge of the bed, and jump onto her feet in a fighting crouch.

"I recognize you from picture," a huge man with a low, gravelly Russian accent said. "You are wife who does not live with husband."

"Who the hell are you?" she demanded.

He pulled a pistol from his waistband. "I will ask questions."

She straightened but kept her fists raised, near her chest. Her mind quickly worked through her limited choices. *I need to be ready to strike if he gives me the opportunity.*

"Why you here?" he asked, closing the door behind him and flicking the overhead room light on.

"That's none of your business," she said defiantly. "Who are you? Where's Carter?"

He took another step, pointing the gun at her head. "You not listening. I ask questions. You answer, or you die."

Just come a little closer, she thought. Still two or three meters away, he wasn't close enough. "How do you know my husband?" she asked, trying to distract him.

"I make clear for you. You answer me, or I shoot you in head. If you ask question, I shoot you in head. If you refuse to answer, I shoot you in head." He growled.

"I have something he needs to sign. That's all." *He obviously knows that we're married but not living together, so he may not know whether I'm a friend or foe to Carter.* Her mind raced. "It's part of our divorce settlement, and he left before signing it. The sooner he does, the sooner I can get out of here." She feigned a tone of irritation. "Not that this is your business, whoever you are."

He eyed her, clearly wondering whether she was lying. "Give this settlement to me." He extended his other hand. "I take it and you to your husband. You better for trade than girl's grandfather, I think."

Even though she had hoped he would order her to hand it over to him, she was puzzled by his statement. *Now I can get a little closer.*

"Give to me." He shook his open hand.

Mary pulled an airline envelope from the back pocket of her jeans. She stepped closer, holding the envelope in her right hand and keeping her left hand near her chest.

When the large man snatched the envelope from her hand, she sprang. She snapped her right hand toward the wrist of the Russian's gun hand while slapping the side of the gun barrel from the opposite direction with her left hand. This created an awkward torque on the weapon, and the gun popped out his hand, skidded off the top of the small dresser, and fell into the narrow space between the dresser and the wall.

Damn! She was hoping to have been able to hold on to it and twist it around on him, but her barrel slap had been too hard.

The man seemed shocked, but he recovered and swung at her head with an agility and force that astonished her. She ducked, but he landed a glancing blow on the back of her head, causing sparks of pain.

She pivoted, sprang back up, and rammed her right elbow into the crown of his nose. Hearing a satisfying crunch and seeing blood pour from his nose, she was surprised when he didn't flinch.

He looked furious. He grabbed her by the neck and lifted her up. Only her toes touched the carpet. "Enough!" he screamed, spitting blood. "Perhaps I finalize divorce now."

She felt the man's foul breath on her cheek. She clutched at his hand, but with his vice-like grip, she could no longer breathe. Thousands of tiny dots flashed in front of her eyes. In a desperate attempt, she raised her leg and drove the heel of her shoe into his kneecap. The kick was not as hard as she might have hoped, but it was enough.

He yelped, releasing her, and fell hard against the wall, clutching his knee.

Mary dropped onto her feet. She knew she could not allow him to recover. He was too big and strong. When he pushed himself upright, she flattened her hand and drove the side of her palm into the man's Adam's apple.

He gasped and grabbed for his throat. He fell onto the dresser and rolled to the floor.

She didn't know if she had hit him hard enough to crush his trachea and kill him, but when she saw him reaching around the dresser, she knew she hadn't.

She leaped over his legs and ran out, slamming the door behind her.

She had no idea how long she would have to escape, but hoped her kick to his knee would slow him down. Her car was only a few steps from the room. She opened the door, jumped into the driver's seat, and hit the start button just as the light from the opening motel room door washed over part of the front hood. Panting hard, she threw the car into drive, spun the wheel, driving over part of the concrete walk-way, and circled back into the parking lot. Her tires spun on the soft gravel, kicking up dust. Three bullets pinged into her trunk before she swerved onto the highway and out of range.

"Ouch!" Carter yelped as the nylon cord ripped through his hands, tearing a thin layer of skin from his palms. He had started to pull the cord after he received the two tugs. He thought something might be wrong, but when he felt the cord's massive jerk, which almost yanked him into the water, he knew something was very wrong.

What happened? "Is Royce okay?" Carter asked, pulling hard. The cord didn't budge. He eased up, not wanting to break it. It was his only connection to Royce.

Your friend is in trouble, Fiogry said.

"Is he alive?"

Yes, but he does not have much time.

"Can you help him?" he pleaded.

A portion of the cave and exit tunnel has collapsed, trapping him. The tunnel opening is too small for me. If I tried to force my way in, I would make it worse and doom him.

He worked through possibilities in his mind, but he could only think of one that might work. He threw on the second set of goggles, grabbed the small spare air tank, and shoved the regulator in his teeth. He wrapped the strap of the second flashlight around his wrist, took two deep breaths, and rolled into the water. The cold felt like a million needles pricking his skin. Soon, it would be hard to think.

Hand over hand, he pulled himself along the cord toward Royce. He reached the mouth of the tunnel in under a minute.

He would have only a few minutes more before hypothermia would claim his body. Grateful that he did not have time to think about diving into such a small, dark space, he dragged himself through the tunnel entrance until he saw the end of the cord buried in mud and rock. He feverishly scraped away the dirt and stones around the cord, stopping only to clench and unclench his fists. His cold hands cramped and ached.

Progress was slow, and it took him several tries to punch a small hole around the cord. His hands were numb, and it became harder to clench. Now he used his hands more like scoops. They bled, but he could no longer feel them.

His heart skipped when Royce's hand reached through the small hole and grabbed his. Carter redoubled his efforts. He now could see Royce's hands working from the other side. They would widen the cavity, only to have the slipping mud and rocks erase their progress. It was maddening.

Royce held up three fingers, and Carter realized he was signaling that he only had three minutes of air.

Carter checked his own. The reserve tank was smaller, but it still held fifteen minutes. Royce shoved something through the hole.

Not understanding and not having much room on his side of the tunnel, Carter accepted what looked like two stacked wooden lids from a chest tied with cord, and slid them under his body. His large frame pressed more tightly against the top of the tunnel as the men continued to work on widening the hole.

Royce stuck his hand through the hole, with his fingers curled and touching his thumb. He was out of air.

Carter knew they needed to buddy breathe with his tank. Unable to clench or feel his hands, he had to use both hands to remove his mouthpiece and stick it through the hole.

Royce took a couple breaths before returning the mouthpiece. He tried to squeeze through the hole, but it was still too small. Carter saw him slip off his scuba tank, and they exchanged the mouthpiece several more times while they worked to widen the hole. Slowly, Royce wriggled his head, shoulder, and one arm through, pushing Carter back and away.

They were now face-to-face at the bottom of the tunnel. Carter shoved the mouthpiece into Royce's mouth. When he saw Royce nod, he took it back.

He tried to inch backward to give Royce more room to come through the hole, but the angle was steep. He couldn't feel his arms or legs, and he and the package slid back down.

The cold made thinking difficult, but he knew he was in trouble.

Royce finally worked his legs through and under his body. He was surprised that Carter had not offered him the mouthpiece again, until he saw that Carter wasn't doing well. Royce put his hand on the mouthpiece and Carter nodded limply. Royce removed it, took a couple breaths, and returned it to Carter's mouth.

Unfortunately, the tunnel exit was almost three meters up and Carter was less and less responsive.

Royce dug his knees in and shoved the Golden Quipu and Carter up the hole, but they kept sliding back. He felt the hole that they had dug behind him shrink and mud and dirt sliding down over his calves. He knew the rest of the tunnel could collapse at any moment. He put his hand on the mouthpiece, but Carter didn't nod. His eyes were only slits, and he had wrapped his arms around the lids, clutching them as if they were a warm pillow.

Royce pushed hard, lifting Carter almost a meter this time, only to see him slide back again. He took another breath from the mouthpiece and returned it. He also knew they did not have much more time. *Please help us!* he prayed.

No sooner had Royce finished his thought than Carter rocketed backward and out, still clutching the lids containing the Golden Quipu under him. Royce was startled but didn't delay. Before the light from Carter's flashlight faded, Royce saw Fiogry had a portion of the nylon cord in her teeth and had pulled the lids and Carter toward the surface.

Royce kicked hard, and his lungs ached by the time his head broke the surface. He gasped and whipped his head around. Carter was floating on his back but not moving. He heard a few faint breaths from the regulator still in Carter's mouth. *He's still alive*, but Royce worried he wouldn't be for long.

To Royce, Carter felt like dead weight. He pulled the side of the raft down and rolled Carter's head and torso in, leaving his legs and feet dangling over the side.

Carter spit out his mouthpiece, mumbled something incoherent, and rolled the rest of the way onto his back. Even in the dark, Royce saw his skin was sickly pale and his body started to convulse.

Royce knew Carter's internal organs would shut down if they couldn't raise his core temperature. "Can you help him?" he begged Fiogry.

Do not worry, John, she said with a twinkle in her eye. She extended her long neck over the raft and lowered her snout to just above Carter's shaking form. Then, she opened her massive jaws and forcefully exhaled.

Though he floated a short distance from the raft, Royce felt the warmth of the great beast's breath. Carter stopped convulsing. After a few seconds more, he opened his eyes and gave Royce and Fiogry a weak thumbs-up sign.

"You okay?" Royce asked him. "I thought we were about to lose you."

"So did I, and I saw that light. I thought maybe I was supposed to walk toward it, but it came to me. Am I sunburned?" His voice sounded stronger.

Royce wasn't sure what he was talking about and wondered whether he might be delusional, but he looked fine. "Sunburned?"

"Yeah, you saw it, right? It was the brightest, whitest light I've ever seen. I closed my eyes, but the light still came through my eyelids, as if they were open. It felt like the light from a thousand suns warming every cell in my body for what seemed like hours. I almost didn't want to come back, but I knew I needed to."

"Carter, I didn't see any light." Royce shook his head, more than a little confused. "I saw Fiogry warm you with her breath, and then I saw you return to normal color within a few seconds."

"A few seconds?" Carter's mouth hung open.

Fiogry backed slowly away as Carter sat up. And Royce heard, *That light was for you and you alone, Carter Porter.*

"Thank you," Carter said. He clenched and unclenched his fists, and then made room in the raft for Royce.

You are most welcome, Carter Porter.

He turned toward Royce. "So, did you find it?"

"I think so." Royce tugged on the nylon cord, pleased at still feeling a heavy weight at the other end. "You know what you did was seriously mental, right?" He lifted the lids into the raft. "You could have died."

"I assumed that you needed help down there." He winked.

"You shouldn't assume, but thank you for saving my life," Royce said in earnest.

"You're welcome." Carter laughed, noting he didn't call Carter an arse for assuming, and nodded.

As they paddled to shore, Royce looked back and saw Fiogry's head just above the water's surface. "Thank you too," he said. "Would you protect the rest of the treasure, both the portions that are inside and outside of what remains of that cave, until either Carter, Hassie, or I return for it?"

It will be my honor, John, Fiogry responded.

Chapter 29

CARTER WAS FIRST out of the raft. He waved to Hassie in the car as he helped Royce, who was carrying the bound wooden lids. "You found it? Is that the Golden Quipu?" Hassie asked excitedly.

"We think so." Royce held up the package.

"Any trouble?" she asked, accepting the small scuba tank, goggles, and regulator from Carter as he pulled the raft out of the water. "I was getting worried."

Royce gave Carter a look. "Yes, but not more than we could handle, working together." He placed the still-tied lids in the back of the car.

The three and Scrounge hopped into the car, and Carter and Royce explained what happened in the cave on their way back.

—

"Please stop up ahead." Carter gestured toward the Inn's surface parking lot, which they were fast approaching. "We need to tell the Russian we have everything and then try to drive the decision on where we'll make the trade. I still want to be careful about where we turn on Hassie's phone."

Royce glanced at Carter but said nothing.

"Thank you both for everything." Hassie reached over the seat and patted Carter's shoulder.

"You're welcome, but you know this won't be a simple exchange." Carter turned to look her in the eye. "They may still want you, whether it's because you obtained the leigheas fala or because they think you know something else about the treasure. They could try to grab you and keep your grandfather as leverage to force your hand. We won't let that happen, but we'll need a plan."

The clock on the dash indicated that it was a little before two a.m. when Royce pulled over and stopped.

Carter powered Hassie's phone on and was about to text the Russian when he saw several missed calls and texts from Mary's phone. He didn't listen to the voice mails, but the last text in the string stated that she was in Inverness and heading to his hotel. "Uh oh!" He turned off the phone and yanked out the battery. "Royce, I need to use your phone instead." He grabbed it from the drink holder.

Royce glanced at Hassie, who shrugged.

"Mary, it's me, Carter," he said as soon as she answered. "If you're already here, don't go to the Red Regency Hotel. It's not safe."

"Carter!" Mary shouted. "Where are you?"

"Mary, don't go to that hotel," he repeated urgently.

"I've already been to your hotel, and you are right, it wasn't safe. Some huge guy tried to kill me, and he knew you."

Carter's stomach knotted when he heard that. "Are you okay? Are you safe?"

"Yes, I'm safe, but I have a few bullet holes in my rental car. In fact, I'm just pulling up to the police station to report this. Now, where are you and who was that guy?"

"Thank God you're okay," he exhaled. "I can try to explain most of it, but please do *not* go to the police."

"Are you insane? That guy tried to murder me!"

Carter saw Hassie shaking her head vigorously. "I know, but

reporting it to the police could make things worse at this point," he said, not really liking the way that sounded.

He heard her let out an exasperated breath. "Where are you?"

"I'll give you the address of where we're heading, and I'll try to explain when you get there. Right now, please trust me and don't go to the police. There are other lives at risk," Carter said, giving her Royce's address.

Mary's drive to Royce's duplex did not take long. Carter waved as her headlights swept over him. He met her in the driveway, alone.

"What are you doing in Scotland?" he asked.

"That's your first question to me?" She stopped and looked like she was about to explode.

He rushed to her, obviously realizing his mistake. "No, I mean I'm glad to see you. I'm just surprised."

"You're essentially AWOL, while facing the threat of discharge. You left the country and told nobody. The police in Maryland may issue a warrant for your arrest, in connection with the death of the Uber driver. Then, you drunk-call me, babbling on about being in some danger." She took a deep breath to calm herself. "Carter, what I heard in your voice was pain and fear. That's why I'm here."

"I'm sorry, Mary. I'm sorry for everything." He shook his head. "I'm glad you're here. I really am, and we do have trouble."

She stared into his eyes. They were sober and he sounded sincere. "What's going on, and who was that huge guy at the hotel?" she asked in a quieter voice.

"Please come inside and meet my friends. There's a lot to explain." He smiled.

It had been a long time since she had seen Carter with a brightness in his eyes. He was sober, clear, and decisive. Maybe it was the night's shadows, or maybe it was just her imagination, but for a brief second, he looked and sounded like the man she once knew. She had no idea what was going on, but at this moment, he was giving her more reason to trust him than he had in the last three years. She followed him into the kitchen.

After making introductions, Carter began to debrief her, starting with the journal his father left him and the letter inside. He detailed the attacks, narrow escapes, how he met Hassie and Royce, Alastair's abduction, and finding the treasure and the Golden Quipu.

"So, this is just about the gold. They thought you knew where the treasure was and wanted to trade the grandfather for the gold?" Mary rubbed her temple, trying to catch up.

"Not exactly."

"What? What else are you not telling me?"

Carter looked at Hassie and Royce, clearly asking for some kind of support. Mary was getting even more frustrated waiting.

Hassie shrugged.

"Well, she's not a man," Royce said flatly.

Carter screwed up his face with a quizzical expression.

"Fiogry said tell no *man*, and your wife is not a man. Words have meaning, remember?" Royce smiled. "Tell her."

Carter cleared his throat and told her about the farmer who sent him the first-class ticket, the voice that Hassie heard from Loch Ness, and the mysterious distortion of light that shielded them from view. He continued with the miraculous healings of Hassie's grandfather, Royce, and Scrounge. Then, he recounted seeing their daughter, seeing Fiogry at Urquhart Castle, and finally, how Fiogry had saved him on the raft a short time ago.

When he finished, Mary studied his and then Royce's and Hassie's faces. *Are they all delusional? Nessie? Really?*

Royce held up the mesh sack of gold and the two groats, obviously sensing her doubts.

"And you're saying that Nessie communicates telepathically?" Mary asked, trying not to sound as skeptical as she felt.

"Yes." Hassie nodded. "You hear your own voice in your head, but somehow you know that it's not you. I know it sounds impossible, but it's true."

"It's true," Royce chimed. "It was hard for me to believe until I experienced it. Once we saw Fiogry—and she does prefer the name Fiogry, not Nessie, by the way—the voice was stronger and clearer."

Mary continued to stare. She couldn't make sense of it, but she couldn't deny that the Russian at the hotel was real, and the sack of gold coins Royce held was real. She was not sure whether she actually believed everything else, but it was evident that her companions did. "So, you think that what they really want, besides the mounds of gold, is that quipu thing?" She pointed to the tied wooden lids.

"Yes. The Golden Quipu and the leigheas fala." Carter held up the Irn-Bru bottle containing the vegetable juice.

"May I see the quipu?" Mary asked.

Royce grabbed a kitchen knife and sliced the nylon cords, then slowly removed the top lid.

Mary sucked in her breath. The Golden Quipu sparkled under the kitchen lights. Intricate carvings were etched into the borders, and the golden strings, with their jeweled knots, glistened as if they were still wet.

"Wow!" Carter whistled.

"It's even more breathtaking than I remember from the cave." Royce leaned over the table to get a closer look.

"That must be worth a fortune." Mary gasped.

"No, it's worth a life! It's worth my grandfather's life," Hassie said, her hands firmly on her hips.

"Understood." Mary nodded to Hassie. "Do you know what it is or why they want it, besides its obvious gold and jewel content?"

"Honestly, we have no idea." Hassie lowered her hands and shook her head. "We know why they may want the leigheas fala. Fiogry told me that they would use this miracle liquid for evil, which is why we cannot give it to them. We'll give them the quipu and a fake leigheas fala. They know what the Golden Quipu looks like. They told us about it. But the leigheas fala is different."

"Different in what way?" Mary gently rubbed her index finger over a ruby hanging on one of the golden strings.

"Well, I've been thinking about this. I believe that they only know of its effect, not what it looks like or where it really came from. They're asking *us* for a sample. I think they may only know its name because they forced it from my grandfather. I can't bear to think what they might have done to get that out of him." She shivered and lowered her head.

"If they got that information from your grandfather, what makes you think that he didn't tell them more, like where it came from and what it looked like?" Mary asked.

"For two reasons." Hassie raked her hand through her hair. "My grandfather is almost completely blind, so he couldn't tell them what it looked like. The leigheas fala cured him of everything, except his blindness."

"And second?"

"My grandfather didn't know where it came from. I didn't tell him, because I didn't know until a few hours ago. So, there is a good chance they won't know that our bottle is a fake." She pointed to the bottle with the vegetable juice.

"That makes sense, but it's still dangerous. Why do you think they may still want you?" she asked Hassie.

"I've thought about that too. If they really don't know anything about it, other than its name and its effect, then they would want someone who does know. They need someone they think knows how to obtain it, like me."

"You seem to have put a target on your back, young lady." Mary frowned.

"She has, and we need a plan that will keep Hassie safe," Carter said.

"I still think our plan should be to call in the police, but it's not my grandfather whose life is at risk," Mary conceded. "So, what is our weapons inventory?"

Carter tossed Mary the old side-by-side shotgun.

"This is it?" Mary asked incredulously. "It looks like it hasn't been cleaned in a decade. This could blow up in my hands." She frowned at Carter, chastising him with her eyes for handing her a weapon in such an unacceptable condition.

"Don't forget these." Carter smiled and flipped the dusty and decayed box of shotgun shells to her.

She opened the box lid. "So, we have an old shotgun and seventeen cobweb-covered shells."

"We do have superior determination, if that helps." Carter laughed.

"Well, we'll just have to adapt and go with what we have." She turned to Royce. "Do you have any gun oil to clean the shotgun? If not, do you have any motor oil?"

Royce shook his head. "No, sorry."

"Okay." She pinched her chin, thinking about what else she could do. "I guess I can drain some motor oil from my car."

"Improvise, adapt, and overcome." Carter smiled.

She grinned back. "Right, and on that front, let's talk about the exchange process. When we make contact with the abductors, we need to try to drive the exchange process, dictate where it will be, and pick a zone of action that might give us some protection, if not an advantage."

"Why does she sound more like a soldier than you do?" Royce asked Carter.

"Because she is more of a soldier than I am."

Mary noticed there was no sarcasm but a hint of pride in his tone. "Thank you," she said, before turning back to Royce. "However, as Carter knows, he and I are Marines. Marines are *not* soldiers. We are much, much more than that. Many Marines feel it's an insult to be called a soldier."

"No, that certainly wasn't my intent." Royce apologized to Mary, then nudged and whispering to Hassie, "Well, this seems to be the evening for unintentionally offending by calling someone the wrong name."

She nodded.

"Hey, why didn't you object to being called a soldier earlier?" Royce asked Carter.

"Probably because I'm more of an officer's candy." Carter chuckled.

Mary laughed, but Hassie and Royce looked confused.

"An officer's candy is the round, scented blue cake at the bottom of a urinal," Mary explained, and they smiled.

"Again, I don't want to offend you, particularly with respect to your military service." Royce held up his hand. "It was a huge honor for my grandfather to be in the Royal Scots Dragoon Guards. I wanted to join, but they wouldn't take me because of my heart."

"Well, it was their loss, I'm sure," Mary said.

"Thank you," Royce responded. "In fact, I can even make my heart to skip if I . . ."

"Is everything okay?" Hassie asked, noticing his changed expression.

"Yes, but I think that the leigheas fala not only cured my leg, it also cured my heart."

Mary tried to return the conversation to their plan. "We should consider the best place to make the exchange and who should be there. Any chance that they would agree to a public square of some sort?"

"I doubt they would want to bring her grandfather into a public place. There would be too many variables," Carter stated.

Mary nodded. "Other thoughts?"

"What about Urquhart Castle? That's where we found the key to the treasure, and they already know that we've been there," Hassie proposed.

"Interesting." Mary rubbed her bruised neck. "We would probably need to schedule the exchange soon, before any staff arrives."

"Agreed. We don't want to risk any other lives." Carter tapped his fingers on the kitchen table, obviously considering it. "I can make the exchange, and you can position yourself in Grant Tower or on top of the guard house. In an elevated position, you could cover me, if things go south. I don't trust these people to walk away after they get what they want."

"You're probably correct." She nodded. "I like the idea of a location with close proximity to the water. We should use the water as part of our exit strategy. If they assume we will be on foot or in a car, they may plan accordingly and fail to address a water exit. Any chance that we can get a boat?"

"All I have is a small inflatable with no engine," Royce answered.

"It's not a boat, but the Inn has Jet Skis for rent," Hassie offered.

Mary thought for a moment. "Actually, those could work. Can you get to them?"

"Yes, I think so. I know where they store them, but the Inn keeps the keys in an electronic safe, which requires you to type in a room charge to release them. Since Carter is still registered as guest, I could charge his room." Hassie looked at him.

"Sure, in for a penny." He shrugged.

"How many do we need?"

"Two, I think." Mary stretched, cracked her back, and rolled her shoulders. "You and Royce can be on the Jet Skis with the Golden Quipu and the sack of gold, on the opposite side of the Loch. Carter will hang on to the fake leigheas fala. If things go well, then Royce can bring the items across the Loch for the exchange. If we make the exchange, then Hassie's grandfather can ride out on the back of Royce's Jet Ski. We can figure out later where we'll meet downstream. If things do go wrong, however, you two can jet out of there in any direction, with the treasure."

Hassie's eyes went wide. "Jet out and leave you and my grandfather?"

"If the circumstances require it, yes." Mary nodded. "It would be suboptimal, but it may be the only way to save your grandfather. If things do go wrong, then they will still have your grandfather and, perhaps, one or both of Carter and me. As long as you stay safe and hang on to the Golden Quipu, we still have something to bargain with. You will live to fight another day. If they succeed in capturing you along with the Golden Quipu before your grandfather is freed, then it's game over for everyone."

Hassie bit her lower lip. She clearly didn't like it, but she slowly nodded.

"That's also why Royce should be the one to bring the Golden Quipu to shore." Then, turning to Hassie, Mary asked, "Is there any place on the opposite side of the Loch from the castle where you could hide the Jet Skis until you are ready to make the exchange?"

"It's not directly across, but there is a good-sized dock on that opposite side." Hassie grabbed a piece of paper and a pen from the kitchen counter and drew a rough sketch.

Mary looked over her shoulder and pinched her chin. "Good. It'll be dark. You can park your Jet Ski on the back side of the dock. Royce can park his Jet Ski out front." She pointed at the relative positions.

Both nodded in agreement.

"If they're available, you should wear helmets. From a distance, we can hope that they will confuse Royce for Hassie, at least until he gets close to our shore for the exchange. That way, we'll never give them a chance to grab her. You both should stay near the opposite shore. Royce should come over only if a signal is given. Is that clear?" Mary looked each of them in the eye, and they said they understood.

"Carter, use my phone to take a few pictures of the gold and the Golden Quipu." She handed him her phone. "For the quipu, don't take a picture of the whole thing, and make it a little out of focus if you can. Again, we need to show them that we have what they want, but we don't want to give away too much. Do the same for the vegetable juice." She picked up the Irn-Bru bottle and placed it on the table.

"Then, send those pictures to Hassie's phone so you'll have them to send when you need them."

"It's a little after three a.m.," Carter said, consulting his watch. "If we are going to do this, we should head to Urquhart Castle and get things set up before we invite the Russians to our party."

"On the way, you two can drop Hassie and me at the Inn, for the Jet Skis," Royce said.

Hassie bent down and scratched Scrounge behind his ears. "You need to stay behind this time, boy."

"I can borrow some of my neighbor's dog food for Sir Scrounge. They keep it out back." Royce pulled out a bowl from the cupboard.

"Good. Thanks." Hassie smiled.

"Now, let's get a couple pictures of the mesh bag of gold," Mary told Carter.

Carter lifted the heavy bag and set it on the table to stage it for a picture. He removed a few of the coins and placed them in front of the bag. "Man, it would be nice to keep just a little of this."

"That is only a tiny fraction of what's in that cave, but we would never have been able to keep any of it," Royce said.

"Wait, what?" Carter jerked up straight, like he had accidentally stuck his finger in a light socket.

"The gold. We could never keep it. It's against the law. It all belongs to the Crown Estate, of course."

"That's correct, unfortunately," Hassie affirmed. "I found that out the hard way."

"So, we've gone through all of this, and we were never going to be allowed to keep the gold?" Carter shook his head.

"Those are the rules, like it or not. You usually get some kind of reward, and it could be—"

"Stop, please!" Carter laughed. "No need to explain further, my friend. I absolutely believe you. Of course we wouldn't be allowed to keep it."

Mary shook her head. "Let's just stay focused on what we have to do."

When they finished taking pictures, Mary went to drain some motor oil from the car, leaving the kitchen door ajar.

"Carter, your wife is a badass. How could you let her get away?" Hassie asked.

"Yes, she is, and I can only blame it on the fog of stupidity."

Avery had paced and scratched the back of his hand in his office at the T-Farm for well over an hour before Lewis forwarded the pictures of a small mesh bag, a bottle of red liquid, and what looked like a bejeweled artifact. The text message instructed him to bring Mr. Douglass to Urquhart Castle at 5:45 a.m. for the exchange.

Avery had just finished reading the texts and looking at the pictures forwarded from Lewis when his phone rang.

"The castle, yes or no?" Avery demanded.

"We can make it work," Lewis answered confidently. "My men were there earlier. They know layout."

"I admire their boldness, believing that they control this process. We will take our patient via a helicopter to a van near Inverness. I want you to be in the van when we make the exchange," Avery ordered.

"*We*, sir?"

"I forwarded the picture of the artifact to my expert, but I know it's real. It has to be; and I have to be there to receive it. I've waited too long not to be."

"Sir, I strongly recommend you let me and my men make exchange. This could be trap. If something goes bad, better that you not there. Agreed?"

"You're probably right, and that would be easier; but I have to be there to receive it. It's mine." Avery's voice quivered. *I am so close.*

"Sir."

"Enough!" Avery shouted. One of his fingernails caught and tore a piece of skin he scratched on the back of his hand, and it started to bleed. He took a couple of deep breaths. *Control yourself.*

He knew Lewis was right. His presence at the exchange would complicate things, and he couldn't allow anybody who saw him there to survive. His presence wasn't logical, but he didn't care, not this time. He stared at the growing droplet on his hand. *The Golden Quipu is mine, and I will hold it in my hands.* He couldn't stand the thought of anyone else even touching it.

"Understood, sir. What about girl? The message did not mention girl. Soldier will not give up girl easily, I think."

"I suspect you are correct. Our primary objectives are to obtain the artifact and the leigheas fala. Grab the girl if you can. If you cannot, then eliminate her. With a sample, we should be able to reverse engineer it, and we can interpret the quipu for ourselves. If some peasant girl could accomplish it, how hard could it be?"

"Understood."

"Get your men to the site early, and make sure there are no police or other surprises. If there are, call me."

"Yes, sir," Lewis answered. "Much to do, but we have about two hours."

"Good. Make it happen." He hung up and clicked over to an incoming call.

"Mr. Darrow, do you have it in your possession?" the breathless woman asked.

"Doctor Thresher, is it our Golden Quipu?" It didn't bother him that he had awakened her at such an early hour to review the picture he had forward to her. That is what he paid her for.

"Mr. Darrow, if that's real, it's a miracle," she replied. "Please let me see and study it. The pictures you sent me were incomplete and the clarity was lacking."

"Doctor Thresher, please answer my question."

"I am sorry, sir. I cannot be entirely sure until I study it in hand, but from what I could make out from the picture, it appears to fit the description. It could absolutely change history," she added with the awe of a child. "When we publish our report in the *PNAS Journal*—"

"Doctor! You would do well to remember the terms of our agreement."

"Yes, yes, of course, sir," she stammered. "Mr. Darrow, I would never divulge or print anything without your consent, ever. I simply meant that when—"

"Good. Otherwise, I would be required to enlist the services of another."

Dr. Thresher's contrite response was barely above a whisper. "Sir, I can assure you that that will not be necessary. Please, I'm very sorry."

Avery smiled. He had no interest in altering history, much less publishing anything, unless it benefitted him. "I accept your apology. Now, can you decipher it?"

"Sir, the opportunity would be a dream and the greatest honor of my career. It would require time with the artifact, but yes. Much of the interpretation depends on relative lengths between knots, color choices, and a host of other factors, which cannot be confirmed through a picture, much less a partial and blurred pict—"

"Excellent, Doctor. With a little luck, both of our dreams will come true soon." He hung up and joined the passel of white-lab-coated medical personnel pushing Alastair Douglass's corpse on a gurney by his office door toward the elevators.

"Mr. Darrow, I understand that you wish me to participate in the exchange, correct?" Dr. Naj Aggarwal asked.

"Yes, Doctor. You will join us. It is imperative that they believe Mr. Douglass is merely sedated, not dead."

"There will be no way to hide the ventilator. As you can see, it is strapped to his face."

"Yes, that is why you will accompany us. You will remove the ventilator immediately before the exchange, and not before."

Dr. Aggarwal looked uncomfortable. "You should not let anyone get too close to the body before the exchange. Pallor mortis will start to set in as soon as we remove it. We used makeup to cover the skin lesions, but this ruse will only work from a distance."

"I agree. You and Mr. Douglass will remain in the van until the actual exchange. Remove the ventilator just before you exit. Keep your white lab coat on. I want you to look like a doctor," Avery said without a hint of irony.

Chapter 30

"WEREN'T WE JUST HERE?" Carter joked as Hassie and Royce pulled up close to the shore in front of the castle on their Jet Skis.

"Hopefully there will be less digging this time." Royce pointed to the hole and the dirt mounds at its edge. "We need to clean that up later."

"Yeah, but you'd lose more than a few pounds if you shoveled all that in your wetsuit. At least you look warmer than Hassie in that sweater."

"Hey, Royce loaned it to me and it was better than nothing." She picked at the chunky knit sweater. "It's cold on the water, and I'm glad he had it in the back of his car."

"Hopefully neither of you will have to be out there long. I've already texted the Russian, and we should expect visitors at any moment," said Carter. "These guys are professionals, and they will send scouts to make sure they're not walking into a trap."

Hassie tucked a loose lock of hair under her helmet. "Where's Mary?"

"She's getting into position." Carter jerked his thumb toward the tower. "Royce, you stay close to Hassie. Remember to position yourself in front of the dock over there, like Mary said." He pointed across the Loch. "If we're good to make the exchange, I'll signal for you to come over. You can take Alastair back to Hassie. We parked the car not too far from the Inn so the three of you could head there. The keys are on the tire, under the back fender."

"Okay." Royce nodded.

"Hassie, you hang on to the Golden Quipu and the gold until we're ready for Royce to come over with them," Carter instructed.

"Me?" she asked, sounding confused. "I thought you said we wanted to keep the puzzle pieces separated as much as possible."

"I know, but I thought more about this on the way over. You position yourself behind the dock, out of view. If things go wrong, let Royce jet out first in one direction. Hopefully they'll follow him. When it's safe for you, you can go in a different direction with the goods. That way, if they catch Royce, they'll still come up empty. It's a risk either way."

"Okay, I guess." Hassie shrugged.

"If things go well and they honor the exchange, place the stuff on the edge of the dock and then hide under the dock until Royce retrieves the items."

"What's the signal?" Royce asked.

Carter pulled out his flashlight. "If I give three quick pulse flashes followed by one long, steady flash, that will be our signal that we are ready. But if I give any other signal or wave the flashlight wildly, then you are to hightail it out of there."

"Okay."

"You both need to be ready to move. Agreed?" He looked each one of them in the eye.

"Agreed."

"Carter, you can also tell them that if they refuse to make the exchange or if they insist on taking me, then I'll drop the Golden Quipu in the middle of the Loch," Hassie added.

"Yeah, we put the bag of gold and the quipu in a stainless-steel warming tray Hassie found in the Inn's kitchen and then sealed it shut with some electrical tape." He pointed to the tray sticking out of the open side compartment of Hassie's Jet Ski.

"Why?" Carter asked, confused.

"The middle of the Loch is over three hundred meters deep. As dark and murky as the water is, visibility gets even worse in deeper water. If we dropped it, the tray will sink and mask the gold from any long-range metal detector search. The steel will look like any other metal debris down there, assuming their detectors could even reach that far," Royce explained.

"Good. I like it." Carter smiled, then turned to Hassie. "Don't take any risks with your life. If they double-cross us on the exchange, follow the plan."

Hassie bit her lip and nodded. "Just make sure you don't take any unnecessary risks with my grandfather's life."

"We won't. I'll be near the castle entrance, making sure they see me, and Mary will be on top of the guard tower with the shotgun."

They glanced up in that direction.

"Don't worry, she's there," Carter assured them. "I'm also leaving Hassie's phone on so they can track it."

"Thank you again, and let's hope this works." Hassie smiled, gave a gentle twist on the accelerator, and rode away.

Royce gave Carter a thumbs-up sign and followed Hassie.

Carter ambled back to the concrete walkway leading into the castle's main entrance. It was a little over an hour before they were supposed to make the exchange, but he knew the action would start before that.

A few minutes later, the phone tucked in his pocket vibrated. It was a text from Mary. *3 coming from grassy area behind castle, body armor, be careful.*

Carter's heart quickened. He took a few deep breaths and reminded himself that this was part of the plan. He started to pace near the front of the castle when he got the second text from Mary, and his heart beat even faster.

—

Mary's second text said, *at dry moat now, 1 has sniper rifle, 2 with night vision, coming to U, around sides.*

Not good, he thought. He had expected the Russian to send an advance team to sweep the location for police or signs of a trap, but he now wondered whether their plan would work at all. A sniper could eliminate any advantage of the Jet Skis. Briefly, he wondered whether they should abort the plan but texted Mary: *stick to plan, roll with it.*

He hopped on the balls of his feet, trying to stay loose. He knew this next part of the plan would be dangerous, and he and Mary had not shared all of it with Royce and Hassie. Pacing across the concrete walkway to the castle entrance and back again, Carter let the three men see that he was alone, no police, and that he did not possess the Golden Quipu or the treasure. He also had to pretend like he didn't know they were there. It was a dangerous game.

His pulse raced. He was the bait, and things rarely worked out well for the bait.

It was hard for him not to look for the men he knew were there or at the dock. He didn't want to draw any attention to Royce or Hassie. For a moment he stopped, keeping his back to the castle, checking his watch, and looking out toward the parking lot. It was almost ten minutes after five a.m. He turned on his heel and returned to pacing. Each time he lingered in the arched entrance tunnel next to the guard tower a little longer before returning to the walkway. On the third trip, he caught some movement under Mary's location.

Mary knew the sniper was likely heading to her position. The guard tower provided the best view and a superior angle. That was why she'd chosen it. Access to the top required her to go through the Guard Room near the castle entrance and up a spiral metal staircase. The spot she initially had chosen to position herself was in a small notch in the stone façade next to the staircase that allowed her to see Carter and the dock.

As soon as she saw the man with the rifle striding toward the Guard Room, she ducked down and scooted farther down the walls of the guard tower, toward Grant Tower. She desperately looked for a place to hide, seeing only open, notched stone areas, many covered by metal bars.

In the quiet darkness, she heard the creak of someone stepping onto the metal staircase. Mary squeezed through the wide bars stretched across one of notched areas only a few meters from where she had originally positioned herself. She hoped she was far enough away that the sniper couldn't see her when he reached the top, but since the area was open and potentially visible to those on the ground, she knew the thermal imaging in night-vision goggles could pick up her heat signature if she crawled too close to the edge. Just inside the front edge, she held the loaded shotgun close to her chest, with her right index finger on the trigger guard. She tingled with nervousness, not sure what to expect and feeling very uncomfortable with such limited weaponry. *Remember your training*, she told herself, hearing the creak of a few more stairs.

The rustling in the grass directly below her position told her one of the other men, who remained on the ground, had made his way around to this side of the castle. She pulled her feet up, careful to make no sound. She tried to maintain her primary focus on the approaching sniper. She knew he was closer and more of a threat.

Her senses on overdrive, she couldn't miss the sound of rubber-soled shoes scuffing the stone as the man reached the top of the stairs and slowly approached her hiding spot. Moving her index finger to the trigger, she pressed herself farther into the shadows.

She knew that the sniper's immediate objectives would be to confirm whether there were any threats on the roof, then find the optimal spot to position himself. He took another step, now only a meter away.

He exhaled in the cool early morning air; she slowly maneuvered the shotgun barrel to a few millimeters behind the notch's edge. She leveled the gun at the height that would take out the man's kneecap, if not his entire lower leg. She had no illusions of what these men were capable of doing. They had already killed and would kill again. There was only one reason to bring a sniper to this exchange. She breathed in through her nose and out through her mouth, ready to fire, but he turned and walked back to the top of the stairs.

Hearing his steps move away from her, she stole a quick glance out. The sniper had found what he was looking for, selecting the same spot she initially had, just to the right of the top of the stairs. He lay down on his stomach, set up a small tripod stand, and fastened his rifle into it. Then he turned a couple of the adjustment knobs on his scope and settled in.

She breathed a little easier and moved her finger off the trigger. The man on the ground, just below her elevated position, said something in a whisper. She leaned closer to the edge until she could see the top of his head. He was not the large man from the hotel.

"We are here. Alexei is on roof and confirmed site is clear," the man said. "No police, only soldier, and he is waiting at entrance to castle, alone. I do not see treasure or girl." He paused before continuing. "Right. We will remain here on sides of castle. Yes, after exchange made, we will wait for signal, and then, we make it clean," he said, ending the call.

She and Carter suspected these men would never honor the exchange, and as soon as he gave them what they wanted, the sniper would open fire. *That must be why they didn't bother wearing any face coverings,* she thought

Mary pulled her head back. Careful not to let her own phone give off any light, she texted Carter that the man had reported in that the site was clear and that they intended to leave no witness after the exchange. She texted the location of the sniper and the man on the ground under her. Then, she added, *Game on!*

Carter lingered inside the archway, reading Mary's texts. It was dangerous to make a play like this without knowing precisely where the third man was, but they were out of time. The others would arrive soon and then it would be too late to act.

He stepped out, but he didn't return to the walkway. Instead, he hugged the outer wall of the guard tower. He was careful to place his feet on the grass to reduce noise and stay out of view of the sniper. When he got to the corner, he removed his flashlight. He raced around the edge below Mary's position and beamed the light straight into the man's goggles.

The man recoiled, ripping off the goggles, but Carter was on him, connecting with a powerful roundhouse punch to the man's jaw. Carter was heavier and the extra weight made him a little slower, but he could still throw a hard punch. The man staggered but didn't fall. He fumbled for his gun, and Carter hit him again. He fell backward against the wall. Flailing but with his weapon freed, he started to raise the gun.

In one swift move, Carter grabbed the man's neck and slammed the back of his head into the stone. He heard a sickening crack of bone and watched his limp form slump to the ground.

Carter knew the man was dead, and he felt no remorse. The guy was a professional killer and would have killed them all. Carter relieved the man of his Heckler & Koch nine-millimeter pistol. Only then did he recognize the guy as the same one he'd previously clubbed with the bottle. A slight crackle came from the dead man's earpiece. Carter removed it and put it in his own ear.

"Gavrie, are you okay?"

Carter thought fast. His Russian accent had worked once, and maybe it would work again. "Da."

"I thought I heard you make noise?" the voice asked.

"I drop earpiece. Be quiet now," Carter demanded, not wanting to say much more for fear they would realize he wasn't Gavrie. Not sure how long the ruse would last, he ran, sticking close to the castle wall and pausing to peek around each corner. He stopped to catch his breath and hoped he might surprise the third man from behind.

The third man was thirty meters away, with his back to Carter. Too far away for the flashlight trick to work and with too much space to cover without the guy hearing him or sensing movement, Carter considered just shooting him. But unless he had to, he didn't want to make any noise. *That could put Mary in danger*, he thought, maneuvering slowly around the last corner with his gun at the ready.

"Gavrie, Alexei, do either of you see soldier? He did not come back to walkway," the man asked in a whisper into his headset.

Carter moved a few more steps closer to the man. If he could reach him, he might be able to take the man from behind, quietly and without firing a shot.

"*Nyet*, Leonid."

"Gavrie?" the man asked into the device.

Carter was too close to try to respond and pretend to be Gavrie again. Leonid was still almost ten meters away, and Carter wished that he had taken Gavrie's Kevlar vest.

"Gavrie?" Leonid asked again.

Less than five meters away, the man twirled and pulled his pistol. Carter fired twice into the man's chest.

Even with his Kevlar vest, the force of the shots knocked him to the wall, but it didn't prevent him from firing back.

The stones to the side of Carter's head exploded. Carter fired three more times, moving forward. The first bullet slammed into the man's shoulder. His second and third hit the man's temple and lower jaw. Before the man even hit the ground dead, Carter raced toward the main entrance.

"Alexei? Gavrie? What is happening?" Carter's earpiece erupted.

Mary heard the first shots below and saw the sniper frantically spin his rifle on the tripod from side to side. With the sniper's attention directed away from her, it was time for her to exit the crawl space, which would be tricky. If the sniper turned his head before she could get to her feet and aim the shotgun, she was dead. She had pulled herself forward under the bar using one hand while holding tight to the shotgun with the other, careful not to let the gun scrape against the metal bars.

When she heard the second round of gunfire below, she gave up her efforts at being stealthy. She shoulder-rolled the rest of the way out and jumped to her feet.

The sniper must have heard the movement behind him and started to pull the rifle up and around.

She pointed the shotgun at his head and squeezed the trigger.

She didn't feel the buck or hear the discharge, only an empty click. She pulled the trigger again. Another empty click.

Damn! She knew it was loaded. Normally, she would have test fired any weapon she intended to use, but there had not been time, and there had been no place to test it without drawing unwanted attention. She knew her mistake had just cost her her life.

The sniper smiled and finished swinging his sniper rifle, pointing it directly at Mary's chest.

"*Dasvidaniya*, pretty lady!" A broad sneer of yellow teeth crossed his face.

Everything moved in slow motion. She felt her breath leave her body, and she saw the man's finger tightening on the trigger. Then, she heard a single shot.

Chapter 31

CARTER SAW THE sneer on the sniper's face as the bullet from Carter's gun entered the bottom of the man's chin and exited through the top of his skull.

"Mary, you okay?" he asked, still pointing his pistol at where the sniper's head used to be.

"Yes."

Relieved to hear her voice, Carter started to climb the metal stairs.

"Stop! Go back down," she yelled.

"Don't worry. I already killed the other two."

"No, I see lights entering the parking lot," she said. "It's them. You need to get back down. They need to find you on the walkway and believe that their men still have you surrounded. I'll take point up here with the rifle," she said. Carter saw her roll the body away from the rifle. She lay down and made a few adjustments to the scope.

"Okay," Carter said. "Grab his earpiece so we can talk to each other, if needed. Be careful. When the others get here, that headset may become a party line," he said, opting to leave the other two men on the ground where they'd fallen. Neither would be visible from the walkway. Then, he tucked the pistol into his waistband, covered it with his shirt, and trotted back out.

A blue van hopped the curb and drove around the visitor center, pulling up twenty meters from Carter. It turned around so the back of the van now faced Carter, and the large Russian jumped out of the passenger's side.

His nose looked like a purple plum, he had dark semicircles under his eyes, and he walked with a noticeable limp.

Carter smiled. "I see you met my wife."

The man glared at him as he hobbled to the back of the van.

Carter saw a man in a white lab coat slip from the driver's seat into the back of the van and out of sight.

"You have Golden Quipu, leigheas fala, gold, and girl?"

"I have the leigheas fala." Carter unscrewed the top of the Irn-Bru bottle and held it up. "This is all there is, and if we don't get what we want, I'll pour it out here on the walkway. The Golden Quipu and a sample of the gold, along with the location of the rest of the gold, will be collected and provided after we confirm that you have Mr. Douglass. The girl was not part of the deal, ever."

"No, please don't spill it," the doctor pleaded from inside the van.

"Shut up, idiot!" the large Russian scolded the doctor without taking his eyes off Carter. Then, he looked over his shoulder toward the Loch. "Where is girl?"

"She's not part of the deal. You should listen better," Carter taunted the big man again. "Give us Mr. Douglass and you will get everything you wanted, other than her. You can ride out and declare victory."

Carter didn't know whether the Russian was going to balk. He just stared. It was unnerving.

"Mr. Douglass? This is Carter Porter. Are you in there?" he yelled.

Receiving no answer, Carter eyed the big Russian. The sound of a boat motor caught his attention, and he turned. Running lights of a speedboat approached their shore.

That was not part of our plan. He slumped, knowing that a speedboat could give an easier chase to someone on a Jet Ski.

Someone from inside the van slapped at the back doors, and the large Russian opened them.

Carter saw a hospital gurney and the van's driver at the far end of the bed. The two men pulled the gurney out, and the one in the white coat moved to the head of the bed. Carter barely recognized Alastair. "What the hell did you do to him?"

"He is only sedated. Mr. . . ."

"Enough, you idiot!" the Russian shouted.

The doctor nodded sheepishly.

Carter stared at Alastair. Even in this pre-sunrise dark, the old man looked sick, nothing like how he had at the hotel.

Is that merely a function of the sedation, the cold night air, or something else? What became obvious was that the remainder of their plan had just gone up in smoke. Alastair was not conscious and could not get on the back of Royce's Jet Ski. They needed a plan B.

"We deliver grandfather. Now, you deliver."

"Not the girl," Carter insisted as he pulled his pistol and pointed it at the Russian.

The large Russian shrugged. "Without girl."

Carter eyed him for a second. "Good, as long as we understand each other." He knew the man had no honor, but he still needed to drive home the point.

"Yes, we understand each other," the large Russian said before pulling out his own pistol and placing the barrel at the temple of Alastair's head. "But you should drop gun now."

Carter looked at the Loch and saw that the speedboat had stopped about fifty meters from the shore. He couldn't help himself and glanced over at the far dock. He only saw Royce's outline. He thought it would be easy enough to shoot the man and the doctor, but he couldn't guarantee he could do it before the Russian shot Alastair.

Quickly running possible options in his mind, Carter thought even if he or Mary could shoot these men and manage to escape with Alastair in the van, Royce and Hassie would have to fend off the speedboat. If these people had one sniper here, he knew they could have another on the boat. Any risk to Hassie and Royce was too great for him. He was confident that Mary would make the same calculations, but he dared not glance back in her direction. "I was just trying to keep things honest," Carter responded but not yet lowering his gun.

"Drop gun or old man dies, then you die and we find girl."

Since Mary still had him covered, Carter was about to drop his pistol when he heard a voice. It was Fiogry.

I am sorry, child. Your grandfather is gone. They told Carter that he is merely sleeping, but there is no light or colors emanating from his mortal body. Alastair Douglass has left this world. Fiogry spoke to Hassie, but Carter could hear her too.

Carter didn't have to ask; he knew instantly that what she said was true. Alastair was dead.

A soulful scream erupted from across the Loch, and Carter heard the roar of a distant Jet Ski firing up. *No! That's not the plan.*

"Well, that must be girl." The Russian smirked.

"You killed him? You killed Alastair," Carter shouted, enraged.

"You will kill grandfather if you not drop gun now. I not ask again." He pushed Alastair's head a little with the barrel of his gun.

"Run! Alastair is dead!" Carter screamed, waving his flashlight wildly. He didn't know whether Royce had received Fiogry's message, but he also wanted to alert Mary that the game had changed.

The Russian recoiled, clearly surprised by the sudden outburst.

Carter tossed the open bottle of Irn-Bru at the large Russian and raised his gun.

The doctor leaped for the flipping bottle. More than half its contents splashed out and across the hospital bed before it landed on the sidewalk.

Carter shot, aiming for the Russian, but the bullet tore through the doctor's back. The doctor collapsed onto the pavement, next to the emptying Irn-Bru bottle.

Carter fired again. His second bullet hit the Russian in the center of his chest, but he didn't fall. *Kevlar vest*, Carter thought.

The Russian righted himself, and with amazing speed and agility, he leveled his gun at Carter and fired just before Carter heard a second shot from behind him.

Dropping his own pistol and falling to his knees, Carter watched a red stain expanding on the front of his shirt. He looked up to see the big man fall like a bag of dirt, the top of his skull missing.

"Carter, how bad are you hit?"

He heard the alarm in Mary's voice. "Mary, help Hassie and Royce," he panted into his headset.

"I will, but how bad are you hit?" she repeated.

"Thank you, thank you for everything," he said in a weak voice as he relished a vision of Courtney. She was smiling at him. He smiled back, reached for her, and fell the rest of the way to the ground.

Mary desperately wanted to race down and check on Carter, but she knew she still had a job to do. Hassie and Royce were in harm's way, and Carter would not want her to leave her post until they were safe. There was no way for her to know if Carter was dead or alive at the moment, and as hard as it was, that knowledge wouldn't change what she needed to do.

From the roof of the guard tower, she perched the rifle on the wall and focused the thermal imaging scope toward the speedboat. Unfortunately, the top of a clump of trees near the edge of the Loch impeded her view. She could make out portions of a couple of heat signatures, and she thought she saw one of them holding something large to their face, like binoculars directed toward the shore. Unfortunately, she had no clear view.

She swung her scope to the far side of the Loch. Hassie's thermal image was moving quickly. She had no idea why Carter had yelled that

Alastair was dead or why Hassie had fired up her Jet Ski early, but she had to roll with it. She heard a second Jet Ski fire up, but when she scanned for Royce's thermal signature, she saw nothing.

Confused and frantic voices came from the deck of the speedboat, but they were too far away to understand. The speedboat's engine roared to life.

She suspected that the people on the boat were part of the group who had kidnapped Hassie's grandfather and just shot Carter, but until she knew with certainty or until they made a move on Hassie, she couldn't kill them in cold blood, even if she had a clear shot.

Her suspicions heightened when she saw the speedboat headed on a direct intercept course with Hassie's Jet Ski.

Hassie had never experienced such inconsolable rage, but it now consumed her. *They murdered him! They treated him like a piece of refuse.* Tears streamed down her face. She had no plan. She just gunned her Jet Ski faster.

The speedboat was a little more than two hundred meters from her and closing fast. She no longer cared. She would plow right through it if she had to, but she was going to make it to her grandfather.

The cold spray mixed with her tears made it hard to see, but she felt a hand on top of her own twisting the accelerator and slowing her to a stop. Royce appeared next to her out of nothingness.

"What are you doing?" Royce asked breathlessly. "That speedboat is coming for you. Remember what Carter said. We have to get away."

The sight of Royce at her side and knowing that he was only trying to help her eased her anger, if only for a moment.

Child, please calm your mind and heart, Fiogry pleaded with her. *I am losing you. You are in danger, but I cannot help you unless you calm yourself.*

Fiogry's words seemed more distant and harder to hear.

"Fiogry, you can save him, right? Like you did before for him, and for Sir Scrounge?" she yelled.

I am sorry, child. Alastair Douglass's light and colors have returned to their creator. His mortal life has ended. The leigheas fala can heal the flesh, but once gone, it cannot restore the light and colors of life to a vessel.

Hassie strained to hear the response, but she understood the answer was no. "You won't help me, even with all your powers?" she screamed. "Why did you give me the gold coins or the leigheas fala? Why did you call to me and come into my life? If you had not, then my grandfather would still be here. Why?" she demanded again but heard no answer.

She reached for her accelerator, but Royce grabbed her hand. "Hassie, please don't."

"They murdered him, Royce!"

"Yes, they did," Royce acknowledged. "I'm sorry. They also shot Carter. I saw him fall. He wanted us to run. Please, unless you turn and head in the opposite direction with me, they will get you too. You'll be giving them exactly what they want."

"It doesn't matter anymore!" Hassie screamed. "You can run if you want. Just leave me alone." She pushed his hand away and twisted the accelerator.

"Hassie, no!"

Out of the corner of her eye, Hassie saw Royce reaching for her wrist, but she leaned away from him. His hand fell, hitting her knee and then fell to the edge of the open side compartment as she tried to pull away. She felt her Jet Ski jerk a little toward Royce's and watched him being pulled out of his seat.

"Let go!" She twisted the accelerator as hard as she could, not caring that she might yank him into the cold water. Initially, she felt a little drag, but then she lurched forward. She heard Royce yell to her again, but she didn't look back.

The running lights of the speedboat grew brighter, only fifty meters away now. She would not let them stop her. She would get within fifteen meters and then make a hard veer to the right and slip around it. She knew the speedboat was fast, but it was not as nimble as her Jet Ski.

Hassie tensed her shoulders and prepared to jerk the handlebar. The speedboat made an almost ninety-degree turn, cutting a huge swath of water right in front of her. She had just yanked the bar right, only to wrench it left to avoid hitting the nose of the speedboat.

Traveling at over thirty-five knots, the sharp turns combined with the large wake caused the Jet Ski to flip over. She managed to hang on with one hand as she rolled under.

The icy water was a shock, and she gasped when the bottom-weighted Jet Ski popped right side up. Panting, she pulled herself onto the seat.

The speedboat made a wide turn and circled back for her. Her heart was in her throat as she tried to restart the Jet Ski, without success.

Water must have gotten into the engine when it flipped. It's dead in the water. And so am I.

Chapter 32

THE SPEEDBOAT SLOWED and pulled up alongside Hassie. A large man was at the wheel, and a smaller, thin man had a smile that chilled her more than the freezing water. She glared daggers at both men.

Hassie focused her attention on the smaller man wearing an expensive jacket and tweed flat cap; his commanding presence suggested that he was in charge. The one driving the speedboat reached over and grabbed the back of her sweater, easily yanking her off her Jet Ski and dropping her on the deck.

"Thank you, Mikhail," the smaller man said with an unsettling calm.

Hassie popped to her feet and swung her tiny fist at him.

Mikhail caught her arm and threw her down onto the deck.

"I do apologize for the rough treatment, Miss Douglass, but we are on a bit of tight schedule. My name is Avery Darrow, and I can assure you that this will go much easier for you if you simply choose to cooperate."

"Murderer!" she screamed as she jumped into a crouch. Acting on pure rage, she lunged at Avery.

Mikhail stepped in front of her, and she slammed into his torso, which was like hitting a brick wall.

Mikhail stood her up and slapped her across the cheek. Sparks flew in front of her eyes. She reeled onto the deck, then rolled over onto her stomach and tried to push herself back onto her feet.

He grabbed her right arm in a vice grip. Twisting the arm behind her back, he then lifted her to her feet.

She gasped. She tried to kick at him from behind, but he wrenched her arm higher. "Try again, and I break it," he menaced.

Her mind reeled from the pain.

"Please, Miss Douglass," Avery said as if speaking to an unruly child. "We did not kill Alastair Douglass. In fact, we had a team of doctors trying to save him. We wanted him to live, to better study the effects of the leigheas fala."

Her anger rose even higher when the man used her grandfather's name and mentioned the leigheas fala. To hear words that represented something so good and pure coming from the mouth of someone so evil unhinged her.

"Liar!" she spat. "You kidnapped and killed him. Murderer!"

"Miss Douglass, we really do not have time for this. Where is the Golden Quipu and the rest of the gold? We know that Mr. Porter did not have them with him onshore. And where is your companion on the other Jet Ski?"

She looked out on the dark waters but didn't see Royce. *Good. He ran*, she thought. She had pushed Royce away, but at least he was safe.

The speedboat's lights illuminated the side of her own drifting Jet Ski, and she saw that the open side compartment was empty. She looked at Avery with a satisfied smile and laughed. "You just lost your Golden Quipu when you dunked me. It was on my Jet Ski, and now it's at the bottom of the Loch." She sneered. "You'll never get it now!"

Avery's jaw tightened, and his eyes became slits. "If you are lying to me, I promise that you will suffer," he said, dripping malevolence. He nodded at Mikhail.

He twisted Hassie's arm further, and she screamed.

"Now, is this the truth, Miss Douglass?"

"Yes, it's the truth," she gasped through gritted teeth.

Avery studied her with a dubious expression.

"It's the truth," she repeated, trying to convince him.

"Mikhail, as soon as we finish with Miss Douglass here, please mark our current coordinates so we will know where to commence the search."

The large man nodded.

"Miss Douglass, we do not have much time, and you no longer have anything to bargain with. Therefore, it is important that you answer my questions quickly and honestly."

Hassie simply glared at him with pure hatred.

Avery sighed, nodding to Mikhail again.

With a pop, the pain exploded in her shoulder. *He's tearing my arm off.* Her shoulder was on fire, and she felt dizzy. "Okay." She winced.

He relaxed the tension on her arm a little, but he held a firm grasp on her wrist.

"Excellent. Now, how were you able to decipher the Golden Quipu to make the leigheas fala? And what is the formula?"

What? She must have misheard him, or he must be playing some sick game. She thought these people might not know everything about the leigheas fala, but it stunned her to hear them connect these two treasures. She couldn't think of how to respond. If this was merely a test and he really knew that the blood cure was unrelated to the Golden Quipu, then a lie could be a death sentence. On the other hand, if he really didn't know about the leigheas fala, she didn't want to offer any information that could help him.

Avery rolled his eyes. He opened his mouth for what Hassie was sure to be an order for Mikhail to break her arm, when Hassie saw Royce's Jet Ski suddenly appear, floating near her abandoned Jet Ski.

Avery turned and drew back. "Where the hell did he come from?"

"Let her go, now!" Royce held the warming tray over the water.

She realized he must have taken it from the compartment before she sped away. "No, Royce! Run!"

"You don't want to test my resolve." Royce's eyes darted back and forth between the two men holding Hassie. "I'll drop this. So let her go, now."

"Royce, drive away, please!" she screamed again.

Mikhail shook Hassie's arm and told her to shut up. With his other hand, he pulled a pistol from his jacket and pointed it at Royce. "Why should we care what you do, and why should I not just shoot you?"

"Inside this container is the Golden Quipu and a bag of gold coins from the treasure." Royce lifted the container a little higher. "If you shoot me, I'll drop it. If you hurt Hassie, I'll drop it. If you don't let her go now, I'll drop it. The water here is very deep, and there is no visibility below ten meters. With the currents from the river feeding into the Loch, this container could drift a hundred meters or more in any direction on the way down."

Avery turned to Hassie. "You lied to me." His tone wasn't angry, but almost respectful and impressed that she had been able to maintain a lie even under extreme torture.

Avery returned his gaze to Royce. "What you hold is mine, young man. Nobody takes what is mine, *ever*."

"Just let her go. She can swim over, then I'll toss you the Golden Quipu. I will tell you the location of the rest of the treasure gold."

Mikhail adjusted his pistol and pointed it at Royce's chest.

"This man is a marksman of the highest degree," Avery informed Royce. "At this distance, he would not miss. If I give the order, you will die."

Royce looked scared, but he didn't back down. "My arm is starting to tire." He shook the tray. "Let her go and you get what you want, but wait much longer and there may not be a choice for any of us."

"Let's all just take a deep breath. There is no need for further violence," Avery said, softening his tone a bit.

Hassie noticed Royce didn't look at Avery but kept his focus on the big man with the gun.

"Mikhail, please do not shoot this young man."

She sighed in relief. She was terrified that Royce was about to get himself killed for her sake.

"Mikhail, please shoot this young man's Jet Ski," Avery ordered calmly. "If he drops the container, please shoot him as well."

Hassie's relief disappeared and her heart sank. The shock on Royce's face said everything. Clearly, he had not considered this possibility. In fact, Hassie suspected he hadn't considered any of the possibilities other than trying to save her.

"Yes, sir."

Two bullets slammed into the lower back part of the Jet Ski, about a half meter behind Royce's right leg. The engine sputtered but continued to run. Mikhail fired a third time, and Hassie thought she heard the bullet ping against something metal.

"Stop!" she screamed, terrified that one of the bullets would hit Royce. The situation was untenable. She couldn't do anything, and unless Royce did something, neither one of them would have any chance to escape.

Royce had obviously made the same determination. He stood, swung his arm, and whipped the tray in a high arc over the back corner of the speedboat.

Mikhail released Hassie's wrist, dropped the gun on the deck, and jumped high. At the top of his jump, his outstretched fingers wrapped around a back leg of the metal warming tray. He slapped his other hand on top and landed, but he lost his balance and fell over the side, holding the tray.

"Jump, Hassie!" Royce screamed.

Avery raced to the back of the boat where Mikhail had gone over, and Hassie threw herself into the water.

Her wrist felt broken and her shoulder dislocated. She used every piece of energy and stamina she had to keep from drowning.

"Hand the tray to me!" Avery screamed.

Hearing Avery and Mikhail yelling behind her, she knew she didn't have much time and swam with her legs and one good arm to reach

Royce. He pulled her onboard and twisted the accelerator. The Jet Ski sputtered and moved, just not very fast.

"Go!" she urged through chattering teeth.

"I'm trying," he responded with desperation in his voice. "The gunshots must have damaged the engine." He aimed the Jet Ski for the castle shore, but it still puttered and moved at a snail's pace.

"I think the gunshots also damaged the steering," Royce announced. "I can't turn it."

Hassie kept her eye on the speedboat. Her rage and anger subsided and was replaced with worry for Royce's safety and guilt over putting him in such danger.

Avery crouched on the deck, peeling back the electrical tape covering the edges of the tray to pry a corner open. He peered in and saw the sparkling artifact. *It's mine!* He laughed. *It may have taken years of searching and millions of dollars, but it's mine.* He carefully pressed the electrical tape around the edges, resealing the lid.

"What about those two?" Mikhail asked, dripping water on the deck as he retrieved his pistol.

Avery thought the sun would be up soon, and the lying girl was now just a frustration. "I believe we have what we need and we do not want any witnesses."

Mikhail nodded, moving to the opposite side of the deck.

With the speedboat stationary, the waters of the Loch calm, and given how slowly his targets moved, Avery knew this would not be a difficult shot for his hired hand. He watched Mikhail raise his pistol and take aim. Mikhail's finger moved to the trigger and began to squeeze, when a sickening thud hit the side of his chest. Avery's man slumped and fell over the side into the unforgiving darkness of the Loch.

Avery watched in stunned silence until, to his horror, he saw chunks of wood from the deck exploding next to him. He heard the sound of a rifle's report a split second after the bullet hit the deck near him.

Who is shooting at me? Terrified, his mind raced. He had seen the soldier fall and knew it wasn't him. With Mikhail dead, he wasn't safe out in the open. Leaving the sealed tray, he crawled to the ship's control area. Another bullet hit near his leg, and he felt some of the wooden splinters strike his ankle. Crouching down to keep his head and body as low as possible, he pushed the throttle forward and down.

Hearing no shots for a few moments, he lifted his head enough to peek through the windshield.

The pair on the Jet Ski were far to his left. He had no gun—he relied on his hired muscle for that—but he knew he could eliminate these witnesses by grinding them under the boat's powerful propellers.

Struggling to keep his balance, since he was not in the captain's chair, he rotated the steering wheel and angled the boat toward the escaping Jet Ski and slammed the throttle all the way forward.

As the first signs of the sun washed over the Meall Fuar-mhonaidh overlooking Loch Ness, Avery watched in disbelief as the Jet Ski and its two occupants evaporated into thin air.

Hassie heard the speedboat engine fire up behind them, and she hugged Royce tighter. "Thank you for coming back for me." Her teeth still chattered. "I'm so sorry I put you in this position."

"I told you before, I don't have so many friends that I can afford to lose one."

The Jet Ski crept along, and looking over Royce's shoulder, the shore seemed impossibly far.

Royce turned when the Jet Ski made a final sputter and came to a complete stop. She saw the panic on his face.

We're not going to make it, Hassie thought but noticed a shimmering curtain between them and the boat. *Thank you,* she said silently.

She realized the speedboat still raced toward their position. Even if the speedboat driver couldn't see her, she remembered Fiogry saying her distortion of light would not prevent physical contact.

"We're going to have to jump," Royce yelled.

She wasn't sure that she could. Her arm was numb and her legs ached. If she jumped, she doubted she could make it out of the way in time.

Be still, children. I am with you, and I will not leave you.

Fiogry's words were not lost on Hassie. They were the same words she had uttered to Scrounge when she thought he was about to die. Shame and guilt flooded her for lashing out at Fiogry.

The speedboat was moving incredibly fast, straight at them, but somehow, all she felt was a warmth. At what should have been the most terrifying moment of her life, she was at peace.

The water behind them exploded. Fiogry shot up like a breaching humpback whale between the Jet Ski and the speedboat. She rose ten meters or more in the air until the tip of the boat's bow slammed into her fleshy belly and tore through the incredible creature with a savage ferocity. It was the most horrifying sight Hassie had ever seen.

The front of the speedboat crunched like an accordion, and the great beast forced the front of the boat underwater. The back end rocketed up, and Avery slammed headfirst into the windshield. His limp body somersaulted through the air before smacking the water. He floated facedown for only a moment and then sank. The metal tray with the Golden Quipu had launched like a rock flung from a sling-shot, and Hassie saw a splash thirty or forty meters away.

Her eyes were drawn to the speedboat, which had flipped all the way over and landed on top of Fiogry. The great beast crashed back onto the water's surface. Her long neck and head slapped the water about five meters from the Jet Ski.

"Fiogry!" No longer thinking about the cold water or the pain in her shoulder, Hassie jumped into the water.

Using her one good arm, she swam over, only to see a terrible sight.

The boat had torn Fiogry's midsection. An open wound at least two meters wide was visible, but it could have been larger, since much of the beast's torso was still under the wreckage. Her blood turned the water fizzy and pink, like soda. The inside of the beast bubbled and foamed too, as if the water was dissolving her in front of Hassie's eyes. The bright and shimmering pink dewlap under Fiogry's chin was now pale, white, and empty.

It is almost finished, child.

Hassie lifted part of the beast's head, but Fiogry winced.

"I'm sorry." Hassie moved her hand away. She felt helpless, watching the beast suffer in tremendous pain and agony. "Please don't die."

Still on the Jet Ski, Royce used his hands to paddle closer.

"This is my fault," Hassie cried.

No, child. This was my choice, and it was a good choice. Your life and Royce's life are lives worth saving, and I had the ability to save them.

"Why me? Why did you . . . ?" Hassie's sobs prevented her from finishing.

Because many are called, but few choose to listen. You heard my call, you answered, and you took action. You did all of this on faith without having to see me first. Thank you, child. You helped me to help others. Fiogry's voice sounded more and more faint, almost a whisper now.

The open gash in her midsection expanded. As more water poured in, the great beast's life poured out. The wreckage of the speedboat gurgled and sank, pulling the weakened Fiogry down with it.

Hassie's grandfather was gone, and now this incredible angel of the light was gone. Surrounded by gallons of the pinkish, fizzing fluid, Hassie felt alone.

Chapter 33

CARTER AWOKE TO a knock on his hospital room door.

"How are we feeling this morning, Mr. Porter?" The cheerful nurse checked the levels of the medicines hanging from his IV pole and added a new bag.

He forced a smile. "Better than I deserve, I'm sure."

"Well, for someone who survived a bullet, two broken ribs, and a collapsed lung, I think you look great. Let me know if you need anything," the nurse offered before she strode out.

"You're still here," Carter said, reaching for Mary's hand.

She sat in a chair by his bed. "Still here," Mary answered, furrowing her brow at her phone.

"I'm glad," he said. "How long have I been here?"

"Four days. You lost so much blood, they weren't sure you'd make it. You drifted in and out for most of that time. It's good to see you more awake."

He nodded. "How are Hassie and Royce?"

"Both fine," she assured him. "Hassie left a few minutes ago. She's making arrangements for Alastair's memorial service and didn't want to wake you."

Carter bit his lip. He was so confused he had to remind himself of everything that had happened, including Alastair's death.

"Royce is on his way up now," she added.

"Okay." He studied his right hand. It was immobilized in a plastic holder with tape around the IV-line connections.

"Are you wondering what they are pumping into you? Antibiotics. And the doctors prescribed some detoxification medicines to reduce some harmful side effects of alcohol withdrawal," she said without anger.

"Good." He looked down again. "Actually, I was just glad that this wrist restraint for the IV wasn't a handcuff." He laughed.

She smiled. "It certainly could've gone differently, but the forensics backed up our story, and we had the text messages from Hassie's phone. In short order, the authorities were able to connect the men who kidnapped Alastair and who tried to kill you, Hassie, and Royce to a man named Avery Darrow. Does that name mean anything to you?"

"Nope." Carter shook his head with a puzzled look. "Who is he?"

"Some pharmaceutical industrialist who wanted the treasure."

"So, is he in custody?" Carter frowned.

"No. He died when the speedboat wrecked."

"Wrecked?"

"Yeah, I didn't see it. I took out one of the men on the boat when he aimed his gun at Hassie and Royce, but when the second man, Darrow, drove the speedboat back toward our shore and bore down on Royce and Hassie's Jet Ski, the tops of the trees blocked my view and any reasonable shot. I picked up the sniper rifle and ran for the stairs to get down by the shore. By the time I got down there, it was all over."

"What did it hit?"

"The authorities really can't explain it. They said the boat was moving at a high rate of speed when it crashed into something that flattened the front of the boat. They think it may have been a rogue wave or sudden change in current, since they found nothing in the water to explain it."

Carter nodded.

"Hassie and Royce told me the speedboat smashed into your Fiogry. With urging from them, I agreed not to share anything about the beast with the authorities. Our story worked without it, and the mention of this beast would have created more suspicion."

"That makes sense, and Fiogry asked us not to tell anyone, or at least no man, about her."

Her tone turned more somber. "Carter, Hassie told me that Fiogry died saving them. They told me she threw herself between the speedboat and them, and the boat gutted her."

"Dead?" He exhaled loudly, his throat tightening.

"That's what she said. She told me that the creature suffered massive wounds and somehow, the exposure to the water killed her. Dissolving her insides, if you can believe that."

He thought about what Fiogry had told them, and he knew it must be true.

"When the authorities raised the sunken speedboat, all they found was a smashed boat. They found Avery Darrow's body and the man I shot a distance away. This made the decision not to say anything about Fiogry easier," she continued. "Of course, it was easier for me, since I never saw the beast, like you all said that . . . like you all did."

He couldn't explain it, but he felt like he had just lost another parent. His chest felt heavy and his world less grounded.

Mary reached out and squeezed his hand. She must have seen the pain in his eyes. "Hassie debriefed me on what she told the authorities. She and Royce told them the atrocities committed by the Russian: murdering Royce's friend, shooting Royce, kidnapping Hassie and then her grandfather, and trying to kill you, all to obtain the treasure."

"Do you think they bought it?"

"Well, Royce and Hassie still had a copy of the first letter, and he took them to the cave and the rest of the gold."

"So, the treasure is gone too." He shook his head, wondering if it had all been worth it. "What about the Golden Quipu?"

"Hassie said she considered not saying anything about it to the authorities, but there were too many references to it in the phone texts, as well as a blurry picture of it. So, she mentioned it but made it clear that none of you had ever heard of it before the kidnappers made it part of the ransom. Royce told them about the frantic search for the treasure so they could deliver what the kidnappers demanded. He also told them he'd tossed the Golden Quipu to Avery on the boat. Hassie told them that on the boat, Avery revealed to her he believed it held the formula for something he called the leigheas fala, and he falsely believed that she somehow knew how to decipher the gold and jeweled artifact, which she assured them was ridiculous." Mary chuckled a little to herself. "She's a great little actress. She also said that she told the authorities she believed Avery was delusional, as well as dangerous. Of course, that last part had the virtue of being true."

"So, did they recover the Golden Quipu?" Carter asked, thinking about its inestimable value.

"No, apparently it was lost in the Loch."

Carter rubbed at his eyes, trying to take it all in. "Mary, I think those men may have killed Dad too." He paused. "When Dad died, I was told that he repeated something he asked an orderly to tell me. He told me he thought it was 'keep on' and 'hold on.' I thought Dad was trying to encourage me, but I now think he was muttering 'Golden Quipu.' They killed him for it." Carter clenched his fist. "To be honest, part of me is glad that thing is gone."

Mary squeezed his hand again, and his fist unclenched.

He exhaled as if trying to purge the negative thoughts from his mind. "Thanks. I'll be okay."

She smiled at him.

He smiled back and then changed the subject. "So, you really didn't see or hear Fiogry at all?"

"No, I'm afraid not."

"I'm sorry. She was miraculous."

Mary cocked her head. "I'm not sure I can recall you ever using that word."

"It's the truth," he said sincerely with pain in his voice.

She fidgeted and rubbed her jaw. "Carter, I'm sorry to tell you this, particularly now, but just before you woke up, I read an email about your court-martial hearing. The navy is going to discharge you with an OTH. With the blood and urine evidence, your prior history, and your absence without leave, you're fortunate they didn't pursue a prison sentence. There may still be a chance for appeal, but Bobby says that the odds—"

He waved her off. "Mary, stop, please. It's okay."

"What do you mean 'it's okay'?"

"No, really, it's okay and it's the right decision." He looked into her beautiful eyes. "Mary, I've made a thousand bad decisions, which have led me to this point. The decision that the navy made was the correct one. I need to start being more accountable for my own life, even if that means retracing some steps and starting over."

She paused and then slowly nodded. "Maybe you're right. Maybe it is the right decision." She patted his arm in support, then added, "And it takes courage to admit it."

"Thanks. I wish it could've turned out different, but I wish a lot of things could've turned out different."

"Well, in the spirit of complete candor, there is one more thing I should tell you." She gave him a wry smile.

"What? I'm not sure how much more bad news I can take," he half joked.

"Do you remember Chuck Reynolds from CID?"

He nodded. "Yeah, sort of. Wasn't he a sniveling little piece of garbage?"

"Yes, he still is," she agreed. "There was a chance that I could have had your blood and urine samples conveniently lost and by extension the current charges against you dropped."

"Really? Are you serious?"

"Yes, if I had just agreed to sleep with Chuck." She made a face like she was retching.

"You said no, right?" He laughed.

"Yeah, I said no. I may have lowered my standards with you, but I still have some standards." She punched his arm.

"To think the navy is going to keep and probably promote a scumbag like that while they drum me out." Carter shook his head. "Gosh, I wonder what Chuckie would have offered if *I* had proposed to sleep with him," he asked mockingly.

"He probably would have tacked on ten years in Leavenworth." She snickered.

Carter pretended to look hurt. He loved to see Mary laugh and smile. It had been a long time since he had seen anything other than worry or anger on her face. He was about to ask her something else when he heard another knock.

Royce pushed the door open. "Hey, Mary told me that you were improving. That's fantastic." He had something large wrapped in brown paper under his arm.

"I hear you gave our treasure away," Carter said with a lilt.

"Yes, well, sorry about that." Royce shook his hand. "We kind of had to, under the law. You, Hassie, and I will receive credit for the find, but yes, we turned it over to the Treasure Trove Unit for assessment three days ago. Failure to turn it over could have exposed us to fines, or worse."

"I remember." He smiled and waved his hands in surrender. "Oh well, easy come, easy go. What's a hundred million dollars between friends?"

"I'm sorry for your suffering, but I don't think you will be left wanting once you hear what we are likely to get." Royce beamed.

"Get?" Mary asked. "You mean like a finder's fee?"

"Sort of, but it's usually more than a traditional finder's fee."

"And?" Mary asked.

"Hey, I'm the one entitled to a third of it," Carter teased.

"Hey, I'm still entitled to a half of your third." She playfully slapped his arm again.

"Yes, you are, and probably more." Carter grinned and turned to Royce. "So, how much are we talking about, buddy?"

He cleared his throat. "Well, we should get a final valuation in a few weeks. They're still assembling the complete valuation committee made up of experts to determine a true market value for the find. However, the preliminary estimates of the historic and intrinsic value of the treasure could exceed four hundred million pounds."

Carter almost choked. He didn't expect to hear that they could receive a life-changing amount of money, particularly when a government agency was involved. He looked at Mary, and then back at Royce. All of them burst into laughter.

"That's crazy!" Mary said.

"Of course it's crazy. This is Scotland! Unicorns are our official mascot," Royce said with pride.

When the laughter subsided, Carter looked at Royce. "Thank you, my friend, for everything."

"You are most welcome, Carter." The two men shook hands again. "I actually have one more gift for you." He handed him the uneven package wrapped in plain brown paper.

Carter tore at the cheap paper. As soon as he revealed a corner, he knew it was the Golden Quipu. It shimmered and glistened even more under the bright, sterile lights of the hospital room.

"I thought that was at the bottom of the Loch!" Mary said, shocked.

"It was. Yesterday I remembered that the mesh bag I put the gold coins in contained a GPS-GSM tag. We use the tags in marine studies to tag and track sharks and sea turtles," he explained. "I tracked the mesh bag and found the metal serving tray."

"Awesome!"

"Hassie and I agreed that you should take it, Carter."

"Listen, thank you, but don't you have to turn this in with the other treasure? Isn't keeping it, you know, kind of against the rules?" Carter crinkled his brow.

"Some of your bad habits must be rubbing off on me." Royce chuckled. "Technically, since you are one of the three people credited with finding it, either you, me, or Hassie can turn it in. Once I give you possession of it, then it will be up to you to determine whether or not the rules are broken."

"Now that sounds more like the Royce I know." Carter laughed. "Any idea what this Golden Quipu thing really is?"

"No, not a clue, other than it's a priceless artifact." Royce shook his head. "Any idea how long you'll be in the hospital?"

"I'm not sure. It could be another week or even two. I guess it's a shame we don't have any more of that leigheas fala."

Royce's smile disappeared.

"Yeah, Mary told me Fiogry died," Carter said, seeing his friend's reaction.

"She did. She died for us." Royce's voice cracked a little.

"At least we had a chance to experience her before she died," Carter offered. "You also experienced the healing power of the leigheas fala. Is it still working?"

"Yeah, it appears to be." He tapped his chest.

"Does that mean you will be joining the Scottish army and maybe become one of the Royal Scots Dragoon Guards like your grandfather?" Mary asked.

Royce shook his head. "No, I don't think so. I can't believe I am saying that. Only a week ago, I would have given my arm for an opportunity to join the army. When people tell you so many times that you can't do something, you start to feel cheated. Suddenly, what you're not able to do takes on greater and greater importance."

"I can understand that." Mary placed a gentle hand on his shoulder. "I've known a few who wanted to serve but couldn't, for a variety of reasons."

"Yeah, well, one thing that Fiogry brought into blinding clarity for me was how much time I've wasted focusing on gifts that were not bestowed to me instead of embracing the talents and gifts that were. I have a real talent and love for marine science. Who knows? Maybe someday marine science research will lead me to another Fiogry."

"For what it's worth, I think you are making the right choice," Carter stated. "It's the right decision for you."

"Still, I have to admit that I would have enjoyed being saluted," Royce said, smiling.

Mary looked at Carter and he shrugged.

"I'm game if you are. We should do it soon, since they are about to kick me out of the Marine Corps."

"Attention!" Mary said loudly. She stiffened to ramrod straight, feet together, head up, and all expression wiped from her face.

Carter sat up straight in the bed as best he could and similarly wiped all expression from his face.

"There is a superior officer on deck," Mary announced firmly, shooting up her right hand in a crisp salute.

Carter's hand, IV tubes and all, snapped up as well.

"Thank you both. I know this must seem silly, particularly to two career military personnel like yourselves," Royce said, clearly touched.

"My friend, there is nothing silly about wanting respect." Carter rested back onto his pillow. "I can assure you, whether you're wearing a uniform or not, and whether or not others salute you, you are respected. You are one of the most courageous people I've ever met, and it has been my honor to know you."

"Thank you, Carter. You, too." Then, Royce turned to Mary. "Thank you, too."

"You're welcome, and I couldn't agree more with Carter. I just wish that I had experienced what you all did with Fiogry. It certainly appears to have had a positive impact on your lives."

"So, you really didn't hear the voice say that Alastair was dead?" Carter asked her again.

"No, but there was a faint something. I chalked it up to my

imagination or the power of suggestion, but it had nothing to do with Alastair." Mary pinched her chin, recalling it.

Carter screwed up his face. "Really? What did you hear?"

"Well, at one point, before you were shot, I could've sworn I heard a voice say, *Your colors are strong, even if you have an unfortunate name.*"

Carter and Royce laughed.

"What?"

"Fiogry didn't like to be called any name derived from where she lived, and I sort of mentioned once that your name was Mary and you were from Maryland."

"Really?" She smiled teasingly. "After meeting you, Carter, I would've assumed the unfortunate name Fiogry referred to would've been my last name."

EPILOGUE

FOUR MONTHS HAD PASSED since Hassie lost her grandfather and watched Fiogry sink into the darkness. She deeply missed and grieved for both. With her grandfather, she missed the life she knew and that they shared. With Fiogry, she missed the life that could have been and the opportunity to experience more of the creature's love.

Thinking about what Fiogry told her about the original light and colors made her feel a little better about where her grandfather was now. The first days were difficult, but she found that focusing on helping others helped her get through it. She visited Carter in the hospital, of course, but caring for Scrounge was the most rewarding. The dog needed her, and she needed him.

On this cool, overcast Tuesday afternoon, Hassie and Scrounge sat on a small bluff overlooking Loch Ness, not too far from the Inn.

Scrounge bounded up to her with a stick in his mouth and dropped it at her feet. She picked it up and scratched the fur on the side of his face. When she didn't throw it again, he nudged her side with his snout and sneezed twice.

"I know, boy, it still smells like him, doesn't it?" She looked down at her grandfather's sweater. She grabbed a large swath of the wool near the collar and held it to her nose. "I hope that never changes, and I'm going to hang it back up in the same place in his closet when we get back to the flat," she told him, glad that she was able to convince her landlord to let her keep Scrounge as long as she agreed to pay twice the rent.

She had no idea what she would do with the rest of the money she'd received for the treasure. She was not yet old enough to drive, so buying an expensive car would be frivolous, and she knew that her grandfather would have frowned on such conspicuous displays of wealth.

Aside from the increased rent, she allowed herself to spend some of the money on only two other things. For one, she made a sizeable and anonymous contribution to the City of Forres, with instructions for them to use the money to repair its broken sewage line. She giggled to herself. *I still feel a little guilty about what my little lie caused.*

The second thing she allowed herself to spend money on was paying for take-out orders from the Inn's restaurant for Scrounge. She tossed the stick to him a few more times before checking the time on her phone. *I still have a few minutes before I have to leave for my shift at the Inn.* Even though she didn't need it, keeping her part-time job provided some normalcy for her, which she valued. She squinted against a strong gust of cold air coming off the Loch.

Hassie pulled the two ancient groats from her pocket. Sometimes she clicked them together, as Royce had shown her, but she could never bring herself to blow into them. It would just remind her of what she had lost. On more than one occasion, she brought the coins with her to the Loch, believing she might throw them in as a tribute to Fiogry, but she couldn't do that either. She returned them to her pocket.

It was hard not to think about the great beast when she was at Loch Ness. Her memories were all she had left of the creature.

She heard a young boy laughing a short distance away. He and his mom were finishing a picnic lunch. She recognized them; they had stayed at the Inn a few months back.

The mother waved at Hassie, and the boy ran over and asked if he could pet her dog.

"Of course; he doesn't bite. He's a sweetie." She scratched the dog's neck.

"What's his name?"

"His name is Sir Scrounge Douglass, Honorary Knight of the Round Pail." She smiled with pride. When she'd formally adopted him, Sir Scrounge Douglass, Honorary Knight of the Round Pail was far too long to include on the license form, so his legal name was Scrounge Douglass.

"Your dog is a knight?" the boy asked excitedly.

"Yes. It's only an honorary title, so he's prohibited from jousting in formal competitions. Besides, he has a terrible time staying on top of a horse. However, except for maybe my friend Royce, you are looking at the bravest in all of Scotland."

The boy seemed confused by her answer. "But he's a real knight, right?"

"Absolutely." She grinned, which earned a gleeful smile from the boy.

"I hope Joey is not bothering you," the boy's mother said, trotting up behind him.

"Not at all, ma'am. Sir Scrounge loves the attention." Hassie giggled.

"You work at the Inn, don't you?" the mother asked.

"Yes, and you all stayed with us a few months ago."

"We did." She introduced herself and said, "This little handful is Joey." She tried to get him to stop petting the dog long enough to properly introduce himself to Hassie, but his mother lost that battle. "Sorry, he is four going on five, with all that that implies."

"No worries." Hassie laughed.

"Still, he is my *gaol mo bheatha*." She bent over and mussed his hair.

Hassie's throat caught at her reference, but she just smiled.

"We actually just moved here. We stayed at the Inn when we came out to look for a home. Joey loves to come here and walk the shores, looking for Nessie."

Hassie nodded and was tempted to correct her, but she stopped herself. "Well, that is one of our national pastimes, isn't it?"

The boy picked up the stick and threw it, laughing when Scrounge raced after it, picked it up, and brought it back to him.

"Joey, leave the nice dog alone. It's time for us to go," the boy's mother directed, with a level of sternness.

Hassie knew her tone and decibel level would have to grow before she would persuade him.

"We're about to leave and we have an extra Irn-Bru, if you would like one," the mother offered, pulling a bottle out of a small, insulated cooler just as Scrounge ran up to Hassie's side, with Joey following.

"Mom!" Joey tugged on the back of his mother's skirt.

"Please don't interrupt, Joey," she chastised, still holding the Irn-Bru out for Hassie.

"No, thank you." Hassie shook her head. She knew it would be a long time before she could bring herself to drink another Irn-Bru. "We were just getting ready to leave too. It was nice to meet you both, and I'm sure Sir Scrounge will enjoy having another playmate around here." She half turned and prepared to leave.

"Moooom!" Joey exclaimed, clearly excited about something.

Hassie took a few steps away, assuming that the boy's urgency was likely a request for them to get a dog just like Scrounge.

"What?" his mother finally said in exasperation.

"Mom, look," Joey pointed out at the Loch and laughed.

"What?"

"Fiogry!" the boy exclaimed, with the absolute joy and wonder of a four-year-old.

Hassie heard the name and spun back around on her heel. She looked at the boy, who was giggling. Then she scanned the Loch but saw nothing.

An inner warmth washed over her, as if she had just arrived

home—something she never thought she would feel again. Pulling the two groats from her pocket, she stared at them before gently returning them to her pocket. Tears of joy streamed down her cheeks.

As if on cue, Scrounge barked and chased his tail.

"You'll never catch that bird, you silly dog."

END

AUTHOR'S NOTE

ALMOST ONE HUNDRED YEARS after John Paul Jones's death in France, General Horace Porter thought it was a travesty that the Revolutionary War hero was not buried in the United States and made it his personal mission, as ambassador to France, to find the lost cemetery and Jones's corpse and return it to the US. He spent years lobbying Theodore Roosevelt and Congress for resources, ultimately using some of his own funds to support the search. All of this is true, and now the body of Jones really is interred below the Naval Academy Chapel at Annapolis. And there is a plaque in the exhibit (described in the Prologue) thanking General Porter for his efforts to find and return Jones's body to the US.

In addition, Jones was born in southern Scotland, and all the information about the first three ships Jones sailed on starting at age thirteen—the *Friendship*, the *King George*, and the *Two Friends*, with the last two being slave ships, and the name of the captain of the first ship being Benson—is all true, as is the timing of Jones's father's death in 1767. The next year, Jones became so disgusted by the slave trade that he left the *Two Friends*, even though, at the time, he was in the lucrative position of being first mate of that ship and entitled to a share of the profits.

Jones's father, John Paul (Jones added the surname "Jones" later) really was a gardener. Now, whether his father was a Jacobite and an abolitionist, I don't know, but I included that because I thought it worked well in the story. When I originally came up with the idea for this book, I considered having Jones himself be the recipient of the Jacobite gold from Dr. Archibald Cameron, but the timing didn't work. When Dr. Archibald Cameron, whom Bonnie Prince Charlie had sent to Scotland to recover the gold, was captured without the treasure by British forces and executed, Jones would only have been around five years old. So, I had to go a different route and use Jones's father.

The information about David's Tower—built in the 1300s, largely destroyed in the 1500s, almost immediately covered and encased by the Half Moon Battery, and then lost to history for hundreds of years before being rediscovered in the early 1900s and used to hide some of the Scottish Crown Jewels in WWII—is also true. King David II is also the only Scottish monarch known to have visited Urquhart Castle.

The information about John Cobb, the man who tried to set a speed record in Loch Ness in the 1950s, is factual. When his speedboat unexpectedly crashed during the speed test and Mr. Cobb tragically died, people were confused because nobody saw anything in the water that would have caused the accident. With the boat traveling at over 200 knots, investigators ultimately surmised that the boat must have encountered either an extreme change of current in the Loch or a small, rogue wave; but the crash became part of the Nessie lore, and Loch Ness enthusiasts speculated whether the boat really may have hit the creature. I thought it would be fun to include a reference to the incident in the story, and you can still find a video of the actual crash on YouTube.

Currently, Loch Ness contains only one island, Cherry Island; but formerly, there were two islands. The smaller, natural island, Dog Island, submerged when the water level of the Loch rose, just as described in the story.

The Scottish law on treasure trove and the information regarding the Scottish Crown Estate having little accountability to the people of Scotland and little oversight by Parliament is real.

The information about the Incan quipu, their treatment by the Catholic Church, the difficulty of modern experts to decipher quipus, as well as the Incan adopted god, Pacha Kamaq, is all true, but the idea of a Golden Quipu and its possible tie to Juan Ponce de León was my own invention.

ABOUT THE AUTHOR

HUNTER H. WHITE is an energy transactions lawyer in Houston, Texas, and creative writing is his love.

Author photograph by Shirley Tucker